SAVAGE DESIRE

THE INFINITE CITY #5

TIFFANY ROBERTS

SAVAGE DESIRE

He's violent, volatile, and loves a good fight. She's small and sweet—and everything he craves. But can he make her his without hurting her?

Thargen wanders the sprawling Undercity streets with one goal—a drink. Well, maybe a few drinks and a good old-fashioned bar fight to let off some steam. But the moment he sees Yuri working behind the bar, he's overwhelmed by a new desire —her.

Yuri is his opposite in so many ways—delicate, soft, beautiful— and he knows the primal, uncontrollable rage in his heart makes it too dangerous for him to have her. But he wants her. He *needs* her.

And when an unexpected series of events sees them stranded on a hostile, unknown planet together, it becomes almost impossible for him to resist her. Lost on a mountainside teeming with ravenous skeks, Thargen must rely upon his survival skills and the ferocity burning at his core to protect Yuri until they can get back home.

But who will protect her from him?

—

Check author's website for content warnings.

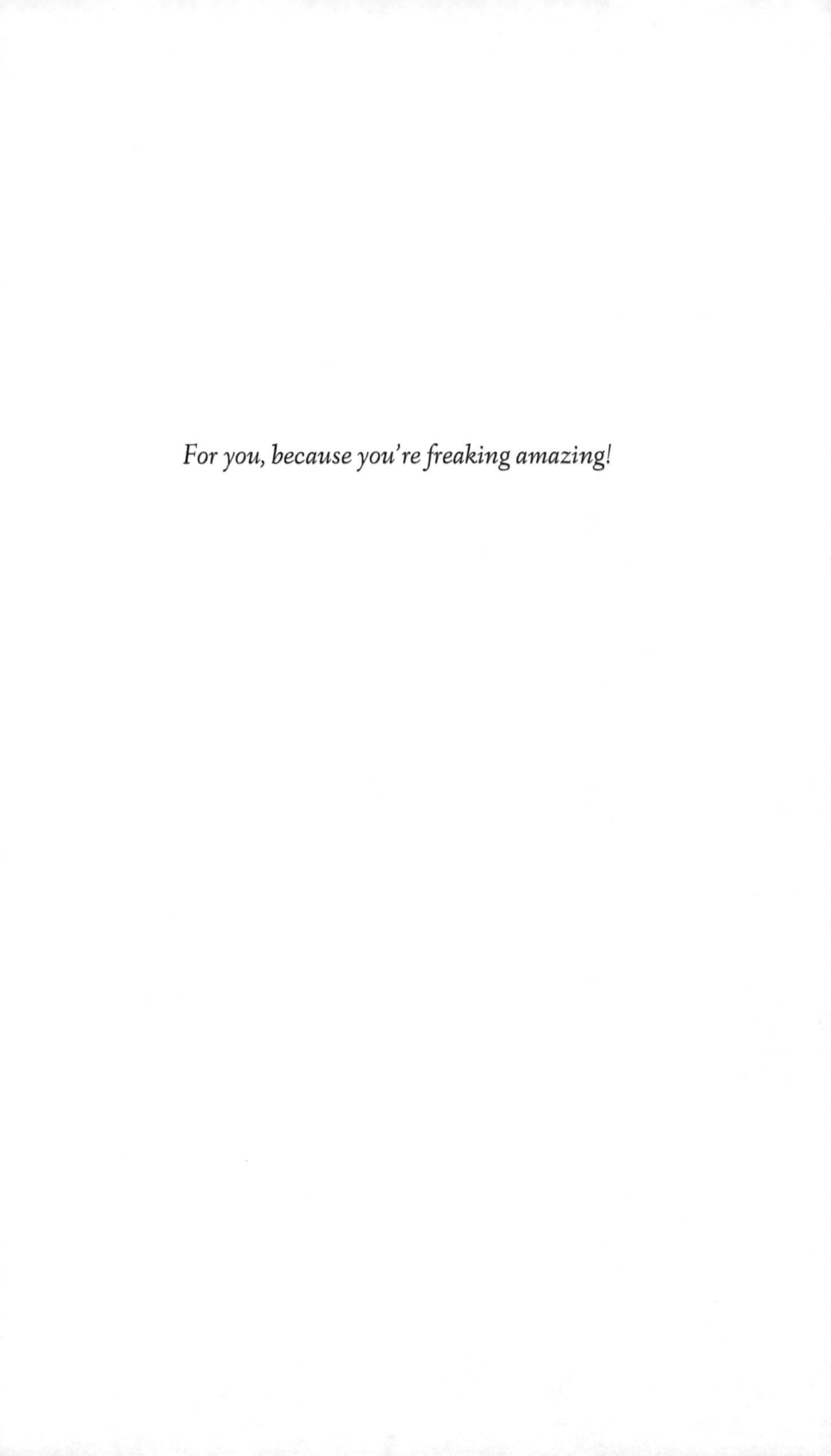

For you, because you're freaking amazing!

THARGEN
SAVAGE DESIRE

ONE

Arthos, the Infinite City
  Terran Year 2107

IF THARGEN SQUINTED JUST RIGHT, these Undercity streets were not unlike a battlefield. The bright lights cast all the right colors—red for blood, orange for explosions, white and blue for sizzling plasma bolts and thrumming energy weapons. All that color was backed by grungy metal and patches of darkness, the latter of which simulated the holes blown through a soldier's awareness by the chaos of battle. The voices of the pedestrians, who were speaking and shouting in a thousand languages, created a din reminiscent of war cries and death wails. Puddles of unknown liquid reflected much of it—at least when they weren't obscured by the crowd.

Most of the battlefields he'd fought on had been wet—if not at the onset, then by the end. Blood, fuel, hydraulic fluid, sweat, melted flesh; it all came together to create mucky, shimmering pools and a stinging stench.

Why the hell are these streets always wet? It doesn't rain down here.

He scanned his surroundings without slowing his walk. The buildings on either side of the street stood at varying heights, no two alike in shape, design, or signage. A perpendicular street cut through the airspace overhead, elevated on huge pillars. Beyond all the buildings was a blend of darkness and machinery—bare pipes and ductwork, conduits, struts, supports, metal plates, and transmission antennas bleeding into the black backdrop. Tiny marker lights glowed throughout like sickly stars, serving as warnings for the endless streams of hovercars flowing through the open spaces above.

The Undercity had plenty of air—all of it stale and recycled—but no sky.

"By Klagar's balls, I need a drink," he muttered.

Thargen had lived in Arthos for years and had walked this street more times than he cared to count, but he'd never been this...this *what?* Thoughtful? He'd never spent a moment worrying over what the Undercity's puddles were made of, and there was no reason to start now.

Rage circled the edges of his consciousness like a predator seeking a moment of vulnerability in its prey. His tribal ancestors had called it *Hruk*—the primal force within every vorgal that drove them to immense feats of strength, courage, and ferocity. The beast that dwelled in their hearts. And thanks to his years in the Rokkoshi Vanguard, his Rage was stronger and more savage than most.

He needed a distraction to ward it off, needed a drink or twelve.

Or he needed to bloody his knuckles.

That quickly, he found himself scanning the nearby pedestrians. There were a few attractive females here and there, but he didn't let his eyes linger on them. Sex could sate the impulses sparked by Rage, but it was dangerous. His aggression and savagery didn't vanish when he stuck his cock into a slit—they just took a new form, a new direction. Losing control in combat had saved his ass on numerous occasions. But losing control in bed, especially with a female of a more fragile species?

It was best for everyone if he kept it in his pants, even if that meant months—or years—of an aching groin.

He focused instead on searching for someone who could provide him the fight he wanted, with the challenge he craved. Most of the people in his direct path either moved out of his way or were knocked aside by his forward momentum; they weren't the ones. Even those who offered protests only did so weakly, displaying no willingness to back up their words with action. None of them had that spark he sought.

His chest and throat tightened, his heart quickened, and his balls firmed up; Rage was exerting more influence now, preparing him for the scuffle it desired. But Thargen couldn't lie to himself. He wanted it, too.

A group of rough looking males were gathered at the entrance to a dark alley ahead. Each wore the same symbol on his clothing—a red sun with the silhouette of a battle-axe against it. They were Ergoths, an Undercity gang that claimed ties to some ancient warrior tradition or another. Maybe all five of them were enough to provide the challenge he needed.

More likely they were just a bunch of pretenders hiding behind gang symbols to look tough.

He walked past the Ergoths and continued his search as a voice in his head—barely comprehensible over Rage—said this was a bad idea. He should've stayed at the party, should've had another slice of that delicious cake Samantha had baked for Leah. He wasn't so far gone yet that he would've caused trouble with his friends.

Before he could pursue that path of thought any further, a figure caught his attention—a tralix who had to be nearly three meters tall. His skin was a mottled blend of blue and green with splashes of purple and pink on his shoulders and atop his head, and his bare arms sported a few jagged scars that looked like old energy blade wounds. The tralix's hands were big enough to individually engulf Thargen's head—and probably crush his skull in one squeeze.

Thargen's heartbeat became rolling thunder, became the thumping of an artillery barrage. Rage induced strength flowed through his muscles.

A one-on-one fight with a tralix in the middle of a busy street would make for one hell of a story.

The tralix was walking toward Thargen, moving with the slow but relentless pace of a being that knew it would easily win any potential collisions with other pedestrians—and probably most small hover vehicles. Thargen drew in a deep breath. Tralix were notoriously easy to provoke; they viewed smaller, weaker species as things to be crushed whenever necessary.

Now it was Urgand's voice that spoke in Thargen's head.

Take it easy out there.

"Fuck," Thargen growled. He altered his path only a second before he would've collided with the tralix, stepping around the huge being without making contact.

His chest tightened further, his guts twisted, and fire amassed in his throat. It felt like he'd swallowed a fresh plasma bolt. Rage did not appreciate being denied, and it had no qualms about making its displeasure known.

Well it can go squat on a battle-axe. Twelve drinks it is.

At least.

Thargen increased his pace. He was close to the bar, and the sooner he arrived, the better. Even if he didn't understand the whole terran birthday thing, he knew Shay wouldn't be happy if he got into trouble and needed to be picked up from an Eternal Guard holding pen on little Leah's birthday. And in some ways, Shay's anger was more intimidating than a pissed off tralix.

As though his urgency had thrust him through a tear in space, Thargen found himself suddenly at his destination—the entrance to a narrow alleyway, where glowing signs jutted out into the main street. The second sign from the bottom was all that mattered; it said *BAR* in Universal Speech. The best places cut through the shit. They didn't need clever, catchy names so long as they had the goods. Booze basically sold itself.

He turned into the alley, strode to the far end—through several of those unidentifiable puddles—and hurried down the steps to the bar's entrance. He placed his hand on the door and pushed.

Thargen's shoulder and face slammed into the door, halting him abruptly.

Uttering a confused curse, he staggered back. Rage simmered in his stomach and warmed his blood, briefly resurging during his disorientation. Why the fuck was the door locked? He'd been coming here off and on for the last year or so, ever since Drakkal and Arcanthus relocated their operation to this sector, and it had never once been closed.

How could the place with the best *gurosh* in town be closed when Thargen needed a drink?

It was only then that he noticed the sign on the door.

NOTICE TO THE CITIZENS OF ARTHOS FROM THE CONSORTIUM COUNCIL OF PUBLIC HEALTH

Thargen's brow furrowed. What did the Council of Public Health have to do with a little Undercity bar?

With a grunt, he forced himself to continue reading. Most of it was some sort of Consortium ordinance, written in that particular sort of obscure, legal language that made words lose all meaning and inflicted severe headaches upon any who tried to decipher it. But the parts toward the end made sense.

Several patrons of this establishment have reported cases of violent illness that may have been caused by contaminated beverages served within.

IN THE INTEREST OF PUBLIC SAFETY, THIS ESTABLISHMENT IS CLOSED UNDER CONSORTIUM AUTHORITY PENDING FURTHER INVESTIGATION.

"Berrok's bare ass, what the fuck does that mean? How is it the bar's fault if some weaklings couldn't handle their booze?"

Sighing, Thargen turned around and started back down the alley. The *gurosh* in this place had usually managed to drown out his Rage after about a dozen tankards. There was no telling how many it would take at another establishment, or if those drinks would even taste good, or how willing the staff would be to call the Eternal Guard at the first sign of trouble.

As though those uncertainties weren't enough, a new realization struck him as he neared the alley's exit—he didn't even know any other bars in the sector. This had been the only place he'd come to since leaving Nyssa Vye.

He stopped just outside the alley and turned his head to check along the street in both directions. People moved up and down the street in long streams, occasionally breaking apart or altering their courses like water flowing around boulders in a rushing river.

Thargen knew this street. He'd walked past that cheese shop dozens of times—and had smelled it many times more. He'd bought surplus military equipment from Nokorg's Vorgal Outfitters, only a few storefronts away from the alley. He even had a few hazy memories of inebriated walks home during which he'd paused to stare at the diners inside the nearby restaurant, wondering if the wide, tall windows were meant to display the people inside as being on the menu.

He turned left—because it was just as good as right—and worked his way into the flow of foot traffic. Rage clawed at his mind. He tried to ignore it, to shove it back down into the recesses of his subconscious, to silence it so he could focus on his search, but it fought him at every step.

That internal battle soon clouded his senses to the world around him. He was aware of his feet moving, of people around him, of lights and sounds, but it was all distant and unimportant. Rage demanded his attention; it wanted control.

When he finally growled and shook off that haze, it took a few moments for his vision to clear. For that time, all he could hear was the pounding of his own heart. He looked up to find himself on a street he did not know in a sector he could not name.

Thargen lifted his wrist to check his holocom. Nearly two hours had passed since he'd left the closed bar.

What was it that he'd heard Sam and Shay say?

Time flies when you're...looking for fun?

No, that didn't sound quite right. But it didn't make a difference. He didn't need abstract terran sayings right now—especially when his own people had so many, like *a blade doesn't care if your gut's empty or full when it punctures your flesh.* What the hell did that mean? Of course blades didn't care—they were tools with no minds of their own.

Not that he would've been surprised if he were told that some scientist had built a knife with its own adaptive artificial intelligence.

Would be interesting to have a conversation with my weapon, though...

Anyway, all he needed was a damned drink, not more empty words. And now he was in an unfamiliar sector, one that looked relatively modernized and clean, where the buildings were packed together a little less densely, the streets were decorated with the occasional living plant, and the pedestrians were dressed just a little bit nicer than most places he went. Perhaps many of the differences were subtle and, individually, easily ignored, but all together, they made Thargen feel like he'd wandered into a different world.

He should've felt out of place here, should've been aware that his military-style casual wear probably stood out like a tretin at a volturian dinner party, should've simply turned around and gone back the way he'd come. He also should've been concerned that he'd lost two hours of time and several kilometers of travel with little recollection of it but for the bars he'd passed...but Thargen had never been one to concern himself with such matters.

A few minutes later, he stopped on the outskirts of a street that was bathed in the cool glow of blue and purple signs, many of which were animated to draw attention to themselves. But only one sign caught Thargen's eye—partly because its vibrant pink letters were a flash of heat amidst the cooler colors, but mostly because the bottom word on that sign was *DRINKS*.

He ran his gaze over the rest of the sign. *MUSIC* and *DANCE* were the next words up, topped off with a holographic image depicting people of undetermined species dancing in a very intimate fashion. The place was called Starlight Trance, and the signage firmly established it as a place he would never have entered under normal circumstances.

Thargen lifted a hand, tucking back a few loose strands of hair that had escaped his braids. His fingertips skittered over the hard, uneven scar tissue on the right side of his head. He could barely remember a time when he didn't have those scars, and yet they still felt wrong, still seemed out of place.

"Damn, you're in a fucking mood tonight, Thargen," he muttered. "All this thinking and brooding just means I'm spending too much time with Arc and Drak. Between them and little Leah, I'm going soft."

Without wasting another second, he turned and strode to the entrance of Starlight Trance, which was right on the main street—a big door set in a recess a few meters wide and about half as deep. He would've preferred a dank, seedy alleyway entrance.

The security guard posted at the door was a borian with broad shoulders and narrow hips who stood a few centimeters taller than Thargen. He didn't have any visible weapons, but his stance was strong and confident.

Thargen walked up to the guard.

The borian arched a brow. "Move on, vorgal."

"Not gonna buy me a drink, then?" Thargen asked.

The borian scowled, extended a thumb, and gestured down the street. "Keep walking. This isn't your kind of place."

Thargen frowned and folded his arms across his chest. "You serve *gurosh*?"

Jaw muscles bulging, the borian offered a curt nod.

"Sounds exactly like my kind of place." Thargen offered the borian a wide, toothy smile that was meant to be charming and friendly, though he knew it wasn't—he'd looked in a mirror recently. Intimidating was probably more accurate.

Thargen didn't miss the way the guard's eyes shifted to the Vanguard tattoo on his cheek. Those symbols were as much a badge of honor as a sign of warning.

Silence filled the space between Thargen and the borian, broken only by the background sounds—hovercars zipping by high overhead and distant conversations, mostly. Well, there were the persistent whispers from Thargen's Rage, too, but he wasn't listening to those right now.

"Fine," the borian finally spat. He turned to the wall beside the door, punched something into a small control pad, and stepped aside as a heavy-duty tristeel drawer slid out of the wall. "Check your weapons here."

Thargen laughed as he reached down to unbuckle his belt. "Nothing but good old-fashioned bare-knuckle brawling in here, huh?"

The borian's scowl deepened. "You make trouble, vorgal, and my team will have to drag your bloody, unconscious ass into the alley when we're done with you."

"Don't tease me with a good time." Thargen tugged off his belt and placed it—along with his holstered blaster and knives—in the drawer.

The borian grunted and tapped the control panel again. The drawer slid shut with a clang. An instant later, it vanished, leaving the spot totally indistinguishable from the rest of the wall.

Thargen raised a hand, holding the tips of his forefinger and thumb a few centimeters apart. "Do I get one of those little tokens or tags or whatever for when I pick my stuff up?"

The borian gestured to a wall-mounted scanner. "Hold up your ID chip. It'll register to your weapons."

"You can't just remember which were mine?" Thargen asked as he stepped forward and raised his left arm. "Feels like an invasion of my privacy."

The control panel beeped softly.

The borian positioned himself in front of the now concealed drawer and folded his arms across his chest. "You going in, or you waiting for me to realize how stupid I'm being?"

"Yeah, yeah. Want at least a couple drinks in me before you drag me into that alley, and since you aren't buying..."

Thargen barely held in his laughter when the borian's already expression darkened save for the tiniest glints of heat in his pupils. It would be easy to capitalize upon the borian's irritation, easy to escalate this to violence—easy to succumb to Rage and give it the outlet it craved.

He pushed through Starlight Trance's front door. It let him into a short, dimly lit hallway with dark walls and flooring. The hall was quiet, almost preternaturally so, but for an underlying pulse so deep it was more felt than heard, steady and frantic like a heartbeat at the height of Rage. Brows falling low, he continued to the double doors ahead. They slid open, vanishing into the walls on either side, before he could even reach forward to touch them.

A wave of sound swept over him—not a thumping heartbeat but a drumbeat, layered with other instruments to form relentless, repetitive music that lost little of its power despite the sound dampeners undoubtedly in place to contain it.

The dance floor was directly ahead, at the base of a low, wide set of steps, and it was beautiful chaos. The press of bodies made individuals indiscernible from one another. The dancers writhed and bounced to the rhythm, many of them sporting vibrant, glowing designs on their clothes and skin that turned into blurs of color, obscuring their features and making them even harder to tell apart. Lights flashed in sync with the various instruments all over the club—on the walls and ceiling, on the bits of floor visible between legs and feet, and in the form of floating holographic shapes in the air that constantly moved and morphed.

The scene was hypnotic, a blur of mesmerizing colors dictated by that pounding music. But even amidst the spectacle—or perhaps because of it—the guards were easy to spot. They were all big, all stood relatively still, and the vibrancy and motion around them turned them into dark, brooding statues positioned around the edges of the dance floor.

It was the left side of the huge room that ultimately claimed Thargen's attention, however—the side that was dominated by a long bar. Behind it were more bottles of alcohol than he could count and rows and rows of mugs and glasses, all lit by steady pink and purple backlights that stood out from the chaos just enough to serve as a focus to anyone who found themselves thirsty.

The patrons gathered at the bar were easier to identify. There were a lot of volturians and borians, many of them dressed in casual finery that would've made Thargen's skin itch had he worn similar. Most had glowing paint and adornments on their clothing and skin—beyond the natural, glowing markings of the volturians—and the lighting at the bar only enhanced the contrast between light and dark.

Absently bobbing his head to the infectious beat, Thargen approached the bar. There were at least five bartenders serving drinks. He meant to gauge their speed against the number of people waiting in front of each, to perform that subconscious calculus that was the only sort of math he tended to do in his adult life—*which one will get me a drink fastest*—but his attention froze on the middle bartender.

The female was small. Delicate. She couldn't have stood much taller than a hundred and sixty centimeters, just about to his chest. Long, lustrous black hair fell past her shoulders and framed her face—a face he couldn't quite make out through all the conflicting darkness and neon light. But he could see her full lips, which glowed bright pink.

Thargen grinned and ran his gaze over the rest of her. Her bare arms were adorned with intricate, luminescent designs, and she wore a short neon-painted crop top which displayed her flat stomach. His eyes caught on a tiny, bluish glint at her belly button—a piercing, catching reflections from the various light sources as she moved. Insignificant as it should've been, it sent a surge of lust through Thargen like he'd not felt outside of Rage for a long, long time.

He'd met his first terran when one had come to see Arcanthus two years ago, and though she'd been in and out of his life in the blink of an eye, the other three he'd met since then were good friends—they were family. Especially Shay, who understood Thargen on a deep, soldier-to-soldier level despite having never actually served in a military force. But none of them had sparked such desire in him, not even remotely.

He found himself suddenly eager to meet this terran, too. That eagerness was undoubtedly driven by the fact that she was petite and beautiful in a way only terrans seemed capable of, and something about her easy though slightly awkward smile made her seem approachable.

There were so few terrans in Arthos—so few terrans in his life—and they all seemed so out of place in this often rough, unforgiving city. Odd as it was, his instinct was to protect this terran, just like he would've protected Sam, Shay, and Leah.

White teeth flashed as the female grinned at the volturian in front of her. She set down a glass, grabbed two bottles from beneath the counter, lifted them high, and twisted them. Two streams of liquid poured into the waiting glass, one ultraviolet and the other white. When she was done, she set the bottles down and pushed the drink toward the volturian, speaking words Thargen couldn't hear, before moving to the next patron.

Though that subconscious math suggested one of the other bartenders could get him a drink faster, Thargen fell into line at the terran's section of the bar—not that the jumble of patrons could rightly be called a line even by the most generous standards. Normally, he wouldn't have hesitated to shove his way to the front. These situations were first come, first serve, and with all the light and noise, it was usually the loudest patron who received their drink first. But something held him back now.

Maybe it was because he wanted to make a good first impression on the terran, or maybe it was just to allow himself more time to watch her. She moved with confidence, poured every drink with a flourish, and freely offered smiles to everyone. Her features became a bit more discernible with each step closer he took.

When he arrived at the bar, he leaned an elbow atop it and watched her serve a tall, lanky cren. She was petite all right, but her form-fitting black pants showed off her feminine curves and a pert little ass that would fill his hands perfectly.

He suddenly found himself wanting a drink of *her* more than anything else.

Thargen's heart sped when she finally turned to him. Her thin, shapely brows rose slightly, and her gaze met his.

Her eyes were green—like him.

She's mine.

TWO

Whoa, Thargen, slow down. Where the fuck did that come from?

The female smiled wide and raised her voice to speak over the pumping music. "Hey! What can I get for you?"

Though she'd smiled at everyone Thargen had seen her serve, this smile seemed like it was just for him.

How about a taste of you?

He smiled around his tusks, hoping it looked warm and friendly instead of his usual savage or intimidating. "*Gurosh*. In the biggest mug you have."

"You got it." She grabbed a tall glass mug from the racks behind the bar and set it under the tap, opening the flow of delicious, golden *gurosh*. "Haven't seen you around here before. You new?"

"Usually stick to the nicer volturian clubs, you know? I fit in better at those places."

She laughed and eyed him up and down. "They kick you out because you put them all to shame?"

Thargen's lips stretched into a grin. "Yeah. Guess something about me made them more aware of their own inadequacies or something."

Someone harrumphed nearby. Thargen turned his head just in time to catch a glare from the well-dressed volturian beside him. The volturian turned his nose up, snatched his drink off the bar, and walked away.

Thargen laughed. "See? I can't help it."

The terran ducked her head with a snicker and shut off the tap. "Totally not your scene." She set the mug in front of Thargen, tapping the counter next to it. A scanner appeared beneath the surface. "Scan your ID here."

"What is it with this place wanting to scan my ID?" he grumbled, reaching into his pocket to fish out a credit chip.

She grinned. "A mysterious stranger, huh?"

"Mysterious? Nah, I'm no good at mysterious. What you see is what you get, and no, it's not too good to be true. But that fucker at the front door already made me scan my ID once, and that's more than enough for me today."

"This one's just to open a tab for you."

He tossed the chip onto the counter. "This should cover whatever I drink tonight."

She picked up the chip and pressed the little button to display the amount of credits loaded onto it. Her eyes widened. "Oh wow. You'd have to drink a lot—like *a lot* a lot—to spend all this."

Thargen lifted the mug to her in a salute. "Guess I'd better get started while the night's still young."

She laughed. "Well, looks like I'm your personal bartender tonight. Enjoy. I'll check back with you in a minute."

Tipping his head back, Thargen took a long swig of *gurosh*. It was cold but fiery, stinging but sweet; it was everything he'd been looking forward to since he'd left home earlier. He stopped himself after two-thirds of the drink was drained and set the mug down.

For a few moments, he squeezed his eyes shut and focused on the lingering burn of the *gurosh*, letting all the other sounds and smells around him fade away. It'd be a while before the booze hit him hard enough to drown out his Rage, but this was a start.

When he opened his eyes, he let his gaze wander the club, noting the positions of the security staff and the doors he could make out through all the clashing light and darkness. It was always good to have an idea of where everything and everyone was in case shit went bad.

And it usually went bad for him.

The dancers continued their revelry, mostly through pelvic gyrations and bodily contact only a step removed from dry humping, and the music continued its frantic beat. He could only imagine how loud it was on that dance floor.

He sipped the remainder of his drink a little at a time, his eyes drifting time and again to the terran. She was in constant motion as she served the patrons, and her smile—that beautiful fucking smile—never wavered. He found himself chewing on his bottom lip whenever his eyes dipped lower. That piercing at her navel was especially alluring; he wanted to twirl his tongue around it.

His cock throbbed, fueled by a spark of Rage—but that Rage felt different, somehow.

When she finally made her way back toward him, her smile widened—or at least it seemed to. It could well have been his subconscious making him see what he wanted to see.

"Ready for another? Or something else?" she asked.

Normally, he stuck with *gurosh*; it was the drink preferred by his friends, and it also happened to be a vorgal drink. But this seemed like a good night to venture away from the typical, to break his routine—especially since his routine had already been broken.

"What do you recommend?" he asked. "Any good terran drinks here?"

She laughed; the sound was warm and light. "Not quite enough demand for those to convince the owners to import any alcohol from Earth yet, I'm afraid."

"Well, how about you surprise me then? I always order the same damned thing. Help me get out of my rut."

The terran narrowed her eyes, pursed her lips, and shifted them to the side in thought. Then she grinned. "I got it."

She placed a shot glass on the bar top, grabbed a bottle of glowing, bright-red liquid, and flipped it, filling the glass halfway. She picked up a smaller, darker bottle as she put the first away, but only allowed two drops from the second to fall into the glass. The mixture bubbled for an instant, and the glowing red liquid turned vibrant purple. "Try that."

Thargen reached forward, took hold of the glass, and threw back his head, downing the contents in a single gulp. If *gurosh* was liquid fire, this was something on a whole new level—closer to drinking plasma, maybe, with a burn so strong that it obliterated his sense of taste for a few moments.

He winced, lips peeling back, and released a breath that burned almost as much as the drink had. He raised the empty glass and eyed it with an arched brow. "Damn, what the fuck is this stuff?"

She laughed. "It's a cren drink. They call it void venom."

How had his cren friends not told him about this stuff yet? They were getting an earful when he went home.

Grinning, Thargen settled the shot glass on the bar and slid it toward her. "And what do they call you?"

She snorted and rolled her eyes as she refilled his glass. "Puny terran."

"I'd say beautiful terran fits better. You have a name, or that it?"

Despite the uneven lighting, Thargen saw her cheeks darken before she shifted her eyes away from him.

"Yuri," she said, sliding his drink back toward him. "My name's Yuri."

Thargen's fingertips brushed over her hand for an instant as he took the drink from her, long enough for him to feel how soft, smooth, and warm her skin was. His hand was easily twice the size of hers.

"Yuri," he repeated, lifting his drink in another salute. "Name's Thargen. To new friends."

The blush on her cheeks only darkened further. "I'm not allowed to drink during my shift."

"Ah, well"—Thargen downed the drink, hissed against the burn, and slid the glass to her again—"I'll have to have one for you, then. Don't worry, it's on me."

She chuckled and poured him another void venom. "I'll be back. Don't pass out on me."

"Gonna take a lot more than a little cren drink to knock me out," Thargen said with a laugh before gulping down the next shot. He shook his head hard, willing away the sting, and slammed the empty glass on the bar top. He was already feeling a buzz that would normally take eight or nine mugs of *gurosh*; he'd have to slow down if he didn't want to make a complete fool of himself before long.

While Yuri helped some of the other patrons, Thargen turned his focus to the collection of bottles and glasses lined up on the wall behind the bar. The lights hitting them seemed so much more vibrant and colorful now, and the music, punctuated by that relentless beat, was that much more hypnotic. Suddenly, he wanted to dance, wanted to feel the bass in his chest and the press of bodies all around him, wanted to get swept up in that hypnotic rhythm.

And you aren't nearly buzzed enough to pretend you don't know how that would end, you idiot.

He frowned. Maybe it would be fun out there for a little while, maybe it would be freeing to lose himself to the music. But eventually, the sweet bliss of oblivion provided by the alcohol would fade and the noise, the heat, and the crowd, would trigger something deep within him. They would stir up memories he couldn't summon himself and wake his Rage, and then what? A fistfight in his old bar wouldn't have caused any fuss for anyone, but here it was likely to see him arrested by the Eternal Guard.

One of the other bartenders approached him and asked if he wanted something else. Thargen shook his head and kept his hand around the shot glass. His attention crept toward Yuri again; she was pouring drinks a few meters away. When she bent down to retrieve something from under the bar, his eyes dropped to her ass. A fresh wave of lust shot through him, and his cock twitched, straining against the confines of his pants. He groaned; fortunately, it was drowned out by the music.

He'd gone a long time without sex, and for good reason—he didn't want to hurt anyone, at least outside a fight. So why was he allowing himself to ogle a terran now, knowing nothing could come of it, knowing she'd break so damned easily? Why was he torturing himself?

I want her.

But I can't fucking have her.

Despite his healthy buzz, Rage roiled beneath the surface of Thargen's mind, and his good mood deflated. He thought he'd learned his lesson long ago—good things could never be his. Yuri seemed like a good person. A kind person. He wasn't naïve enough to think that she couldn't be acting, playing a part to make her patrons a little more generous with their tips, but he didn't think that was the case. She seemed genuine.

The world in which he existed wasn't a place for someone like her.

Oh, but it is the place for Samantha, Shay, and Leah?

You know that's not the same thing. Shay is as tough as any of us, and she has Drakkal to look out for her and Leah. Sam has Arcanthus, and he isn't...broken.

Not like me.

Thargen clenched his jaw and squeezed his eyes shut against the sudden, piercing pain at his right temple. As potent as this void venom was, apparently it wasn't enough to dull the headaches he was sometimes prone to.

It's because I'm overthinking. Gonna take a few more drinks than this to muck up my brain enough to prevent that.

Why was he causing himself all this trouble over a terran he could never have? There was no sense in it. Arc and Drak had terran mates now, and they were both happy, and Thargen could be happy for them. That didn't mean he needed to run off and find a terran of his own.

But he hadn't run off to find a terran. Meeting Yuri had been a matter of chance, and she was friendly and beautiful, and her smile made his chest warm, and his cock—

Fuck, I need another drink.

He opened his eyes and nearly jerked back from the bar. Yuri was directly in front of him, elbow leaning on the countertop and chin propped on her hand, staring at him with those damnable alluring green eyes.

Her lips curled into a smile. "Is this where I act like the clichéd bartender from every movie and ask what's troubling you?"

Thargen arched a brow and willed his heart to slow. "Why

would a bartender ask anything other than *ready for another one?*"

Yuri chuckled. "Sorry. Too many movies." She tilted her head, eyes moving as though she were searching his face. "Though you do look like something's bothering you."

He released a heavy breath through his nostrils. It was stupid to think she actually cared, yet he couldn't help believing it all the same—and he definitely couldn't talk to her about what was bothering him right now.

But she was a terran; maybe she could help him with something else.

"I got a hypothetical situation for you." He folded his forearms atop the bar and leaned toward her. "Maybe you can help me figure it out."

Yuri mimicked him, folding her arms on the counter and bending closer until their faces were only a handspan apart. "Ask away."

Her scent drifted to him, momentarily overwhelming him. It was soft and sweet, feminine and exotic, unlike anything he'd ever smelled—a scent from another world, from another universe. "Uh. Well. Say I was friends with this terran, and she had a baby. And that baby had a birthday party. First birthday—not that it makes sense, because she was born a year ago, so you'd think *that* would be her first birthday. Anyway, I needed to get a gift. Would a high-quality tristeel combat knife be an appropriate purchase?"

One of her brows quirked. "Uh, that's quite the specific hypothetical question."

"Yeah, I just want to be thorough."

"Well, for a baby, any kind of weapon is definitely not an appropriate gift. I would say you're better off getting something...softer?"

"Like...an energy blade?"

"Something more...cuddly, you know? Something you can hold and squeeze? Not something the baby could stab themselves with."

Thargen frowned. "I had my first knife before I could walk."

She eyed him skeptically. "That why you have those scars?"

He laughed and brushed a hand over the side of his head. "Yeah, maybe. Got time for a follow up question?"

Yuri glanced down the crowded bar. One of the other bartenders, a tall female borian wearing strips of neon clothing, paused and looked her way. Yuri flicked her finger, gesturing to herself and Thargen. The borian nodded.

"Yeah," Yuri said, looking back at Thargen with a smile. "You're my top paying customer right now, so you're my priority."

"Ha! I knew you didn't like me just because of my good looks."

Yuri laughed with a shrug. "What can I say? A girl has to eat. But I'd say your good looks are a bonus."

There was a strange fluttering in Thargen's stomach, and his smile softened. He didn't know why it felt so good to talk to this female, but he wasn't about to stop. "All right, so... Say that same baby had that party, and I maybe were to suggest drinking during that party, and when I was told it was not appropriate, I left. Would that make me an asshole?"

"Well, it would wholly depend upon the mood of the party before you left."

"I mean...I stayed for presents and cake."

"It's usually okay to leave after the presents are opened and the cake is served." She groaned and rolled her eyes up. "I would honestly kill for cake right now. I haven't had any since I left Earth a couple years ago."

Thargen chuckled and smacked his lips. "It was damned good cake, too. Probably should've stayed for one more piece."

She reached out and lightly slapped his arm. "Tease."

His Rage perked, but in a way he'd never experienced—it fed directly into his lust, pumped blood straight to his groin, and nearly made him groan again.

He wouldn't have been averse to another slap—and maybe some hair-pulling or scratching to go along with it.

"If there's any leftover when I get back, I'll put some aside for you," he said. "Can bring you a slice tomorrow."

"Don't make promises you can't keep."

"Not lying, terran."

She perked. "Really? You'd seriously bring me some cake?"

"Yeah. I should warn you, though, if you knew some of the people I work with, your hopes of any leftovers would be slim."

She stuck her bottom lip out in a pout. "Now why'd you go and get my hopes up?"

"Guess I just like seeing you smile."

Though her pout was adorable, too.

Yuri smiled again, and something in her eyes softened.

A tall, lean, four-armed dacrethian squeezed in beside Thargen. "Give me a glass of Turian wine."

Thargen turned his head to glance at the newcomer. "Get in line, buddy."

The dacrethian scowled.

Yuri straightened, her eyes on the dacrethian. "I'll be with you in a second." She returned her attention to Thargen. "You ready for another refill?"

Thargen glanced down at the glass and sighed. A couple more shots of void venom and he'd be too far gone to know what he was saying, and he wasn't likely to remember much of this by tomorrow if he hit that point. He *wanted* to remember her—every second, every detail. "I'm good for now. Gotta let my insides recover before I have any more. Go ahead and help this impatient asshole."

The dacrethian growled.

"Okay! Turian wine coming up!" Yuri said, giving Thargen a scolding look with her eyes, though a smirk lingered on her lips. "I'll check back on you in a few."

"I'll be here." He watched as she poured the dacrethian's drink, entranced by her confidence, efficiency, and subtle grace. It was a deceptively simple thing, serving drinks, but those simple things often revealed so much about a person.

She was a little flashy, but she was precise and didn't seem to waste any motion. And she was quick. Within ten or fifteen seconds, the dacrethian had his drink, and his scowl faded as he walked away with it. Yuri moved on to her next customers without missing a beat.

A soft vibration on his left wrist called Thargen's attention to his holocom. He lifted his arm and opened the little screen to find a message from Urgand.

Everything good?

Had Thargen known what was about to happen, he would've cackled at his own reply—*Doing fine. Haven't even been in one fight.*

Urgand's response came immediately. *Keep it that way and get back soon. You have first shift tomorrow.*

The space left by the dacrethian was quickly filled—and forced wider—by a group of three males. The volturian was several centimeters shorter than Thargen, gray skinned with red *qal* marks on his face. He was accompanied by a sharp featured kaital with bluish skin and large ears, and a four-armed onigox who stood at least a head taller than Thargen and had vibrant red skin. They were all well dressed, but Thargen couldn't help noting the identical neon orange accents on their clothing. Even in a place filled with people wearing bright, glowing patterns and adornments, something about these seemed too uniform to suggest the volturian, onigox, and kaital were just some friends out for a few drinks and some dancing.

The onigox slammed one of his meaty fists atop the bar, rattling glasses and mugs. "Terran!"

Yuri glanced at the onigox, nodded, and lifted one finger before returning her attention to her current customer and finished serving their drink.

"Allow her a few moments, Mortannis. Terrans are too primitive to handle more than one task at a time," said the volturian in a smooth, cultured voice.

"I'm thirsty, Firios. Now, terran!" Mortannis banged his fist again. Several glasses toppled over, and a couple of them rolled onto the floor to shatter.

Some of the people closest to the onigox quickly cleared the space.

Yuri's brows furrowed as she approached Mortannis. Once she was in front of him, she leaned forward slightly, tilted her head back, and raised her voice so it could be heard over the music. "I'm going to have to ask you to stop doing that."

"Perhaps if your service were faster," Firios said, "my friend wouldn't have to resort to such methods."

Thargen gritted his teeth. Not only did this volturian talk just like his kind did in the overly dramatic shows Razi always watched back at the compound, but he was being passive aggressive with Yuri. What a fucking coward.

Aggression should never be passive.

"Your friend needs to learn a little patience and simply wait for his turn." Yuri looked from Firios to Mortannis with one eyebrow quirked. "Now that you have my attention, what do you want?"

Mortannis braced two of his hands on the bar and leaned

down, placing his face closer to Yuri's. "Well, I've never had a terran before."

Yuri stared at him unflinchingly. "I'm sorry, terran isn't on the menu."

"She does not know who we are," the kaital said, thin lips twisting into a smirk.

"Well, Garegon, I suppose we must be the ones to teach her, mustn't we?" Firios asked.

"Look, if you're not going to order a drink, I have other customers waiting," Yuri said, turning to walk away.

Mortannis reached over the bar and caught Yuri's upper arm in one of his big hands, halting her in her tracks. "*Ji'tas*, you haven't served—"

Rage poured into Thargen's blood, hot as magma flowing through the veins of a planet. His hand trembled around his shot glass.

Yuri swung around and slapped the onigox across his face, producing a *smack* loud enough to resonate over the thumping music. Her eyes widened, as though her own reaction surprised her. She tugged her arm. "Let me go."

Mortannis's lips curled into a scowl. He raised a hand, balling it into a fist, and yanked her closer. "You're going to pay for that, you little—"

Thargen lunged at Mortannis, slamming the shot glass into the side of the big red bastard's face. The glass shattered; Thargen distantly felt the pain of it slicing his palm, but he only pressed harder, grinding the shards into the onigox's cheek.

There was a scream from somewhere—Thargen didn't know if it was from Yuri or not—and Mortannis staggered aside, releasing the terran.

Chaos unfurled over the next few moments. Mortannis kept on his feet, but Thargen pressed his advantage, slamming his knee into the onigox's midsection repeatedly. Fists hammered Thargen's back; he barely registered the blows through the waves of Rage coursing through him. Thargen twisted away from Mortannis, throwing an elbow back. It caught Firios in the face, knocking him backward.

More people cried out around him. Each cry sounded farther away than the last, sounded less important. Thargen knew in the back of his mind that the security guards would come soon. He had perhaps ten or fifteen seconds at best. He planned to make them count.

Releasing a guttural laugh, Thargen returned his attention to Mortannis, hammering his fists and knee repeatedly into the alien's body. His foe's pained grunts were a sweet battle song, underscored by the dull *thwaps* of flesh striking flesh.

Someone slammed into Thargen from the side; it must've been the kaital, Garegon. Thargen's ribs hit the edge of the bar, knocking a bit of the breath from his lungs. He clamped his hands on the sides of his new attacker's head and twisted, slamming the kaital face first into the bar top. He followed it up with a hard knee to Garegon's sternum.

Mortannis wrapped a powerful arm around Thargen's neck from behind. Thargen caught it with both hands, digging his nails into the onigox's flesh, just as Firios punched him in the face. Laughing again, Thargen raised a leg just high enough to brace his foot on the bar and kicked back with all his strength, throwing his weight against Mortannis.

They crashed to the floor together, Thargen's full weight landing on his foe. The onigox's hold loosened. Thargen twisted around and straddled the larger alien, pinning Mortannis's lower arms under his knees as he rained blows on the onigox.

Thargen's vision was stained redder than the onigox's skin now, and that crimson haze deepened with each thunderous beat of his racing heart. He bared his teeth and kept swinging. Something hit him in the back of the head, knocking him forward slightly. He shook off the blow and kept attacking.

Harsh shouts sounded immediately around him. He slammed his fist into Mortannis's jaw one more time and pushed himself up, meaning to turn toward his new foes, ready for more, *eager* for more.

Strong arms looped beneath Thargen's—not quite big enough to belong to the onigox—and a pair of hands locked behind his neck, restraining him. His new assailant heaved back, dragging Thargen away from Mortannis.

Thargen growled. Rage flooded his muscles with a fresh surge of strength, more than enough to break that hold on him.

"Wait! Stop!" A soft hand settled on Thargen's forearm before he could break free.

That voice, that touch, broke through his battle haze. He shook his head, clearing away some of the fog, to find Yuri standing in front of him. Her face looked paler than before, but it could've just been because the lighting was different behind the bar.

She stepped closer and placed her other hand on his chest, meeting his gaze. "It's over now."

A portion of Thargen's Rage burned away in that instant, drifting off like ash on the wind. The feel of her palm against his skin, over his pounding heart, was unlike anything he'd ever experienced; he wanted to feel that touch *everywhere*.

"Get back, Yuri," the male restraining Thargen said. "He's dangerous."

Yuri shook her head and looked up. "He's the one that stopped them from attacking me. Let him go, Ruunok."

"Did you see what he just did to these guys, Yuri?" Ruunok asked.

Yuri's gaze held Thargen's. "Thargen won't hurt me."

All Thargen could do was stare into those eyes. Those deep, beautiful, green eyes, so full of kindness and compassion. Had he ever seen their like? Some of the tension in his muscles eased.

Ruunok grunted; if anything, he'd only strengthened his hold on Thargen. "You sure?"

Thargen drew in a deep breath. The situation was suddenly clear to him now—the male holding him was one of the security guards. There were guards in his peripheral vision, dragging Mortannis, Firios, and Garegon to their feet.

"I'm good," Thargen said, his voice as rough as loose gravel. "I'm done."

"Let him go, Ruunok, so I can take him in back and get him cleaned up," Yuri said, lowering her hands and stepping back.

The flesh that she'd been touching felt immediately cold. Ridiculous as it was, Thargen felt like a part of him had just been wrenched away.

"All right, Yuri." Ruunok reluctantly released Thargen. "But you know the boss will have your ass if this vorgal steps out of line again."

Thargen rolled his shoulders, willing away his remaining tension. Heat lingered in his muscles, his skin was tingling, and his body itched for motion, for action, but he could feel the pain on his palm now. It was dull, throbbing, and warm. He knew it would sharpen as his Rage continued to fade.

He turned and stepped back so he could see both Yuri and Ruunok. "I'll, uh...I'll pay for the glass."

Ruunok—a burly, black-furred azhera—grunted. "You're lucky you were helping her"—he pointed at Yuri—"or we'd be tossing you out on your ass right now."

Thargen's Rage flared a little in response—at the challenge inherent in Ruunok's threat. Taking on the entire security staff of a nightclub...that'd be a good fight. He shook off that foolish urge. Pissing off security would get him banned from this place, and while it wouldn't have been the first bar he'd been banished from, he didn't want to add this one to the list.

He wanted to be able to see Yuri again.

"Ruunok, can you let Lyrani know I'm taking a break?" Yuri asked.

"Sure, Yuri," Ruunok said. "You're okay, right? That big bastard didn't hurt you?"

"I'm good." Yuri smiled up at Thargen. "This vorgal got him before he could hurt me." She took hold of his wrist, her fingers not even wrapping halfway around it, and tugged him toward her. "Come on, big guy. Let's get you cleaned up."

Thargen didn't resist; he had the sense that he'd happily allow her to lead him *anywhere*.

THREE

Keeping a gentle but solid grip on Thargen's wrist, Yuri led the big vorgal through the crowd of onlookers toward the concealed door at the back of the club. His muscle was hard, his skin almost feverishly hot; she focused on the feel of him and kept herself moving forward. Even if she told herself that she was only holding onto him to lead him where they needed to go, the contact was a lifeline to her. Her outer calm was little more than a mask; inside, she was trembling like a leaf in the wind that was on the verge of being torn away from its branch. Thargen was the only thing keeping her grounded.

This incident with Mortannis wasn't the first time an alien had been rough around Yuri, and it certainly wouldn't be the last, but it *was* the first time she'd nearly been pulverized. She hadn't meant to slap the onigox but—

Come on! The big jerk had it coming to him. He deserved it.

Touching the staff was off limits in Starlight Trance unless that staff member had granted explicit permission, and Yuri sure as hell hadn't given Mortannis the okay. So, it served the onigox right that Thargen had kicked the shit out of him. Yuri knew Ruunok and the other bouncers would've taken care of it whether Thargen had intervened or not, but how much damage could Mortannis have caused in those precious seconds?

Would she have even survived?

She'd been lucky to land a job here shortly after immigrating to Arthos; a lot of humans had trouble finding good work in the city, still seen as exotic and untried. The pay was decent, and it had paired well with the Consortium guaranteed income she'd received during her first year here—well enough to enable Yuri and her younger brother, Takashi, to rent a relatively nice little apartment. And the owner of Starlight Trance, Lyrani, cared about her staff's wellbeing. She didn't take kindly to anyone—including other staff members—harassing her employees.

When Yuri reached the concealed door, she raised her wrist and held it up to the ID scanner. The tiny light on the panel flashed green, and the door slid open. She stepped into the hallway beyond and pulled Thargen in behind her. The air was noticeably cooler here; she welcomed its soothing touch.

The door closed, plunging the hall into a silence that was almost deafening after spending so long with the thumping music and dozens of indistinct conversations as a backdrop.

Yuri glanced at Thargen over her shoulder. "Almost there."

He nodded.

There was blood spattered on his face, but she didn't relinquish her hold on him even though that glimpse of blood made her stomach flip. A little voice in the back of her mind whispered that she should be just as afraid of him as she'd been of Mortannis. Thargen had fought three opponents, one of whom was significantly larger and heavier than him, without a hint of fear or hesitation—and had displayed a savagery she'd never seen in person.

But he did it to protect me.

She led him around the corner and stopped at the first door on the right, tapping the entry button. When the door slid open, she leaned her head through the doorway. The breakroom was deserted—no one was at the tables or on the couch, and the holo screen in the corner was turned off. That sent a pulse of relief through her; even if a little part of her said she shouldn't be alone with Thargen, she didn't want to answer any questions from her coworkers, didn't want an audience.

Yuri released Thargen's arm as she stepped into the breakroom. "Go ahead and take a seat while I grab the medical kit."

He strode to the nearest table, pulled out a chair with his foot, and sat down, leaning back casually with thighs spread wide apart like nothing important had happened and he was just here to hang out.

Like he wasn't covered in blood.

Well, *covered* was a severe exaggeration, but to Yuri, there was little difference between a few drops of blood and a bucketful.

Yuri turned her face away from him as she walked across the room to the cabinet over the sink. Opening one of the cabinet doors, she stood on her toes and reached blindly for the med kit that was always up on that high shelf.

Yuri *knew* there were races here on Arthos that were the same size as humans—and many that were even smaller—so why did it seem like half the stuff in the city was built for giants?

Her fingertips brushed the side of the kit, pushing it back.

"Damn it," she muttered, lifting a knee onto the counter to boost herself higher. "Come on."

A large hand passed over her head. For an instant, Thargen's hard, hot body pressed against her from behind. His scent enveloped her—earthy amber, almost honeylike, with hints of leather and metal—and she breathed it in greedily.

Yuri's heart quickened, and heat flooded her in a rush. Her stomach was all aflutter from his nearness.

And had any man ever smelled so damn good?

Thargen plucked the med kit off the shelf and stepped back.

She climbed down, turned, and looked up at him. His lips were stretched into a grin around the pair of five-centimeter-long tusks jutting from his lower jaw. She realized suddenly that this was her first real look at him under normal lighting, without all the pulsing neon and ultraviolet lights out on the club floor.

He was big, of course—easily around two meters tall—and he was powerfully built. When he'd joked about being good looking, she hadn't feigned her agreement; he had a strong, squared jaw, a wide mouth with dark, full lips, and a narrow nose that was slightly crooked, as though it'd been broken a few times, but that didn't take away from his attractiveness. His skin —which had appeared much darker at the bar—was a light olive green, nearly the same color as her eyes.

Long, black, slashing brows rested over his intense golden eyes, and there were several hoop and studded piercings in his pointed ears, one of which was covered by his long, black, braided hair. The right side of his head was shaved to display the jagged, wicked scars that ran from his temple to the back of his head; they only added to his dangerous allure. There was a crimson tattoo on his right cheek. Yuri recognized its central symbol as a battle-axe, but the markings surrounding it were meaningless to her.

Her gaze dipped lower. He was dressed in a vest, a pair of black pants, and heavy looking combat boots, granting him a militaristic flair. But she didn't know of any soldiers who wore uniforms that kept their brawny arms bared, displaying every scar and sculpted muscle openly. The collar of that vest plunged particularly low, as well, giving her a nice view of his broad chest and the top of his toned abs.

Watch it, Yuri. You probably got some drool dribbling from the corner of your mouth.

But he's so damn yummy.

"I know it's hard, Yuri," he said in a deep, rumbling voice.

"Hmm? What?" She blinked and returned her gaze up to his. "What's hard?"

"Hard not to stare. That's why I don't keep any mirrors in my room."

Yuri laughed. "So...you just wake up looking that good, huh?"

"Funny enough, I *did* just wake up looking like this one day," he said, lifting his bloody right hand to tap the scars on the side of his head.

The sight of that blood reminded Yuri why they were here—and, unfortunately, made her stomach churn, killing whatever mood might've otherwise built through their flirtation.

She swallowed thickly and waved a hand toward the table he'd been sitting at a few moments ago. "Let's, uh...get you taken care of."

Thargen tilted his head. "You all right, terran? You're looking a little green. No offense, but it doesn't look as good on you as it does me."

She forced her eyes away from his hand, and an embarrassed chuckle escaped her. "I...don't really like the sight of blood."

He grunted thoughtfully and held the med kit out to her. "You take this, then. I'm gonna wash up. If that doesn't help, it's okay. Wouldn't be the first time I had to patch myself up, and I heal pretty fast, anyway."

His thoughtfulness touched her as much as it relieved her, but those feelings were followed by a hint of sadness. From what she could see, Thargen was covered in scars. How hard had his life been? What horrors had he witnessed, what pain had he endured?

Yuri took the medical kit from him, walked to the table, and pulled out a chair. She sat with her back toward him. "It's kind of funny, actually."

The faucet turned on, and the sound of flowing water was disrupted a moment later, likely because he'd put his hands in.

"What's funny, Yuri?"

A thrill swept through her. She *really* liked the way he said her name, all rumbly and gravelly. It did all kinds of things to her body.

"My mom was a nurse, and I was so eager to follow in her footsteps when I was younger. Nurses work hard, you know? They do so much to help people in need, to heal them and comfort them, and I wanted to do that. So I went to nursing school right out of high school. The standard UTF programs have nursing students doing hands-on training after the first eighteen months. I'd been a top student before then, but once I had to look at *real* blood..."

She laughed again and shook her head as she opened the kit and found the items she'd need to tend his wounds, setting them aside one at a time. Last was the medtool, a ten-centimeter-long device with a curve leading to a little metal disc at one end. It was a deceptively simple looking tool; according to Yuri's mother, these little things had all but revolutionized emergency medical care when they were first introduced on Earth about thirty years ago.

"I only fainted outright once or twice," Yuri continued,

"but I almost always felt like I would—and like I was going to puke. I made it into my second year before I had to face reality. I just...couldn't do it."

"This might sound strange, and probably runs the risk of scaring you away"—Thargen turned off the water—"but sometimes I wish the sight of blood made me sick."

Yuri furrowed her brows and twisted to look back at Thargen. "Why?"

His hands were in front of the drying pad on the wall. The pad released a soft *ding* before he pulled away from it and turned toward her. He'd washed his face, leaving glistening droplets of water in place of the flecks of blood that had been on his skin only moments before.

Thargen's expression was grave as he walked toward her. "Because a big part of me *likes* the blood. I've been a fighter for as long as I can remember. That's all I know. And I like it."

She cringed. "Is that how you got all your scars? Fighting?"

"Yeah, in some war or another." He eased onto the chair beside Yuri, moving slowly as though to avoid startling her. "I'm not some rogue lunatic, Yuri. I mean, I have my moments, but... I was a soldier. That's where most of my scars came from. I'm told I fought for my people with courage and honor."

Yuri smiled and held out her hand. "Give me your hand and let's see if we can keep from adding to those scars."

Thargen hesitated as he extended his arm. "Sure you'll be okay?"

Yuri gave him a deadpan stare. "I promise I won't puke on you."

He grinned. "Don't make promises you can't keep."

"You're not allowed to throw my words back at me until you deliver on that cake," she said with a laugh.

He chuckled and laid his arm atop the table, palm turned upward. "All right. I'm counting on you, little terran."

There were several cuts on his palm, and the overhead light made a few of the bits of glass embedded in those cuts gleam like tiny, bloody gemstones.

Her stomach protested immediately.

Knock it off. You can do this.

She flicked on the medtool, activating its little projection screen, and ran a quick scan to pinpoint the shards stuck in his palm; she could spot all of them with her naked eye but one. After setting the medtool aside, she opened one of the antiseptic wipe packets and used the corner of a wipe to sanitize the tweezers. She took careful hold of his hand to draw it closer and started removing the glass.

Each time blood seeped from his wounds, Yuri wiped it away with the antiseptic cloth and swallowed her bile, affording herself the briefest glimpses of crimson as possible. If she was hurting him, he made no indication of it apart from the occasional twitch of his fingers.

"You said you were *told* you fought for your people with courage and honor," Yuri said. "What'd you mean by that?"

"Just what I said, I guess. This happened"—he turned his head to gesture at those wicked scars—"and pretty much erased most of my memories of everything before. I see flashes here and there, but nothing I can really hold on to. I remember a lot of impersonal stuff, vorgal history and traditions and all that, but that's about it."

"Oh." Yuri frowned as she ran her eyes over the scars. "From the looks of it, you're lucky to be alive."

"Luck's a big part of it, yeah. Also had a really good friend watching my back. He was a combat medic." He turned his gaze back to her, brow furrowing. "How you holding up, terran?"

She chuckled. "I'm not puking, so that's a good sign." She flashed him a smile before dropping her eyes to the mess that was his palm. Her stomach revolted, making a mortifying gurgle. She ignored it as she wiped more blood away and plucked another tiny shard from his torn flesh.

A flash of cold swept through her, and her heart raced.

I can do this. I can do this.

It was the least she could do after Thargen stopped that onigox from pulverizing her.

"If it means anything, I'm trying to bleed as little as possible." Thargen covered her hand with his, engulfing it completely and halting its trembling—which she hadn't even noticed. "Take a minute, Yuri. I promise I'll be okay."

She stared at his hand, tracing the crisscross patterns of his faded scars with her eyes. It helped. His hand was warm, and its heat flowed into her soothingly. He had a really, really nice hand. Like, a sexy as hell hand—big and strong with long fingers, black nails, and defined knuckles, made all the sexier by those scars. She was seriously a sucker for hands like his.

Oh, who was she kidding? She was a sucker for *him*.

Yuri inhaled deeply through her nose and slowly exhaled through her mouth. She hated feeling so weak over something as minor as a few cuts. All she needed was something to keep her mind occupied as she worked—something other than Thargen's strong hands and sexy body. She needed to have at least a little focus left for the task at hand.

"Distract me," she said. "What do you do when you're not at a bar guzzling booze and breaking heads open?"

THARGEN CHUCKLED and shook his head. A little part of him wished he was guzzling more booze right now. His Rage had subsided, but it had burned away his buzz, leaving him with nothing to dull the sting of his cut-up palm. Maybe smashing the glass against the onigox's face hadn't been the smartest move, but it had seemed the best one at the time. Mortannis had possessed the advantage in size, reach, strength, and limb count, so a surprise attack, coupled with a bit of dirty fighting, had been Thargen's best bet.

Besides, smashing a glass into the unsuspecting bastard's face had been nothing compared to Mortannis laying hands on this tiny terran. Cowards like him didn't deserve a fair fight.

"It depends," he said. "Sometimes I sit in a room kinda like this one and guzzle booze. Sometimes I break heads open. Mostly I stand guard at doors or monitor security feeds."

And on very rare occasions, he went to new places and broke heads open, but those weren't instances that needed to be mentioned now.

Yuri gently took hold of his hand and lifted it off hers, guiding it onto the table. Her eyes briefly met his before she resumed her work. "You're a security guard then?"

"I prefer the title security specialist. Sounds more dignified."

She chuckled. "What's wrong with guard?"

Thargen shrugged, watching her little hands move and keeping his fingers as still as possible despite the flares of pain. "Guess it just reminds me of the boring parts. A lot of it is just sitting or standing around, waiting for something to happen. *Wanting* something to happen, even though I don't really want that because it puts my friends in danger."

Yuri ran the antiseptic wipe over his palm, sparking a fresh burn. "I think I got all the glass." She set the tweezers down and looked away from his hand, her gaze suddenly far away and unfocused. Her pale skin still had that slight green tinge. "Is that why you came here? Hoping for a fight without involving your friends?"

He wasn't sure why he was being so open with her, or why he felt so at ease around her, or where this gentleness he was showing her had come from. All Thargen knew was that he wanted her to feel safe around him...and talking to her helped lessen the weight of his Rage.

"Honestly, I just wanted to go out for a drink, and my usual place—where I was pretty much guaranteed a fight—was closed down. Some fucking Consortium health code violation or something." He released a heavy sigh and willed the tension that had been building in his hand to ease. "I wandered until I got tired of wandering, and this was the first place I noticed."

She smiled and picked up the medtool again. "I'm glad your usual place was closed." Yuri stiffened and sucked in a sharp breath, snapping her gaze up to his. "I mean, that is, uh... Well, I *am* glad to have met you, and I guess I'm being a little presumptuous in thinking... That is... Ugh!" Cheeks pinkening, she ducked her head, drew his hand closer, and set the medtool to work sealing the cuts on his palm. "You're hot."

The medtool's tiny lasers traced warm, faintly stinging sensations on Thargen's hand, but he barely registered them in his confusion. His brow furrowed. "Guess I did get a little worked up back there, but I feel all right. Unless... Am I running a fever or something?"

Her eyebrows drew together, forming a little crease between them, and she peeked up at him. "Huh? No, you're fine... Oh!" She laughed and shook her head. "You took that literally, of course. Stupid translators." Biting her bottom lip, she sealed his final cut. "Look, I'm not good at this kind of stuff, flirting and all that. What I meant was...I find you attractive."

A slow grin stretched across his lips, and heat spread through his chest. His Rage whispered again—that lustful beckoning that produced a tingle low in his belly. "I'd worry if you didn't. Can I tell you something, Yuri?"

She groaned, releasing his hand, and pressed her palm to her face. "*Please* don't tell me you're married or something."

He leaned forward on his arm, making the table creak beneath his weight. Yuri's scent—without the smells of hundreds of other aliens to compete with—grew stronger as the space between them shrank until it engulfed his senses, sweet and heady and arousing.

When his face was close enough for her to feel his breath on her skin, he grasped her wrist and guided her hand down from her face. In a deep, gravelly voice, he said, "Look at me, Yuri."

Her eyes met his. Her pupils were huge and impossibly dark, and from this close, he could see the little veins of darker and lighter green running through her irises.

"Oh, believe me, I've been looking," she said.

For an instant, he caught his lower lip between his teeth. "Me too. And you're pretty fucking hot yourself."

A tremor ran through her, and she released a shaky breath. Yuri's gaze dipped to Thargen's lips; his gaze dipped to hers. Just a little closer and he could taste her. Just a little closer and he could touch her for real, and they could tear off each other's clothes, could—

No.

However much he wanted her, he couldn't let things go beyond this point or he'd have no chance of maintaining self-control. He'd protected her from the thugs at the bar, but he couldn't protect her from himself. He knew these terrans were far tougher than they looked...

But his Rage was too much.

Just a taste though... That's not too much, is it?

He leaned infinitesimally closer, groaning at the ache in his cock. The sound vibrated across his chest in a rumble.

Just a quick taste.

Yuri closed her eyes—and closed the remaining distance between their mouths.

Heat flooded him, and thrilling tingles spread outward from his lips. Yuri's mouth was so damn soft and small, and it fit perfectly in the space between his protruding tusks. Her lips tentatively caressed his.

That hint of hesitance in her roused a fierce possessiveness in Thargen.

Lifting his free hand, he caught the back of her neck and held her in place as he slanted his mouth across hers. Her gasp of surprise only encouraged him to kiss her harder, deeper, to flick his tongue past her parted lips to taste her.

He growled as her flavor swept across his tongue, even sweeter than her fragrance, even more enticing. He crushed her lips against his, ravishing her mouth. He wanted more—*needed* more. He couldn't get enough.

Something clattered on the table, and Yuri grasped the edges of his vest with both hands, tugging it as though to draw him somehow closer. Her mouth moved beneath his, returning the kiss, and a small moan escaped her. The sound made his cock throb, made it fucking ache with desire. Hunger and Rage roared through him and made his limbs tremble with over-whelming need.

Fuck.

He knew then that he wouldn't be able to resist her—and that by giving in to these urges, he was likely to do more damage than the onigox could've.

The breakroom door whooshed open.

Like a switch had been flipped, Thargen's Rage shifted from lustful to protective, pouring molten strength into his limbs. He tore away from Yuri and shoved himself upright, baring his teeth and positioning his body to shield her as he turned to face the new threat.

The azhera who'd restrained Thargen at the bar—Ruunok —came to a sudden halt just inside the doorway. His brows fell low over his clear blue eyes, and one of his big hands dropped to his belt, where his claw-tipped fingers curled around the handle of a collapsed stun baton.

Instinct urged Thargen to attack. This azhera was a threat, a real threat, both to Thargen and Yuri. Thargen clamped a hand down on the chair, hooking his fingers beneath the backrest. It would make a clumsy, crude weapon, but all he needed was an extension of his reach to counter that stun baton. His muscles tensed, and his skin pulled taut over them.

A gentle hand fell upon his arm. The contact sent a cool, soothing current through him that washed away the haze of his Rage. Yuri stepped in front of him and met his gaze. She was so small, so fragile looking, and so unafraid of the fury and aggression he'd just displayed.

"Hey, Ruunok," Yuri said as she turned toward the azhera. "Everything okay out there?"

The azhera's gaze flickered between Thargen and Yuri, his mouth turned down in a deep scowl. "Yeah, everything's fine. What's going on here?"

Thargen clenched his jaw, forcing away the lingering tension in his neck, before twisting his lips into what he hoped was a casual smile. He lifted his right hand. "She just finished patching me up. Probably bled everywhere, though."

Ruunok stepped farther into the room, keeping his hand on the stun baton. "Yuri?"

Yuri cleared her throat and peeked up at Thargen. Her lips were swollen and red, and her flushed cheeks seemed to be darkening by second. She was undoubtedly a female who'd been well and thoroughly kissed. Thargen barely resisted the urge to lick his lips, wrap his arms around her, and smash his mouth against hers again to stake his claim right in front of the azhera.

"I'm good, Ruunok. Thargen and I just finished up," she said.

Ruunok's scowl eased, but only slightly. "You finished *something* up, all right."

Yuri pointed at the azhera. "That part is none of your business."

"When you're doing it in the breakroom it is."

"Did I say anything about that cren you were necking with last week?"

"Hey now, that was diff—"

Yuri crossed her arms over her chest and cocked her hip. "You were doing it right in front of the restrooms. While you were on duty."

Finally, Ruunok bowed his head and lifted his hands—leaving the stun baton on his belt. He laughed. "Okay, okay. You win, terran." The azhera leveled his gaze on Thargen, and a bit of that hardness returned to his expression. "Just be careful, Yuri. I know he helped you before, but this one is dangerous."

Thargen drew in a deep breath, filling his lungs near to bursting, and let it out through his nostrils.

Just smile, Thargen.

He stretched his lips into a grin. "Yeah, I'm dangerous. But I'm a pretty good kisser, too."

Yuri laughed, and the sound eased Thargen a bit more. "As crazy as it might sound, I trust him."

The warmth Thargen had felt in his chest while she'd talked to him at the bar flared again, spreading outward slowly from his center. He wasn't sure if it was pride, happiness, or some deeper, unfamiliar emotion, but it didn't matter. It felt...*good.*

Ruunok grunted, one corner of his mouth pulling back in an expression that clearly stated he did not share Yuri's assessment of Thargen. "You're a grown female. Anyway, Lyrani wanted me to check on you and let you know you're free to head home if you want. And I'm sure she'd want you to know that she thoroughly chewed us out over being so slow to respond to what happened." The azhera's features softened again, more so than before. "I'm really sorry, Yuri. I fucked up on this one."

"Hey." Yuri walked over to Ruunok, placing a hand on his arm.

That possessiveness she'd woken in Thargen roared in his mind. He clamped his mouth shut and didn't allow his feet to move. He had no right to be jealous when she touched another male—he'd only known her for an hour or two.

"It's fine, Ruunok," she said. "It all happened so fast, I don't think you or anyone else would have made it in time. Thargen was only able to help because he was right there." She grimaced. "And I...probably escalated it by slapping him. It wasn't the best thing to do, but I, uh...wasn't really thinking. I just kind of reacted, you know?"

The azhera nodded. "Yeah, not the best reaction, but..."

Thargen barked a laugh. "Should've seen the look on the big fucker's face. Hell, I wish I'd have seen the look on his face after that scuffle—at least what was left of it."

Ruunok let out a long, heavy sigh. "Yuri, you *sure* you want to trust this vorgal?"

"He won't hurt me, Ruunok." She said as she walked back to the table, her voice brimming with confidence and certainty.

Don't think I deserve that trust, but I'm definitely taking it.

Yuri gathered the supplies and returned them to the med kit. "Anyway, yeah, I'll take the boss up on heading out early. Can you thank her for me?"

"I will. You should probably slip out through the loading dock out back. That onigox and his friends were wearing Zulka colors, and gangs like that aren't above seeking revenge. Employee entrance might be too visible."

Zulka; that's what those colors were. Thargen had thought the orange highlights looked familiar. They were smugglers or gun runners or something like that, weren't they?

"Greeeat." Yuri moved to the cabinet, placing the med kit on a lower shelf before sidestepping to the sink to wash her hands. "Yeah, I'll go out the back way. Thanks, Ruunok."

"I need my belt," Thargen said. "Borian out front had me check it."

"So go get it," Ruunok said, scowl returning.

Thargen spread his hands to either side. "It's the least you can do after I helped you out tonight, right? I even let you pull me off that onigox without hitting you once."

Yuri turned off the sink, dried her hands, and walked back toward Thargen and the azhera.

"You didn't *let* me do shit, vorgal," Ruunok replied. "I'll have someone bring your gear back to the loading dock. You're not getting it till you're out, got it?"

Yuri poked Ruunok's shoulder. "Oh, stop being all growly."

The azhera grumbled something, not looking away from Thargen.

"I got it," Thargen said. "Just tell your crew that I know *exactly* how many knives were on that belt and if even one is missing, I'll be coming to find it."

Ruunok stared at Thargen for a few seconds more before shaking his head, turning away, and stepping into the hall. "Nice knowing you, Yuri. Send me a message if you make it home safe."

When the door slid closed behind the azhera, Yuri turned to face Thargen, eyes narrowed suspiciously, and put her hands on her hips. "You're not going to take me into a dark alley and stab me, are you?"

I might. But not with a knife.

His balls tightened, and his cock twitched. Arousing as that thought was, it was also *wrong*—and that she deserved so much better than a rut in a dank alley was only one of many reasons why.

"If you were half a meter taller and a whole lot meaner looking, I might try just for the challenge of it," he said, "but no. I think tonight I'll settle for just getting you home."

"Good, cause I have a mean slap and I'm not afraid to use it." She raised a hand and blew on her fingers—just like actors did to smoking, overheated blasters in those ridiculous action movies Thargen often watched with his friends. She cringed and dropped her hand, hiding it behind her back as she flashed him a self-conscious smile. "Sorry, that was really corny."

Thargen grinned and chuckled. "Not sure what *corny* means, but that was funny." And cute. Why the fuck did she have to be so cute? "Tell you what, you feel the need to slap anyone, I'll back you up. Pretty sure if you'd hit that volturian first he would've dropped."

She laughed. "Now you're just trying to make me feel better."

"Is it working?"

"Maybe." Her smile softened, and she tilted her head. "You're really going to walk me home?"

"Yeah, if you aren't worried about a big, creepy vorgal who owns a lot of knives knowing where you live."

She walked up to him and reached out, slipping her hand into his. "I'd feel safer, actually."

Thargen's smile fell abruptly, and he found himself staring down at the point of contact between them—at her pale, delicate fingers wrapped around his large, rough hand, a perfect representation of the stark differences between him and Yuri. Her skin was warm and soft, her touch gentle but sure.

Holding hands was the kind of thing Shay would've referred to as *sappy shit*, but that never seemed to stop her from holding Drakkal's hand.

Hell, just about everything Arcanthus and Samantha did together was sappy shit by Shay's definition, but the joy it sparked in those two was undeniable. And this...well, this felt fucking good. This trust, this little bit of innocent intimacy. But it was also a little scary, too.

Thargen was pretty sure he'd never done anything like this; nearly all the memories he had left were of violence. Combat had defined his entire life.

"Guess my theory of security guarding is finally paying off," he said, lifting his gaze to hers.

"Oh? And what theory is that?"

"The most important thing is to look scarier than anyone you might be guarding against. Doesn't hurt if you're also better looking, too."

Yuri quirked a brow. "So it's all about appearances, then?"

"Basically. I put a lot of time into"—what was it Arc would say?—"cultivating this look."

Yuri chuckled and raised her other hand, patting his chest. "Then don't worry. I'll protect you. Come on." She stepped away without releasing his hand, giving it a little tug. "Someone should be waiting for us at the loading dock with your stuff."

For a second, he was tempted to resist, to pull Yuri against his chest, lean down, and kiss her again instead of following her. But he wouldn't have been able to stop himself the first time had Ruunok not interrupted. He couldn't count on outside interference to distract him a second time. As much as he liked Yuri, as much as he wanted her—and he really, *really* did—he couldn't have her. He had to be satisfied with the brief taste he'd already had.

It would be best for both of them if he just saw Yuri home

safely and then returned to the compound. No more drinking, no more wandering. Just home, where he could trust himself to behave until his Rage resurged and forced him to seek release again.

The training facilities in the compound basement had given him enough of an outlet before. They'd have to be enough next time, too.

He forced his feet to move, following Yuri's lead. She stopped in the hallway to retrieve her jacket from one of the lockers built into the wall and continued through the employee-only corridors, offering smiles and warm words to the coworkers she passed. All of them seemed quite friendly with Yuri—and quite suspicious of Thargen. He brushed off their stares for her sake. She'd seen enough trouble for one night.

When they reached the loading dock at the back of the club, a pair of security guards—one of whom was the borian from the front entrance—opened the smaller door beside the big bay, allowing Yuri and Thargen to step into the back alley, and thrust Thargen's belt at him once they were outside.

Yuri released Thargen's hand then, and he couldn't ignore the pang of loss that struck his chest at the severance of that contact.

Thargen insisted the guards keep the door open as he inspected his equipment, somehow managing to mask his petty delight at their annoyance. When he was done, he jabbed a finger toward the guards. "You're lucky it's all here."

The borian glared at him. "Sure you don't want us to call a hovercar for you, Yuri?"

Yuri had a hand over her mouth like she was stifling laughter. "Yeah, I'm sure, Eroe."

Eroe grunted, cast Thargen another glare, and nodded to Yuri. "See you."

Yuri waved, and Eroe closed the door. She swung her

jacket onto her shoulders, slipped her arms through the sleeves, and turned her face toward Thargen. "You really don't have to walk me home."

When she pulled the sides of her jacket together, covering the bare skin of her midriff, Thargen barely kept himself from frowning. He put on his belt to distract himself, taking extra time to ensure his weapons hung exactly as he preferred once it was fastened. Though he had no qualms about fighting unarmed—and often enjoyed it more just for the enhanced rush—he felt more complete with his weapons at hand. Most people in the Infinite City weren't interested in a fair fight, especially against a vorgal with a Vanguard tattoo on his cheek.

"Not giving you a choice, terran," he said once he was satisfied with his belt.

She grinned. "I'm not complaining."

"Good. Besides, if that gang causes more trouble, I'm not gonna let you have all the fun kicking their asses."

She raised her right hand and blew on her fingers like she'd done before. "More like slapping their asses." That lovely pink returned to her cheeks. "Wait! That *really* didn't come out right."

"Yeah, I can't get behind that," he said with a chuckle. "But tell you what—you can slap mine if it means that much to you."

Yuri laughed and moved closer to him, looping her arm around his. She rested her hand on his forearm, tilted her head back, and met his gaze. "We'll consider it a reward if you get me home safely."

"I do like a good challenge."

They walked arm-in-arm, like they'd known each other for years rather than an hour or two.

Thargen still couldn't understand just what he was sharing with her. His comfort and ease around this little terran, the sense of closeness he already felt toward her, was unlike anything he'd ever experienced. Though his Rage had been present throughout his time at Starlight Trance, it hadn't been able to break through—at least outside of those brief, lustful bursts—while he was talking with her. Something about Yuri seemed to keep the worst of him at bay.

For a fleeting moment, he imagined her driving away his Rage completely. He imagined kissing her without the threat of him losing control, imagined the things he'd do if he wasn't worried about harming her.

"Can I tell you a secret?" Yuri asked as they neared the alley's exit. "It's kind of embarrassing."

That fluttery warmth in his chest reasserted itself. He glanced down at her from the corner of his eye. "You can tell me anything. No need to be embarrassed."

"You might think differently after I tell you." She tightened her hold on his arm, leaning against him, and guided him to turn left onto a quiet side street. "So, on Earth, before humans ever knew aliens existed, we had these fantasy beings that were in old books, movies, and games. *Elves, dwarves, dragons, and...orcs.*"

Thargen furrowed his brow. Those last words held no meaning to him despite his implanted translator. "What do you mean *fantasy beings?*"

"Things that were just make-believe. Things we didn't believe existed—well, at least not anymore—but that were created through our imaginations."

"So...your people just made up entire species?"

She chuckled. "Yeah, we did. My older brother and my dad were really into gaming, especially virtual roleplaying games. They got me and my younger brother hooked at an early age. Anyway, when I was a kid, I used to call the volturians and borians *elves* because they really resembled the *elves* in those fantasy games. But my favorites were the *orcs*, and my brothers used to make fun of me because I kind of had a crush on the *orcs* when I got older, and I guess everyone expected me to like the pretty races instead."

Yuri turned right at the next intersection, leading Thargen onto a narrower street. "Some people in school, um... Well, some of them called me a monster lover, and since they knew I'm half-Japanese, they'd give me all this crap about tentacle *hentai* and other weird stuff that I didn't even know about until I looked it up. *That* was enlightening, and some of it was pretty hot...buuuut that's all beside the point. I realized later that it was also pretty racist of them to make fun of me like that. I mean, my dad was from Norway, but they didn't make fun of me for being a *Viking* or ask if I'd sacked any villages lately or anything like that. Uh, I'm rambling, aren't I?"

Maybe she was, but Thargen was grinning. He found her rambling endearing, and the passion behind it—though under-stated—was something he could relate to. "You're fine. Gotta be honest, though, I only understood about half of what you said."

"Sorry. Guess I'm a bit nervous."

"Don't worry, Yuri. I'm not the fastest when it comes to absorbing new information, but I'll get there. I find all this terran stuff kinda interesting. Now, you were talking about...*orcs*, right? What did they look like?"

"That's the embarrassing part." She walked the fingers of her free hand up his arm, leaving little tingles in the wake of her fingertips, before flattening her palm on his bicep. "They, well...they kind of looked like you. Except you're *much* hotter. I've...always liked green."

"Say that again," he rasped.

Yuri coyly looked up at him. "I *really* like green."

The huskiness that had crept into her voice sent a thrill up his spine that arced along his every nerve, flooding his body with desire from top to bottom. His lips peeled back, and he sucked in a breath through his teeth, drawing to a halt. Yuri stopped beside him, keeping her gaze locked with his.

There was an undeniable glint in her eyes, a heat that was the perfect match to the fire burning deep in Thargen's chest and low in his belly. He knew instant attraction was a very real thing, knew such attraction could be mutual, but he'd never imagined a connection like he felt with Yuri being forged so quickly, so strongly.

His cock throbbed with need. His pants had never felt so stifling, their fabric never so abrasive. And it was all the worse knowing he could not have her. The sorts of relationships that Arcanthus and Drakkal had found with their terrans weren't for someone like Thargen—but that didn't stop his yearning.

"I could fucking eat you up right now," he growled.

The flush on her cheeks darkened, and she laughed. "I really hope you don't mean that in the literal sense."

"Terran, I'll mean it in whatever sense you want."

"Oh, well, in that case, I..." She glanced away and inhaled deeply before looking back up at him. "I *really* don't make a habit of this with strangers, but you... I don't know, I just feel this strong—ouch!" She winced, her brows dropping as she released his arm and twisted to move her hand toward her ass. "Did something bite me? I didn't...I didn't...know there were...bugs..."

Yuri swayed as though suddenly drunk, and her pupils dilated so big they nearly swallowed her irises. Thargen's already accelerated heartbeat quickened further as he placed a hand on her shoulder to steady her.

She lifted her hand from her backside and stared down at her open palm, upon which lay a small metal dart with a tiny glass viewport on it. The needle at one end had a tiny smear of blood on it.

Her blood.

"That doesn't...look..." Yuri's eyelids fluttered, and her knees gave out.

Something small struck Thargen's left shoulder, its impact accompanied by a prick of pain, but the sensation was dulled by the bestial roar in his mind. He caught Yuri in his arms, drawing her against his chest; she was completely limp, head lolling to the side.

A hundred simultaneous thoughts tumbled through his mind, but they were all swept aside by the simplicity of Rage—Yuri was in danger. Yuri needed to be protected. Thargen needed to *kill.*

A group of dark figures entered his peripheral vision. Thargen filled his lungs with a ragged, fiery breath and turned his head to the left. He recognized two of the five beings in that group. One was the onigox from Starlight Trance, Mortannis. One side of his face was swollen, his flesh criss-crossed by freshly sealed cuts and patches of dark purple bruising. The volturian, Firios, stood to Mortannis's left; he'd escaped with only a cut on his temple, courtesy of Thargen's elbow.

"Hit him again, Ir'esh," said the one at the center of the formation—a tall, broad-shouldered borian with slicked back, silver hair. The borian's clothing didn't have the same orange highlights as his companions', but his posture indicated all Thargen needed to know; this was the one in charge.

One of the aliens to the borian's left—a bronze-scaled ilthurii—raised a gun and fired. The projectile hit the front of Thargen's neck, grazing off the hardened tendons flanking his trachea, and clattered to the ground.

"Shit," Ir'esh hissed.

Despite his Rage, Thargen gently lowered Yuri to the ground; even with his primal instincts taking control, he recognized her as friendly, as important, as *his.* His limbs trembled with overwhelming strength, and his thundering heart was already beginning to drown out the city's ambient sounds.

"Again, damn it!" the borian said. "Get on him *now*."

Once Yuri was down, Thargen's conscious thought ceased.

Movement from his opposite side called his attention. Four more aliens were advancing from the other end of the street; he and Yuri had been surrounded during their little exchange. The aliens' features were indistinct to him, but they were unimportant. All that mattered were the orange highlights adorning their clothing.

Thargen's leg muscles bunched for an instant, like coiling springs, and he leapt at his assailants. The roar that tore from his throat echoed off the nearby buildings.

His existence became a blur of motion, a cacophony of shouts, grunts, and crackling stun batons. He threw wild punches and kicks—attacks that should've thrown him off balance, that would've left him wide open for counters were he in any other state. But the return blows were nothing to him. His knuckles smashed flesh and crunched bone, and the warm splatter of blood on his hands was a welcome feeling whether the blood belonged to him or not.

At least two more darts hit his back. He ignored them.

One of the gang members lunged at him with an extended stun baton. Thargen shifted aside, caught the attacker's wrist, and used his opponent's momentum to throw the alien face first into the nearby wall.

Another stun baton connected with his leg. His knee buckled, and he dropped onto it heavily. Twisting, he threw out his arm and caught the crackling baton in his hand. The electric shock pulsed up his arm, threatening to seize his muscles, but he simply growled and wrenched the baton down, snapping it in half.

Shards of ice stabbed into his blood, creeping outward from the impact points of the darts on his shoulder and back.

No!

The shout in his mind forced another roar from his chest, a wordless sound that was pure Rage. There were more foes close by now, at least six of them, each little more than crimson-tinged shades that needed to be destroyed. He shoved himself to his feet and lunged at the closest enemy.

His fingers closed around a throat. He dug his nails into the soft flesh and squeezed.

Another burst of electric hit him on the lower back and raced up his spine, mixing with the darts' deep chill to rob him of control for an instant. The being in front of Thargen tore out of his hold.

Something hard hit the back of his head—he heard the blow more than he felt it, a resounding *thunk* that vibrated through his bones. But he would not be taken down, he *could* not be.

He had to protect Yuri.

He twisted around and threw himself at the newest threat. He collided with a huge foe; undoubtedly the onigox, back for more.

Mortannis fell backward. Thargen came down atop the big, four-armed alien, his elbows, knees, and fists striking the onigox repeatedly. Strong hands grabbed at him, but Rage was pumping impossible strength through his burning limbs. The crimson haze over his vision deepened.

He was going to drink their fucking blood before he was done with them.

Another dart struck him in the neck, and this one stuck. He raised a hand, meaning to pluck the dart out, but his fingers were sluggish and unresponsive—and a stun baton struck his side before he could force his fingers to work. He tumbled off the onigox.

Thargen was aware of several enemies looming over him—and the pulsing white of their stun batons—just before they attacked. Several batons hit him simultaneously, and his entire body seized.

"Dart him again," someone said.

Thargen barely registered the impact of another dart on his belly through the consuming pain of the batons' shocks.

Thargen couldn't be sure whether a few seconds or a thousand years had passed when the electricity finally subsided. Rage burned in his mind, but his body was cold, and his limbs were slow and reluctant to obey his command when he willed himself to his feet.

His vision blurred, and the surrounding street grew darker. He let his head turn aside as he clawed internally for some final burst of strength.

Yuri lay unconscious on the ground nearby, but even if he could move his arm, she was just out of reach.

"You idiots," someone growled; was it the borian? "Did you not see that mark on his face? He was a fucking Rokkoshi vanguard!"

The ice in Thargen's veins crept up his neck, and its long, thin fingers brushed along his still-clenched jaw.

He wanted to call Yuri's name, but his lips wouldn't move, and no sound formed in his throat. Everything hurt even though he couldn't feel anything, everything was cold despite the fires in his soul, and he knew then that Rage couldn't stop this.

"Do you see what he did to me?" Mortannis said, sounding like he'd spoken through mangled lips.

"I don't care how fucked up your face is," the borian

replied. "Shipment is leaving in twenty minutes, and you're going to get both of them into the hold."

"Since when do we capture them?" someone asked.

"Since you botched this. After all this trouble you made, you can be fucking sure I'm going to turn a profit off this if I can. Now get moving, or you'll be part of this shipment, too."

Yuri...

Her features grew indistinct as Thargen's vision darkened. He tried to reach for her, visualized his arm sliding over the ground, his fingers clawing the pavement to move in her direction, but his body didn't move.

The void consumed his awareness, and he knew no more.

FOUR

Yuri had never been much of a drinker; she'd always been a lightweight with alcohol. There'd only been one time when she'd drank so much that she'd passed out, and the consequences the following morning had ensured she had no desire to repeat the experience—she'd suffered one hell of a hangover and had spent hours bowing to the porcelain god. It was all made worse by the fact that she couldn't even remember the night before. Definitely not worth it.

But this time, Yuri was sure she hadn't drunk a single drop. She never did while working.

So why did it feel like her head was going to explode, and why was her mouth so dry it could put the Sahara Desert to shame?

Yuri groaned and lifted her hand to her throbbing temple. Judging by the cold, hard floor beneath her, she must have passed out in her bathroom. The chill seeped straight into her bones, wracking her with a shiver. She moved her hands to adjust her clothes, seeking some warmth, to place a barrier between her and that cold, but all her palms encountered was bare skin.

She was bare-assed naked.

Why was she naked?

"So, the terran finally wakes," someone said in a gruff voice.

Yuri's eyes snapped open, and she gasped, shoving herself upright. Everything within her froze.

Not my bathroom.

Not my bathroom.

I'm not in my bathroom!

The floor was so cold because it was made of metal. The walls in front of her and to both sides were metal, too—metal bars. Like an old-timey jail cell.

Or a cage.

Eyes wide, Yuri surveyed her surroundings. Beyond those bars were more cages, all seemingly the same size as hers—maybe three meters by three meters at best. The cells were contained within a long room that was lit by a few dim lights over the central walkway, which itself led to a door at the far end of the chamber. Between the poor lighting and the rows of bars obscuring her line of sight, it was difficult to see into all the other cages, but each seemed to contain an alien being who was just as naked as Yuri.

There was a female volturian and a female cren in the cages across from Yuri, a willowy female kaital to her right, and a big male azhera with black fur in one of the cages at the end of the walkway, opposite the chamber door. She glimpsed a groalthuun, a borian, and several others, their features difficult to discern. One cell farther down even seemed to have two occupants, a sedhi and an ilthurii. There had to be at least a dozen people held in here, if not more.

Someone chuckled in the cell to her left, and long fingers curled around the shared bars of the two cages as the yellow-skinned cren within leaned forward, grinning around his tusks. "Come a little closer, terran. Let Iljibi get a good look at you." He licked his lips.

A surge of fear pushed back Yuri's shock and confusion, instilling her with a chill more intense than the metal beneath her ever could.

This...this can't be happening. This isn't *happening.*

Trembling, she crossed her arms over her bare chest and scooted back. She made it a few centimeters before bumping into something. She flinched and whimpered, but the sound was cut short when she turned to see what was behind her.

"Thargen," she breathed.

The vorgal lay on his front with his face turned toward her, his eyes closed, and his arms bound behind his back by a pair of thick metal manacles. There wasn't a stitch of clothing on his large, muscled body. Even in the weak light, the myriad of scars on his arms, legs, and back were clearly visible, and Yuri could see several spots where his green flesh was much darker, as though it were bruised.

She placed a hand on his shoulder and shook him gently. "Thargen? Thargen, wake up."

He released a groan and a huff of air but did not otherwise stir.

"Thargen, *please* wake up," she begged, unable to keep the desperation out of her voice as she shook him a little more firmly.

The cren chuckled again. "Think that vorgal's gonna be gentle with you when he wakes? You want attention, little terran, you come over here to Iljibi."

Ignoring Iljibi, she kept her eyes on Thargen and eased closer to him. With a shaky hand, she brushed his braided hair away from his face and tucked it behind his pointed ear. "Thargen, you need to wake up."

He groaned again, and this time he did move; his expression contorted, eyes squeezing more tightly shut and lips peeling back. His voice was deep and raspy when he said, "Fuck."

Relief flooded Yuri, and she clutched his shoulder. "Thargen?"

Moving slowly—and with a series of grunts that suggested, at best, great discomfort—he rolled onto his side, drew in a deep breath, and swung himself up into a sitting position with his muscular legs spread to either side.

Yuri's breath hitched, and her eyes rounded as they dipped to his groin. He was hairless down there, and even flaccid, his cock was *huge*. But that wasn't the only thing that caught her attention. She counted at least five piercings along the top of his shaft, running from its midpoint to just under its head, each bar capped by a metal ball at both ends. Their spacing and pattern was reminiscent of the rungs of a ladder.

What would those feel like inside her? How big was he when erect? And would that thing even fit if they were to—

Not the time, Yuri!

She forced her gaze up, meaning to return it to his face, but stopped when she saw the glint of two more piercings—one in each of his dark nipples. Yuri couldn't hold back the rush of desire that warmed her core at the sight of him. He was...a god. He was the type of male she'd always dreamed of, except...*better*.

She shook her head and finally looked at his face just as he opened his eyes. "Are you okay?"

"I've felt better," he said, blinking as though trying to work away grogginess in his eyes. "Felt worse, too." After a few seconds, he swept his gaze over his surroundings and muttered, "Fuck, not again."

Yuri's brows creased. "Again? Have you woken up in a cage before?"

His jaw ticked. He closed his eyes long enough to take in another deep, steadying breath. "I don't make a habit of it, but shit like this happens to everyone once in a while."

She frowned. "I would have preferred it not happening." Drawing her knees to her chest, she wrapped her arms around her legs. A flare of tenderness on her left wrist as it touched her leg had her lifting it away, not due to hurt but curiosity. She turned her arm toward the walkway light to find a small, red mark on the inside of her wrist—a cut freshly healed by a medtool, from the looks of it. And that cut was right about where her Consortium ID chip had been implanted.

Yuri brushed a fingertip over the cut. It was sore, but not painful. She probably wouldn't have felt it at all a few hours from now. "Um...I think they might've removed my ID chip."

Fire flashed in Thargen's yellow eyes. "Magama's flailing teats, these fuckers are—" His mouth curled into a brief grimace, and he grunted, letting out a little hiss through his teeth before he seemed to compose himself. "Feels like a tralix stomped on my head."

Yuri could relate; her head was pounding. At least the light was dim, if not enough so to mask everyone's nakedness.

As though of their own accord, Yuri's eyes dipped again, running over the expanse of Thargen's chest and his rippling abs. It wasn't like she could help it—Thargen was just so...big. Her gaze moved lower still to his pierced cock. Big *everywhere*. He commanded her attention, and she was helpless but to obey.

"You want cock, *ji'tas?*" Iljibi asked.

The cren's words were enough to snap Yuri out of her trance. Thargen's body was a good distraction from the current situation, but it wasn't enough to make her forget she was naked in a cage. She turned her head to look at the cren.

Iljibi had eased closer to the wall separating their cells. Fortunately, the bars were too closely spaced for him to fit an arm through, but he'd apparently found good use for the hand that wasn't clasping the bars—it was pumping his erect shaft. She looked away quickly, grateful that the shadows had spared her the details.

"That vorgal don't deserve a taste of terran slit. Iljibi can feed you, terran. Come closer and open that mouth."

Thargen was suddenly up, and before Yuri could react, he lunged at the cren. His body struck the bars heavily, and he slammed his head against them, making the metal resonate with a deep clang.

Yuri gasped.

Iljibi started and fell back onto his ass, kicking himself away from the bars.

Thargen snickered. The muscles of his arms, shoulders, and back bulged. "Stick it through, cren. Don't be a fucking coward."

The cren laughed; the sound was tinged with nervousness despite the bars between him and Thargen. "What you gonna do? You don't got a collar, but you're trussed up better than any of us."

The air in the cage seemed hotter than before, as though Thargen were somehow putting out far more heat. She recalled how hot his skin had been after the bar fight; he'd only begun to cool while she was tending his wounds.

Thargen grunted so deeply it seemed to make the bars vibrate. "Don't need hands to deal with the likes of you, you skeks-spawned shit stain."

"We in cages. Nothing you can do."

In a low, low voice, Thargen said, "We're in cages *now*. You don't wanna be on my bad side when we get out." He stepped back from the bars and turned to face Yuri. His legs bent as though he were about to sit, but he paused, and his eyes widened as he raked his gaze over her.

Before her eyes—literally, as her head was nearly level with his crotch—his cock pulsed and swelled...and the distance between the rungs of his metal-studded ladder increased along with it.

Oh yeah, definitely a grower.

And as his erection angled upward, she saw he had those same piercings on the underside, as well.

She'd never thought anything about body piercings on a guy before, but seeing them on Thargen...she liked them. She *really* liked them.

Her sex clenched, and her nipples hardened to achy little points, making her especially glad that she'd covered her chest. She knew this wasn't the time or place, but that didn't stop her body's natural reaction to his.

His cock wasn't too different from a human's with the exception of the thicker bulges on the sides of his shaft and a collection of little nodules on the underside of the head. His heavy scrotum seemed little affected by the cold.

Yuri dragged her eyes up to find him still staring at her body.

"You're naked," he said.

Fresh heat suffused her. She cleared her throat. "Uh, so are you."

"Yeah, but I'd already noticed that."

"How are you not freaking out right now?"

He shrugged, and without looking away from her, carefully lowered himself into a sitting position, belying the deadly speed with which he'd charged the cren not a minute before. Once he was down, he stretched his legs out, placing them to either side of her.

Not going to look again.

"It won't do any good," he said. "Not yet."

She crossed her ankles and hugged her legs tighter to her chest. "So...we just wait?"

"Yup. It'll give my head a chance to stop spinning."

Yuri quirked a brow. "I'm sure headbutting the bars didn't help."

"Nah, that has nothing to do with it. I have a naturally hard head." His gaze drifted up toward the ceiling, and he nodded to himself. "It's probably that void venom you served me. Hit harder than that onigox could. And *maybe* whatever shit they darted us with, too."

The dart. How had she forgotten about that? She and Thargen had left Starlight Trance through the loading dock, and they'd been talking as he walked her home. Then she'd felt a wasp sting her backside—only it hadn't been a wasp, but some kind of tranquilizer dart. Even now, her ass felt bruised, though the coolness of the floor had dulled the soreness.

"Doesn't mean much, but I'm sorry, Yuri."

Yuri frowned. "Why? This isn't your fault."

"Said I'd get you home. Unless you wanna pretend we're taking the long way, I fucked up pretty bad."

"Thargen, I don't blame you for this. And they darted you, too, right? What could you have done?"

He made a sound that was half-grunt, half-laugh. "They did. Four or five times, I think. And hit me with a bunch of stun batons. Hard to count...memory is pretty fuzzy, and I was pretty focused on punching everything within arm's reach."

It was no wonder he was covered in bruises. Having seen him in action, Yuri could only imagine how much damage he'd inflicted before their assailants had finally brought him down. And despite having done everything he could, Thargen was blaming himself for not protecting her. That made her chest ache.

Yuri shifted a little closer to him, her movement restricted by her unwillingness to expose herself to any onlookers—particularly Iljibi, whose gaze she could feel upon her like it were a physical, stomach-souring touch. "Thargen, you don't need to apologize. Maybe...maybe it's because of me that you're here."

He laughed, and that laughter was so genuine and good-humored that it caught Yuri completely off guard. "We haven't known each other long, but come on, Yuri. If it weren't this, you know I would've found some other kinda trouble before the night was through. If you wanna say this isn't my fault, it definitely isn't yours."

Thargen pressed his heels against the floor and bent his legs, dragging himself closer to her. The more his body blocked her view of the other cells and filled her awareness, the better she felt.

He tilted his chin down, and his intense golden eyes held hers. "I'm gonna get you out of this," he rumbled, voice low—these words were just for her. "I'll get you home."

"As long as you're safe, too," she whispered.

"Don't worry. I've been through much worse than this."

She wanted to say more—wanted *him* to say more—but a mechanical whir called her attention toward the far end of the room before anymore words could be spoken.

Thargen climbed onto his feet and turned to face the sound, his movements allowing Yuri a glimpse of the open door at the end of the walkway.

A tall borian with broad shoulders, a narrow waist, and long, silver hair stepped through the open doorway. He was dressed in a coat that looked like black leather, snug gray pants, and tall boots. The door slid shut with a metallic bang a few seconds after he'd crossed the threshold.

Many of the caged aliens recoiled from the walkway as he

strode past, retreating into the meager solace of the shadows gathered at the rears of the cages.

The borian ignored everything until he reached Yuri and Thargen's cage, where he stopped and turned to face them. He had those chiseled, elfin features common to his race, accented by thick, sharply angled brows and a mean slant to his mouth.

"Good. You're both awake. That means I won't have to repeat any of this," the borian said.

"Might as well just open the cage now," Thargen replied. "It'll save you a lot of trouble later."

The borian's hard expression didn't change. "You have a lot of fight in you, vorgal. I respect that. Hell, I would've tried recruiting you if you hadn't kicked the shit out of three of my people. I'm sure you understand that I couldn't just let that go. Especially not when there was a terran involved."

His eyes—the cool, pale gray of bare tristeel—shifted fully to Yuri. She cringed away from his stare, moving farther back in the cell until her back was against the solid wall.

Thargen stepped in front of her, blocking the borian from her view. "You don't get to talk to her."

"After last night's display, I know you have a thick skull," the borian said, "so let me explain this simply. You're both slaves now. We had this shipment ready to go to a buyer on Caldorius, and you nearly caused us a delay in our departure. Vrykhan does not like to wait for his goods, and my boss doesn't want trouble with that tretin. You fucked with us at the wrong time. So now I'm making an example of you and getting paid for the trouble you caused. Your little terran *ji'tas* will fetch prime credits on the market, even if we don't offer her as a sex-slave, and you...a half mad vanguard should get some good bids on the arena scene."

Thargen's hands curled into fists, and the muscles and

tendons of his arms bulged. Once again, the air around him warmed.

"Any other night, I would've had my people beat you to a pulp and move on," the borian continued. "We're smugglers, not slavers. Consider yourselves special for having pissed me off just enough to make me dip my toes in flesh wrangling."

Thargen shook his head and chuckled. "You have a name? I wanna know what to call you when I tell my friends about how fucking stupid you were."

"Taeraal," the borian replied evenly. "That's the name you can curse every time they're about to throw you in the fighting pit. The name she can spit right before her new owner plunges into her tight little slit."

"I'm not always good with names, *Taeraal*, but I'll remember yours," Thargen said. "I'll be sure to tell you mine right before I spill the last few drops of your blood on the ground."

"You don't seem to understand your situation, vorgal. That's not how this ends for you. We'll touch down on Caldorius in a week, and I'll be gone within a day of offloading you—a fuck of a lot richer and with a couple fewer headaches. For you, though...well, that's just the start of your suffering."

"I understand fine. You're a talker. You talk shit and have your *people* back it up." Thargen leaned toward the front of the cell. "When I talk shit, *I* back it up. I'm going to kill you, Taeraal, before this is all done. It's just gonna be you and me, and no one will back up your talking. And my only regret when I'm done is that I won't be able to kill you a second time."

Taeraal uttered a brief, humorless laugh. "And I don't need to kill you, vorgal, or the terran. Because what you're going to face is so much worse. Now settle in and get comfortable. You have a long ride ahead."

The borian's boots clomped on the floor, and he crossed

into Yuri's view as he strode to the door, opened it, and went through, all without a backward glance. The door clanged shut behind him.

That sound echoed with a dreadful finality.

This is real. Oh God, this is real.

Some part of Yuri had held out hope that this was some fucked up dream, a nightmare, an alcohol-induced hallucination. That it was anything but reality. This was so far removed from the virtual games she'd played back home. She couldn't just shut this off, reload a previous save, or start a new game. This was *real*, and it was everything her parents had warned her and Takashi about when the siblings had announced their decision to immigrate to Arthos.

Yuri's throat tightened, and her breaths came short and quick, each more of a struggle than the last. Pain seized her chest. She shifted a hand to cover her heart, which pounded rapidly beneath her palm. Uncomfortable heat was spreading just beneath the surface of her skin, contrasted by a chill so deep that it set her to trembling. Her vision narrowed, dimming, as her head swam. It felt like the room were spinning around her.

She turned her body so she was perpendicular to the wall, leaned her shoulder and forehead against it, and closed her eyes.

"Yuri," Thargen said gently, his voice breaking through the ringing in her ears.

She opened her eyes to find him kneeling beside her, torso leaning close.

"Breathe, Yuri. Deep breaths," he said, holding her gaze. "In and out."

Yuri took in a long, shaky inhalation through her nose and slowly released it through her mouth.

"That's it, terran. Keep breathing."

She obeyed without looking away from his golden eyes. Gradually, the tightness in her chest eased and the heat under her skin faded.

"I will get you out of this, *zoani*," Thargen said in that low, just-for-her voice. "Remember? I still owe you a slice of cake."

Unbidden, a small laugh escaped her, pushing away her lingering panic. She blinked, and tears fell down her cheeks. "I hope it's chocolate."

"Anything you want. Even if I have to take you to Earth to get it." His lips quirked in a smile that had no business being as charming as it was. "Fair warning, they may not let me onto your planet if you don't vouch for me very thoroughly."

Yuri laughed again as she reached up and wiped her cheeks. "I would. And that means something, since my sister, Kaiya, works for the Ministry of Interplanetary relations. I'll even buy you a few rounds when we got there."

"You talking ammunition or drinks?"

She smiled. "Which would you cause the least amount of trouble with?"

Thargen grinned around his tusks. "Doesn't matter. We're bound to have an interesting time either way."

Yuri was simultaneously amused and horrified by his nonchalant attitude. How could he be so calm? How could he so easily act like everything would work out fine? But oddly enough...she did find comfort in his demeanor, in his confidence, no matter how crazy it should've seemed.

The tension seeped out of her body, and the last of that heat vanished, leaving only cold in its wake. Shivering, she squeezed her legs tighter against her chest, but the chill would not diminish.

Wordlessly—and more than a bit awkwardly—Thargen walked forward on his knees until he was at her back. With a series of soft grunts, he shifted a foot forward, gently nudging her hip away from the wall to slide his left leg alongside her. He moved his other leg into position on her opposite side, leaving his knee bent to create a little wall between her and the cold, bleak little world she was currently trapped in. Heat radiated from his body. She longed for more of it, and he obliged a moment later by scooting forward until he was snug against her back—including his thick, pulsing shaft.

"Lean against me, *zoani*," he said. Though his voice was soft, she felt it rumbling in his chest. "I have plenty of warmth to spare."

Yuri looked at him over her shoulder. His eyes were even more heated than his skin, and even though those golden, predatory orbs were the sort of thing you were supposed to run from in the middle of the night, there was a gentleness in them that made her feel safe.

She turned her body again, this time to face the wall, and shifted her weight onto her hip so she could lay against his chest. She kept her knees drawn up and her arms wrapped around her. His skin was as hot as a furnace, and she soaked up as much of that heat as she could—while trying hard to ignore that club of a cock jutting against her side. She rubbed her cheek against his pec and closed her eyes. His heart pounded beneath her ear, strong and steady.

Think of the positive, Yuri. This situation may be shit, but you have your very own sexy orc right here letting you cuddle him like he's a big ole teddy bear. It could be much, much worse.

She sighed contently and murmured, "This is nice."

"Wish I could put my arms around you," he rumbled.

"Me too."

FIVE

Thargen tipped his head against the wall, closed his eyes, and took in a deep breath through his nostrils. The air had that stale, recycled taste typical on many spaceships—but it was sweeter than any he'd ever breathed thanks to Yuri's fragrance permeating it.

They'd sat like this for a long while, with his shoulder on the wall and Yuri tucked against his chest. He had no way of knowing how much time had passed. Hours, most likely, though it could've been days for all he knew. The multitude of aches in his body flared and faded with no discernable pattern. Most of them were from the street fight, and would be healed soon enough, but the worst by far was the discomfort in his shoulders, caused by the unnatural position in which his arms were restrained.

And as far as he'd seen, he was the only one in any of the cages with manacles on. Everyone else—except Yuri—had metal slave collars around their necks. His restraints made sense; though his memory of the capture was hazy, he knew he'd inflicted heavy damage on his attackers. They feared him.

What he didn't understand was why he and Yuri hadn't been fitted with those collars. As far as he was aware, slavers and slave owners used those things pretty often to keep their slaves in line.

That usually meant remote shocks on par with those delivered by stun batons.

Yuri and Thargen's lack of collars supported Taeraal's claim that he and his crew were smugglers rather than slavers; if they had decided to take Thargen and Yuri at the last moment, it stood to reason that they simply hadn't had any spare collars on hand.

Fuck reason, Rage growled in the back of his mind. *We can break these restraints. Free us. Kill them all.*

Klagar's balls, you're back already? Guess the tranqs are finally out of my system.

Who was he fooling? Rage was *always* with Thargen. Even when he quieted it, even when he buried it deep, it was always there—and it always would be.

He turned his mind away from Rage; there were plenty of other things to focus on. Like just how much his arms were killing him. That was unfortunate—he would much rather have had them killing the slavers, or smugglers, or whatever the fuck they were. There were all those aches to occupy his attention, too, like the hint of a sting lingering on his left wrist. That one was probably the result of his ID chip having been removed, just the same as Yuri's.

So much for Arc being able to track me by my chip.

So this Taeraal was stupid, but not clueless. That was good to know.

It would've been easy to focus on Yuri, too. Her little body fit against him perfectly. Her skin was warm and soft, and her black hair tickled his chest and teased his abdomen whenever she moved her head. But there were only two paths his thoughts could take right now if he focused on her too much—and each led to Rage in its own way.

Firstly, there was the fact that they were both naked. He'd been painfully attracted to her even before he'd seen her bare body, and that attraction had only deepened by an impossible degree despite the current circumstances.

She was...delectable.

Her hand had relaxed while she slept against him, allowing him a glimpse of her breast with its bronze nipple. Her feminine curves seemed to have been shaped perfectly for his hands, her skin beckoned the touch of his tongue, and she'd been pressed against his throbbing cock the whole time they'd been sitting here.

His erection hadn't wavered for even one damned second, and he wondered how there was any blood left for his brain to produce a single coherent thought. It *hurt*, and even if he couldn't put his hands on her, it would only take a slight change of her position to give him what he so desperately needed.

Maybe restraints are a good idea. Maybe...maybe they could make it possible.

He clenched his jaw and forced himself to take another slow breath. That was a dangerous path for his mind to wander, and it would drive him mad if he dwelled there too long.

These restraints will not hold you, his Rage said, helpful as ever.

But that interjection highlighted the only other path Thargen's thoughts could follow, a path of fury. He'd only known Yuri for a day—or two or three, depending on how long they'd been in this cage—but he *knew* she was a good person, knew she was genuine and kind. That she was an innocent. Her only crime had been to defend herself from an aggressor—not a crime at all, by the standards of most people. She didn't deserve any of this. She shouldn't have been sitting here, locked up like an animal, in a cold cell, forced to snuggle against a half-mad vorgal to keep warm.

The anger that this situation instilled in Thargen went well beyond Rage. There was fire in it, yes, a whole fucking inferno, but it also had a hard, icy edge. He couldn't claim to know much about justice or the law, but he did know about revenge—and he'd always been good at killing people who needed killing.

Somewhere aboard this ship was a whole crew of assholes who needed killing. Just the thought of them and the ugly orange accents on their clothing poured magma into his blood and threatened to make his breathing ragged, and what would that accomplish? He could break the manacles. Great.

Then what?

He couldn't break down the cell door. He knew just enough to understand that these cages were reinforced tristeel, and the bulky latches on their doors looked a hell of a lot like maglocks. Maybe Arcanthus could've managed it with his cybernetic limbs, but even that was doubtful.

As much as Thargen usually tried to roll with the situation, this feeling of impotence, of helplessness, would only enhance his Rage and make him throw away any opportunities to escape that might later arise.

Need to maintain my outward calm. For her.

So what was he to do, then? He wasn't going to turn his attention toward the other captives. That would just result in ceaseless speculation about who they were, why they were here, what their lives had been like before. And if they were staring at Yuri, like Iljibi had been, that meant more people on Thargen's eventual kill list, which was only fun if his enemies put up a decent fight while he pummeled them into a gooey, unidentifiable mass.

By the looks of them, none of these prisoners could provide any challenge—except maybe the azhera in the cage at the end of the walkway, but he'd been sleeping so long that he might as well have been in hibernation.

Thargen was suffering from another discomfort that he hadn't let himself dwell on for long, exasperated by Yuri being pressed against his cock—not the ache in his balls, but in his bladder. He had to piss something fierce. His raging hard-on only made that pressure so much worse.

Yeah, thinking about that will sure help. The fuck is wrong with you, Thargen?

His lips curled into a small smile. His friends would've offered quite a few entertaining answers to that question, were he with them. He hadn't really spent much time apart from them over the last several years; those excursions to local bars had rarely kept him away from his adopted home for more than a single night. He missed the banter, missed the good-natured insults, missed little Leah's giggles and smiles.

But I have Yuri now.

She grounded him, and her sense of humor was different from what he'd grown accustomed to—it was goofy, light-hearted, flirtatious, and so, so warm. That was refreshing. Though she'd delivered an impressive slap to Mortannis at the bar, she clearly wasn't a fighter, but she harbored a warrior's spirit in her heart. Thargen admired her inner strength—it didn't require physical strength to fuel it, and that seemed to make it all the more special. He'd had honest, heartfelt conversations with Urgand and Shay, but talking to Yuri was so easy, so natural, and felt so good.

She felt good.

Fuck!

He gritted his teeth; he could feel seed seeping from the tip of his cock, marking her skin.

Marking her as his.

The mechanical whir of the chamber door sliding open

shattered the silence. Yuri jolted awake with a gasp, pushing herself up straight by thrusting her elbow against his shaft and shoving hard.

Thargen grunted and curled slightly inward, arms straining reflexively to reach for his cock and ease the new ache.

"I'm so sorry!" Yuri said as she turned to him, eyes rounded. She reached toward his shaft as though she meant to soothe it, but hesitated before making contact. She placed a hand on his chest instead—giving him a full view of hers.

"I'm good," he groaned, eyes fixed on her full, pert breasts. The touch of her elbow had been the perfect blend of pleasure and pain; it had brought him to the verge of exploding. And his current view seemed like it'd be enough to push him over that edge without the need for another touch.

Brows drawn down in concern and confusion, Yuri followed Thargen's gaze with her own. She sucked in a sharp breath and crossed her arms over her chest, skin flushing pink.

Under different circumstances, Thargen would've taken those tempting nipples into his mouth, would've laved them with his tongue, would've sucked them hard—and maybe would've even asked her to slap his cock a time or two. But this wasn't the best place, and it definitely wasn't the right time.

Thargen took another steadying breath and focused past those desires.

He lifted his gaze to look toward the front of the room. Someone had entered and was moving from cage to cage, but the bars from the neighboring cages prevented Thargen from getting a good look at the newcomer until they'd moved closer.

It was Firios, the volturian from Starlight Trance.

Rage stirred along the edges of Thargen's consciousness, slithering like a serpent, searching out the breach through which it could enter. He'd only had a chance to hit Firios once from what he could remember, and it had been done blindly. That wasn't nearly enough.

As Firios drew closer still, his task became apparent—he was carrying a bucket in one hand, into which he dipped the other as he stopped at each cage, taking out one clear, gelatinous water cube and a single beige meal bar. Thargen watched the volturian toss the cube and the bar into a cell across the walkway and to the left.

The male groalthuun inside reached forward with a trembling hand to snatch up the rations before retreating to the rear of his cage.

Carrying himself with a disinterested air, Firios stepped to the next cage. The female volturian within stepped forward, standing straight and seemingly unconcerned with her nakedness. Her red *qal* markings shimmered faintly on her dusky gray skin. They were the same red as Firios's *qal*, and their patterns were similar.

"You are a disgrace to our *qalar*," she said in the smooth, flowing Volturian language.

Firios lowered his hand into the bucket. Maintaining that indifferent manner, he tossed a meal bar at the female's feet before reaching into the container to produce a water cube. He threw that higher; it struck the female's chest with a dull *thwap* and fell to the floor.

"The *qalar* can go fuck itself," he replied in the same tongue, somehow making the words sound dignified and graceful.

Fucking volturians.

The female was unfazed. "I will see that you face justice on Korous."

"The only thing you are likely to see is your new owner's cock just before he thrusts it into your mouth to shut you up."

Expression unchanging, she leaned forward and spit at the

male's feet. "I do not accept your disgrace, traitor. You are disowned."

"Spare me your sanctimonious whining. It would serve you better to turn your efforts toward making peace with your situation, because it will only worsen from here." Firios turned away from the female and stepped up to Thargen and Yuri's cell.

Fixing a cold glare on Thargen, the volturian dipped his hand into the bucket and produced two water cubes. He angled his hand to let the cubes slide off. They landed at the very front of the cell, barely inside the bars.

"I gotta take a piss," Thargen said as the volturian reached into his bucket again.

"I doubt you let anything stop you before. Is there a problem now?"

"Guess I didn't hit you hard enough the first time, huh?"

"The *only* time." Firios dropped a pair of meal bars into the cage. "There is a hole in the corner. Piss away."

"Oh, my God," Yuri whispered in horror.

Firios turned away to toss meager rations into the remaining cages. As soon as he was done, he walked to the door and exited the chamber.

Yuri looked at Thargen with a frown before she stood up and crept to the front of the cell, giving him a lovely view of her ass. She crouched, collected the meal bars and water cubes, and returned to her place beside Thargen, all while keeping one arm banded across her breasts.

Her eyes flitted from Thargen to that arm clamped over her chest. That enticing blush hadn't faded from her skin; if anything, it deepened further now. "It's stupid, isn't it? Being concerned about modesty in a place like this when everyone else is...as naked as I am."

Thargen offered her as gentle a smile as he could. "Not stupid. You're taking what control you can, that's all."

She nodded and hesitantly lowered her arm from her breasts, using that hand to wipe the water cubes clean. "I'll, uh, hold these if you want to...pee."

The sound of his own chuckling was all that snapped Thargen's attention away from her chest.

"Yeah. Before I embarrass myself, I guess." He forced himself to rise, pausing when he was up on one knee to meet her gaze. "So you know, you have *nothing* to be embarrassed about. I would tell you to cover up, but that's only because none of them deserve to see you."

Though a glimmer of shyness remained in her eyes, she smirked. "Oh, but *you* do?"

"Fuck yeah, I do," he replied as he climbed to his feet. The motion reminded him how stiff his legs had become while sitting with her and introduced a new ache at the base of his spine. He scanned the floor until he found the hole Firios had mentioned—it was in the corner to Thargen's right, no wider than his hand.

Thargen stepped over to the hole. He shifted his gaze from it to his still erect cock, flexed his hands, which were locked securely behind his back, and frowned.

"This should be fun," he muttered.

If he let loose now, he'd just piss all over the wall, and he wasn't going to do that—at least not in Yuri's presence. And he'd be damned if he was going to ask for her help; as much as he wanted her hand on his shaft, *this* was not how he wanted it to happen.

He lowered himself onto his knees sand bent forward, pressing his head to the wall. Slowly, and not without a few frustrated grunts and muttered curses, he shifted his knees back, simultaneously angling his pelvis forward to direct his cock toward the hole as best he could. His abdomen burned with exertion, forced to support more and more of his weight at this unfavorable angle. Pressure and heat built in his face as his position grew increasingly precarious, and he was soon forced to bury his chin against his chest just to see where he was aiming.

Finally, the head of his cock was pointed at the hole in the ground; if his angle were any lower, he might as well have been lying on the fucking floor.

A soft, muffled sound came from behind him—something suspiciously reminiscent of a giggle.

"I know you're not laughing at me," he grated. His words were followed by a drawn out, grateful moan as he finally let it all out. His eyelids fluttered shut. This wasn't full relief—it'd take far more than a piss for that—but it was a hell of a lot better than a few moments before.

"I'm not. Swear," Yuri said, though the amusement in her voice suggested otherwise. "You're, uh...surprisingly flexible. For such a big guy, I mean."

"This is at least a little bit your fault." Despite her teasing, his flow continued unbroken. Were he not in such an uncomfortable, ultimately unsustainable position, he might've found the duration impressive. But it was difficult to appreciate the possibly record-breaking piss while his muscles were burning, and his scalp was being ground between his skull and the wall.

Iljibi laughed. "You not the only one she making suffer, vorgal."

"If you show her your dick again, cren," Thargen growled, "I am going to tear it off and shove it down your throat."

"Sorry. Iljibi will go get dressed."

"Fuck your sarcasm. Now shut up, I'm busy."

It might've been ten seconds or twenty minutes later when Thargen finally finished. Placing that much more strain on his muscles, he rocked his hips from side to side to shake away the last few drops.

"You want Iljibi to give it a few taps for good measure, vorgal?" the cren asked.

Clenching his jaw, Thargen shifted his knees forward and straightened. He opened his eyes as he stood up. "If you hadn't treated this terran the way you did, you and me might've got on all right. But now you're on the fucking list."

"You want to fuck Iljibi?" the cren laughed. "Not interested, vorgal."

Thargen walked back to Yuri and sat beside her. She was facing the wall again, legs drawn up with knees close, and had her head bowed as though to hide her smile. Thargen couldn't blame her for her amusement.

"Did, uh...everything come out okay?" she asked.

"You tell me. You were watching."

Her eyes shot up to his. "I was not!"

Thargen grinned and leaned his shoulder against the wall. "Maybe not the whole time, but I know you were watching my ass flex. We already know our neighbor was transfixed by it."

"He's just a nasty pervert. I was trying to give you some privacy." With her cheeks flushed red, Yuri edged closer to Thargen and raised one of the meal bars to his mouth. "Here."

"You wash your hands?" he asked, brows falling low.

"Yep, with fancy soap and everything. Now eat."

"Guess my business did take a while. You could've skinned and roasted a whole glehorn while I was over there pis—"

Yuri shoved the end of the bar into his mouth.

Thargen snorted and bit the bar in half. It was oddly tasteless and dusty, but he supposed it was at least on the same level as some of the food he'd been forced to eat on the front lines back in the day.

She lowered the remainder of the bar and stretched out her legs, waiting as he chewed. When he swallowed, it felt like a fistful of dirt tumbling down his throat to pile in his gut, and it only made him hungrier—for anything but the rest of that unidentifiable meal bar. He opened his mouth dutifully and leaned his head toward her.

Yuri smiled and held the bar up again. Thargen extended his tongue and swept the whole bar into his mouth, getting the faintest hint of salty and sweet from her skin; that sample of her was the best thing he'd tasted since the birthday cake.

"Best to eat crap like this quick," he said as he chewed. "Longer you take, the worse it tastes."

She gave her own bar, which lay on the floor beside her, a disappointed glance. "Guess we're lucky they're feeding us at all."

He choked down the food in his mouth. "That's the spirit, terran. Look at the good. Another positive is that you get to stare at me as much as you want."

She chuckled, plucked a water cube from her other hand, and raised it to his lips. "I'd say that's the best thing about this."

Thargen dipped his eyes, letting them linger on her body—particularly her navel piercing. "Second best."

He sucked the water cube into his mouth. It was cold, rubbery, and had a very faint chemical taste, but he was grateful for it as the gelatinous, slowly melting outer layer released water that washed away the lingering taste of the meal bar.

Yuri drew her knees up, grabbed her meal bar, and took a bite. She grimaced as she chewed, seeming to have a harder time of it than he had. "You're right. Even though it's tasteless, it tastes like crap."

Thargen squished the last bit of the water cube's outer layer, making it dissolve, and laughed. "Doesn't make any damned sense, does it?"

She glanced longingly at her water cube before taking another, much larger bite of the meal bar, nose wrinkling in disgust. When she finally swallowed, her grimace was even deeper than before. She looked up at him, her expression suddenly serious.

"I know we talked about this a little before," she said in a soft voice, "but...I need to ask again. How are you not scared by any of this, Thargen?"

His smile faded, and he longed more than ever to be able to put his arms around her. "Want the inspirational, full of shit answer, or the real one?"

"As much as I'd love to be told everything is going to be okay, I...I think I need to hear the real one."

He nodded and glanced upward as though the perfect answer were scribbled on the metal panels of the ceiling. "I should be worried. I know that. But I've stared death in the face so many times, Yuri, I don't know when to flinch anymore. I'm either too crazy or too stupid to be scared."

Thargen scooted a little closer to Yuri, sliding a leg past her and bending it to press his calf along the outside of her thigh; it was as near to a hug as he could manage. "But the truth is, fear is *good*, and there's no such thing as courage without it. There's no shame in being scared. It's natural, it's smart. And you should take pride in the fact that you're still functioning despite that fear. You're brave, *zoani*."

Her eyes met his. "I really don't feel brave. I'm scared out of my mind right now. What Taeraal said...what they plan to do with us..." She looked down at the partially eaten bar she was holding in her lap. "For what it's worth, I'm glad I at least got to meet you."

"Oh, you and me have a lot more to do yet, Yuri. A fuck of a lot more. Look at me." When she obeyed, he tilted his chin down and stared into those beautiful green eyes of hers, unwilling to let her look away. "We're getting out of this, together, no matter what I have to do."

SIX

Yuri sat huddled with her back against the wall, letting her gaze wander the room for lack of anything else to do. She didn't know how long it had been since she'd woken in this cell; however difficult she'd found it to gauge the passage of time in the subterranean Undercity, it was a million times harder here.

Everything was so still, so gloomy, and other than Iljibi's crude commentary and remarks to rile Thargen, the other captives had been relatively silent.

Her eyes shifted toward the violet-skinned female kaital in the next cell. The kaital's long ears were drooped, and she was shivering. The metal collar around her neck looked huge in comparison to her lithe body.

That was one thing Yuri could be thankful for—at least she hadn't been collared. She'd seen what those things were used for.

Firios had returned earlier to toss one more water cube to each captive. The female volturian had stepped forward again, looking just as proud and defiant as before, and given him another tongue lashing—or at least she'd started to. This time,

Firios took a small control out of his pocket, directed it at her, and pressed a button.

A light had flashed on the female volturian's collar, and she'd convulsed as though being hit by a strong electric shock. Her strained cries had ended after a few seconds, when her suddenly limp body pitched forward. She'd barely caught herself on hands and knees, and had remained in that position, panting, as Firios calmly put the remote away and tossed in her water ration.

That felt like it had happened hours ago.

Yuri squeezed her thighs together, tipped her head back against the wall, and closed her eyes as though any of it could ease the discomfort in her bladder. That dreaded moment had come, just as she'd known it would.

She'd have been stupid to expect her body to comply with her wishes and just...not have to freaking pee. It was a natural bodily function—and she'd been holding it for a long, long time. Now, the pain was becoming unbearable. She hugged her legs desperately.

Please, please, please just...absorb back into my body, or magically disappear or something!

She fidgeted again, crossing her ankles and pressing her toes down on the metal floor.

"Just go," Thargen said.

Yuri lifted her head and opened her eyes to look at Thargen, who was standing at the front of the cell. Though his back was toward her, he'd twisted slightly to look over his shoulder, giving her full view of the shaved side of his head and those wicked scars.

Despite her discomfort, she couldn't stop her eyes from dipping to his taut ass.

"What?" she asked.

He turned to face her fully, and for a moment, her pain was

eclipsed by the glory of his sinfully sculpted body. A rogue thought flitted through her mind—apparently, the whole *erections lasting longer than four hours* warning didn't apply to vorgals.

"You've been fidgeting for a while, terran. You gotta piss, right?"

Yuri's face warmed, and she covered it with her hands, replying with a muffled, "Yes."

"So just go," he said. "No reason to torture yourself."

She watched through the gap between her fingers as Thargen stepped closer to her and glanced at Iljibi's cell.

Thargen returned his attention to Yuri. "I'll act as your personal privacy shield, or whatever."

Iljibi, who was lying on his side, facing away from them, waved a dismissive hand. "Just shut up so Iljibi can sleep."

"Now this fucker wants some quiet, huh?" Thargen grumbled, shaking his head.

Yuri lowered her hands, certain that her expression was the same one she might've worn when facing her own imminent death. What choice did she have? It was either pee in the hole or pee while she was sitting here on the floor. She couldn't hold it in forever.

Pushing herself up to her feet, she moved to the corner of the cell and looked down at the hole. It was pitch dark inside. At least it wasn't just some bucket collecting all their...excrement. Though now that she thought about it, sitting on a bucket might've been a little more dignified than squatting over a hole in the floor—not that anything about this situation left much room for dignity.

She felt Thargen just behind her. It was more than the heat he always seemed to emit, more than his masculine, earthy-sweet, leather and metal scent. His presence itself had become a physical feeling to her. It blanketed her with comfort, wrapped her in security, instilled her with a calm that probably shouldn't have been possible given the circumstances.

She glanced over her shoulder to find him with his back turned to her, but he was looking over his shoulder, too. Their gazes met, and he gave her a small nod before facing forward.

You can do this, Yuri. It's...just a stupid hole. Should be easier than peeing in a cup, right?

She positioned herself over the hole and groaned inwardly as she squatted down, resting her elbows on her knees and covering her face with her hands as though she could fool herself into thinking she were alone. Then she let it flow. Her cheeks burned with embarrassment, but the feel of an empty bladder was such a relief.

That relief was tainted by another complication.

There was nothing to clean herself with. What was she supposed to do, give it a good shake like a man?

"I'm never taking private toilets for granted again," she muttered.

"Not that I want to get into a pissing contest with you, but I think I had it a little worse," Thargen said.

Though she was mortified, Yuri couldn't help but laugh. "Yeah, you did." She dropped her hands from her face and gave her bum a little shake before standing back up. "I'm done."

She turned around to face Thargen. His back was still toward her, and his huge body made this corner of the cell seem even tinier than it was. Given the amount of space he took up, he actually provided more privacy than some of the public toilet stalls back on Earth.

As he stepped forward, Yuri noted the tension in the muscles of his back, the stiffness in his movements. He was likely sorer than she could imagine, having had his arms bound behind his back this whole time, but something about him was increasingly reminding her of a caged beast—temporarily muzzled, perhaps, but increasingly agitated and dangerous. It was an instinctual recognition, a gut feeling, driven by changes in him that were so subtle she might not have noticed had she not been here with him for so long. It should have unsettled her.

She didn't doubt the humor he still offered from time to time—it was genuine—but there was definitely something darker beneath.

And even after glimpsing that darkness, I don't fear him.

Have I already gone insane?

Yuri hadn't taken more than two steps away from the hole when total darkness swallowed her. She stilled, body tensing as her heart leapt. Fear trickled down her spine, sending goosebumps over her skin. "Thargen?"

"I'm here, *zoani.*"

His voice, deep and rough, staved off the terror that sudden darkness might otherwise have instilled in her. She raised her hands and held them in front of her, creeping forward until her palm pressed against him. Yuri moved her hand over that expanse of flesh, seeking his shoulder, until her fingers brushed a bit of metal and a nub of harder flesh—she was touching his chest, not his back, and that had been his nipple.

She felt his chest rumble, though it was too low to produce a sound, and she had to chew her lip to stop herself from acknowledging that she'd just stroked his nipple.

Yuri quickly shifted her hand to the center of his chest, settling it in that valley between his powerful pecs. The feel of his skin against hers grounded her the rest of the way and robbed the darkness of its lingering bite.

"What's happening?" she asked. "Do you think something's wrong?"

He grunted, and his chest swelled against her hand as he drew in a deep breath. When he exhaled a few seconds later, he said, "No, still feel that hum in the air from the engines. Probably just giving us a night cycle—or putting us in the dark to fuck with us."

Though she couldn't sense the hum he'd referred to, she accepted his answer; the only time she'd spent on a spaceship had been during the trip to Arthos, and she knew almost nothing about them.

As seconds passed, she slowly became aware of light ahead of her—thin vertical strips of it so dim that they must have been a trick of her mind. But those strips of light grew clearer with time until she finally realized she was seeing faint reflections on the bars of the cells. She turned her head toward the chamber's entrance; there was a soft light over the door which, apart from casting that barely noticeable glow on the bars, only seemed to deepen the shadows in the room.

No, even that was wrong—there were two more sources of light, one a few cages closer to the door than Yuri's and the other directly across the walkway. Both were from *qal* markings; the farthest belonged to the sedhi, the closest to the female volturian. Those *qal* didn't seem to cast light on anything, and the volturian's was weaker than ever, its orientation suggesting that she was lying on her side.

"Might as well lie down and try to get some rest," Thargen said.

Yuri wanted to argue that she wasn't tired, that sleeping was the last thing she wanted to do right now, but she knew he was right.

Keeping one hand on Thargen's chest, she extended her other arm in the direction of the solid wall—at least what she *hoped* was its direction—and waved around blindly. She'd only taken a few dang steps away from it, hadn't she?

Thargen chuckled. "Put your arms around me, terran."

Yuri turned her face toward Thargen, narrowing her eyes.

She could almost detect his shadowy outline. "Uh, Thargen, I don't know if this is the time to...uh, you know. *Do* stuff. I didn't mean to, um, *touch* you."

"Not saying I'm not ready, but that's not what I had in mind. I was just gonna guide you toward the wall."

Heat flooded her face. "Oh. I knew that."

Sure, right, Yuri. You totally did. We know what's been on your mind. It's not like you haven't been sneaking peeks at his ass and cock the entire time, and you know *he's been looking at you. He's probably checking you out right this...*

"Wait, can you see?" she asked.

"Mmhmm." His reply made his chest rumble; the vibrations flowed into her arm, making her toes curl, her sex clench, and her nipples harden into firm little buds.

Why does his voice have to be so damn sexy?

He can see you, Yuri!

"Damn it." She crossed her arm over her chest to hide her body's reaction, but it was likely already too late.

"Thought we were past that, *zoani.*"

"Well, you... How are you supposed to rest if you're ogling my chest?"

Thargen chuckled again. "That's my problem to deal with. Come here, terran."

Cheeks burning, Yuri stepped close to him and slipped her arms around his waist, pressing her chest against his. His hard cock probed her belly. She flinched her hips back out of reflex.

A soft but unmistakable groan escaped Thargen's lips. "It's not gonna bite, Yuri."

"But you might."

"Oh, I *will.*"

Before she could respond, Thargen sidestepped, forcing her to move with him. When he turned, leading her along, she almost felt like they were in some sightless, stilted dance—and couldn't help wondering if Thargen knew how to dance, or if he was willing to try it. Then he guided her backward another step. Her back touched the cold wall, and her breath hitched.

Thargen leaned over her, caging her between the wall and his big, solid body—his cock a hot brand against her belly—and pressed his face to the side of her neck. He inhaled deeply, like he was taking in her scent. That was followed by a low, appreciative growl.

A pleasurable shiver rippled through Yuri. She could feel Thargen's warm breath and the cool, hard touch of his tusks on her skin as he brushed his lips over her neck and shoulder, and she closed her eyes, instinctively tilting her head to give him more room.

When his tongue trailed up her neck to flick just behind her ear, heat flooded her core, and Yuri squeezed her thighs together in an attempt to alleviate the sudden ache between them.

"Thargen," she rasped softly, digging her fingers into his back as she gripped him tighter; she needed him closer.

Thargen tensed, his muscles becoming as solid as tristeel, and he turned his face away from her. He drew in a harsh, shuddering breath. She felt his cheek against her ear, and just a tiny bit of moisture on her belly where his cock, still hot and throbbing, was trapped between their bodies.

Even if she couldn't guess at what conflict was raging inside Thargen at that moment, she felt it radiating from him; her arousal wasn't strong enough to make her miss how torn he was, how *tortured*.

And her recognition of his inner torment was like a bucket of ice being dumped over her head.

She and Thargen were locked in a cage, surrounded by other captives. It didn't matter that it was dark—if Thargen could see, who else could be watching, who else was listening?

For that brief, delightful moment, Yuri had forgotten where they were. All that had mattered…was him.

Yuri relaxed her grip on him and turned her face toward his, grazing his cheek with her lips. "Thargen?"

"Lie down," he grated, voice rougher than she'd ever heard. He stepped back, and she let her arms fall away.

She froze, eyes widening in the dark. "What?"

Surely, he wouldn't…

"Don't know everything about terrans, but I *know* you don't sleep standing up."

"Oh." Right. He meant for them to lie down and sleep, not to… She laughed nervously as she lowered herself to the floor. "No, we don't."

She lay down on her side facing the wall, curling her arm to use as a pillow. The floor was cold and hard, but what choice did she have? It was either this or sleep sitting up—and that wall was just as cold and hard as the floor. The important thing was that she rested when she could. What better time than now, while she was blanketed in darkness?

And how exactly am I supposed to fall asleep?

Though her arousal had diminished, it still thrummed through her with dull insistency. She tried hard to ignore the cool, wet spot on her belly where she knew his seed was drying, but it was impossible.

Thargen grunted softly, and there was a muted thump behind Yuri. A few seconds later, his chest was against her back, and she could feel his breath through her hair. His voice was low and gruff as he said, "Not here, *zoani*. I wouldn't take you here."

Yuri allowed herself to relax against him. Guilt, confusion, and arousal battled inside her, making her chest tighten and her stomach twist into knots. "I'm sorry."

"For what?"

"For thinking you would."

He sighed heavily, scooted a little closer, and placed a surprisingly gentle kiss atop her head. "Get some sleep, Yuri."

Something warm and soothing bloomed within her chest, easing the tension. Thargen didn't look like someone who had a gentle side—he didn't look like the kind of person who knew the word *gentle* at all. He was rough, could be crude, and took to violence with little hesitation and at least some enjoyment.

Yet Thargen had shown her nothing but care and consideration in the short time they'd known each other. Whether he blamed Yuri or not, he was here because he'd helped her. And he was the only thing keeping her grounded when all the uncertainty and terror in the universe was clawing at her mind from every side.

She lay there, taking comfort in his closeness, his warmth, and the sound of his breathing until it slowed and deepened, and she knew that he'd fallen asleep. But sleep eluded Yuri.

Her attention drifted to the other sounds in the room—the faint hum of the ship, which must've been what Thargen was referring to before; the whispers coming from the other side of the room, letting her know she wasn't the only one awake; Iljibi's droning snores.

Finally, after what felt like hours, a sense of heaviness settled upon Yuri, and sleep claimed her.

A growl startled her awake.

Yuri's eyes flashed open, but it was so dark that her groggy mind couldn't immediately determine whether she'd actually opened her eyes or not. She stared into the blackness for several seconds, the passage of time marked only by the thumping of her heart, and listened for the sound—for any sound—in the stifling silence.

Another growl came from behind her, but it was sharply cut off. Thargen twitched. His breathing became labored, and the heat of his body had intensified considerably. A new sound emerged from his throat; it seemed almost as though he were trying to speak, but all that came out was a low, rough groan.

Yuri turned over to face Thargen and reached for him. Her hand touched his shoulder, and she slid her palm across it and up his neck to cup his jaw. Leaning her head closer, she stroked his cheek with her thumb. "Shhh. It's just a dream."

Thargen started with a snarl, his body going rigid and recoiling from her. His breaths were even more ragged now, punctuated by deep rumblings from his chest.

"Shhh." Yuri scooted closer until her body was flush against his, slipping an arm beneath his head so he had something to rest it on as she held him. She tucked her head just beneath his chin and continued stroking his cheek. "I'm here. It's okay. It was a bad dream."

He remained tense—so tense that he was trembling—and his body was damp with sweat that seemed impossibly cold against his heated skin. She felt his heart thundering in his chest like it was the pounding of some immense drum.

For a while, a long while, he just lay there and breathed. Slowly—so slowly it was difficult to notice—he eased. The tension in his muscles faded, his breathing smoothed and slowed, and his heart quieted.

He'd fallen asleep again.

Yuri skimmed her fingers over his jaw, tusks, lips, following the lines of his nose and brow until her fingertips encountered the scars on the side of his head. She traced those scars, frowning, each one making her heart ache a little more.

How much had he suffered in his life? What had he gone through that had left him so scarred both inside and out?

She returned her hand to his cheek and cuddled a little closer to him. She still felt safer with Thargen than anyone else, and maybe...maybe she'd granted him a bit of that security, too.

SEVEN

The next day—or at least the time between when the lights came back on and eventually went off again—passed much like the first. The prisoners were left largely alone. Firios entered the room twice, tossing out rations with his typical aloofness. One meal bar and two water cubes for each captive. None of it tasted good, and it did little to satisfy Yuri's hunger and thirst, but it was better than nothing.

Yuri understood that their captors were providing just enough for survival. She also understood that this journey was meant to break the captives; Yuri and the others were supposed to reach Caldorius as shells of their former selves, ready to bow to any prospective owner so long as there was a chance their conditions would improve.

But she refused to succumb to the despair that constantly threatened to overwhelm her. Maybe the sight of blood made her queasy, but she would *not* be broken by this.

Even when she wasn't feeling particularly strong, she had Thargen with her—and his presence commanded her constant attention. Whenever he spoke, he offered Yuri confidence, reassurance, and encouragement.

But the passage of time didn't seem to be doing him any favors. That sense she'd had of him being a caged predator had only intensified through the day.

His patience seemed frayed, and the easy humor he'd displayed since they first met burned away as untold hours ticked by. Yesterday, Thargen had brushed off most of Iljibi's comments, offering a few snappy retorts that had made Yuri laugh despite everything. Today, he was increasingly hostile toward the cren—and his threats grew more serious and direct in accordance with his demeanor.

Before long, it seemed like Thargen was ready to charge the bars separating the two cages any time Iljibi so much as glanced in Yuri's direction. The kaital female in the other neighboring cage had taken to huddling as far away from Thargen as she could.

Thargen expressed his restlessness in small ways, like frequently changing position while sitting, or repeatedly clenching his fists, often hard enough to make his knuckles pale and the tendons on his forearms stand out.

Not long after Firios had delivered the second round of water cubes for the day, Thargen's restlessness ratcheted up to a new level—he began pacing. The fact that he could cross the entire space in two or three agitated strides only made the cell feel infinitely smaller than it already was.

It was only when the lights went out for another night cycle that Thargen seemed to relax. He and Yuri lay in the same position they'd assumed after his nightmare the night before— face-to-face with her body tucked against him, his head resting on her arm for support.

Right before Yuri drifted to sleep, Thargen muttered, "Wish I had my arms around you, *zoani*."

Thargen woke her once during that period of darkness, having released a troubled growl, but she quickly soothed him back into a quiet slumber.

The next day was just like the prior two, different only in that Yuri was beginning to feel the effects of her confinement and lacking nourishment—and Thargen was even more irritable.

Firios brought more meal bars and water cubes, and Yuri helped Thargen eat.

There was something new in Thargen's eyes—an unsettling gleam that seemed to spark only when he was looking away from her. More than once, she saw him ball his hands into fists and tug against his manacles as he prowled the cage, his movements stiffer and more agitated than they'd been the day before.

She could almost envision a countdown timer over his head, rapidly ticking toward zero—but she couldn't guess what would happen once it ran out.

Yuri looked up at Thargen. He was standing still now, positioned at the front of the cell as though waiting for someone to enter the room, posture rigid and muscles tense.

Her gaze trekked over his form. No matter how often she looked upon him, his appeal never lessened. If anything, her attraction to him only grew with each passing hour. She hadn't been lying when she told him that she'd had a thing for orcs when she was younger. That *thing* had evolved as she'd matured into a woman, expanding into an *appreciation* of a variety of inhuman features—the sort of features that might've prompted some people to call Thargen monstrous.

The sort of features that had initially drawn her eye to him.

Thargen was tall, muscular, savage-looking, and the perfect shade of green, but it wasn't those looks that had locked Yuri in. The person behind those features was interesting, funny, and thoughtful, too.

It was part of her job to be friendly to patrons at Starlight Trance—to laugh at their jokes, to make them feel welcome, to put them at ease. She'd talked to so many people of so many species that she'd lost track of them all long ago, but she'd never experienced as immediate and powerful a connection as she had with Thargen. His golden eyes, protruding tusks, and green skin might've caught her attention, but it was his genuine humor and honesty that had sealed the deal. Even if he hadn't given her a chip loaded with enough credits to buy a round of drinks for everyone in the club, she would've gone back to talk to him again and again.

And during their time in this situation, he had done so much for her. He'd made her feel safe when she had no reason to, and his presence was the only thing keeping her hope alive. She wanted to give back to him, to return the favor—to ease him now that he was slipping. It'd be a lie to say she didn't need the distraction, too, but she wanted to help him beyond the comfort she'd provided during the night.

She drew her knees up to her chest and wrapped her arms around them. "Tell me about where you're from."

His shoulders rose with a deep breath. When he exhaled, a barely noticeable shiver coursed up his spine, shaking away just a little of his tension. "Rather hear about where you're from."

"I can tell you about Earth later, but only if you tell me about where you're from first."

He leaned forward, resting his forehead against the bars. He turned his head slightly toward her before he spoke. "I... don't remember too much. Valgorond is a big world. And spherical, I guess. Like most planets I've been to. Grew up in the Rokkoshi tribal holdings, which border this rugged mountain range that always reminded me of teeth jutting up from a jawbone. Those mountains used to be crawling with skeks, but...that was a long time before me."

"Come on. I know you can give me more details than that." She smiled. "Is the sky yellow, and the water purple?"

He chuckled and shook his head slightly. "Throw out enough colors and I guess you're bound to get one right, huh? Yeah, the water's usually kinda purple. But we don't have a yellow sky. It's somewhere between purple and blue on clear days. And I guess the light from the star Valgorond orbits is weaker, or comes from farther away, because everything Shay's shown me makes Earth look brighter and more vibrant."

"Yeah, we have a bright blue sky with big, white, fluffy clouds, and our water was either blue, green, or gray, depending on where you lived and what was in it." Yuri tilted her head. "Who's Shay?"

Thargen turned around to face her and leaned back against the bars. Though his posture seemed more relaxed, there was still clear strain in his expression—a crease between his eyebrows, a tightness around his mouth, and just a hint of that wild light in his eyes, though the latter faded when he met her gaze.

"She's a friend of mine," he said.

"She's from Earth? She's human?"

He nodded. "Her and Samantha both."

"*Two* female humans?" Yuri's brows rose. "You in a habit of making friends with female terrans?"

"Technically Leah's a female terran, too. So you can say three."

"Huh. And here I thought I was special."

His lips tilted into a lopsided smile. "You are. You're the only terran I know who I don't live with."

She rolled her eyes and looked away from him. "Wow. That totally makes me feel better."

I'm not jealous. Nope. Not at all. Not even a smidge...

Okay, so maybe I am a teensy, weensy, tiny little bit.

At the edge of Yuri's vision, Thargen pushed away from the bars, walked toward her, and plopped onto the floor in front of her. "They're friends. Family, pretty much. And anyway, Sam and Shay both have mates of their own, and Leah's just a year old." That smile of his stretched into a grin with just the right amount of wickedness in it. "You don't have anything to worry about, *zoani.*"

"I'm not worried about anything," she said *way* faster than she'd meant to.

Smooth, Yuri.

Her cheeks warmed as she returned her gaze to Thargen. He was sitting cross legged, a position that only emphasized the powerful muscles of his thighs—but which definitely didn't hide his semi-erect cock.

A semi-erect cock that was working its way toward full mast even as she stared at it.

It's so beautiful...

Focus, Yuri!

She forced her eyes up to find him watching her with a knowing grin.

Busted.

Yuri cleared her throat and said, "You, uh...mentioned buying a gift for a baby before. Was that for Leah?"

"Yeah. Everyone suddenly decided a knife was inappropriate to give a baby."

Her brows rose. "It really is, you crazy vorgal."

"How the hell is a baby supposed to defend itself otherwise if it doesn't have any claws or tusks?" Thargen grunted dismissively. "Anyway, all the terrans I know would tell you that we crazy vorgals are the best kind."

She tilted her head. "Besides my brother and a guy who

works at Starlight Trance, I haven't seen any humans after immigrating to Arthos. Everyone just kind of went their separate ways, and that was it. It's pretty easy to get lost in the Undercity."

"Pretty easy to get lost anywhere in Arthos. It's like the city was built to swallow people up." His shoulders twitched, and his grin faltered. He shook his head and chuckled. "All this time and I suddenly forget I'm locked up. Was about to put a hand on your leg and charm you by saying I'd introduce you to more terrans when we get back."

Yuri wiggled her eyebrows. "You can put your hand on my leg when we get out of here, how's that?"

"Terran, that's just *one* place I plan to put my hands."

Heat sparked in her core. Yuri crossed her ankles, hugging her legs more firmly. She *wanted* his hands everywhere. "You, uh, were telling me about your homeworld."

His smile regained that mischievous slant for an instant; it was just long enough to tell Yuri that he knew exactly what he was making her feel.

"Yeah, I was. Area I lived in, my tribe's lands, is this combination of steppe and highlands. Rugged terrain, not many trees, gets real cold in the winter and too damned hot in the summer. Got this short, scratchy grass that grows all over. In the dry season, it gets these dust storms that make everything turn reddish brown, sometimes for days afterward."

"Why ever would you leave it?" she asked. "It sounds like a lovely vacation spot."

He laughed. "I don't remember much, but I know there's beauty there. Not saying I appreciated it back then, but I'm sure it's there. Joined the military as soon as I could. There isn't any real action on Valgorond anymore, not since the last time the tribes united a few hundred years ago, so I was shipped out to space. I served...seven or eight years, I think. Went back to my homeworld for a few months after my near-death experience had me discharged, but there wasn't anything there for me. Been on Arthos for the nine or ten years since."

"And now you work as a security guard."

"Yep. It has its moments."

Yuri tapped her right cheek. "What does your tattoo mean?"

He shifted his eyes as though to look down at the symbol. "Rank, unit, honors. I was in the Rokkoshi Vanguard, best of the best. First in, last out. Marks along the bottom are completed campaigns."

She ran her gaze over the crimson tattoo again, studying it closer than she had thus far. The central symbol was clearly a double-headed battle-axe—just the sort of thing she would've expected from the orcs in those old fantasy games. But the symbols around it were more abstract. Some looked like alien writing, and the ones he'd mentioned at the bottom looked like a set of thin, pointed fangs. There were eleven of those marks, many with at least one dot over them. The combined symbols gave the tattoo an overall shape reminiscent of a shield.

"That looks like quite a few," she said.

"Woulda had more if not for..." He turned his head to the side, displaying the scars on the right side of his skull.

Yuri leaned forward and reached out to lightly run her fingers over them. "What happened?"

"Iljibi will show you what happens if you don't shut up," Iljibi grumbled, kicking the bars between the cages.

That furious light Yuri had seen more and more of lately flared in Thargen's eyes, and his lips curled back to reveal clenched teeth.

Yuri caught Thargen's chin before he could turn toward Iljibi and forced him to keep his eyes on her. "Ignore him." She lifted her other hand and caressed the scars on his head. "Tell me what happened here."

His nostrils flared, but that primal fire in his eyes diminished. His jaw muscles ticked once, twice, and finally relaxed after the third time. When Yuri was sure he'd calmed, she lowered her hands and wrapped her arms back around her legs.

"Don't remember most of it. Was on some planet, don't know if it even has a name, fighting skeks. We were always fighting fucking skeks. We were...pinned down somewhere..." Thargen's brow furrowed. He searched Yuri's eyes, but there was a sudden vacancy in his gaze that suggested he was lost in his own recollection. "We had wounded. My friend, Urgand, was tending them, but we were being overrun. I tried to hold the enemy back until we could be extracted, but..."

Thargen shook his head, and his eyes regained their focus. "There was an explosion or something. I blacked out. Next thing I remember, I was in the infirmary of a battlecruiser. Urgand had dragged me off that planet, had saved my life, and I couldn't even remember all of it to thank him properly.

"He was discharged and moved to Arthos a few years after me. We've worked together ever since. He's, uh...he's kept me out of a lot of trouble over the years, even if I can't always recognize it at the time."

Yuri smiled. "You kept in contact before he was discharged? Is that how he found you?"

"Heh, no. I didn't keep in contact with anyone after they sent me home. I was just...lost. All I knew was fighting, so my only thought, I guess, was to go and do more of it without breaking too many laws. He tracked me down. One of those things where bleeding together made us brothers, or some sappy shit like that."

Yuri's brows rose. "Wow. So, he was determined to find

you. Kind of like...your guardian angel and the angel on your shoulder at once."

"What's an *angel*?"

She chuckled. "Yeah, guess that's a word the translators wouldn't really be able to define. An angel is...well, I guess they're from these millennia-old religions on Earth, but they've kinda transcended their origins. Angels are supposed to be these beautiful, radiant beings of light, goodness, and right-eousness. Protectors and guardians. Stuff like that."

Thargen tipped his head back to look up at the ceiling. "Don't know about all the radiance and beauty stuff. Guess to most non-vorgals, Urgand looks a lot like me." He returned his gaze to her and grinned. "But he doesn't look as good as me, of course."

Yuri laughed. "Of course not. But I didn't mean that he's literally an angel, just that he watches out for you."

"Yeah, he does. You said you have a brother on Arthos, right? You and him do the same for each other?"

Her smile faded at the mention of her brother, who was undoubtedly worried sick right now and wondering if she was even alive. "Yeah, we do. Takashi and I immigrated to Arthos together two years ago. We live together in Niharin Sector, not far from Starlight Trance. He's...uh, well, he's a dancer in another fancy club. Not exactly something I would have chosen for him, but it wasn't my choice to make, and he seems to enjoy it."

Thargen's eyes rounded, and his grin widened. "When you say he's a dancer..."

Yuri chuckled. "He likes to show it all off—and I mean *all* of it. Not that I want to picture that."

Thargen laughed that deep, booming laugh she hadn't heard from him in what felt like days. "That's great. So many assholes in Arthos are after terrans, I'm glad one figured out how to make a living off it without getting his ass captured." His expression sobered, and he straightened a little. "I just insulted *us*, didn't I?"

"Maybe. What's so special about humans, anyway? I mean, there are so many other species that are more...beautiful than us."

"More beautiful than who? Terrans as a race, or you specifically? Cause if you mean the second, I'm calling—what's that word? Bullshit?"

Yuri smiled as a pleasurable warmth flooded her chest. "I meant as a race." She leaned toward him. "You think I'm beautiful?"

The hungry light in his eyes was all the answer she would've needed, even if he hadn't spoken again. "Of-fucking-course I do, Yuri. And all you gotta do is look at me to know I have particularly high standards."

As though of their own accord, her eyes dipped to his cock, which was standing at full attention. She caught her bottom lip between her teeth as she ran her gaze along his pierced shaft, and the warmth in her chest rekindled the heat in her core.

When his cock twitched, and a bit of seed oozed from its tip, Yuri's sex clenched.

She tightened her hold on her legs and squeezed her thighs together. She wanted more than anything to reach out and wrap her fingers around his shaft, to find out if it felt as hard as it looked, to brush her thumb—or better yet, her tongue—over the head and taste his flavor.

Yuri had never, *ever* wanted anyone like she wanted him.

"Fuck, *zoani*," Thargen said thickly, "keep looking at me like that and—"

The door to the chamber opened with a hydraulic hiss. Thargen snapped his mouth shut and twisted to look toward the entryway.

It felt like it was time for their second daily water cube, but it was impossible to accurately keep track of such things—and Yuri doubted the smugglers kept a regular schedule when it came to tending to their *cargo*.

But it wasn't Firios who stepped through the open doorway; it was the towering, four-armed onigox who'd grabbed Yuri in Starlight Trance and started this whole ordeal—Mortannis. The door slammed down behind him with a resounding metallic clang that seemed somehow more ominous than it had any time before.

Oh, God, what now?

Thargen curled his torso forward slightly and stood up, releasing an undeniably frustrated huff through his nostrils. Yuri caught that primal glint in his eyes just before he turned to face the walkway, his head angled toward Mortannis.

She scrambled to her feet, crossed her arms over her chest, and stood beside Thargen, leaning forward to peer down the walkway. She could already feel his body heat rising.

Mortannis turned and opened some sort of panel beside the door; his bulky body blocked it from Yuri's view. A moment later, there was a machine-like whir underfoot, strong enough to vibrate through her feet and up her legs. She placed a hand on Thargen's arm to steady herself. His muscles were coiled steel, his skin taut and hot.

Yuri looked down to see the floor *change*—thin strips along the edges of the walkway sank down and split apart, opening long lines of tiny drainage slits. When the floor under her feet suddenly moved, Yuri's heart skipped a beat. She spun around and leapt back, pressing herself against the front of the cage.

A section of the cage floor dropped a few centimeters and slid out of sight, leaving a grating with hundreds of tiny holes behind. It was dark beneath that grating—like she was looking straight into the void.

The onigox laughed. "Smells like shit in here. But don't worry. I'm going to fix that."

Thargen released a low growl. He was in the same position as before, attention pinned on the onigox; he'd not so much as flinched when the floor changed. Swallowing thickly, Yuri willed her breathing to steady and stepped forward, away from the cold bars. The floor felt strange now. The holes were too small for even her little toe to fit through, but they were so numerous that she swore she could feel every one of them on the soles of her feet.

She turned to look toward the chamber's entrance again.

Mortannis grabbed something in the wall and pulled. Yuri only recognized it for what it was when he turned, aimed the object at the first cell, and opened the nozzle.

A powerful stream of water sprayed from the hose in the onigox's hold, splashing off the bars and creating an impossibly loud noise that almost completely drowned out the muffled cry from the cage's occupant. Mortannis grinned and laughed again.

After twenty or thirty seconds, he turned closed the nozzle and sidestepped to the next cage. His grin didn't waver as he turned on the water again, and his laughter was a little stronger this time.

"Guess it doesn't matter whether you've been bathing with your tongue, does it, azhera?" he called to the cage's occupant—a female azhera who Yuri had only been able to glimpse a couple times so far. Mortannis turned off the hose and leaned forward, his grin stretching somehow wider.

From somewhere inside the cage, the azhera growled—but the sound faded into a desperate whimper.

Thargen stepped forward, pressing his forehead against the bars. "Pissed because you didn't have anyone to lick your wounds?"

"Thargen, what are you doing?" Yuri whispered, brows furrowing.

Mortannis turned and walked toward their cage, his footfalls heavy upon the metal floor; Yuri could hear his size and strength in every step. In Starlight Trance, Thargen had caught the onigox off guard, but he'd still handled the bigger alien like that size difference was meaningless.

Now, Thargen was restrained and caged. The situation was about as uneven as it could've been.

The onigox stopped in front of Thargen and glared down at the vorgal. His skin, which was a vibrant red, was marred by several blotchy purple bruises on his face, and several paler lines marked the cuts Thargen had opened on his cheek and temple with the shot glass. One side of his face still had a swollen, uneven look to it.

"You say something, vorgal?" Mortannis asked.

"If you can't hear me, why don't you open the cage? I'll get *real* close and whisper it in your ear."

Mortannis bent closer to the bars, placing his face nearly on level with Thargen's. "Sounds like you need to cool off."

Before Thargen could respond, Mortannis opened the hose nozzle. The jet of water struck Thargen in the face. Despite his size and strength, he was blasted away from the bars, backpedaling until he struck the back wall.

Yuri gasped. The water spraying off him and hitting the bars and wall filled the air with mist that obscured her vision. The droplets that hit her skin were frigid, and some still held enough force to sting. She threw up her arms to shield herself as best she could.

Thargen roared. Muscles bulging, he leaned into that relentless stream and walked forward one hard-fought step at a time.

The sound created by the water's impact was almost deafening, but Yuri swore she heard Mortannis laughing just outside the cage.

The jet of water intensified suddenly, growing impossibly louder. Thargen crashed back into the wall again, losing every centimeter he'd battled to gain in an instant, and slipped. He crashed heavily to the floor.

All at once, the spray stopped. The gentle sound of runoff flowing through the grating and dripping to some unseen part of the ship below was surreal after all that noise. Thargen grunted and heaved himself into a sitting position. Water streamed over his skin from head to toe, and huge patches of his face, chest, and shoulders were darker than normal, as though irritated or bruised. When he released a huff, it sent a spray of droplets from his lips.

"See, doing better already," Mortannis said with a chuckle. "And don't think I forgot about you, little *ji'tas*."

Yuri looked at Mortannis, eyes widening a split second before the water hit her. A scream tore from her throat; the impact was like being hit by a train, like being struck by lightning, like being drenched in liquid nitrogen. It knocked her off her feet as though she were an insect being swatted aside, and the continued pressure quickly slid her back until she struck the wall. The pain of her shoulder striking solid metal was nothing compared to the agony of that water.

And now she was pinned between that hard, unmoving metal and that punishing, forceful stream of water. It was at once burning and freezing, sending a numbing sting across her flesh. Sputtering and choking, she turned her face toward the wall; the water blasting her was too strong, knocking her arms and knees aside when she tried to shield herself with them. No place was left untouched.

Her world was water—its force, its sting, its icy chill, its consuming roar. There was nothing else.

Not until she heard him.

Thargen's roar was a direct challenge to that water, just as primal and elemental but infinitely more furious. She felt it even through the pain and cold, felt it resonate in her bones, in her *heart*. That sound should have been terrifying—it was the call of a beast, a force of nature that knew only how to destroy.

And then the jet of water broke. Thargen's body fell over hers, covering her completely and blanketing her with a heat that was scalding in contrast to the iciness of her skin. Yuri coughed, trying to clear her airway. Outside, she was freezing and numb, but her lungs and throat were ablaze and raw.

Thargen was heavy, almost too heavy, but his crushing weight was a welcome change. His muscles strained around her, and his ragged breaths were audible even over the water, each of them run through with a snarl, grunt, or growl. Every sound he made was brimming with pain and rage.

The flow of water ceased abruptly, and Mortannis's laughter boomed in the relative silence that followed. "Brought low by a little water. Not so tough now, are you, vorgal?"

His heavy steps moved away, and the water came on again, just as loud as before. Iljibi cried out, but his voice was drowned out as water filled his mouth, turning words into gurgles.

Still coughing, Yuri squeezed her eyes tighter shut, wishing she could block out sound just as easily. Mortannis moved from cell to cell, cackling at the screams, whimpers, and sputters of the captives as he hosed them down. Shivers wracked her body, and her teeth chattered. The numbness was fading, allowing the chill to intensify and the stinging sensation to spread across her skin from head to toe, both far worse in the places she'd been directly hit by the water.

Thargen shifted his position, easing much of his weight off her.

Yuri turned her face; her forehead touched Thargen's chin. She opened her eyes and looked up at him. The muscles of his jaw were bunched, his lips were peeled-back, and his golden eyes blazed with barely contained fury. His nostrils flared with a harsh exhalation.

With a trembling hand, she reached up and cupped Thargen's jaw. "C-Calm. S-S-Stay calm."

He leaned his face into her touch, and his chest swelled with a deep, shaky breath. His skin was even hotter now, and she could feel his rapid, steady pulse through her palm. For some time, he remained like that—on his knees, leaned toward her but not *on* her, with her hand on his face. Breathing and seething in silence.

"Not time yet," he finally said through clenched teeth, lips barely moving as he spoke.

Yuri reached up with her free hand to brush Thargen's dripping braids out of his face. She looked into his eyes for a moment before she slipped her arms around him and pulled him closer, burying her face against his throat and closing her eyes, desperate to shut out everything outside their cell—the water, the onigox's laughter, the soft cries of the kaital in the neighboring cage.

He shifted, settling a little more of his weight on her as he stretched his legs out and pressed them along hers, further enveloping Yuri in his heat and solidness. She breathed in his scent deeply as she stroked a hand up and down his wet back. Slowly, her shivers subsided.

It wasn't until long after Mortannis had left the room that Thargen relaxed—though she could only consider him relaxed compared to the peak of his earlier agitation. He was still a bow string ready to snap, and Yuri could sense the fury brimming just beneath the surface, could sense his need for release.

Handcuffed or not, she knew Thargen would've ripped the onigox to shreds had the cage door been open.

"I'm with you, Yuri," he rumbled.

His words caught her off guard; it was as though he'd been reading her thoughts and sought to put her at ease.

Yuri's chest constricted with near overwhelming emotion, and she brushed her lips against his neck. "Stay with me."

He groaned. "It'll take a fuck of a lot more than four arms and a hose to pry me away, *zoani*."

EIGHT

Had five days gone by, or six? Had they even been *days* at all? There was no way to tell how much time passed during the cycle of dark and light the smugglers had maintained throughout Thargen and Yuri's captivity—no way to tell with any certainty, at least. Every lost moment, every unaccounted for second, pushed Thargen closer to his limit.

Whether he tracked it or not, time bolstered his Rage.

It didn't matter if the day-night cycle on the ship were comparable to those in Arthos; he knew days had gone by. He couldn't track the time, but he couldn't ignore it, either.

The passing minutes lined up like soldiers preparing for muster, the hours like armored regiments, and the days built up like intergalactic fleets amassing for invasion. Now they were all standing against him, staring him down, their target locked— the tenuous mental barrier keeping his Rage contained. They meant to unleash that Rage, the legacy of his people, and let it run wild in this three-by-three-meter cage.

His skin itched, stretched taut over swollen muscles that twitched with unspent energy, and his breaths were thick and scratchy. His shoulders screamed with discomfort, and his wrists stung where his flesh had been rubbed raw by his manacles. Rage dulled all the other aches and pains he should've felt to the point of making them unnoticeable.

Even now, he couldn't regret having embraced Rage in order to better serve his species. Regrets were pointless—especially when he'd forgotten so much.

He paced in the tiny confines of the cell, moving faster and faster, mindful only of his Rage—and of Yuri. It didn't matter if his chest felt near to bursting or if his head seemed about to split open. It didn't matter if his mind was being seized by the overwhelming need to damage, destroy, and kill.

Or fuck.

His eyes fell on Yuri. Small, defenseless, delicate. Beautiful. His erection throbbed in time with his pounding heart.

No.

He tore his gaze away from her and continued moving. Yuri was his center, his balance. The only thing keeping him grounded. She would not become a target for his Rage. He would hold it in for her sake, protect her as best he could...even if it meant protecting her from himself.

And it was only for her sake that he resisted the urge to slam his head into the bars, to shout and growl, to break his bindings and force the smugglers to come deal with him. That would only bring suffering and pain—because they wouldn't open the cage door. They didn't have to, not until they reached their destination. And when Thargen couldn't break free of the cell, couldn't unleash his fury on his captors, what would he do?

No matter how hard he fought it, he'd eventually turn to Yuri. And that would be worse than anything she'd been forced to endure thus far.

Fight, not fuck. Fight, fight, fight.

Fight what? The fucking cage?

Fuck, fuck, fuck.

No, damn it! This is not the fucking *cage!*

A growl tore up from his chest, and his lips peeled back around his clenched teeth. He needed to punch something, *anything*, but his arms were restricted, and it wasn't time to break them free. What good would it have done him, anyway? His body would break before the cage's reinforced bars.

He swung his gaze around the chamber, but he didn't allow it to land on any of the other captives—not even Iljibi, who would've made a perfect outlet for his Rage. A shouting match was not what Thargen needed right now; he needed action. The cren was especially aware that he was safe in his cage, and he'd grown quite adept at getting under Thargen's skin. Provoking Iljibi would only be a roundabout way for Thargen to provoke himself.

Fuck.

Back home, Thargen had always had ways to release his Rage before it reached this point. Sure, that had sometimes resulted in broken exercise equipment, holes in walls that weren't meant to have holes, or strangers knocked on their asses out on the streets, but at least he'd vented his Rage before it reached the murderous peak to which it was currently rocketing. He'd always spared the people he cared about from having to deal with the truth of what he was.

Rage had been a part of him before his head injury; afterward, it had become him.

Thargen heard the *whoosh* of the chamber door sliding up, felt the subtle breeze on his skin as fresher air swept in, smelled the difference almost immediately—though he'd largely blocked it out, this chamber reeked of body odor, piss, and shit.

He angled his chin down, bared his teeth, and positioned himself in front of Yuri. Even if this was most likely Firios coming with their rations, Thargen would not risk leaving her exposed to another blast from that fucking hose. Her pale skin was mottled blue and purple in the spot the stream had first hit her.

Mortannis was going to suffer for that, but not for long. Thargen wouldn't be able to hold back enough to prolong the ordeal.

Fortunately, it was Firios who entered the chamber now, carrying his bucket of meal bars and water cubes. As he began tossing out those meager rations, he said, "You people produce more of a stink than a menagerie of wild animals would."

"Come here," Thargen growled. "I'll show you a wild fucking animal."

"I see you still have not learned your lesson, vorgal," the volturian said. He dropped a water cube into the female azhera's cage. "Perhaps we should end your journey without food and water to see if you're more cooperative afterward?"

"Thargen, don't," Yuri said, a note of worry in her voice.

But he couldn't stop now. He couldn't keep his mouth shut. He *needed* to get this out, to ease this pressure, to find a release. He needed to take the infinitesimal chance that Firios would be stupid enough to open the cell door.

If Yuri were to have moved closer and placed a hand on him, that might've been enough to temporarily soothe the raging beast within him.

Thargen stalked to the front of the cage before she could. Rage whispered in the back of his mind, its voice rough and seductive, urging him to slam into the bars, to batter them with his body, to bend them to his will. Heat blasted out from his center, suffusing his body and intensifying every sensation. "You won't be around to find out."

Tilting his head slightly, Firios stopped in front of Thargen. "You lost, vorgal. It is finished."

"Do I look dead to you?"

Firios smirked and lifted one shoulder in a noncommittal shrug. "No. But you do look like you are bound and locked in a cage, on your way to the Caldorian slave market."

"It's too bad you'll be dead before you can feel the pain you deserve."

"You really ought to get more creative with your threats, vorgal. Make an effort and take some pride in it."

Thargen didn't need to get creative with his threats, he just needed to *kill*.

The volturian stepped closer, leaning his face close to the bars. "I have you figured out. You're a simple creature. I can withhold your food and water, we can beat you, make you sleep in your own piss and shit, but it will not break you. It won't even bother you. But if I do the same"—his ethereal purple eyes shifted to look past Thargen—"to *her*..."

Thargen lunged forward with a snarl, slamming his head and chest into the bars. He felt the impact only as a dull vibration in his bones. His arms strained against the manacles, making the metal cuffs bite into his flesh. "You do *anything* to her and—"

A muffled but powerful *boom* rocked the ship, rattling the cages and making the lights flicker. Thargen felt the explosion resonate into his feet through the floor; only the ship's artificial gravity kept him steady.

The whir of unseen machinery he'd sensed throughout his time here suddenly became a chugging, clanking, vibrating cacophony that made the floor tremble. Even if he couldn't see the damage, he'd been on enough crippled dropships to know by the sounds that the engines had been hit and were in the process of failing.

Alarm lights flashed on the ceiling, making the room strobe between dirty white and panicked red.

Eyes wide, Firios spat a curse that was well outside his dignified demeanor, dropped his bucket, and ran toward the chamber door.

Several of the captives cried out—a couple in sadistic delight, most in terror.

In his heightened state of awareness, Thargen felt a change in the wounded engine. A faint electric charge spread through the air and tingled across his skin. The machinery below whined, producing a sound so high pitched that Thargen couldn't be sure whether he was actually hearing it or not.

Dread pooled in his gut; he hadn't experienced such a feeling in longer than he could remember. Rage tended to leave little room for true fear.

He spun to face Yuri. Her eyes were rounded and unfocused, darting all over as though she were unable to choose one place to focus her attention, and her skin was even paler than usual.

A tremor shook the ship so violently that it seemed likely to tear apart. The main overhead lights flickered out, leaving only the pulsing alarm lights.

Thargen's stomach fluttered. The familiar, reassuring weight of his body was suddenly nullified, and his feet rose from the floor. Gravity reasserted itself an instant later; fortunately, he'd only been a centimeter or two up.

Fucking grav generators are sputtering out.

Thargen threw away conscious thought; there was no time to plan and assess. Only one thing mattered—Yuri. Rage flooded his veins with fire, and he roared, forcing his arms apart. The manacles resisted, but he was already too far beyond pain to know if they sliced his flesh. The manacles gave slightly, allowing his wrists to separate by a few millimeters. That tiny bit of leeway was all he needed.

The muscles of his arms, shoulders, neck, and chest swelled

with another surge of strength. The connection between the cuffs snapped. Something metallic clinked on the floor.

He moved to close the distance between himself and Yuri. Gravity gave out again while he was midstride, and his body was in the air before he could even bring down his lead foot. Yuri floated off the floor in front of him, her dark hair spread in a wild, restless mass, her limbs waving like she was fighting for balance. For a second, Thargen drifted freely, without anchor, without control.

He thrust an arm toward Yuri, and she reached out to him, grasping his hand. He yanked her toward him. The impact of her body against his, however gentle, created enough force to push him through the air until his back bumped the bars at the front of the cage.

"What's happening?" she asked, slipping her arms around his neck.

The chugging machinery had grown louder and more desperate, and that high-pitched sound had intensified to the point of being painful; it pierced Thargen's skull and made his temples throb.

"Just hold on tight." Thargen banded an arm around her middle, grabbed the bars with his free hand, and pulled himself to the back of the cage.

Facing the corner, he wrapped his body around Yuri as best he could and wedged himself between the rear wall and the cold tristeel bars, holding the latter with one hand. Her grip on him tightened as she buried her face against his chest.

"Oh God, we're gonna die," she moaned, her words barely audible over the noise.

"Not gonna die," he growled. "I got you, *zoani*."

Thargen welcomed another wave of Rage. It surged through him, pumping his muscles with fresh strength, bracing his body for what was to come. At the very least, it would make him a better barrier to shield her. Thargen breathed in; Yuri's scent, exotic, sweet, and calming, filled his nostrils.

The universe burst into primal chaos.

Another explosion rocked the ship—not that *rocked* or *explosion* were adequate words. The roar consumed Thargen, so loud he felt it in his every cell and saw it in flashes of white across his vision. The ship jolted and rattled around him; the fabric of reality itself rippled, making the space within the cage imperceivably vast and infinitely tiny, impossibly cold and searing hot, thin and ethereal but thick and oppressive.

He was blinded by intense light but engulfed in impenetrable darkness, and his body felt like it was being both stretched out over a maddening distance and crushed down to the size of a single atom.

This is what it feels like inside an exploding star.

It was impossible to know whether the ship were thrashing around him or he was being thrown around inside it, but it didn't matter in the end; his body was repeatedly assaulted by the walls and floor, some of the impacts strong enough that they might've shattered his bones were it not for him being amped on Rage. His strength was not enough to keep him unmoving, and his anchors—the hand clutching a bar of the cage, his shoulders wedged against the wall, and his feet braced to either side of the corner—would not have been adequate regardless.

All he could do was hold Yuri and cushion her from as much of the punishment as possible. Her every whimper, grunt, and cry were a direct blow to Thargen's heart, a sign of his failure. And he heard each one of them despite all the other noise. She was the only thing he could identify in that chaos.

The utter darkness was broken by bursts of bright light, but Thargen could not tell if his eyes were open or closed. The thunderous noise in his ears might've been from the ship falling apart, the screams of other passengers, the thundering of his heart, or dead silence. The air against his skin was heated and stifling or chilled and wavering. His stomach flipped, clenched, and knotted.

The ship was spinning, rolling, tumbling, yanking and tossing him, treating Thargen like a tiny pebble in a massive industrial tumbler.

A new roar joined the cacophony, a fiery rumbling from somewhere beyond the walls. Yuri—little Yuri, precious Yuri—clung to Thargen desperately, digging her blunt nails into his skin.

Everything culminated in a crash that sheared the universe apart. Thargen was distantly aware of screaming from either very far off or very close by, and more acutely aware of immense strain in his left arm, which was holding the bar. Both those things couldn't have lasted for more than a fraction of a second before his hand was torn away from its hold and he was launched across the cage with the speed of a plasma bolt fired from a blaster. He didn't feel any impact—he was swallowed by oblivion.

Thargen's perception returned gradually. First there was blackness, as complete as the void. Then silence, deafening in its own right, that was slowly chased away by an intensifying ringing in his ears. Pain came next—or at least its echoes, still held at a distance by Thargen's lingering Rage. The air was different. The usual stench of bodily waste was now layered with the acrid smells of burned electronics, stinging smoke, and superheated metal.

Soft, pained cries drifted to him as though carried by the wind across an expanse of open grassland. He recognized those weak, confused sounds, so laced by suffering. They were the cries of battered, disoriented survivors after a bombing or a direct hit from artillery fire.

He grunted. Though his lower half was in a sitting position, his torso was twisted to one side and slumped over with his back against the tristeel bars. The position wasn't unnatural, but it sure as hell was uncomfortable. And the floor felt like it was at a slant, on top of all that.

There was a small body against his, partially draped over his lap, warm but unmoving.

Yuri!

Thargen's eyes snapped open, and he sucked in a harsh breath. The dust-laden air set him to coughing immediately. He forced himself to survey his surroundings despite the burning in his lungs. There was just enough red-tinged light for him to make out the bars of the cage's opposite wall, but everything beyond was made hazy and indistinct by thick dust in the air.

"Yuri," he rasped.

He looked down. Yuri lay on her back, her spine curved over his arm and legs atop his thighs. Dirt and a dark liquid were smudged on her face. Thargen's breath caught in his throat, and he froze just before he would've jolted upright.

There was something he knew about terrans, something Urgand and the others had mentioned—something important. Terrans...they could be startlingly resilient, but they could also be equally fragile, especially when they were already sick or wounded.

Swallowing thickly, Thargen carefully shifted his arm until it was beneath her shoulders. Now that he was awake and alert, Rage thrummed around the edges of his consciousness, its insistent pounding reminiscent of the beating of frantic war drums. He held it at bay and forced himself to move slowly despite the tremors threatening to course through his limbs.

A tiny bit at a time, he straightened his torso to sit upright, lifting Yuri as he went.

Body stiffening, she groaned and winced before falling into

a coughing fit. Thargen stilled, unwilling to so much as breath until he knew if she was okay.

"Yuri?"

Her eyelids fluttered open. She blinked several times, but her eyes remained unfocused, pupils dilated wide.

Thargen's chest constricted, and his heart stuttered.

Yuri squeezed her eyes shut, coughed again, and released another groan once her coughs faded. She trembled as she pulled her torso up the rest of the way. Thargen kept as much of her weight on his arm as she allowed. She pressed a hand to her forehead and exhaled heavily through her nostrils.

"What happened?" she asked. Her trembling intensified, wracking her entire body.

He wrapped his arms around her as gently as he could, fighting the urge to crush her against his chest and shower her in relieved kisses. It was too soon to celebrate survival. For all the optimism he usually expressed—and as little consideration as he normally held for his own safety—having Yuri here made it impossible for Thargen to ignore the truth of the situation.

Either this was an opportunity to escape or a prolonged death sentence.

"You hurt?" he asked, pressing his cheek to her hair.

"I-I don't know. I don't think so?"

That answer resonated with him; he understood that confusion, that inability to assess the damage to one's body. Rage greatly diminished his perception of pain—sometimes nullifying it completely—and accelerated his healing rate, but it sure as fuck didn't make him invulnerable despite trying to make him believe he was.

He lifted his head and scanned their surroundings again. Some of the dust had settled, strengthening the faint red light from outside the cage. That wasn't a flashing alarm signal—it was the glow of emergency lighting.

The kind of emergency lighting that usually came on when a ship experienced power failure.

Thargen swung his gaze to the front of the cage, and his eyes widened. For a few moments, his mind could not reconcile the half-meter-wide gap in the bars, could not understand the alteration to an environment that had been constant and unchanging for what felt like an eternity.

The door was open.

Fuck yeah.

The ever-burning fire at his core flared and spread outward through his limbs. An open door meant escape. It also meant there was no barrier between Thargen and the smugglers.

Yuri first. She matters most.

But a significant part of him was already fixated on the chance to feel the smugglers' bones crunching beneath his fists, to feel their warm blood splatter his skin, to hear their pained cries—and to cut those cries short.

Yuri.

Killing the smugglers is protecting her.

Rage latched onto that notion and agreed vehemently, grinning the sharp-toothed grin of a bloodthirsty predator in the back of Thargen's mind.

Clenching his jaw, he carefully slid Yuri off his lap and lowered her to the floor.

She grasped his shoulders with shaking hands. "Thargen?"

"Making sure it's clear." Taking her chin in one hand, he tilted her face up and met her gaze. Her eyes were wide and searching, brimming with fear and uncertainty. Rage lashed against his conscious mind like angry waves against a shore, demanding control, but Thargen held it back a little longer for her. "Stay here, *zoani*. Don't move until I say."

She was silent for a couple seconds, her fingers flexing,

before she nodded and withdrew her hands. "Okay. Be careful."

Klagar's balls, he wanted to kiss her. But that wouldn't lead to anything good now, not when Rage was about to take over, not when he had no idea how much time they had to take advantage of this situation.

"Whatever you see," he said, voice growing more guttural with each word, "I will *not* hurt you. Never you."

She touched her fingers to his cheek. "I trust you, Thargen."

He closed his eyes and leaned into her touch for a moment, locking the feel of it away in his memory; for that little while, his Rage was silent, and everything in him was still and peaceful.

Thargen didn't allow himself to look at her when he pulled away.

He rolled onto his hip, braced his hand on the floor, and shoved himself to his feet. As he drew in a deep breath, his senses sharpened, honed by the primal force to which he was surrendering. There were more moans and strained cries from the other captives, and now he could smell blood on the air—the mixed scents of the blood of several species. The red glow in the chamber deepened toward crimson as his vision—or his mind's interpretation of it—altered to focus foremost on motion.

And there was motion all around—pieces of wire and metal dangling from walls and ceiling; a few red emergency lights along the walkway flickering irregularly; a few survivors stirring in nearby cages; small showers of sparks spraying intermittently from a broken fixture toward the rear of the room. But none of those held Thargen's attention—that was claimed entirely by movement at the far end of the chamber, near the door.

Someone was there, features obscured by the poor lighting and still settling dust.

Thargen strode forward, slowing only to kick the cage door. The door swung wider open, its bottom scraping across the floor, and produced a brief but piercing metal-on-metal scream before coming to an abrupt halt. As he emerged from the cage, Thargen turned toward the figure at the end of the walkway.

Leaning to the left to counteract the slant of the floor, Thargen stalked along the walkway. He barely felt the bits of debris scattered beneath his bare feet. The chamber's entrance was straight ahead, the door halfway raised from the floor and stuck at an angle completely at odds with its frame.

The panel beside the doorway, the one Mortannis had pulled the hose from, was open, and the figure that had caught Thargen's attention was clutching the inside lip of the panel with both hands, hauling himself up. He'd only managed to get one foot beneath him.

The figure's bloody features grew clearer as Thargen closed the distance; when the alien turned his head, Thargen caught the faint sheen of red *qal* marks.

Firios's eyes rounded as they met Thargen's. He dropped a hand from the panel to fumble at something on his belt.

"My turn, skeksfucker," Thargen growled. A wave of Rage swept him into a charge. His feet pounded on the metal floor panels, making them shake and vibrate, and the remaining distance between him and the volturian shrank to nothing within the space of a couple heartbeats.

Firios finally freed his weapon from his belt, but Thargen's knee struck Firios's chest before the volturian could raise the weapon in defense. Thargen threw all his weight and momentum behind the blow, driving Firios back into the wall. There was a satisfying crunch, emphasized by a choked grunt and the sound of the volturian's weapon clattering to the floor.

When Thargen withdrew his knee, Firios pitched forward, sucking in a labored, wheezing breath. Thargen clamped his hands on either side of Firios's head, stopping him before he could fall. If Firios struggled against Thargen's hold, his efforts were too weak to make a difference—too weak to be noticed.

Twisting from his hips, Thargen slammed the volturian's head against the wall. The wet, muted sound of the impact was like fuel to the fires of his Rage, making it flare anew. He drew back and swung again and again, faster and faster, pouring more strength into each blow. His furious roar swallowed the sounds of flesh being mangled and bones shattering, of blood and soft tissue spattering the walls and floor.

He didn't know how many times he'd slammed Firios's blood-slickened head against the wall when it finally slipped out of his hands. The volturian slumped lifelessly to the floor. Thargen whipped his arms to the sides, flicking away blood, clumps of hair, and flecks of flesh and bone. For a moment, the scent of the Firios's blood was the strongest and sweetest of them all. Thargen breathed it in deeply.

Too fast. Should've made him suffer. Should've made him scream.

And he should've put up a fight.

Thargen crouched and plucked the fallen weapon off the floor; it was a stun baton, still collapsed and deactivated. He clenched his jaw and stilled his fingers before he could crush the weapon in his grip. The stun baton was a coward's weapon, a crutch...but he couldn't discard it yet. Not while the unknown challenges lurked ahead.

Without rising, he leaned to the side to look through the partially open door.

The dust was even thicker in the next room, making every-thing shadowy and indistinct—but the shapes ahead suggested storage containers or crates of some sort. And there was a light somewhere within that cloud of dust—not the red of emergency lights or the washed out glow of the lights over the cage room walkway, but a pure light that possessed that indefinable, undeniable quality marking it as coming from a natural source.

Daylight.

One corner of his mouth tilted up; there was a way out. There had to be.

Nothing seemed to be moving in that room—nothing but the dust cloud and the air it rode, which was just a touch colder than what he'd been acclimated to on the ship. When he breathed that air in, it made his nostrils sting.

Not done yet. Not out.

He stood up and turned toward the cages. The black-scaled female ilthurii and the gray-skinned female sedhi had emerged from their shared cell, and the male azhera at the back of the room was shoving against the door of his cage, fighting to get it open. A couple other captives were stirring, but Thargen's attention shifted to Yuri, who was standing up in her cell, her eyes looking black in the weak red light.

Conflicting urges held him in place for a few moments. He needed to find more of the smugglers—especially Mortannis and Taeraal. They had to pay for all this. But he also needed to keep Yuri safe...which meant keeping her close. He didn't care what shared trauma he and the other captives had endured here, he didn't trust any of them. Not with Yuri.

Even his Rage was torn between those two motivations, which were at once interconnected and opposed. Fulfilling the first by killing the smugglers meant upholding the second, but doing so would also place her in danger whether he left her behind or brought her along.

The whole thing was confusing enough to dull the edge of his Rage and make his head hurt.

Can't let her out of my sight. Won't.

"Yuri!" He strode toward her.

With arms around one another in support, the ilthurii and the sedhi hurried past him, heading for the open chamber door. He ignored them; they weren't a threat.

Yuri stepped into the walkway a moment later, moving with a staggered gait to compensate for the tilt of the floor, and looked at him.

Despite everything, he couldn't help noticing her delicate body, her feminine curves, her smooth, pale skin. His cock roused immediately, twitching upward as it hardened. Even through all the overwhelming smells layered in the air, he picked up her scent. Thargen halted a few meters away from her.

He curled his hands into fists. The blood on his fingers was sticky and cooling, but his Rage was already rebounding from his confusion, burning hot.

It would be so easy to take her. So easy to sheath himself in her warmth, to fill her with his seed over and over and over again. He wouldn't even have to think; Rage would handle it all, would drive him on with relentless, animalistic eagerness to take what he fucking wanted.

Yuri hurried toward him, grasping the bars of the cages she passed to keep herself balanced. As soon as she was close enough, she reached for him and asked, "Are you okay?"

Thargen jerked back from her hand and drew in a hissing breath. There were other smugglers aboard this ship, he knew there were, and they needed to be his targets—but Rage was only concerned with the immediate. It was focused entirely upon her now. He couldn't accept her touch, couldn't trust himself.

He would *not* hurt his *zoani*.

She halted and narrowed her eyes, sweeping her gaze over him. "Thargen, is that...is that blood? Is it yours?"

Farther down the walkway, one of the cell doors opened slightly. The occupant—the female volturian—grunted. Holding a bar beside the door with one hand, she pulled herself out, shoving the door wider open with her shoulder to fight the angle of the floor. As soon as she was out, the door slammed shut with a resounding bang. She limped toward Yuri and Thargen slowly, favoring her right leg.

Most minor details were usually lost on Thargen during his Rage, but one stood out now—the collar around the volturian's neck.

"Need to go," he said. "Stay right behind me."

Yuri frowned and eased closer. "Thargen, the...the other people—"

"*Now*, Yuri."

She recoiled slightly, eyes widening, and nodded.

He clenched his jaw. Even Rage could not shield him from the stab of guilt that struck him in that moment.

Rather have her scared than dead.

But when he spoke again, his voice was notably softer. "Come."

Thargen turned and strode toward the partially open chamber door, flicking his wrist to extend the stun baton in his hand. Beyond that doorway lay the unknown, and he couldn't deny that part of him was excited to plunge into it—largely because of the chances for battle and mayhem. It was Yuri's footfalls, quiet but unmistakable behind him, that kept his excitement contained.

Mayhem was bad for her. He needed to keep her away from it.

He crouched when he reached the door, and even then, he had to bend forward to fit through. The dust had thinned significantly, but the far ends of the room were still obscured by it—because this was a damned cargo hold. There were crates, chests, and containers scattered all over, much of it buried in plain sight amidst the mangled remains of fallen shelving. There were two figures ahead, features indistinct in the dust, rummaging through items on the floor; likely the ilthurii and sedhi who'd rushed out of their cages.

But it was the source of the light he'd noted before that stood out the most; it was *definitely* natural light, streaming in through a huge tear in the hull to Thargen's left. The contrast between that light and the relative gloom inside the cargo hold made it impossible for him to see anything beyond the breach, but he knew in his bones that it was *outside*, and almost any outside was better than being on this ship.

He paused just inside the hold and glanced back.

Yuri ducked under the door effortlessly. In this light, her bruises—both new and old—were painted in stark contrast to her pale skin. She was bleeding in a few places, too—one of her knees was oozing blood, there were a few little cuts on her arms, and the knuckles of her right hand looked like she'd been in a fistfight. The liquid smeared on her cheek was crimson, having flowed from a cut on her temple.

Thargen normally enjoyed the sight of blood. It had woken a primal thrill in him for as long as he could remember, had somehow made everything more immediate, more...real. But seeing Yuri's blood made his stomach fold into knots and his chest tighten. His Rage growled in fury, hungry to make someone suffer for the damage done to her, but even it seemed to know that such a pursuit wasn't a priority.

He needed to get her out of here. Now.

"On my ass, terran," he commanded, activating the stun baton. It hummed to life.

"Do I get to touch it?" Her brows dropped, and she turned her face away with a cringe. "Wait. Sorry. I'm not...not thinking very clearly. Bad time to joke around."

I think I fucking love her.

Thargen smirked. "You don't start moving, I'm gonna slap yours."

Her eyes widened, but the way she caught her lower lip between her teeth suggested she wasn't *afraid* of his threat.

A deep ache pulsed in his groin, flowing through his balls and along his shaft. Even if Thargen was surprisingly lucid, his body was primed with Rage, ready to fight or fuck. It didn't care which.

But he did.

He turned away from Yuri and moved forward, picking a path through the debris on his way toward the breach. The light from outside fell across a wide section of the floor, illuminating a jumble of items that had spilled from numerous crates and containers, a problem that would've been avoided had the smugglers secured their cargo.

Thargen's eyes rounded as he raked his gaze over the mess; he was looking at a pile of weapons, clothing, and equipment. One glance was enough to tell most of it was military grade.

Apparently, the Zulka ran guns in addition to flesh.

Guess someone has to keep the markets on Caldorius supplied.

Thargen stepped forward, deactivated the stun baton, and tucked it under his arm. He bent to pick up one of several auto-blasters from the floor. "This is some quality shit."

The sedhi and ilthurii—who were a few meters away, digging through the scattered objects—started and turned their wide eyes toward him. The sedhi raised one of her hands, brandishing a tristeel combat knife. Both females had pulled on ill-fitting clothes—the sort of bland gray undershirts that many paramilitary forces favored.

Yuri moved beside Thargen and raised a hand, palm out, toward the females. "We're not going to hurt you."

The sedhi glanced at Yuri before returning her gaze to Thargen. She narrowed her eyes; her orange irises shone with reflected light. It was only when her companion, the ilthurii, placed a hand on her shoulder that she finally lowered the knife.

The two females returned to their scavenging, the sedhi's tail flicking as though in agitation. Thargen couldn't blame the sedhi for her distrust; though all the captives had suffered in those cages, individuals like Iljibi had proven they weren't all friends just because they happened to be enslaved together.

Thargen dropped his attention to the auto-blaster and opened the power cell chamber. He wasn't surprised to find it empty; you had to be dumb not to secure your cargo, but you'd have to be on a whole new level of stupid to transport loaded weaponry.

He tossed the auto-blaster aside. It landed amongst a heap of identical weapons, all useless without power cells.

"The air in here...it kinda burns when I breathe," Yuri said softly.

Thargen flicked his gaze toward the breach but didn't keep it there long enough to adjust to the light. He didn't need a glimpse of the world beyond just yet. "Just the dust. We'll be okay."

Yuri walked forward.

Uncharacteristic alarm flared in Thargen's chest; he had the sudden urge to grab her and pull her back to his side, where he could keep her safe. He resisted.

Barely.

After a few steps, she stopped and bent forward to rummage through the items around her feet, pulling a piece of clothing from the tangle. It was a pair of black leggings, the kind usually worn beneath armor. Compared to her, they were huge.

Yuri stuck one foot in, then the other, and tugged them up her legs, but they sagged. She rolled the waistband a few times until they hugged her hips snugly enough to remain in place.

In his mind's eye, he pictured himself sliding those pants back off, letting his hands run down the outsides of her thighs. He imagined her lower half being revealed a little at a time, and his excitement at that thought was even stronger now that he knew what was beneath.

Well, not *all* of what was beneath. He'd only had the briefest glimpses of her slit, and it remained something of a mystery, a treasure not yet claimed.

His cock throbbed painfully in time with his thudding heartbeat, stiff as a tristeel pillar, and his eyes fell on her breasts as she bent forward again. He clenched his fists against the wave of Rage and desire that roared through his veins.

Thargen jerked his gaze away from Yuri. She was doing something productive; he needed to focus and do the same. The blasters were useless, but there was other equipment here —and there was no telling when the smugglers would arrive to find the would-be slaves rummaging through their illicit cargo. For Yuri's sake, he needed to get her out of here before then.

The female volturian limped into the cargo hold at the edge of his peripheral vision, calling Thargen's attention toward her. Her *qal* was dim, and she was covered in cuts and bruises beyond her injured leg. Her expression was one he'd seen before—far-off and dull, as though her mind had disconnected from her body at some point during the trauma she'd suffered. She wasn't going to last long.

None of them would, if they didn't move quickly.

So get moving, you green-skinned bastard!

Thargen transferred the stun baton to his mouth, clamping his teeth over the grip, and strode into the mess. He bent forward and dug into the debris with both hands, seeking anything that could aid them outside the ship. With each passing second, the sting of the air grew a little sharper. He could only imagine what it would feel like to draw in those first few breaths of pure alien air once he were outside.

He tugged a rumpled piece of cloth from the pile and unfurled it for a quick inspection. It was one of those gray shirts. His eyes were immediately drawn to the smudges of blood on the fabric—blood from his hands.

Ah, shit. Guess we're lucky she's been distracted since she first noticed it.

Thargen used the already soiled cloth to quickly scrub away as much of the blood as he could, wadded it up, and threw it deeper into the hold before resuming his search.

He already had a wad of clothing—all free of bloodstains—tucked under one arm by the time he heaved aside an overturned storage chest to discover a pile of black backpacks. He snatched one up. Its black material was thick but pliable, save for its outside face—that was rigid, as though armored or reinforced.

He turned his attention to Yuri. She was several meters away with her back toward him, in the process of pulling on one of those gray shirts; its hem fell nearly to her knees when she released it.

Thargen bent forward to pluck the stun baton from his mouth and called her name.

She looked at him, and he tossed her the backpack as soon as their eyes met. She flinched, but her hands darted up reflexively to catch the bag.

"Fill it up," he said before returning the stun baton to his mouth. He grabbed another backpack, opened it, and stuffed in the clothing he'd gathered.

There was more movement at the edge of his vision—Iljibi, looking battered and bruised but alert. The cren stumbled toward the breach, his gaze running across the debris-strewn floor. The sedhi and ilthurii seemed to have slipped out while Thargen was searching.

Fleeing into an alien world naked and unarmed was a mistake, but the absence of those two females emphasized a different mistake Thargen was in the process of making—he was taking too long. He'd wasted too much time.

Thargen pushed forward, relying upon training that had become second nature years ago to rapidly assess the objects on the floor, kicking aside everything that didn't immediately register as useful. He was barely conscious of most of the items he picked up and shoved into the backpack; he had no choice but to trust his own unthinking judgment.

When he found the tipped over container that held tristeel knives just like the one the sedhi had brandished earlier, Thargen scooped the sheathed weapons into his backpack by the handful. He didn't bother counting them—you could never have too many blades.

He stood up and turned toward the hull breach, meaning to call Yuri and finally get the fuck out of there, but his eyes caught on a storage container. It was similar in dimension to many of the others—about one hundred and thirty centimeters wide, half as tall and deep—but it was completely different in appearance; its black exterior was trimmed with gold edging that gleamed despite the dust.

It was also one of the few that was unopened.

Curiosity overrode his urgency. He walked to the container, grasped its handles, and turned it upright. His lips stretched into a grin. Thargen knew the symbol emblazoned on the lid—it belonged to Herestion, a famous weapon designer who built many of the elegant but brutal weapons popular in professional fighting circuits.

And undoubtedly in the fighting pits on Caldorius.

Wasting time. Need to go.

Thargen grasped the latch handle and turned it. The lid released a soft hiss as it unsealed, and a moment later it swung open silently.

A pair of identical black weapons lay in cutouts in the interior padding. Their hafts were a little longer than Thargen's forearm, and they were topped with stylized axe heads. Thargen picked one up and turned it in his hand, examining the head; it was blunt, with tiny slits on both ends and a shield-shaped cutout on the back.

His thumb brushed over a slight depression on the grip. When he pressed down, the weapon came to life—an orange hardlight blade formed on the front end, a smaller, more abrupt one on the back, and simple, flowing orange patterns glowed amidst the otherwise black haft and head.

"That's fucking awesome," he said, words garbled by the stun baton between his teeth.

Now it was time to leave.

He deactivated the hardlight axe, knelt in front of the chest, and set his backpack down. Removing the baton from his mouth, he collapsed it and tossed it into the pack with everything else he'd gathered. He secured the axe along the side of the pack using a couple small fastener loops attached to the fabric. Once the backpack was sealed, he slung it over his shoulders, snatched up the other axe, and strode toward the hull breach.

Yuri was a few paces away, crouched over her backpack.

"Time to go, Yuri," Thargen called.

She stood up and lifted her backpack in one hand, reaching inside as she hurried toward him. When she withdrew her hand, she was holding a balled-up piece of black material—probably a pair of pants or something—which she offered to him after swinging her backpack on over her other shoulder.

"Here," she said, taking in a wheezing breath.

He glanced at the pants and was about to reach for them when a new sound commanded his attention. It was soft but distinct—hissing and crackling. Thargen turned his head toward it.

The big door on the wall opposite the cage room was bathed in a reddish glow cast by the plasma cutter slicing along its left edge; someone was trying to get through from the other side. Flecks of molten metal rained onto the floor beneath it. Based on the cutter's slow but steady progress, the door would be breached within a few minutes.

Rage clawed to the forefront of Thargen's mind. His skin went taut, his muscles swelled, and his heart quickened. In a few short minutes, there'd be blood to spill, bones to break, enemies to slay. He'd finally satiate the primal bloodthirst at his core.

Yuri, he roared from the back of his mind. Her name echoed in his skull and made his temples throb, forcing his Rage back just enough for Thargen to maintain control.

"Pants later." Thargen tore the pants from Yuri's hand, tossed them aside, and grabbed her extended arm. He ran toward the gap in the hull, pulling her along.

"Pants not...important. Got it," she rasped behind him.

The thunderous beating of Thargen's heart intensified, drowning out all other sound. The light from outside was intense compared to the shadows gripping most of the hold, nearly blinding him for a few seconds, but he pressed on. His lungs burned more with each breath.

His eyes adjusted to the change in light just as he neared the breach.

The landscape outside was as familiar as it was alien. Gray clouds spotted a blue sky that possessed just a hint of green, beneath which stood huge outcroppings of gray and brown rock with rusty stains. There were tall, rugged trees with clumps of tiny, needle-like leaves beyond the ground where the ship had come to rest, which itself was an amalgamation of short, reddish grass and patches of exposed stone.

"Fuck," he growled.

The ship had come to rest at a slant, and that slant meant this breach in the hull was nearly three meters above the ground.

It was too late to stop.

Thargen yanked Yuri forward harder than he'd meant to. Her little cry of pain pierced the pounding of his pulse, striking him directly in the heart, but he didn't let it give him pause. The instant she was alongside him, he released her wrist, looped an arm around her waist to lift her, and jumped.

She screamed and wrapped her arms around him. With her body tucked against his, he couldn't help the thought that flitted through his mind—*wish she hadn't put clothes on.*

His feet hit the ground, and his knees bent to absorb the impact—which was barely noticeable thanks to the loose dirt and his Rage-enhanced muscles. The ground near the ship had been torn up, leaving a several-meter-wide buffer between the hull and the start of the red grass.

Thargen drew in a breath as he straightened his legs.

The air was like fire blazing down his throat, and it made his lungs feel like they were about to simultaneously burst and collapse. His head spun, and his vision wavered. This shit must've only barely crept into the hull.

Yuri struggled in his hold, one of her hands clawing at her throat while the other clutched at Thargen, nails digging into his skin and scraping. "I can't... It hurts," she rasped between wheezing, desperate breaths.

It had been a long, long time since his body had been

forced to adapt to a new atmosphere on the spot—but he *had* been through this before. He knew this pain, and he knew it would pass. The stuff vorgal soldiers were injected with to enable such reactive mutations was potent, but it was nothing compared to the compound the Consortium pumped into every citizen of Arthos.

Thargen exhaled and forced another lungful of the fiery air in through his nostrils. The sting was diminished now, but only slightly. He shook his head to clear away the fog forming on the edges of his awareness.

"Breathe," he said, his own voice ragged. "You'll adapt."

Her eyes met his. The fear in her gaze was like a kick to Thargen's gut. His Rage growled impotently, incapable of helping her in these moments. Her face was turning a shade of red deeper than any blush he'd seen on her cheeks.

"*Breathe*, terran." Thargen lowered her until her feet touched the ground but didn't release his hold on her. "Fucking breathe."

She took in a deep, gasping breath and nearly doubled over; only his arm kept her upright.

The burning in Thargen's throat and lungs eased a little more. He set his focus on the trees ahead and walked forward. Yuri took a couple staggering steps and sagged against him, coughing, her feet dragging in the dirt.

"Walk, *zoani*." Now he could smell a hint of sweetness on the air—the fragrance of the grass, or the trees, or both? His next breath came easier. "The compound will force your body...to adapt. The stuff they gave you when you came to Arthos."

She drew in another strained breath and tightened her hold on him, pulling herself up to stumble along as he walked. Her next breath sounded a bit smoother.

"Keep breathing, Yuri. Keep walking."

"Remind me...to never go...on vacation to another planet... again," Yuri said. "This fucking *hurts*."

Thargen grinned and increased his pace. "Fuck this planet. But fuck that ship harder."

Hushed voices came from the hull breach, accompanied by more wheezing breaths. Something hit the ground behind Thargen with a thud. An agonized scream followed.

Thargen turned his head to look over his shoulder. The female volturian lay on her side below the breach with her face in the dirt and both hands clutching her injured leg. Another captive dropped down beside her, the male azhera with dark, bristling fur. He cast a single, guilt-laden glance at the fallen female and hurriedly stumbled toward the trees.

Thargen felt Yuri slow and begin to turn as though she meant to look back, but he strengthened his hold and pressed on faster. "Keep going. Don't look back."

"But she's—"

"We can't help her."

The reddish grass was surprising soft underfoot, even more so than the loose dirt that had been kicked up around the ship, but it was contrasted by the cold, hard patches of stone interspersed throughout. The trees looked increasingly alien as Thargen neared them; he didn't allow himself to slow until he and Yuri were beneath those unfamiliar boughs.

Shouts emerged from the ship.

Thargen knew instinctually those shouts weren't from the captives, though he could not make out the words. Rage coursed up his spine, crackling along his nerves and sweeping through his veins. His legs stopped moving only a few meters past the tree line.

Tightening his grip on the haft of the hardlight axe, Thargen released Yuri to turn and look back toward the ship.

The female volturian was writing on the ground where she'd landed. A few flashes lit up the breach; their pure white suggested shock staves or something similar.

A figure appeared in the breach, nearly large enough to fill the entirety of that hole—a red-skinned, four-armed onigox. Mortannis peered out before turning to yell something into the ship.

Running. I'm running from a fight.

Thargen's legs carried him a couple steps back toward the ship. When had he ever run from a fight? Vorgals didn't run. Rokkashi Vanguards didn't fucking run.

Thargen didn't run—unless it was headlong into the fray. He was the front line, the first in, last out, the thing his enemies screamed about in their nightmares.

"Thargen?" Yuri said.

Need to keep her safe.

But now, Rage was resisting him. It growled and laughed, taunting him, calling him a coward. The smugglers, the people who'd hurt Yuri, who'd captured her and intended to sell her into slavery, were only forty or fifty meters away. How could Thargen run? Wasn't he supposed to make those smugglers pay?

"Stay here," he heard himself say. He walked forward a few more steps.

No!

He clenched his jaw against a sudden, piercing pain in his head. For a few seconds, he felt like he was being pulled in two different directions, like his mind was being ripped apart. His muscles trembled with unspent power and fury.

Then Yuri screamed, and the conflict within Thargen was over. His vision was already stained crimson as he spun toward her.

Iljibi stood behind Yuri with his arm looped around her

neck. Her furious struggles seemed to have no effect on the much larger cren, not even her frantic punches to his chest and kicks to his legs. He held an auto-blaster in his other hand, its barrel pointed toward Thargen.

"Iljibi taking this one. Vorgal just needs to move on." Iljibi backed away, dragging Yuri with him.

Yuri reached up, grabbed a handful of the cren's orange hair, and yanked it down. She brought her other hand up simultaneously, raking her nails across his eye. Iljibi snarled and wrenched back to lift Yuri's feet off the ground. She made a choked sound and clamped her hands on the cren's forearm, fighting to break his hold.

The glint of fear in her eyes pierced Thargen to his core and ignited something inside him unlike anything he'd ever experienced. It was Rage, but it was more than that—it was stronger, deeper, and even more primal.

The entire universe shrank down to Yuri, Iljibi, and the distance separating them from Thargen.

Thargen sprinted forward.

Iljibi's eyes rounded. He depressed the auto-blaster's trigger, and his eyes widened further when nothing happened.

Only a few meters remained between Thargen and the cren.

Iljibi shoved Yuri aside, spun around, nearly tripping over his own legs, and scrambled away.

He didn't make it more than a meter before Thargen tackled him.

Fury burst from Thargen's throat in a roar as his arms swung with lethal strength and speed. The pent-up Rage of the last week—of a lifetime—drove him. His conscious mind barely perceived the person pinned beneath him. If Iljibi made any noises, they were lost within Thargen's roar, muffled by the dull sounds of flesh being hacked and pummeled. Warm blood splattered Thargen's hands, arms, face, chest. It was indistinguishable from the crimson haze that dominated his vision.

When Thargen stopped, he wasn't sure how much time had passed. Instinct said it couldn't have been more than a few seconds, but it had felt impossibly longer—and like it hadn't been nearly long enough. His breaths were harsh and ragged, and his heartbeat thumped in his ears as he pushed himself away from the mangled corpse.

He glanced at the axe in his right hand. He didn't remember activating the hardlight blade, but it was on, and blood glistened on its blade, head, and haft.

Shouts sounded somewhere behind him—masculine shouts from the direction of the ship.

The smugglers.

Yuri.

Startled out of his daze, he swung his eyes to her. She was standing a few steps away, breath labored and skin even paler than usual. Her wide eyes were locked on the body behind Thargen. Her lips parted as though she meant to speak, but only a shuddering breath came out. Then her eyes rolled up to display their whites, and her knees buckled.

Thargen lunged toward her, catching her on his left arm before she could hit the ground.

The shouts were louder now. He turned his head to see several of the smugglers outside the ship, a couple of whom had taken the female volturian by the arms. At least three others were walking toward the trees, shock staves in hand.

Thargen deactivated the hardlight axe, peeled off Yuri's backpack, and crouched to lift her onto his shoulder. Her weight was slight, but she was limp.

"I got you, *zoani*," he said gruffly, wrapping his arm around her legs and hooking a couple fingers through the little loop on the top of her backpack.

He drew upon his Rage, willing it to flood his muscles with fresh strength, and ran.

Better not fucking fail me now.

NINE

Yuri groaned, her eyelids fluttering open as she came to—only for her face to slam against something rough and hard. Something equally hard was digging into her stomach, and her weight was driven down upon it with teeth-clacking force each time she bounced.

What the hell?

She grunted and braced her hand against the thing in front of her, peering at it through the tangle of black hair hanging around her face. It was a backpack, which was settled against a span of solid green flesh contoured with toned muscle and raised scars.

Thargen.

She looked down to see the ground rushing by dizzyingly—and his tight ass flexing as he ran.

Why was he carrying her over his shoulder? Why was he running? What had happ—

The blood.

She could *smell* it. Yuri closed her eyes and groaned as nausea swept through her. Though having some of her weight braced on her arms helped reduce the impact on her abdomen, the bile threatening to rise from her stomach grew a little more insistent every time she came down upon his shoulder.

"Thargen?" she said, voice strained.

He didn't respond.

Yuri said his name again, and when he still didn't answer, she reached past the backpack and slapped his ass. "Thargen, put me down!"

He grunted in an oddly pleased fashion, but his stride didn't falter in the slightest. "Can't."

"If you don't put me down right now, I swear I'm going to puke all over you."

"Go ahead."

"*Please.*"

This time, his grunt was decidedly less satisfied. "They're chasing. Can't stop yet."

She swallowed thickly, temporarily tamping down her nausea. "Put me down so I can run with you."

His arm, which was banded around the backs of her thighs, squeezed a little harder. "I'm faster. Close your eyes and be quiet."

Yuri scowled at his back. Reaching down again, she pinched his ass hard.

"*Fuck,*" he growled. "Keep that up and you're not gonna like what happens when I stop."

In some messed up way, his words sent a shiver along her spine that sparked something hot in her core. She knew *exactly* what he was threatening—and part of her was eager for him to fulfill that threat.

"If you won't put me down, then at least carry me a different way. This is making me sick and it hurts."

Thargen muttered something—probably a curse—and slowed, each of his steps slamming a little harder than the last until he finally halted. He bent forward, swinging her torso upright, and let her slide off his shoulder. Yuri staggered backward, hit by an immediate wave of dizziness that made the world spin and forced her to shut her eyes.

Thargen clamped one of his big, strong hands over her shoulder, steadying her. "Take these."

Yuri opened her eyes just as he thrust her backpack and one of the axes toward her. She reflexively wrapped her arms around them, clutching them against her chest.

Before she could do anything more, Thargen stooped down, curled an arm behind her back, and swept her legs out from beneath her. He caught her legs behind their knees with his other arm and drew her against his chest before breaking into a run.

His speed rattled the equipment in the backpacks, and it was anything but a smooth ride for Yuri, but it was much better than all her weight driving her stomach down on his shoulder repeatedly.

She looked up at him, and the warmth drained out of her cheeks. There was blood on his face; that quickly, she was aware of its smell again. Squeezing her eyes shut, she hugged the backpack and axe a little tighter and turned her face against his shoulder, which had been surprisingly clean.

Probably because all that blood is on me now.

"So, what's the plan?" she asked, desperate for a distraction from her resurging nausea.

"Survive."

She wanted to lift her head and give him a blank look, but she resisted the urge. No good would come from another glimpse of his blood-spattered face; a bit smartassery wasn't worth vomiting.

After a while, Yuri's stomach settled enough for her to chance opening her eyes. She made sure not to look at Thargen directly, instead turning her attention to their surroundings, surveying the alien scenery over his shoulder.

Thargen was running across a sloped meadow that was filled with the same rust-red grass that had been outside the crashed ship. Other plants jutted from the grass here and there —strange, pale stalks ending in bulbous orange and violet growths were the most common, the tallest of which must've stood to her knee. But mostly there was grass—and rock.

There was stone everywhere, some of it in patches nearly level with the ground, some in the form of boulders of varying sizes, the largest of which looked as big as houses, and, farther up the slope, in jagged outcroppings that formed cliffs and rises as they climbed up toward a mist-shrouded mountain peak. Fuzzy-looking, blue-green lichen clung to that stone in many places.

Trees butted up against the edge of the meadow far behind Thargen. They were tall with thick trunks, but their branches were incredibly numerous and thin, each spotted with irregular clumps of red and yellow needles. They reminded her of pine trees—though she doubted that the comparison would hold up as she studied these alien plants more closely.

Regardless, the landscape was beautiful. The colors were reminiscent of autumn back on Earth, complemented by a blue-green sky.

There was no sign of the ship or other captives—not even a pillar of smoke in the sky to signify a nearby crash, though she doubted anything like that would've remained visible for long given the rugged, mountainous landscape and thick copses of trees everywhere.

Yuri tucked a few wild strands of windblown hair behind her ear and frowned. "How long was I out?"

"Minute or two," Thargen replied.

"Then where's the ship?"

"Somewhere too close."

They darted past several spread-out trees, and within a few seconds had passed into a forest. Those red and yellow needles blanketed much of the ground, reducing the grass to sparse, scattered patches, though there were still plenty of lichen-covered stones all over.

Yuri furrowed her brows and flicked her gaze across the open field behind them and to the trees beyond it. "Where are the others? Shouldn't we be traveling together? Greater numbers and all that?"

"No." His response was more of a grunt than a spoken word.

"Why?" Not all the captives had been like Iljibi.

"Because."

Yuri glared at him and opened her mouth to ask another question—only to snap it shut when she finally saw past the blood to the person beneath it. Thargen's expression was strained; brows low, jaw clenched, the cords of his neck standing out. Little beads of sweat had formed on his forehead.

He was entirely focused on their escape. And, considering how fast he was running, the weight he was carrying, and his clipped responses, he had little energy to spare for anything else. He very likely had little energy for *anything* right now. The rations they'd been given during their captivity had left Yuri hungry every day, and she was much smaller than Thargen; he must've been weakened and exhausted even before using his body to shield her from the violence of the crash.

Her questions could wait until they'd stopped somewhere safe and Thargen had rested.

Yuri returned her attention to their surroundings. Thargen continued running between the trees, over rock, across grass, and up and down the sloped terrain at an unrelenting pace. He didn't slow, didn't show any signs of tiring but for his steadily intensifying body heat and his heavy but steady breathing.

As they plunged deeper into the forest, the vegetation became more varied. Yuri spotted vibrant flowers with oddly shaped petals, squat plants with jagged leaves, and lush bushes. Some of the plants were decidedly pale, thriving in the shadows of the trees. Alien birds shook branches and rustled leaves overhead as they scattered, startled into flight by Thargen's pounding feet and unwavering forward momentum. She caught only fleeting glimpses of the creatures through the vegetation. It was the same for the small bugs flitting through the air nearby—she often spotted them from the corners of her vision, but they were too fast for Yuri to get a good look at them.

Yuri's weariness caught up with her as time passed. Her head lolled, dropping against Thargen's shoulder, and her eyelids drooped, lulled by his constant, almost hypnotic motion. His skin was hot on her cheek, and she could feel his heart pounding through his chest.

She roused herself sometime later when Thargen finally slowed, blinking away the grogginess from her eyes. Every muscle in her body screamed in protest. Despite Thargen's best efforts, she'd taken a beating during the crash, and she was sure feeling it now. Lifting her head, she looked around to find herself in a small, grassy clearing that was backed on one side by a huge boulder. The light streaming in through the gap in the trees made the surrounding colors just a little brighter.

Thargen walked closer to the boulder, still breathing heavily but evenly, and leaned forward to gently lower Yuri's feet to the ground. Once she was standing on her own, his arms fell away. She tightened her hold on the backpack and axe as she took a step back and looked up at Thargen.

His green skin was a tapestry of scars, bruises, and smeared blood; the only thing keeping the latter of those from making her sick again was her overwhelming concern for him. He was still naked—and his pierced cock, though flaccid, was still as intimidating as it was enticing. His chest swelled and his shoulders rose with another deep, ragged breath.

Thargen raised his hands and tugged his backpack off his shoulders, letting it drop heavily onto the grass behind him.

"Fuck." Moving slow and stiff, he closed the distance to the boulder, bracing a hand on its stone face once he reached it. He winced and turned to lean against the boulder as he lowered himself into a sitting position.

Yuri's eyes widened. She dropped the axe and backpack beside his bag and hurried over to him, placing a hand on his shoulder. "Thargen? Are you okay?"

He released a huff of air through his nostrils and tipped his head back against the rock. "Tired."

She would've expected anyone to be tired after what they'd gone through—she absolutely was—but his response didn't ease her worry. Heat baked off him, and his skin was coated in sweat.

Yuri wasn't familiar with vorgal physiology, but she knew many species could run themselves to death, driven by pure adrenaline—or whatever hormones were specific to their kind. And she had been part of the burden he'd carried. She had increased his exertion.

He should've listened when I told him to put me down.

But she knew in her heart that wouldn't have helped—he *was* faster, and even if she were in peak physical condition, she'd only have slowed him down.

She scrambled to her backpack and heaved it upright. Unzipping it, she dug inside, pushing aside clothing and other items until she found two water cubes. There hadn't been many intact cubes in that mess back on the ship, but she'd taken every one she could find.

Yuri returned to Thargen and knelt at his side. He'd already closed his eyes. Frown deepening, she brought one of the cubes to his lips. "Open."

"Only for a kiss," he said, one corner of his mouth twitching up in a tiny smirk.

"Oh, you stubborn male," she said, but couldn't help smiling herself. "Fine." Leaning forward, she pecked a brisk kiss on his mouth before pulling back and raising the water cube again. "Now open."

"That shouldn't cou—"

Yuri shoved the water cube into his mouth, cutting off his words. "Maybe after you're done resting, I'll have a better one waiting."

He pressed his lips together, and his cheeks sunk in as he sucked on the cube. After a few seconds, he swallowed thickly and grimaced. "Still tastes shitty."

"Doesn't matter." She held the other to his mouth. "Next."

Thargen covered her hand with one of his, pushing it down. He lifted his head, opened his eyes, and met her gaze. "Save it."

"You need to rehydrate."

"It's our only water for now. Save it." Despite his obvious weariness, both his tone and his hold on her hand were firm.

Yuri's gaze shifted from his eyes to their hands and back again, indecision and worry coiling in her chest.

"I'll be fine, *zoani*. Either put it away or take it yourself." He released her hand and caught her chin, forcing her eyes to remain on him. "Stay close. Stay alert."

She searched his face. His golden eyes were intense and flooded with concern—concern for *her*.

"I will, Thargen."

He held her gaze for another moment or two before his eyes drifted shut and he tipped his head back again. His hand fell away from her face, his whole body sagged against the boulder, and his breathing was immediately slow and even. It was as though he'd just...powered down in an instant.

Yuri's heart lurched, and she hurriedly raised her free hand, placing her palm over his forehead. He was burning up. She moved her fingers down, pressing them to his throat to check his pulse. It took some searching, especially because she paused after discovering the hard cords on either side of his trachea. Were they tendons or cartilage, or perhaps something else entirely? When she finally found a good spot, his heartbeat was almost as slow and steady as his breathing—an alarming change from it having been racing only a minute or two before.

She'd only studied human medicine during her time in nursing school. She didn't know anything about vorgals, didn't know if this was normal or something to be concerned about. Thargen hadn't seemed panicked or alarmed by his condition, but that didn't necessarily mean anything.

Dropping her hand to her lap, she sat back on her heels and studied him. His green skin glistened with sweat, some of which combined to trickle down his neck and chest—and a few of which carried a red tinge, having mixed with the blood spattered on him.

Yuri was suddenly reminded of the bloodied, battered corpse they'd left behind near the ship.

"Ugh." She tilted her head back and looked up at the trees, forcing herself to take deep breaths until the lightheadedness passed. "Come on, Yuri. It's just a little blood. Stop being such a damn baby."

The most frustrating part of it was that she knew her problem had nothing to do with being a baby—the medical term for it was vasovagal syncope, and it was fairly common even if most people didn't know what to call it. Best of all was that modern medicine hadn't come up with a cure other than *avoid your triggers.*

Hence the end of her nursing career before it had even begun.

She could still remember the first time she'd fainted because of it. Seven-year-old Yuri had been playing at the park with her siblings when her older sister, Kaiya, ran beneath one of the slides and hit her head. Fortunately, Kaiya hadn't suffered a concussion or anything serious—but she had opened a gash on her forehead. There'd been blood *everywhere.*

Yuri's last thought before passing out had been that Kaiya was going to die. No one could bleed that much and live. Ever since then, Yuri had felt light-headed and nauseous whenever she saw blood. She could usually push through it if she focused on her breathing and closed her eyes, but it still made her vomit or faint on occasion.

She'd hoped to outgrow it, as many people did.

Seventeen years and counting, now...

But after everything Thargen had done for her, Yuri couldn't sit here and do nothing. Lifting her head, she looked at him again and studied his body. Her brows furrowed.

Thargen seemed just a touch smaller than he had a minute before. Not that there was anything really *small* about him, but his muscles appeared just a little less defined. She supposed that was normal; this was the first time she'd seen him truly relaxed since they'd been kidnapped.

More concerning were the discolored patches all over his body—dark bruises, some wider across than her hand.

Though it was difficult to tell given the amount of blood on him, Yuri didn't think his skin had been broken anywhere—at least not this time. She once again found her eyes following the paths of his many scars, and wondered how they'd been caused, wondered how much pain he'd endured. Her gaze dipped lower, running over his abdomen, and she swallowed thickly when it stopped on his cock.

"Enough, Yuri," she said in response to the desire sparking within her. "Now is *not* the time."

Turning, she grabbed her bag and dragged it closer. She carefully put the water cube inside and was rummaging through the backpack's contents when she noticed the dark blotch on her shirt. She looked down at it and stilled—a large blood stain, not unlike an inkblot from those old psych tests, had settled into the fabric all over her midsection.

Her stomach immediately revolted.

She swiftly crawled away and heaved, emptying the meager contents of her stomach. The meal bar didn't taste any better coming up than it had going down.

Yuri spat and took in several calming breaths before she sat up. Groaning, she tilted her head back and closed her eyes, letting her stomach settle.

Once the worst of her nausea had passed, she grasped the hem of her shirt and slowly peeled the garment off over the top of her head, holding her breath and taking great care to keep the blood from touching her face. As soon as it was off, she wadded it up, opened her eyes, and returned to Thargen. She used the shirt to clean as much sweat and blood from Thargen's skin as she could, doing her best not to directly look at any of that blood in the process.

When she was done, she tossed the soiled shirt aside, pulled a clean one out of the bag, and put it on. Knowing she needed to stay hydrated herself, she popped one of the water cubes in her mouth. The cube's thick outer layer melted, and a gush of water sluiced down her throat. Despite its slightly chemical taste, it was heavenly, and helped wash away the taste of vomit.

Sitting back, Yuri ran her gaze over Thargen's face, which was uncharacteristically serene in his sleep.

She felt helpless. Whatever was going on in his body right now, she didn't have the knowledge or the tools to aid him beyond cleaning a little blood off his skin—and she could barely manage even that without passing out or puking.

"You really lucked out getting stuck with me," she said.

She picked up his right hand and turned it so his palm was facing up. Her lips curled into a small smile as she traced her finger over the tiny, barely noticeable scars there—remnants of the wounds she'd mended in the Starlight Trance's breakroom. It felt like a lifetime had passed since she'd first seen Thargen standing at the bar, but she clearly recalled the way her heart and belly had fluttered when he'd smiled at her. That feeling hadn't diminished; her time with him had only reinforced what he'd made her feel from that very first moment.

Even then, her attraction to him had been so much more than her fixation with orcs; she hadn't even noticed he was a vorgal, not right away. It had been those intense yellow eyes, which had seemed to glow under the blacklights, that impossibly disarming smile, and that contradictory air of danger and security he emitted that had drawn her in.

It had been *him*.

Yuri flattened her palm over his. Her hand looked so tiny in comparison. Everything about Thargen was big, and it was just one of the many things she loved about him.

Love.

Something warm flared in her chest, her heart skipped a beat, and that fluttering sensation returned to her belly; butterflies, they called it. Yuri laced her fingers with Thargen's and looked up at his face again.

All this was undoubtedly a chemical response in her body, explainable by science—pheromones and hormones and all that reacting to one another, driven by that deep, instinctual drive to mate, to carry on the species and pass down genes to the next generation.

It was lust.

But to Yuri...it was more.

She'd always believed in love at first sight. And these feelings, these sensations... They were *real*. She believed fate was real.

So many people had called her old-fashioned and ridiculous, had called her a prude, a tease—all because she'd chosen to wait. They'd acted like it was such a stupid little thing. Why wait? Why not explore her options, have a little fun? Who chose to stay a virgin in the twenty-second century? Some people had even tried pressuring her to give in, but Yuri had held firm.

No one seemed to understand that it was simply *her* choice.

Of *course* she'd had urges, of course she'd experienced arousal, but it had never been inspired by anyone she'd ever met. Only her own fantasies had sparked anything in her, and self-pleasure had been enough. She'd never wanted anything more—not without that *fire*, that connection.

Not without the sort of bond she already had with Thargen. No one had made her feel like he did. She'd never felt this pull, this attraction, this *desire*, not even in her wildest fantasies.

She wanted Thargen.

A high, trilling call shattered the forest's quiet.

Yuri started, her heart leaping up in her throat. She turned her head to look around.

There was no one there.

That didn't mean there wasn't someone nearby. She knew the smugglers were out there, somewhere, and that at least a few other captives had escaped. Not only that, but she was on an alien planet—and she'd already glimpsed a few small crea-tures. Who knew what else was lurking out there, looking for prey? And here she was, daydreaming, leaving herself open for attack while Thargen was so vulnerable.

"Okay, Yuri, this sucks and it's terrifying but at least you're not in a cage," she said quietly, pulling her hand away from Thargen's. "You can be useful while he's out of commission."

She crawled to the axe lying in the rust colored grass, wrapped her hand around the grip, and hefted it up. It was heavier than she'd expected, but not unwieldy. Taking the haft in both hands, she slowly turned the weapon, examining it; there was some way to activate the hardlight blade, but she didn't see any obvious buttons or switches.

It was only as the haft was turned to a certain angle that she noticed the shallow depression above the grip. She placed her thumb in it. Nothing happened. Brow furrowed, she slid her thumb up and down the depression, but the weapon remained inactive.

"Just as stubborn as him," she muttered, gritting her teeth and pressing her thumb down harder.

The hardlight blades on either side of the axe head flashed into existence. Yuri started, eyes wide, and fumbled with the haft, nearly dropping the damned thing. Her heart leapt into her throat until she finally firmed her grip and steadied the weapon. She took in a deep breath, and her cheeks puffed as she slowly released the air.

She glanced at Thargen. "You seriously trusted me with this thing?"

He continued to snooze.

Yuri chuckled and shook her head, facing forward. "Of course you did. Mean, scary terran. Rawr. Anyone who comes by will take one look at me, see just how dangerous and fright-ening I am, and run away in terror."

She ran her eyes over the translucent hardlight blade. It was neon orange, with faint hexagonal patterns shimmering in and out of view across its surface in waves. She'd seen what such blades could do, even before today; there wasn't much they couldn't cut through with enough force behind them.

Yuri cringed. "Here's hoping I don't cut my own leg off before you wake up."

Holding the weapon as steady as possible, she pressed her thumb down on the depression again. She had to push so hard it started to hurt a little before the orange blade vanished.

She laid the deactivated weapon across her lap, steeled herself, and quietly stood—or rather *sat*—guard, scanning the surrounding forest constantly. It took no small amount of willpower to keep herself from jumping at every little sound. The alien animal calls, which were rare but distinct, were the hardest to ignore; the only comfort she could draw from them was that they hadn't been made by the smugglers.

She paused every now and then to check Thargen. His skin was gradually cooling, the sweat had mostly evaporated, and his heartbeat remained steady, even if it was slower than she would've liked. But there was something else, something that made her feel like she was going crazy—she swore his bruises were smaller and fainter than they'd been before. She wrote it off as a trick of her eyes; he'd said he healed quickly, but healing that fast without any medical aid?

That was impossible, wasn't it?

And Thargen slept on, unstirring. Even if he was utterly exhausted, Yuri didn't quite understand how he'd gone to sleep so easily, with so little apparent concern. He'd sat down, put his head back, and fallen asleep as though they weren't stranded on an unknown planet with limited food and water, questionably useful supplies, and goodness knew how many dangerous smugglers out to get them.

Yuri was barely holding back a tidal wave of worry regarding the current situation. If she tried to settle down, to sleep, she knew that wave would break through, and it would be strong enough to keep her wide awake for days.

But it probably is *exhaustion. At least mostly. That, and...he doesn't seem to fear anything.*

And why would he? Even unconscious, he was intimidating.

Intimidating and sexy. Very sexy. Lickably sexy.

Stop it, Yuri. Focus!

Yuri turned her thoughts to her family, her parents and her older brother and sister back on Earth, to her younger brother, Takashi back in Arthos, who had likely lost his shit by now wondering what had happened to her. Was *he* okay?

She raised a hand and ran it through her hair. At least she and Thargen were free from the cage. The situation wasn't ideal, but they stood a chance of getting home.

Right?

TEN

At least a couple agonizing hours had to have passed by the time Thargen stirred. He groaned, cut that groan off with a grunt, and shook his head. Just like that, his eyes were open and alert.

"You're awake!" The relief that flooded Yuri was so great that she felt as though she were about to sag to the ground. She hadn't allowed herself to acknowledge just how tense and frightened she'd been until that moment.

Yuri set the axe on the ground, dug another water cube out of the backpack, and moved to Thargen's side to thrust the cube at him. "No arguments."

Thargen's hand snapped up so quick it could only have been reflex, creating a barrier that halted her thrusting arm. "Easy, terran. Give me a couple seconds, and you can shove whatever you want in my face."

She didn't miss how his eyes dipped toward her body—or the hungry light that sparked in them.

Heat crept up Yuri's neck as she sat back on her heels and lowered her arm. "Sorry. It's just that you've been out for hours after running yourself to near death. So as your...your doctor—yeah, we'll go with doctor—I order you to hydrate." She turned her hand and opened her fingers, presenting the water cube on her palm.

Thargen arched his right brow, which was bisected by a little scar. "Have you had one, doc?"

"Yeah, I did."

Keeping his eyes locked with hers, Thargen took hold of her wrist and lifted her hand. He bent toward her at the same time, lowering his head. He didn't break that eye contact as he opened his mouth and pressed his lips down onto her palm around the cube. He sucked the water cube into his mouth slowly before lifting his head.

Yuri's heart quickened, and her sex clenched, aching with desire. "I-I guess you must be...feeling better?"

He swallowed, and his tongue slipped out to run across his upper lip. "Yeah, now that I'm hydrated."

Her gaze locked on his tongue for the brief instant it was out.

Yuri shook her head, clearing her throat as she drew her hand away. "Good." She returned her attention to the backpack, pulling out a pair of pants, which she held out to Thargen. "I, uh, cleaned up most of the blood." She tipped her head toward the wadded up, bloody shirt on the ground without looking at it. "Did the best I could without anything to wash with."

Thargen glanced down at himself and made a thoughtful hum. His expression was softer and more serious when he looked at her again. As he accepted the pants, he asked gruffly, "You did that for me?"

She frowned. "I couldn't just leave you like that. And...it's not like I could do much else."

"I've seen what looking at blood does to you, Yuri. And you

did this for me anyway." Thargen shook his head and lifted his free hand, running it over the scars on the side of his head. "Guess it's just a small thing, but small things tend to mean the most. Thanks."

Warmth flooded her cheeks. "Well, you did just kind of kill someone for me, so..."

His brow furrowed, and the corners of his mouth fell. "Yeah. You, uh...you okay? I know it's not...*normal* for most people, and even if he got what he deserved, I guess that could be...traumatic to watch?"

Yuri reached out and placed her hand on Thargen's arm, looking deep into his eyes. "We...we both know what he would have done with me, and had that blaster been loaded, you would've been... He would have killed you. As horrifying as it was to watch, I'm fine."

"Pfft. You think he could've stopped me?" He thumped his chest with his fist. "I'm your fucking orc, *zoani*. Gonna take more than a perverted cren with a blaster to bring me down."

Yuri laughed, but it took her a couple seconds to pick up on the most significant words he'd said.

Your fucking orc.

My *orc.*

A more intense sort of warmth spread outward from her heart, filling her chest and working into her limbs. Those soft wings resumed their fluttering in her belly, making her body feel delightfully weightless.

"What does *zoani* mean?" she asked, withdrawing her hand from him and placing it on the backpack. "You've called me that several times now."

"And I'll call you that a lot more times before we're through. But I gotta keep a little mystery about me, don't I?" Thargen grinned at her, climbed to his feet, and brushed dirt and clinging blades of red grass off his ass and the backs of his thighs. When he was done, he held up his pants by their waistband and shook them out, letting their legs unfurl. "Can't risk you losing interest."

Not happening, Thargen. You're mine.

Yuri's lips spread into a wide smile as her eyes moved over his muscular body. His cock, which had been flaccid while he slept, now stood thick and erect. Bending forward, he shoved his feet into the pant legs one at a time. Each of his movements made his muscles ripple beneath his skin. Everything about him heated her blood and made her sex ache.

"I don't think that'll happen," she said softly.

He paused with the pants drawn up to his knees and released a heavy breath. There was a sudden, unmistakable tension in him, but it passed in an instant. Had it just been a twinge of pain? He'd taken quite a beating during the crash...

Thargen straightened and pulled the pants up the rest of the way—not without some hard tugs and a few grunts. "I, uh... I'll tell you what *zoani* means when we get back. To Arthos."

Yuri smiled. "I'll hold you to that." She stood up, clasped her hands together, and raised them high over her head, closing her eyes. The stretch felt so damn good after sitting for so long —but it also made her aware of the abuse her body had taken since she'd been kidnapped. She felt like she was made up of bumps and bruises instead of flesh and bones.

Could be worse, Yuri. You could still be in that cage.

When she looked back at Thargen, he was tugging at the fabric around his crotch and adjusting the immense bulge that was his cock. His pants were more like traditional military fatigues than hers, with belt loops, clasps, and pockets, and their material less elastic—but to call those pants form-fitting would've been an understatement.

"Well"—he shifted the waistband from side to side—"guess these pants are good for you."

"Why's that?" she asked, dropping her arms to her sides.

He flashed her a toothy grin. "They're not hiding much."

Yuri laughed. She could definitely appreciate that fact.

He stepped to his backpack and crouched, almost as though to illustrate his point—the pants hugged his toned ass so tightly that Yuri was suddenly jealous of them. Her hands itched to run over him, and she yearned to feel his solid muscle beneath her palms.

Wasn't I always the one who would complain about people having sex at the worst possible times in movies? Now I totally understand. Some things are just hard to resist...especially when they offer a temporary distraction from a terrible situation.

And now she needed a distraction from that distraction before her lust ran rampant—and it seemed that turning her attention back to what was important, like getting back home, was the right way to do that. "So, what's the plan?"

"I'm working on it." Thargen opened the backpack wide, and Yuri's eyes rounded at the sight of its contents. Even in those fantasy VR games she used to play, which were brimming with medieval weaponry, she'd never seen so many knives piled together.

And he looks like he's one item away from declaring his inventory is full.

He rummaged through the backpack, examining the items one by one. He returned some of the objects to the back and placed others on the ground beside him. After a minute or two, he grabbed Yuri's backpack, dragged it close, and repeated the process. The pile on the ground grew.

Thargen grunted thoughtfully. "We have plenty of clothes. Enough meal bars and water cubes to last maybe two days if we're disciplined. But a lot of this stuff looks like attachments for those auto-blasters. The optics might be useful, probably have range finding and scanning functions built in, but the rest of this is dead weight." He gestured to the pile on the ground; most of the items were black and relatively small, devices that seemed to be pieces of greater wholes.

"We're set on weaponry for fighting up close. Knives are balanced enough to throw in a pinch, but we're disadvantaged at range." Thargen nodded, scanning the open backpacks again. "We don't have much, but we'll manage. Just gotta improvise."

Thargen closed the backpacks before scooping the discarded items into his arms. He stood up and walked toward the edge of the clearing, where he dumped the items unceremoniously into the bushes.

Yuri couldn't help but check out his ass as he moved. The man did have a really, *really* nice ass.

He turned to face Yuri and walked back toward her, breaking the spell his glutes had cast on her.

"Why didn't we stay with the others?" she asked—the same question she'd posed while he was running earlier. *Because* wasn't a good enough answer. "Wouldn't we have more of a chance against the smugglers if we all worked together?"

"No, we wouldn't." Thargen bent forward to snatch up the axe she'd set down. "That'd be like laying fresh bait for a predator and then sitting on it to wait."

Her brows creased. "What do you mean?"

Thargen moved to the boulder, raised his free arm, and laid it against the stone. "They all had collars. Even if they were out of range for remote shocks, those things usually have tracking beacons built in."

The axe's hardlight blade flashed on. Thargen shifted his grip up until his thumb was against the metal axe head and pressed the blade down on the manacle binding his raised wrist. His movements were slow and controlled in a way Yuri hadn't yet seen from him despite the tension rippling through his muscles. She pressed her lips together nonetheless, unable to help but worry as she watched him—that blade could slice through his skin as easily as hers.

A few seconds later, he lifted the axe away and shook his arm. The manacle broke apart, its pieces clanging against the rock before hitting the grass with muted thuds.

"Couldn't that axe have removed their collars?" she asked.

"Yeah." Thargen switched hands to repeat the process. "And those smugglers were right on our asses. So think about how that would've gone. Maybe I would've helped one or two of the prisoners before those Zulka fuckers caught up, and maybe I would've killed one or two smugglers in the fight."

The blade of the axe slipped, and Thargen jerked his arm away; the manacle flung off his wrist as the axe sheared through solid stone. He lowered the weapon and met Yuri's gaze. "But their guns would've worked when they pulled the triggers, and shit would've gone real bad. I wasn't gonna take that risk. Not with you."

Not with you.

The combination of his intense, golden eyes and his fervent tone sent a thrill through her. But that thrill diminished as swiftly as it had come.

How long would it be before the other escapees were recaptured? Had any of them even lasted this long? Iljibi had been terrible, but none of the others had shown any such behavior. Yuri was sure many of them weren't much different than Thargen and herself—victims who'd been in the wrong place at the wrong time.

Still, Yuri didn't know any of them, didn't know what this ordeal had done to their mental states. As hard as it was to set aside compassion, she had to remember that any one of those captives might have stabbed her in the back for something as simple as a water cube. Unfortunately, out here...it was everyone for themselves.

But Yuri wasn't alone.

If not for Thargen, she wouldn't have stood a chance. It could easily have been Yuri jumping from that breach and breaking a leg instead of the volturian—if she would've survived the crash to begin with. She was sure that Thargen was the only reason she was still up and moving.

Yuri crossed her arms over her chest. As horrible as she felt for not being able to help the others, she knew Thargen was right.

He deactivated the hardlight axe, moved to stand in front of her, and took her chin in his big hand, angling her face up toward his. "The stuff they were hauling is worth a lot of credits. They're not going to give it up." He lowered his face until it was mere centimeters from hers. "And I'm not giving *you* up."

Yuri reached up and covered his hand with hers. "What now? What are we going to do?"

"Well...the best plans are, uh...fluid, right?"

She arched a brow. "You don't have a plan, do you?"

"I absolutely have a plan, terran." His eyes dropped to her mouth, and he brushed her lower lip with his thumb. "We're gonna find a decent spot to shelter, scrounge up some food that doesn't taste like ass, and then figure out how I'm going to kill every one of those Zulka bastards that didn't die in the crash."

A shiver ran up Yuri's spine. She didn't know if it had been caused by the way he stroked her lip, the desire burning in his eyes, or the promise of violence in his tone.

Seeming to know the effect he had on Yuri, Thargen released her and stepped back. He took a few seconds to locate the fallen pieces of his manacles and throw them deep into the woods before returning to his backpack. After a bit of fiddling with the loops and fasteners, he hung both hardlight axes from his waist, their hafts secured along the outsides of his thighs. He hooked sheathed knives on the waistband of his pants, closed his pack, and swung it up onto his shoulders. A few adjustments to the straps had the backpack snugly in place.

When Yuri put on her backpack, he helped tighten its straps to grant her a more comfortable fit, his large hands surprisingly precise and delicate. By the time he was done, she barely noticed the weight on her back.

Thargen walked forward, twisting his head to look over his shoulder and say, "On my ass, terran."

"On it," Yuri replied, setting off behind him.

Unfortunately, it wasn't long before she was forced to face the truth—no matter how much she wanted to be, she most assuredly was *not* on his ass.

Thargen's strides were long—it felt like she had to take two steps for every one of his—and the exhaustion that had forced him to stop earlier seemed to have no effect on him now. Yuri's body, on the other hand, reminded her that it was aching and tired with her every movement, no matter how tiny. She was sore in places she hadn't even known existed. But more immediate was the new pain on the soles of her feet. The red grass had been as soft as fluffed cotton, but that grass wasn't everywhere—especially not in the thicker parts of the forest.

The fallen needles from the trees blanketed wide sections of the forest floor. They were stiff, and often lay flat enough to avoid poking—but when one of them did jab her foot, it felt like stepping on a damned nail. The stone they crossed over only provided relief when it was covered in soft patches of lichen; much of the rock itself was rough and uneven and wouldn't have felt nice even if her feet hadn't been stabbed a hundred times already.

When her foot came down on a particularly jagged rock, she winced, hissing through her teeth as she quickly pulled her foot back.

Thargen halted and turned toward her. Though he'd been gradually easing his pace throughout the journey—undoubtedly to accommodate her—his lead had steadily increased, and he now stood several meters ahead of her.

"You okay, *zoani?*"

I'm just slowing him down.

The heat of shame filled her cheeks, and she gave Thargen a sheepish smile. "Guess running around behind a bar every night doesn't build the right kind of callouses for barefoot hikes through the woods."

He frowned and strode over to her. He eyed her skeptically, brows low, and dropped to one knee. Before she could figure out what he meant to do, he took hold of her ankle and lifted her foot off the ground.

Yuri wobbled and teetered backward, thrown off balance by the backpack, but Thargen looped his free arm around her waist to steady her, and she threw her hands out to grasp his shoulders. Once she'd reclaimed her balance, Thargen lowered his arm and turned his attention to her foot.

"Yuri," he said in a low rumble as he angled her foot so its sole was facing him. He lightly brushed a finger forward from her heel.

She flinched, nearly yanking her foot out of his hold as a small burst of laughter escaped her. "That tickles."

"And this?" He pressed the tip of his finger to a spot on the ball of her foot.

This time, she gritted her teeth, cutting off a whimper, and dug her fingers into his shoulders. "Hurts."

He straightened, and his eyes—which were pretty much

level with hers while he was kneeling—met hers. "How long's it been hurting?"

Yuri looked away from him. "Not long."

Thargen caught her chin and firmly guided her face back toward his. "Don't lie to me, terran."

She blew out a frustrated breath, scowled, and threw her hands up—only to hurriedly return them to his shoulders to prevent herself from falling backward. "I'm a burden! What use am I? I'm slowing you down because I can't even walk."

Frustration flashed across his features, straining his expression and adding a hint of darkness to his eyes. Still holding her chin, he released her foot and stood up suddenly, looming over her. Yuri reflexively moved back, but he caught her with an arm around her waist.

The look on his face promised anger, reprimand, a taste of the fury she'd seen him unleash on Iljibi earlier. And yet...a glint of hunger lingered in his gaze.

He pulled her flush against him and leaned down, smashing his lips over hers. Yuri started, eyes flaring wide. The kiss was unrelenting, charged with fire and lightning that coursed from her mouth all the way down to the tips of her fingers and toes. It demanded everything from her—and offered everything in return.

Closing her eyes, Yuri looped her arms around his neck, leaned into him, and parted her lips to grant him the access he commanded. His tongue swept in and danced with hers, stroking sensually and exploring her mouth. Yuri flicked her tongue out, licking along his tusk.

Thargen growled. The arm around her back dropped so he could take a handful of her ass and draw her tighter against him as he tilted his head and slanted his mouth over hers, deepening the kiss.

Yuri moaned as her conscious thought faded away. His kiss

was a drug, addictive and intoxicating, filling her veins with an insatiable need for *more*. Heat flooded her core, and her sex clenched, aching with want, tormented by a raging, unfulfilled desire.

He pulled back abruptly, breaking the kiss.

Desperate, Yuri tried to follow, unwilling to let it end, but his hold on her chin prevented her from closing the distance he'd placed between their lips. Brows drawn down, she opened her eyes.

Thargen's mouth was mere centimeters from hers, and his half-lidded eyes were even more intense than before. "You're not a burden, *zoani*," he said, his voice a low, rough rumble. "You're the only reason I'm still going."

Yuri released a shaky breath. She could feel the heat emanating from him, could see the lust burning in his eyes, could still taste him on her tongue.

He held her gaze for several seconds, his eyes searching and ravenous, and she swore his head tipped infinitesimally closer. But before she could battle his hold to claim another kiss, he released her and stepped back. He hooked his fingers under the straps of her backpack and slid them off her shoulders. Taking hold of the backpack in one hand, he swung it to Yuri's front, holding it there for her.

She dazedly hugged it to her torso.

Thargen stooped and swept her into his arms, cradling her against his chest. His motions were so easy, so smooth, as though she weighed nothing at all, and he hadn't already carried her across *at least* several kilometers of wilderness a few hours ago.

As he started walking, he said, "Tell me next time. I need to know so I can keep you safe."

Yuri sighed and rested her head against his shoulder. "Okay."

He continued through the forest at a brisk but steady pace, carrying Yuri and both their packs over the uneven terrain without showing any signs of increased exertion. The sky dimmed steadily, creating pockets of gloom between the alien boughs, and a chill crept into the air.

She didn't know how long they'd traveled when Thargen stopped at the edge of a small clearing, where he set Yuri down on a soft patch of grass so they could relieve themselves. No problem. Yuri was a pro at this after peeing in a hole for days. Going on the ground outside was a cinch.

And at least there are leaves to clean up with.

Once they were done, he picked her up and moved on without hesitation.

Neither of them talked much during the journey; for some reason, the quiet felt appropriate. Even if they'd made occasional jokes since this whole situation had begun, Yuri knew it was serious. People had died—and more people were bound to die before it was all done.

Yuri just had to believe that she and Thargen weren't amongst the doomed.

The forest eventually opened again, giving way to a wide, hilly stretch of land that was even rockier and more irregular than the places they'd traversed thus far. That red grass was in abundance here, covering all the ground that wasn't bare stone —and even growing in clumps and tufts from some of the little cracks and crevices in the rocks.

The mountain loomed to Thargen's right, seemingly closer than ever, its top still blanketed in mist. The sky, which had been a soft cyan when they'd first emerged from the ship, had become a deep teal as it darkened, with hints of cerulean closer to the mountains. This new area was bathed in twilight shadow.

As nice as it was to be in the open after a week in a cage

and hours in a sometimes oppressive forest, the air was colder out here—and the breeze, though gentle, only made it worse, carrying a downright icy bite.

Yuri curled up against Thargen's warmth. "It's getting cold and dark. We should stop."

A low hum rolled from his chest, and he turned his head to look toward the misty peak. "Yeah. Wind shifted downslope already, and it's only gonna get colder."

"Well, thankfully I have my own personal heater," she said, giving his chest a pat.

The corner of his lips quirked. "Could say the same about you, terran."

"I don't put off nearly as much heat as you do. I think you got a raw deal."

"Now, my memory isn't always so reliable," he said as he walked toward a large rock formation ahead of them and to the right, "but I know we already established this. You're fucking hot, *zoani*. Definitely sparked fire in my blood."

Yuri laughed and looked up at him, her gaze tracing his strong jawline to his wide, full lips, where his tusks jutted out. The memory of their last kiss was fresh in her mind—and it ignited a heat in her core that had her squeezing her thighs together.

She pried her attention away from him as they reached the rock formation. From its base, it was an imposing cliff, at least ten meters high, that ran roughly parallel to the peaks farther upslope. Thargen walked along the rock face until they reached a point where it cut briefly back upslope, leaving a sheltered pocket a few meters deep and across.

"This is about as good as we can hope for," Thargen said, stepping into the space.

As he set Yuri down on her feet, she noticed something was missing—the breeze. The air was still cold, but not nearly as cold as out in the open. The red grass ran almost directly up to the rock face, separated by a bit of bare dirt and loose rocks.

Yuri wiggled her toes in the grass. It really was soft—and it would be a million times better than lying on a cold, hard, metal floor.

Stepping away from Thargen, Yuri set her bag down as she knelt, opened it, and rummaged inside.

Thargen dropped his pack next to hers. "Pretty nice compared to that cage, isn't it?"

Yuri chuckled as she withdrew a meal bar and two water cubes. "This is like a five-star luxury hotel." She held out the bar and one of the cubes to him.

He accepted them, popped the cube in his mouth, and broke the meal bar in half, handing a portion back to her. "Eat, terran."

She took it from him and bit into it. The meal bar was as bland and dry as ever—and yet somehow tasted so much better now that she was out of that cage and away from the ship.

"Water, too," Thargen added after she swallowed her mouthful.

"You're being bossy."

And I think I like it.

Staring up at him, Yuri slowly raised the water cube to her mouth and slipped it past her lips.

Even in the rapidly deepening twilight, the hungry gleam in Thargen's eyes was clearly visible. "If that's what it takes to keep my terran safe."

He opened his backpack and tugged out several pieces of clothing through the jumble of knives inside. Once the clothing was piled on the ground, he laid the bag near the base of the cliff. "It's only gonna get colder, and we can't risk a fire."

Thargen removed one of the hardlight axes from his thigh and placed it on the ground near the bag. Lying down on his side, he dragged the backpack a little closer, adjusted its position, and rested his head upon it. He looked at her and grinned, holding his arm open. "Come on, *zoani*. Get in here."

Yuri pulled another shirt out of her bag and crawled toward him. Once she was close enough, she turned and lay down in front of him. Together—with little grace and a few laughs—they draped the spare clothing over their bodies like a pile of too-small blankets. When they were done, Thargen wrapped his arm around Yuri, drawing her back against his chest. Heat radiated from him, and she sighed, snuggling even deeper into his embrace.

His big bicep made a surprisingly comfortable pillow.

Darkness descended swiftly, and now that Yuri was finally still, she was more aware of the sounds around her. The wind rustled the grass and sighed around the rocks. Unknown animals made strange night calls in the distance. Faint chirruping, not unlike that of some insects back on Earth, rode the breeze, oddly soothing despite its alienness.

Yuri looked up at the sky, and her breath caught at the beauty of it. Countless sparkling stars glittered against a dark backdrop that was run through with a cloud of deep violet, blue, and touches of pink—a galactic cluster painted across the heavens. It was beautiful, the sort of sight that couldn't be seen save in the remotest parts of Earth thanks to light pollution, but that wasn't even the most amazing part.

She stared at the wavering, mist-like light flowing above the horizon—a river of violet and red, accented by flares of green, its course ever shifting but its direction constant. An aurora. She'd never seen one in person.

"I haven't seen the sky in over two years," she said softly, "but I never imagined *any* sky could look this beautiful."

Thargen's hand spread across her belly, and he curled

around her just a little bit more. He lifted his head and turned his face skyward. "It's okay."

Brow furrowing, Yuri looked back at him. "Just okay? Tell me what's more beautiful than that."

He met her gaze, and his eyes flashed faintly as though with reflected light. "You."

Yuri caught her bottom lip between her teeth. Those tiny wings in her belly took flight again as a thrill swept through her, spreading warmth across her skin that had nothing to do with his body heat.

Thargen moved his hand up and brushed his thumb across her lower lip, coaxing her to release it with his gentle touch. His fingertips trailed over her cheek and along her jaw, barely skimming her skin, until he cupped her neck.

Her heartbeat quickened. For a moment, Thargen's hand tensed, and she was certain he'd angle her face toward his, certain he'd claim her with another kiss.

But he lifted that hand away, returning his arm to its previous place over her stomach—where their skin was separated by the thin but stifling fabric of her shirt.

Thargen laid his head down, pressed his nose to her hair, and breathed in deep. He released the breath in a low, appreciative rumble that vibrated into her. "Sleep, terran."

Body thrumming in with unfulfilled arousal, Yuri released a quiet, shuddering exhalation as she turned her face forward and closed her eyes.

How many times could he tease her like that and leave her wanting before she simply came undone? How could anyone sleep while their bodies were so consumed by desire that the slightest touch could make them ache at their center, could make them wild with need?

How could she sleep while she was tucked against his big, solid body, while she could feel his throbbing cock through their pants, pressed against the back of her thigh? He was so warm, so strong, so...safe.

Her body eased into his heat, into his security, and grew heavy. Her breathing evened out, and her heart slowed.

How could she sleep when all she wanted was *him*?

But exhaustion didn't care what Yuri wanted. It dragged her down into the darkness, and she soon drifted into soothing oblivion.

ELEVEN

Thargen surged out of sleep. He snapped his eyes open and lifted his head to stare downslope at a rocky landscape dominated by deep shadows, instinctively searching for any signs of movement, for anything amiss. The shimmering light that had flowed across the sky earlier was gone now; even Thargen's eyes could not penetrate all the darkness here by starlight alone.

A warm, tingling sensation pulsed at the back of his neck, lingering at the base of his skull.

He'd heard something.

He drew in a deep breath and held it, listening.

The wind sighed over the land, making the grass whisper a subtle song. Farther away, alien trees creaked and groaned restlessly. A spark of Rage lit at Thargen's core. The animal sounds that had been evident when he and Yuri had gone to sleep were absent.

That Rage flared when another sound shattered the night—the boom of an explosion echoing across the mountainside.

Thargen slid his arm out from beneath Yuri to shove his

torso up, and she jerked awake with a gasp, sitting up abruptly. Some of the loose clothing they'd covered themselves with fell away. He kept his left arm around her middle; she was trembling.

"What was that?" she asked, her breath forming a small, wispy cloud in front of her.

The sound came again, repeated in quick succession, this time followed by another noise that was quieter but no less distinct—the low whine of blaster fire.

Not explosions. Gunshots.

"Fuck," he growled. Even though the sounds were distorted echoes, made faint by what had to be kilometers of distance, they were unmistakable. He'd heard them too many times to forget—even after his head wound had stolen so many of his memories.

And in his experience, there was only one prevalent species that preferred old-fashioned projectile weaponry.

"Thargen?" The trembling had entered Yuri's voice now, and she'd turned to look at him, eyes wide and pupils dilated.

"Fighting. Back in the direction of the crash." He sat up beside her and slipped his other arm around her shoulders, drawing her against him again. "It's far away, I promise."

The gunfire continued, answered by the piercing *whumps* of blasters and occasionally punctuated by shouts so weak compared to the other sounds that they could've been tricks of the wind. But when those howls tore across the night sky—a chorus, raw and deep, that undulated and rose into a piercing trill—he knew exactly what was happening.

"*Fuck,*" he repeated.

Yuri tensed. "Thargen, what was that?"

"Skeks. Those were fucking skeks."

"You mean...like when people say *spawn of a skeks*? Like it's some...*demon*?"

Thargen withdrew his arm from around her middle and reached behind him, feeling blindly around the backpack until he closed his fingers around the haft of the hardlight axe he'd laid down. He settled the weapon on the ground beside him without relinquishing his hold on it. "Don't know what a *demon* is, but there's a reason everyone uses skeks as an insult."

"What are they?"

"They're big, strong, mean, and will eat just about anything they can kill. But they prefer to take prisoners. They like having fresh meat on hand."

"You mean they'd eat...us? *Alive?*" Her hand flew up to cover her mouth, and her words were muffled when she spoke again. "I think I'm gonna be sick."

Thargen strengthened his grip on the axe as his Rage intensified. Just the thought of Yuri coming to harm, of a skeks so much as laying a finger on her, was nearly enough to send him over the edge.

He inhaled through his nostrils and, making his voice as gentle as possible, said, "No getting sick, *zoani*. They're far away, and even if they weren't...they should be afraid of *us*. I spent a long time fighting them in a lot of places. Even with as much as I've forgotten, I still remember how to kill those fuckers a million different ways."

Yuri took Thargen's right hand between both of hers, drawing his arm just a little more snugly around her shoulders. "You've fought them before?"

"Yeah. Old legends say the skeks might've originated on Valgorond. No one really knows if it's the truth, because we weren't the best about recording history for a long time, but we've been fighting them as long as our people remember. Drove them off our planet, but they're like an infestation. They rove around the universe looking for planets to scavenge and hunt. They don't care about treaties or borders, don't care about governments, don't care about much of anything but eating and breeding."

More howls echoed in the sky, and her grip on his hand tightened. "And they're here. The crash likely led them right to the ship."

Thargen looked down at the top of her head and frowned. "We're not at the ship, *zoani*. Not even close."

"Should we...should we keep moving then? Put more distance between us and them?"

The Rage pressing in on Thargen's mind railed against that idea; he'd already run from a fight with the smugglers, how could he allow himself to flee another enemy? Even if so many of his battle memories had been lost and those remaining were blurry at best, just thinking about the skeks ignited fury in his gut. They were his enemies on a primal level, the same beings his ancestors had battled in the mountains and foothills of his birth...but even more so, they were a threat to his Yuri.

"We will," he replied. "Tomorrow. Need to rest as much as we can before sunrise."

Yuri tipped her head back and looked up at him. There was a worried crease between her eyebrows. "How can you sleep now, listening to that? What if...if they find us here while we're sleeping?"

The fear in her eyes and the slight wavering in her voice was nearly his undoing. The sounds of battle, the screams and blasts and howls, were nothing new to Thargen; in some ways, they were *his* sounds, as much a part of him as his bones, muscles, and blood. None of this was normal for Yuri. None of this was anything she'd dealt with before.

She was exactly the sort of person he'd sought to protect when he joined the Rokkoshi Vanguard—an innocent, unscarred by the horrors of the universe...or at least not so badly scarred. Not yet.

"Ah, terran, trust in me." He lay back slowly, coaxing her to follow with a gentle tug on her shoulders.

She resisted for only a moment—and only weakly. Once she was lying with her head on his arm, he shifted onto his side and draped his other arm over her middle, dropping the axe onto the grass next to her, where it would be within easy reach. He settled his now free hand on her hip and pulled her close, turning her so her back was tucked against him.

"I do trust you," she said, rubbing her cheek on his arm. "I just...don't know how we're going to get back."

Don't know if we're going to get back. She didn't say those words, but he heard them in her voice.

Thargen squeezed her hip, holding her a little more possessively than he meant to. His *zoani* needed comfort—he recognized that well enough, understood what it meant, but he wasn't sure how to give it to her. What he considered comforts —fighting and drinking—wouldn't have done her much good even in better circumstances.

"We'll find a way, Yuri, even if it means I have to fight my way into a skeks camp to steal a ship."

"They have ships?" she asked.

He chuckled. "Yeah, though *pieced-together hunks of shit* is probably a better term. They scavenge parts constantly. Seem to have a knack for building sort of functional stuff from scrap. Some of their ships just explode without warning, but most of them work."

"That's...not encouraging."

Fuck. Doing a great job so far, buddy.

"That's just our backup plan. Don't worry about it."

"Then what's our plan right now?"

"Survive."

She fell into silence, leaving them both to listen to the battle sounds for a few more seconds before those, too, went quiet. The echo of the final gunshot stretched out, lingering far longer than seemed natural.

"Is it over?" she whispered.

"Sounds like it."

"What do you think happened?"

Thargen grunted. "Either the skeks killed or captured everyone on the ship or got scared away. If it's the second, they'll go back another time with a larger group."

Several more seconds of silence stretched between them before she said, "You're not very good at this comforting thing, are you? You're supposed to ease my worries. Take my mind off our impending doom."

As gently as she'd spoken—and though he'd known that truth before she'd said it—her words were still a blow. He wanted to give her everything she needed, and that drive came from a place so deep in him that he couldn't rightly identify it.

Can never get good at something if you don't try...

He lifted his hand from her hip to drag some of the loose garments back over their bodies before settling it back into place. The night air was chilly, and Thargen knew she felt it far more than him. "How long do terrans live, *zoani?*"

She snuggled closer to him, her backside fitting perfectly within the curve of his body—tucked right up against his cock.

Thargen gritted his teeth to hold back a groan. That pressure, that warmth, wouldn't have meant much with anyone else; he would barely have noticed. But with Yuri...

Supposed to be comforting her, damn it.

"I think the average lifespan is around a hundred years," she replied.

He drew in a deep breath; that it was scented by the soft, sweet fragrance of her hair didn't help him ignore his rekindled arousal. "How old are you?"

"I'm twenty-four."

"So you have a long, long time before you have to worry about doom, or whatever."

Yuri turned her head toward him, eyed him, and laughed. "Yeah, I guess I do." When she faced forward again, she lightly pressed her lips to his arm in a small kiss. "What about you? How old are you, and how long do vorgals live?"

Thargen squeezed his eyes shut for a few moments, trying to think beyond the lingering thrill created by the brush of her lips against his skin. "I, uh... Not sure. Somewhere between thirty and forty, I guess."

"You don't know how old you are?"

Though she was turned away, her tone painted a clear image of her expression in Thargen's mind—brow furrowed and lips downturned; confusion with a hint of sorrow.

"We don't really do that whole birthday thing, and there were a lot of years that got all mucked up in my head. Can't piece together enough of it to figure out dates. I do know that vorgal lifespan has two curves."

"Curves?"

"Yeah, like...those chart things they use to measure numbers or whatever?"

"What are the two curves?"

"You got civilian life expectancy, which is close to what you said for terrans, and military life expectancy. Pretty sure I'm already past the peak of the second one."

Yuri kissed his arm again. "And you've got a long time before you reach the peak on the first."

Hearing that out loud put Thargen's time with Yuri into perspective. For so many years, he'd drifted through life like he was caught in the current of a speeding river—no direction, no reason to swim against the flow. He'd found joy, had found a family—as fucked up as that family could be sometimes—but largely, his existence had been hollow between those colorful flares of Rage. He'd looked for fights because they were the only time he'd truly felt alive. And though he'd never sought it directly, he'd always known that he'd eventually find his death in some bar or alleyway. It was inevitable. There'd been no need to consider a future that was never going to be his.

In the short while he'd known her, Yuri had changed all that. For the first time, thinking about that distant future didn't seem pointless, and that future didn't seem out of reach. With Yuri, it was something he craved—something he *yearned* for.

She'd given him a sense of purpose he hadn't possessed in many years. She filled in all those hollow moments with vibrancy, warmth, and pleasure, even while they'd been locked up in a cage to be sold as slaves. Yuri had taken what he felt during combat—that fleeting feeling of being *alive*—and spread it across all his moments, even during the heights of his Rage.

Somehow, this little terran had soothed his Rage, had brought him back, not once but on several occasions. As small and delicate as she looked, she'd proven herself a tether stronger than any he could imagine.

More than that, she looked at him with the same hunger he felt toward her, with the same light in her eyes; he recognized it even if she tried so often to hide it. She looked at him like she *wanted* him. But there was an earnestness to that look, a depth, that went well beyond any longing glances he'd received from females over the years. He'd long ago learned to ignore such looks; he couldn't ignore it from Yuri. He didn't want to.

But he couldn't take her, couldn't have her as his own—he was too big, too hard, too brutal, and he couldn't bear to hurt her. Thargen didn't know if he could maintain control once his Rage roared to the forefront like it always did during sex. It was too much of a risk.

Maybe I can't take...but I can give.

What was it that brought female terrans immense pleasure?

He'd overheard Arcanthus and Drakkal talking about it once. A clit? A tiny bud on the outside of female's sex at the top of her slit?

He could give her the pleasure she deserved and take her mind off her worries for a little while. And, even if he couldn't sink into her warm, tight body and seek his own release, he could take some enjoyment in making her feel good, in feeling her writhe within his arms.

"I don't think I'm going to be able to go back to sleep, knowing they're out there," Yuri said.

Thargen grinned.

Perfect excuse.

He slid his hand from her hip and cupped her between her thighs; only the material of her pants separated his hand from her sex. Yuri's breath hitched, and she jumped, her backside bucking against his cock. A thrill jolted through Thargen, heightening his desire.

He moved his head closer to her, so his mouth was just behind her ear. "Might know a way to distract you, *zoani*. You want it?"

Warmth radiated from her, and it took everything within Thargen to keep his hand still, to keep from thrusting his hips against her. He watched as her brow furrowed, as she curled her hand into a fist on the ground and caught her bottom lip between her teeth, and finally—*finally*—gave him a single nod.

"Yes," she whispered.

Rage roiled up in Thargen's mind, demanding control, demanding action, demanding he tear off her clothes, spread her legs, and rut her *now*. A deep ache resonated in his cock, which was so close to the source of her heat—maddeningly close.

But this was about Yuri. This was *for* Yuri.

Thargen hooked the hem of her shirt and drew it up to her

midsection. The soft skin of her belly quivered when his fingertips brushed over it. She released a shuddering breath when he let go of the shirt and reversed the motion of his hand, sliding it under the waistband of her pants.

His fingers brushed over her pelvis, through a small patch of soft hair, until they encountered her slit. He grazed it lightly with a fingertip.

Yuri shivered, and parted her thighs slightly. "Thargen," she breathed.

"On your back, terran," he growled, struggling against his Rage-fueled need. "And spread those legs."

She rolled onto her back, turning her face toward him. Her eyes met his as she spread her thighs wide. He felt her sex blossom beneath his fingertip, felt her petals open and bloom, felt the dew as his finger delved lower. Even without pushing inside, it was clear that her channel was tight and hot; he could almost imagine the feel of it around his cock, the pressure, the delightful friction.

Though now it was her outer thigh rather than her ass pressing against his cock, his desire hadn't diminished. He was only a few quick movements away from burying himself in her. And all he had to do was push his finger in to have that taste, to feel the strength of her inner walls clamping down on him hungrily.

He couldn't let himself do that. He couldn't trust himself with that sort of temptation.

As he ran his finger back up, it brushed over a little nub at the apex of her sex. Yuri twitched, her lips parting with a soft gasp.

Found it.

Thargen fixed his gaze on her face as he circled her clit with the tip of his finger, keeping his movements slow and gentle. Her lashes fluttered, and she tilted her head back as her hips subtly rocked in time with his strokes. When he inhaled, there was a new scent on the air, faint but heady, teasing him with a sweetness that made his cock impossibly harder; he knew instinctively it was the fragrance of her arousal.

Despite his raging desire, despite his near-painful need, he couldn't deny the pleasure in this—in learning her body through his touch and her reactions to it.

He increased the pressure on her clit just a tiny bit.

Yuri whimpered and clamped a hand on his forearm, squeezing—but she didn't stop him. As he continued to stroke around her clit, her movements grew steadily stronger and more desperate, and the tiny reflections of starlight in her eyes became lust-hazed gleams.

Her breath quickened. She lifted her other hand to cup his jaw, brushing her thumb down one tusk and over his lower lip.

"Kiss me," she begged.

Thargen groaned. His heart was thumping, his blood was hot, the pressure in his groin had built to a startling degree, and seed had seeped from the tip of his cock. His control was as tenuous as a frayed rope—but he could not deny her now, no matter the risk. He dipped his head and captured her lips with his own as he swept up some of the dew from her lower sex to spread across her folds. When his finger returned to her sensitive little nub, he sped its movements and pressed harder.

She gasped against his mouth and she moved her hand up to clutch a fistful of his hair. The sharp sting on his scalp stoked his Rage—not in anger, but in pleasure. He growled and crushed his mouth against hers, sweeping his tongue past her lips for a deeper taste. But he wanted more—*needed* more.

Can't.

Yuri undulated her pelvis against his hand, and soon, she was writhing beneath him. Nectar flowed from her sex, and the sweet, intoxicating scent of her desire filled his senses. He swallowed each of the ragged moans that rose from her throat; they were *his*, just as much as she was his.

"Thargen," she rasped, tearing her mouth away. Her moans came in rapid succession, broken only by her panting breaths. She tightened her hold on his hair, increasing that delightful sting on his scalp, and the nails of her other hand dug into his forearm.

By blood and fury, he yearned for more of that. He wanted her nails raking his back as he thrust into her, wanted her pulling his hair, wanted her clamping her little teeth down on his shoulder as she was caught in the throes of ecstasy. He wanted to feel her sex squeezing his cock and milking it for every drop of his seed.

All at once, Yuri's back arched off the ground, and her quivering body went rigid for an instant. Then she threw her head back and cried out as a fresh rush of liquid heat spilled between her thighs. Her cry of pleasure rang out into the night sky.

Thargen covered her mouth with his again to muffle that cry, keeping his finger moving relentlessly. Her thighs snapped together, locking his hand in place as she continued to come undone, feeding her desperate cries directly into him. Tremors rocked her entire body, and her hips bucked against his hand erratically.

It wasn't until those tremors finally waned and her cries fell into soft, breathless moans that Thargen slowed his finger, easing her down from the peak she'd summited.

He forced himself to breathe deeply and slowly as he lifted his head to look down at her. His balls felt full near to bursting, his cock was so hard it seemed about to tear through his pants, and his blood flowed through his veins like molten metal, but he focused only on Yuri.

Even in the poor light, the flush on her cheeks was clear.

Her dark hair was tousled, spread over his arm and the grass beneath, and her parted lips were kiss swollen.

She was as beautiful as ever—*more* beautiful.

Yuri opened her eyes and looked up at him, a soft smile spreading across her lips. She released her grip on his hair and slid her palm to his cheek. "I changed my mind. You're *very* good at comforting."

Thargen stilled his hand, cupping her sex possessively. Her words pierced the haze of Rage and desire in his mind, making it a little easier for him to resist even if that haze had not been fully cleared. It didn't matter how much he *wanted*; he'd done this for her. To make her feel good, to comfort her. That was enough.

"Always been good with my hands," he said as he finally withdrew his fingers from her pants. The air was icy compared to her warmth, the cold enhanced by the moisture on his fingers.

He didn't waste any effort in trying to stop his next action; he knew it would've been futile. He raised his hand, slipped his fingers between his lips, and sucked Yuri's essence off them. A low groan rumbled in his chest. Her taste was even better than her scent had promised—sweet and tangy, as delicious as a succulent fruit.

Yuri's breath caught, and her eyes flared. "I...think I just came again."

Got pretty close myself.

Thargen resisted the urge to clamp his hand over his erection, setting it over her stomach instead, where he stroked his thumb over her navel piercing. "Next time, I'll drink from the source."

The flush on her cheeks somehow deepened, and the lustful gleam in her eyes brightened. Hunger burned at Thargen's core.

Don't have to wait until next time...

His muscles were already filling with heat and strength, and his heart was quickening; his body was priming for what he wanted, what he *needed*.

He drew in a deep breath, closed his eyes, and clenched his jaw before turning his face into her palm. Her skin was soft, soothing, grounding, providing him just enough clarity, just enough willpower.

Thargen's Rage had been given an outlet today. It wasn't gone—it never would be—but it wasn't strong enough to take control from him for now.

He pressed a gentle, lingering kiss on Yuri's palm and pulled his face away, opening his eyes. He wrapped his arm around her, turning her onto her side as he drew her close, and tucked her against his body.

"Thargen?" she asked, looking up at him. "What's wrong?"

"Sleep, Yuri," he replied as he pulled the loose clothing back into place over their bodies. "Long day ahead."

"We could just get a head start. I'm not"—she yawned—"tired. Okay, so maybe I am. Your clever hands did good."

Thargen snickered. "Don't think any part of me's ever been called clever, but I'll take it, terran."

She chuckled. "I don't think I could move if I wanted to."

"Guess it's good that I can carry you if necessary." He willed his body to relax, a process that was not aided by having her pressed against him again, nor by her scent in his nostrils and her taste lingering on his tongue.

She released a soft, sleepy sigh. "Yeah. I like your arms around me."

"Me too."

Within a minute or two, her breathing had slowed, and her body had eased, snug and secure against Thargen. He couldn't help a flare of envy; normally, he could get himself to sleep anytime, anywhere—it had been a necessary skill during his time in the Vanguard, when rest was never guaranteed. But that wouldn't be the case tonight.

Lust and Rage pumped through his veins, and his cock—again tucked against her delectable backside—was hard enough to drive a nail.

But there was only one sort of hammering he was interested in right now.

Fuck.

Reluctant as he was to leave her alone even for a few seconds, he was tempted to slip away, take himself in his fist, and empty his seed into this red alien grass. It wasn't at all what he wanted, but it was *something*—and it would provide at least minor relief.

But he couldn't move away from her, not while she was vulnerable, scared, and cold. And he knew that any relief he could provide himself would only be temporary—and that his hunger would come back twice as strong afterward. Right here was where he belonged, with his arms around her. Easing her discomfort, soothing her suffering. Protecting her.

His own discomfort was irrelevant. This was nothing new—his time with Yuri had been spent in a near constant state of arousal, and the lack of an outlet for that arousal had made it almost painful. But she was worth it. He'd suffer like this for the rest of his life so long as it meant he could be near her and keep her safe.

Thargen could survive the ache in his balls; he'd lived through far worse.

His cocked pulsed painfully as though to challenge that idea.

Fuck. This is gonna be a long night.

TWELVE

"How the hell do you walk if your feet are so soft?" Thargen asked as he wrapped Yuri's right foot with a strip of cloth he'd torn from one of the spare pieces of clothing.

"Usually I just wear shoes, but I guess I must've forgotten them at home," Yuri said with a roll of her eyes.

The sky was bleak, shrouded by dark gray clouds and forsaken by a sun that hadn't yet risen above the mountain—which itself was completely hidden by mist thicker than Yuri had ever seen. The air was colder than it had been yesterday, its chill bolstered by strengthened winds, and possessed a hint of unsettling energy that had nothing to do with the skeks attack the night before.

Those clouds held the threat of rain.

It would've been easy for Yuri's imagination to run wild with speculation about how miserable this place would be in the rain, but she didn't allow it to. Despite her fear of both the known and unknown dangers of this world—the skeks scared the hell out of her—she was in a *really* good mood.

She turned her attention down to Thargen's hands—particularly his long, thick fingers, which moved with precision and confidence belied by their appearance. She shifted on the rock she sat upon, but no matter her position, the slight tenderness at the apex of her thighs would not diminish, serving as a reminder of what those fingers had done last night. Her sex throbbed, and her core ached; even with the release he'd granted her, she was in no way satisfied. She wanted those hands on her again, those fingers inside her.

She wanted *him* inside her.

Thargen grunted, and one corner of his mouth lifted in a smirk, pulling his lips tight around his tusks. "Next thing you'll tell me is that you forgot to bring the food, too."

She threw her hands up. "And the booze. I knew I should've made a checklist before we left."

He secured the cloth around her ankle, tying the ends off and tucking them away. "Last time I trust you to plan a trip, terran. Other foot."

Yuri chuckled and lowered her foot from his knee, replacing it with the other. She wiggled her toes.

"Soft, small, and cute," Thargen muttered as he stretched out the next strip of fabric.

She grinned. "You should see them when my nails are painted green."

"Fuck, terran," he groaned, dropping a hand to his groin—to his very visible *erection*—and squeezing. "You're killing me."

Yuri bit her lip, staring at the outline of his cock, recalling every little detail of what was hidden beneath the fabric. "I could...help you with that."

His grip tightened, making the tendons on the back of his hand stand out. After several seconds of silence, he finally huffed through his nose, withdrew his hand from his groin, and positioned the fabric strip beneath her foot. His voice was strained when he said, "We need to get moving."

She knew he was right, but that didn't stop the pang of disappointment that struck her chest.

Thargen brushed a finger across the tips of her toes. "I expect them painted when we get back, *zoani*. No teasing me."

Yuri chuckled, wiggling her toes again. "Oh, they will be. As green as you want them."

He began the wrapping process, crossing the fabric over itself as he covered her foot with it, keeping it snug. "It's nice to meet a female who understands that green is indisputably the best color in the universe. There is one shade better than the rest, though."

Yuri ran a finger over his shoulder and down along his arm. "Yours, of course."

"Oof. It suck to be so wrong?"

Laughter bubbled out of her. "Now what color could be better than yours? I thought for sure that was the best."

Thargen folded the cloth over her toes and started wrapping it back toward her ankle. He lifted his gaze, locking it with hers, and leaned a little closer. "Yours is. Your eyes."

Yuri's cheeks warmed. "Let's agree to disagree."

"Nope." He glanced down only long enough to tie off the cloth strip and tuck the ends away before his eyes were on hers again. "It's all right to be wrong, terran. Which you are in this case."

Yuri snorted. "Keep telling yourself that. Things are gonna be rough for you until you accept the greatest truth of them all."

He cocked his scarred eyebrow and tilted his head. "And what's that?"

"I'm *always* right, even when I'm wrong. And I'm never wrong, since I'm always right."

Thargen shook his head and chuckled, gently guiding her foot off his knee. "Keep up with that kinda talk and you'll make my head hurt, terran."

"I might be willing to stop"—she waggled her eyebrows—"if you concede that I am, in fact, correct."

Perhaps it was childish to playfully argue about which green was better, but Yuri needed this light-hearted distraction. Soon, they'd be traversing dangerous, unfamiliar land, and there was no telling when they'd have a moment like this again—if they had any more at all.

"You could tell me this grass is blue," Thargen said as he turned away and scooped up his backpack, "or that I'm a damned volturian, and I wouldn't argue with you. But when it comes to questions of your beauty, *zoani, I'm* right."

He slung the straps over his shoulders, muscles rippling beneath his skin; despite the cold, he hadn't put on a shirt, and Yuri certainly wasn't going to complain if he was comfortable shirtless. He snatched up her pack and turned to face her again. "Now get your sexy ass over here, terran."

Grinning, Yuri stood up and walked toward him. It felt strange having her feet wrapped up, but it'd be considerably better than rocks, sticks, and fallen pine needles constantly digging into her bare soles.

"It's all yours," she said, holding her hand out for her bag.

"Oh, I know." Thargen passed her the backpack; the instant it was in her grasp, he stepped close and swept her off her feet, taking her in his arms.

She released a startled gasp, followed by a laugh. "What was the point of wrapping my feet if you're just going to carry me?"

"I thought you liked being in my arms?" He started down the slope, his steady, casual pace eating up ground thanks to his long stride.

Yuri leaned toward him and kissed the corner of his mouth, relishing the feel of his hard tusk against her lips. "I do."

He made a rumbling sound in his chest—a blend of a grunt and a groan. "Think I like it more every time."

She smiled and looped one arm around the back of his neck while adjusting the bag in her lap with the other. "Yeah, but shouldn't we be conserving your strength while I'm able to walk on my own?"

"I got *plenty* of strength, little terran. The gear I had to haul around every day in the Vanguard was heavier than you are."

She chuckled and lightly raked her nails along the back of his shoulder. "I do like a male with muscles."

"This male," he growled, his hand flexing on her thigh. "You like *this* male with muscles."

Yuri hummed thoughtfully and lay her head against his shoulder. "Yeah. Yeah, I do."

Thargen strode forward, leaving their little campsite behind.

The sky only darkened further as the gray clouds gathered, swept along by that cold wind. The landscape felt more alien than ever under that dreary lighting. It seemed a place caught in time, frozen. Trapped. Yuri thrust those thoughts aside as quickly as she could, knowing they would just lead her back to that cage—and from there they would undoubtedly turn to the current situation. She didn't want to kill the good spirits Thargen had helped her maintain.

She didn't want to face the reality of just how hopeless this was.

He moved steadily downslope, crossing red grass and passing around, over, and between large rock formations. After what felt like an hour or so—not that Yuri's concept of time mattered much here—she asked him to set her down so she could stretch her legs. He did so without argument, stepping back once she was on her feet.

She swung her backpack on and followed close behind him

when he resumed walking. The cloth bindings on her feet worked on the hard, unforgiving stone they crossed, providing just enough cushioning to prevent pain and thus allowing her to keep up with Thargen's steady but relatively easy pace.

They hiked onward—leaving the ship a little farther behind with each step—through an increasingly rough and rocky landscape that further limited their range of view. Yuri was surprised by her own endurance. Her body was sore and definitely weaker than it had been before she was kidnapped, but sleeping with Thargen last night had left her surprisingly well rested. She didn't expect that to last long, though. Those bland meal bars were in short supply and would only get Yuri and Thargen so far. They needed real food, fresh water, and a safe place to hide. Without those things, their lives were going to get miserable very quickly.

Her first taste of that misery came sooner than Yuri had hoped. After what felt like hours of walking—and occasionally climbing—her legs were heavy and wobbly, her muscles burned, and sweat coated her skin, enhancing the chill in the air. She labored for breath as she followed Thargen up another rocky rise, feeling as though even a mild gust of wind would be enough to knock her over and send her tumbling back down to where they'd started.

By the time Thargen halted, his lead on her had opened to several meters. He stared out over that rise for a few seconds before looking at her over his shoulder and offering a grin. "Come on, terran. I think you'll like this."

Yuri paused, glanced up at him, and quickened her pace. The tone in his voice, combined with his sexy grin, sent a burst of energy through her, making that last bit of distance between them a piece of cake.

Mmm, cake.

Her mouth watered at the memory of the super sweet

frosting that topped birthday cakes. She'd been reprimanded a few times as a child for dipping her finger into the icing on the bottom of the cake when she thought no one was looking.

I am so holding Thargen to his promise when we get back.

He turned and extended a hand to her as she neared. Yuri took it gratefully. As he helped her up the last meter or two, she asked, "What is it? Is it a—"

The question died on her lips. She was looking down on a valley, where the cliffs and rock formations they'd been navigating were broken by rolling hills blanketed in red grass and copses of those tall trees that reminded her of pines. But it wasn't the sudden proliferation of vegetation that was most striking.

A slow-moving river flowed along the base of the valley, flanked by steep embankments and clusters of trees save for a wide section not far off. There, the water was shallow and filled with countless smooth, rounded stones, and patches of tall, reed-like plants growing along its banks.

Yuri reached up and swept her wind-blown hair out of her face. "Is that... That's real, right? My eyes aren't playing tricks on me? That's actually a river down there?"

"Better be real, or I'm gonna be pissed," he said in a tone that was somehow threatening and good-natured at once. "I'm not above fighting a hallucination."

Arching a brow, Yuri looked up at him. "You say that like you've done it before."

Thargen nodded, running his gaze over the landscape below. "I have. Long story. Remind me to tell you another time."

Yuri returned her attention to that dark water, and a fully-formed scene crept into her mind—Thargen in the shallows, growling, punching, and kicking the river.

And *of course* he was bare-assed in that mental image. It

sent a little thrill through her, sparking that now familiar heat at her core. At least part of that imagining could come true—her big, powerful orc naked in the river with water running down his toned green skin in rivulets.

She grinned. "So, what are we waiting for? There's water!"

Without giving him a chance to respond, she started back down the way they'd come, which was *so* much easier than hiking up.

"Slow down, terran," he called from behind. "Don't need you spraining an ankle for some maybe-real water."

Yuri laughed and slowed down, falling into place beside Thargen once he caught up. They had to double back quite a bit before they found a way down from the higher ground they were on. An hour ago, that would've driven Yuri mad and emptied her already diminished stores of energy and morale, but the promise of cool, clear water had reinvigorated her.

Thargen bypassed the wide section of the river they'd seen from atop the rise—he said it was too exposed to stop there—and pushed farther along to a place where the trees grew densely almost right up to the water. The world around them seemed to shrink the instant they crossed the tree line. Everything was close and oddly muted, as though the fallen needles carpeting the ground were absorbing most of the ambient sounds.

It wasn't silent by any means—the trees creaked and sighed as they swayed in the wind, and the river's burbling grew more distinct as they neared it—but it *felt* that way. If she'd been alone, Yuri probably would've been unsettled by it. With Thargen, it seemed a slice of paradise, a welcome reprieve from the biting wind and uncompromising stone that had dominated their travels today.

They stopped on a stretch of riverbank that was relatively level and free of the rocks and fallen branches common in many other spots. A swath of dark clouds was visible over the river, flanked by tall trees on either side.

Thargen moved to the edge of the water, knelt, and leaned forward, inhaling through his nose. "It's real, *zoani*, and it's safe."

Yuri's brows furrowed. "You can tell it's safe just by smelling it?"

He twisted slightly to look back at her. "You can't?"

"No. I mean, we can tell if water smells sour and such, but not if it's teeming with bacteria and all that."

"How the hell did you terrans survive long enough to make it into space?"

Yuri crossed her arms over her chest and shifted her weight onto one leg, jutting a hip out. "Asks the guy who was ready to beat up the river?"

"Oof. That hurts, terran, but good point."

"Not everyone is born with the same...advantages," she said as she walked toward him. "Our peoples adapted to different circumstances on different planets, and at totally different times. Vorgals were probably in space hundreds of years before us."

Smirking, Thargen sat back on his heels and braced his hands on his thighs. "So, your planet has soft carpeting everywhere?"

Yuri dropped to her knees beside Thargen and poked his arm. "Don't make fun of my soft feet."

"I like your feet, terran. There's not a part of you I've seen that I haven't liked."

Yuri's cheeks flushed as she turned her face toward the river. She would have thought any self-consciousness about her body would've been obliterated after sitting naked in a cell for days, especially considering that Thargen looked at her like she was the most beautiful and desirable woman in the universe.

At the corner of her vision, Thargen leaned down, dipped a hand into the water, and lifted it to his mouth to drink. Trusting his judgment, Yuri bent forward and did the same.

The water was cold—almost freezing—and it was the most delicious thing she'd tasted in days. She drank handful after handful, filling her belly with the precious liquid.

"Slow down, Yuri," Thargen said, catching Yuri's wrist before she could scoop up another handful. "It won't taste nearly as good coming back up as it did going down."

"I know," she said, only noticing how cold her hand was now that the wind was blowing over her wet skin. "But it's just so *good*."

"And it's not going anywhere. There'll be plenty to drink later." He released her arm and glanced skyward as he stood up, lips downturned and a troubled crease between his brows. "We need to find shelter."

Yuri wiped her hand on her thigh and looked up. The clouds, which had been that dark gray all day, were closer to black now. The static charge in the air seemed even stronger than before; she could almost feel it tingling across her skin, like her little hairs were about to stand on end. Dread pooled in her stomach.

She'd always enjoyed rainstorms back on Earth, but she'd never been stuck outside in one. And this was an alien world. Who knew how intense or unforgiving the weather here could be?

As if her thoughts summoned it, the sky lit up in a flash of white-violet. Yuri flinched, looking down and blinking rapidly to clear the blurred white afterimage from her eyes. A prolonged, crackling boom tore through the sky, rumbling the ground, making the very air around her vibrate.

Now, her little hairs *did* stand up.

The smugglers, the skeks, the uncertainty of having food

and water, the prospect of never getting home—all those were frightening things, but they weren't insurmountable. There was hope of overcoming them.

This impending storm felt different. That taste of power, that brief demonstration, shook her on a primal level. It couldn't be overcome, couldn't be fought or reasoned with. And it certainly didn't care about a wild vorgal and his little terran.

Thargen grasped her arm and hauled her to her feet. "Time to go, terran."

Before she could respond, he scooped her up in his arms, clutching her against his chest, and hurried away from the river. Yuri threw her arms around his neck. Another flash lit up the sky, briefly turning the branches and needles overhead—most of which were thrashing in the strengthening wind—into dark silhouettes.

"I can run," she said, her fingers curling to dig her nails into his skin as another peal of thunder shook this alien world.

"I know." He didn't relinquish his hold, didn't slow his pace —not even as the gentle upward slope he'd been traversing steepened and became more irregular. After leaping up onto a large boulder, he paused and scanned their surroundings.

The rain started in that moment, a torrential downpour so immediate and intense that it made Mortannis's punishing hose seem like an eyedropper in comparison. The trees offered little protection from the rain; Yuri was soaked within a second or two, as thoroughly as though she'd jumped into the river.

It was just as cold, too.

Thargen released a huff of air that sprayed water from his lips, bared his teeth, and glared up at the sky, seemingly unaffected by the rain pelting his face. There was a wild gleam in his eyes for a moment, and his body heat intensified despite the cold engulfing them.

Yuri swept her wet hair back from her face and wiped her

eyes. The chill was already sinking straight into her bones. She returned her arm to its place around Thargen's neck and held tight.

He swung his gaze to her, and the menacing light in his eyes faded. His grip on her strengthened infinitesimally. Everything he might've said, everything he could've said, everything that mattered, was conveyed by his expression and that little action—*I have you, Yuri. You're mine, and I have you.*

She couldn't shake her deep-seated unease, couldn't silence the primal part of her brain that was screaming about the danger, but she knew Thargen would keep her safe. They'd survived the crash and had managed to evade the smugglers. This was just one more obstacle to overcome.

"Fuck this storm," Thargen growled. He ran forward, his heavy footfalls jolting through his body and into hers as though in defiance of the wind and thunder. "I've been in public toilets more dangerous than this."

Despite everything, the corners of Yuri's mouth tilted up. "Well, we needed a shower, right?"

He laughed. It was a guttural but genuine sound, as savage, raw, and good-humored as Thargen had proven himself to be— but a hint of tension and strife flowed through its core. Though he'd not shown any signs of it during the day, she knew he was still caught in that internal struggle that had made him so restless and irritable in the cage.

Yuri's backpack jostled as Thargen ran, its straps pulling at her shoulders; she just squeezed him tighter and ducked her head to keep the harsh rain from hitting her face. When she glanced over his shoulder, the river—which couldn't have been that far behind them—was already out of sight thanks to the heavy rain and the mist it was creating.

As Thargen finally slowed, Yuri turned her attention forward. It took a moment for her brain to decipher the large, dark shape in front of them, which was made indistinct by the gloom and mist.

She was looking at a huge tree—an *ancient* tree, she had the sense—that had fallen over. Many of its upturned roots were jutting into the air like gnarled, skeletal fingers, and the exposed wood was almost entirely blanketed by reddish mossy growths. The dirt around those roots had settled in a mound that bulged off the slope—a mound with a wide, low opening. Water dripped from the top of the mound and flowed in little streams around it, but the hollow was facing downslope, and seemed to be spared the wet.

Thargen stopped a few paces away from the natural shelter and set her on her feet. "Wait here."

Yuri crossed her arms over her chest, trying to hold in some of her body heat, as he took one of his axes in hand and stalked forward. Without the protection of Thargen's body, the freezing rain and wind blasted her anew, making her shiver and her teeth chatter. Lightning flashed overhead, briefly illuminating the nearby trees. Even though she was expecting it, she still jumped when thunder boomed a few seconds later.

Thargen crouched at the entrance to the mound, braced his free hand on one of the exposed roots nearby, and leaned into the darkness. He remained like that for several seconds—during which Yuri's imagination suggested all sorts of terrifying beasts and monsters that might've been dwelling in that darkness.

Finally, he drew back, turned, and waved her over. She hurried toward him, and he placed his hand on her back to guide her through the opening. Yuri ducked inside. The sound of falling rain was thankfully muted within the hollow. After a few moments, her eyes had adjusted to the meager light just enough for her to make out some of what lay before her.

Though the ceiling was low, the inside of the hollow was open and spacious. Exposed roots ran in tangles through the dirt overhead and poked out in a few places along the walls. The floor was a combination of bare dirt and wide patches of pale moss, scattered with what looked like dead vegetation, pine needles, sticks, and tiny bones; it was too dark to tell for sure, and she found herself not really wanting to know if she was right.

Thunder rolled outside, making Yuri start; the hollow definitely didn't dull that sound.

Shivering, Yuri shrugged off her backpack and caught it with numb fingers before dropping it on the ground. It landed with a dull thump. She drew her hands up close to her chest.

That pathetic light coming in through the opening was snuffed out for a second as Thargen entered the hollow. He had to keep his shoulders hunched and his knees bent to fit inside. He placed his backpack, which he'd already taken off, on the floor beside hers and swept his hand up his face and back across his hair, shedding a small spray of water in the process.

"Clothes off," he said as he swept aside the debris on the floor with his foot.

For a few moments, Yuri stood there with cold, wet clothing plastered to her body, unable to keep her teeth from chattering. His words repeated meaninglessly in her head. Was he...? *Now?* He'd seen all of her already, that wasn't the issue, but her foggy mind could only come up with one reason for him wanting her naked.

Not that she didn't want to do *that* with him. She *really* wanted to. And the authority in his tone sparked a heat in her core.

"Happy to do it for you if you want." Thargen kicked aside the last of the little bones and turned to face her, managing to look imposing, powerful, and sexy even while he was bent to fit in this hole.

Apparently, he'd already spread some clothes on the floor

to create a pallet; how long had she been standing there, dumb-founded?

"Okay," she said, the words coming out quickly and little breathlessly.

Thargen tossed his weapons onto the ground near the bags, unclasped his pants, and pushed them down, keeping his eyes on her. "Okay you're gonna, or you want me to?"

Naturally, Yuri's eyes dropped to his erect cock the instant it sprang free. The piercings along the top glinted faintly as he moved, reflecting the dim light at the opening. She grinned; despite the chill that had seeped into her, she was heating up quite nicely between her legs. "Y-You."

He lowered his brows and pressed his lips together. Fire flashed in his eyes for a moment before he braced a hand on the ceiling and tugged the pants off his ankles, tossing the garment aside after it was off. His nostrils flared as he moved toward her. Somehow, his hunched posture made him seem even larger once he was standing before her—it gave her the sense that he was too big for this space, that he could burst right out of it if he chose to stand up.

"Fuck, terran," he groaned, sinking onto one knee. He bent forward and lifted her feet one at a time to peel off the wet cloth strips. When he was done, he straightened, and a crease formed between his eyebrows—she wasn't sure if it was concentration, torment, or restraint—as he placed his hands on her thighs. He slid them up under the hem of her soaked shirt until they reached the top of her pants.

Thargen's fingers were like branding irons against her skin when he hooked them under her waistband. He drew her pants down, his palms sliding over her outer thighs with his thumbs coming precariously close to where she ached for him most. Once the pants were past her knees, the weight of the waterlogged material dragged them down the rest of the way, allowing her to step out of them and kick them aside.

His hands reversed direction, smoothing over her hips, spanning her waist, catching the hem of her shirt as they continued up her body. He stood up as his fingers crept higher. His thumbs grazed her hardened nipples for an instant. She drew in a sharp breath, her core clenching in need, before raising her arms.

Thargen pulled the shirt off over her head and tossed it aside. It landed amongst the other discarded clothing with a wet *plop*. He lingered in front of her, eyes heated, shoulders rising and falling with ragged breaths. Yuri's skin tingled in anticipation of his touch, of his hands returning to her body to spread his sweet warmth all over. Little droplets of water were beaded on his skin, catching tiny reflections of the light; she wanted to lick every one of them off him.

He stepped back, moving onto the large patch of that velvety moss where he'd arranged the pallet of dry clothing, and lowered himself onto his knees. His cock jutted out from between his thighs, hard and throbbing. "Come here, terran."

Eagerness and arousal thrummed through Yuri. Despite the cold, despite her body quaking, she *yearned*. So damned badly. His fingers touching her the night before had only been a taste of what he could do for her, and she wanted more. She wanted all of him.

Keeping her eyes on his, she closed the distance between them, reaching out to place her hands on his shoulders. Even on his knees, he was several centimeters taller than she was.

Thargen moved his hands to her waist and guided her to turn around. It wasn't what she'd expected, but she could go along with this if he liked to do it from behind. She backed up until her back was flush with his body, and his cock brushed the insides of her thighs. His heat, intensifying by the second, baked into her, and she moaned.

He tensed, leaning his forehead against the back of her head, and let out a slow breath that flowed through Yuri's wet hair to caress her neck. It triggered a thrill that ran down her spine. He removed his hands from her hips and wrapped his right arm around her, tucking it beneath her breasts. Yuri's tight nipples ached for his touch, ached for his strong, calloused fingers to stoke them, to pinch them.

She could feel his heart beating through his chest, could feel his cock's tiny twitches in time with that steady, unrelenting pulse.

This was it. This was finally it. Yuri caught her lower lip between her teeth and placed her right arm atop his.

Thargen leaned to the left, bracing his hand on the ground, and eased Yuri to lay down on the pallet. Once again, she was the little spoon—not that she minded. She really liked being the little spoon, as long as it was his body tucked against hers.

He shifted his left arm beneath her head and pressed his thighs to the backs of hers. His cock was now tucked along the curve of her ass, so damned close to where she wanted it. She arched, pushing her backside against him.

Thargen groaned and moved his right hand to her lower abdomen, spanning his fingers over it and pinning her in place. It, too, was a tease—his fingertips were only centimeters from the top of her sex, but they might as well have been a kilometer away.

Yuri's brows furrowed as seconds passed and they lay there, unmoving, except for her shivering, the rise and fall of his chest with his ragged breaths, and the thumping of his heart. His body cocooned hers, blanketing her with his heat, swiftly chasing away the cold, but leaving a heavy, unfilled emptiness behind.

"Um, Thargen?" she asked.

"Hmm?"

"What are we doing?" She knew there was more to it than this. Like touching, licking, stroking, thrusting. Part A being inserted into slot B. She'd seen enough on holos, and a surprising number of the Undercity's residents didn't seem very concerned about potential onlookers during their intimate moments.

"Warming you."

"Warming me?"

He grunted, and the fingers on her lower abdomen flexed. "You were shivering with cold, Yuri."

Yuri closed her eyes and tilted her pelvis, just begging for those fingers to slip just a little lower. "Mmhmm."

"*Fuck,*" Thargen growled through his teeth as he pressed harder on her pelvis, stilling her hips.

"That's the plan, right?" Yuri asked, lifting one of her knees to spread her thighs. Cold air kissed her sex, sending a wholly different shiver through her.

His laughter was somehow both amused and tortured. He hooked his leg over the top of hers and forced it back down. Still, he made no move to intimately touch her.

"Or...not?" she said with a frown, turning her head to look at him as best she could.

Thargen's expression was tense, and the lusty fires in his eyes bore a wild edge. "Barely in control, Yuri. Be still."

Tendons and veins stood out starkly along his neck and on his arm beneath her hand. This was just like when they'd been trapped in the cell, and he'd been pacing back and forth, a beast bristling with hunger and aggression—but it had taken him days to build to that point. He'd seemed fine a couple minutes ago. Why this sudden change?

Yuri slid her palm along his arm to take hold of his hand; all she needed was for him to lift it away from her pelvis. "But I don't want you in contr—"

Thargen growled, burying his face in her hair. He shuddered, and his hold on her tightened a fraction more. "Just...talk to me, *zoani*," he grated through clenched teeth.

Talk? Why was he wanting to talk? She was basically throwing herself at him.

Yuri's sex ached, and her nipples were so damn hard they *hurt*. Was it possible for women to get blue balls? Yuri was pretty certain she was developing a severe case.

"Thargen, not that I don't enjoy talking to you, but isn't there something else you'd rather be doing?" She wiggled her bottom against his cock. "Like...me?"

Thargen's hips bucked, sliding his shaft along her ass. She felt all the little studs of his piercings as they glided over her skin, and felt a hint of moisture unlike the raindrops that had pelted her outside—this was warm and slick.

He snarled, the sound more animalistic than any she'd heard from him so far, and his body seized around her, every muscle going rigid. When he moved again, his speed was so explosive that she barely registered what was happening.

Thargen flipped her onto her belly and rolled to position himself over her from behind. One of his hands cupped the back of her head, forcing her cheek onto the moss beneath the rumpled pallet, while the other lifted her ass into the air. His weight came down atop her, caging her in his blazing heat.

Yuri gasped, her fingers curling into the soft moss. Something hard, blunt, and even hotter than the rest of Thargen pressed into the entrance of her sex, something throbbing with his rapid, powerful pulse.

A rumble of thunder rattled the earth beneath her.

He froze again. His breaths were heavy and snarling, as though they were clawing their way out of his lungs.

Yuri's heart was fluttering, her skin was aflame, and the heat gathered in her core was reaching critical levels. His display of speed, strength, and dominance was frightening—but it aroused her more than anything. She'd never imagined her first time being like this. A little more foreplay would have been nice, but damn it, she wanted him. She was ready.

And he was poised *right there*.

Her sex clenched around the tip of his cock. She tilted her hips and pushed back, forcing him infinitesimally deeper. His fingers pulled her hair hard enough to produce a sting on her scalp, and his hand on her hip clamped down roughly enough to bruise.

"Fuck," he growled. "*Fuck!*"

Thargen shoved himself away from her, breaking all contact between them and pulling a few strands of her hair out in the process. Yuri winced and sat up, bringing a hand to her scalp as she turned her head to look at him. He stalked toward the opening, and the gray light from outside turned his figure into a dark, brooding silhouette.

"Thargen, wait!" she called.

"Stay here, Yuri," was all he said before he was gone.

Yuri sat back on her heels and crossed her arms over her chest as an entirely new coldness filled her. Thargen was gone, and he'd taken every bit of warmth with him. She was frustrated, confused, and most of all, hurt.

What was wrong with her? Why wouldn't he just...*fuck* her? She knew he was attracted to her. She'd seen how he looked at her, how his body reacted to her. But he was holding himself back. Why?

Shivering, Yuri rubbed her arms and moved toward the backpacks. Her sex was slick, aching with arousal, and she couldn't forget how he'd felt poised there, so close to entering her fully, so close to filling her.

Not helping, Yuri.

With a growl, she opened one of the bags and tugged out some dry clothing. She pulled on the too long pants and overly large shirt, wrapped a second shirt around her shoulders like a blanket, and sat down to wait for Thargen's return.

The rain's heavy droning continued outside, louder and more invasive now that she was alone. Flashes of lightning occasionally lit up the interior of the shelter, always followed by ground-rumbling peals of thunder—but the time between the flashes and the booms seemed to be increasing, if only little.

"Damn that hard-headed, cock-blocking, stubborn orc," she grumbled. "You better come back to me."

Just like that, worry overpowered all the other emotions roiling within Yuri.

"Please, come back," she whispered, hugging her legs to her chest.

The forest outside dimmed gradually, and the rain did not relent. It wasn't long before Yuri's eyelids were drooping. She struggled to keep them open, to keep waiting, refusing to give in to her body's need until she knew Thargen was safe, but her fight was short lived. Without meaning to, she lay down and curled up with her arm folded beneath her head.

Sleep claimed her.

THIRTEEN

Stupid. This is stupid.

Those words had been repeating in the back of Thargen's mind since he'd left the shelter, but he was only hearing them now—the din in his head had been too great before, his thoughts too chaotic and wild. Not that he could consider much of what had been roaring in his head *thoughts*; they were instincts, urges, desires, all with little conscious thought involved.

He was standing in front of a tree now, rain pelting his bare skin but doing little to soothe his inner heat. The trunk before him was battered, its bark cracked and broken to reveal the dark, soft wood beneath. Viscous, purple sap oozed from the cracks and ran in slow rivulets along the bark.

When he'd swept Yuri into his arms and run from the river, he'd been concerned about the most immediate dangers—lightning strikes and flooding. He'd seen the destruction wrought by those forces firsthand, and those memories had been just intact enough to motivate him. His only goal had been to get her to shelter. That concern hadn't extended to his own wellbeing.

He shook his head and shoulders with a growl, spraying water in all directions. Fresh raindrops filled in the cleared space instantly. Tension thrummed in his muscles, and though his heartbeat had slowed from earlier, it was still fast and hard. A dull ache pulsed in his knuckles, which sported a few new cuts, and his balls were tight and uncomfortably full despite having taken himself in hand and pumped his shaft until he hit a jolting, unsatisfying climax. He still felt like he was brimming with enough seed to fill a bucket, and he knew exactly how his mind and body truly wanted to find their release.

Inside his little terran's sweet, hot, *pussy.*

Even now, he had to resist the temptation to drop a hand to his groin and fuck his own fist again. But that wasn't what he wanted, and it wouldn't help anymore.

He'd punched tree trunks and rocks, had broken branches, and even torn up a few sizeable stones from the ground and heaved them down the slope with all his might. For all its bluster, the storm hadn't been able to fully mute the snapping wood and thumping rocks. Those acts of violence and aggression—of which even his masturbation could be counted—had dulled his Rage, if only a little. They'd been the equivalent of opening a valve to let off some pressure, a means of delaying the inevitable overload.

Fucking Yuri would've been far more complete a release. But he couldn't let her pay the price for him. He wouldn't let himself harm her, especially not because Rage—or anything else—demanded he take her.

A burst of lightning lit up the dark clouds and turned the forest into a harsh contrast of stark light and deep shadow for an instant. The thunder that followed several seconds later rumbled right through Thargen's bones.

How long had he been gone? Even teetering on the edge, in danger of falling into his Rage, he'd not wandered more than twenty or thirty meters from their shelter, but the sky was darker than it had been when he left, and both the air and the rain were noticeably colder. Had it been an hour? Two? Four? He wasn't accustomed to this planet's solar cycles, and Rage often made time seem erratic on top of that, turning seconds into lifetimes and hours into minutes.

He shifted his attention back to the battered tree in front of him. The sap, which crept along a millimeter at a time, had continued its slow trek toward the ground. The bark was still broken, wood still cracked and crushed where it had taken the brunt of his fury. Thargen couldn't quite recall hitting this particular tree, but he had no doubt that he'd done so.

Hruk was a hell of a thing.

Turning away from the tree, he scanned his surroundings. The rain hadn't let up, pairing with the deepening evening gloom to reduce visibility even further than before. One of the smugglers—or a skeks—could've walked by only fifteen or twenty meters away, and Thargen might never have known it. At this rate, it would be too dark after nightfall for even a skeks to see, much less Thargen.

And he'd left Yuri alone this whole time.

He'd left her so he could throw rocks, punch trees, and yank on his cock in the middle of a lightning storm, with smugglers and skeks only a day or two's walk away and Thargen himself bare-assed and unarmed.

Stupid, that voice insisted.

"Fuck you," he said, lifting a hand to wipe water from his face and sweep back the strands of hair that had come loose from his braids.

This was stupid, he couldn't argue that, but when the alternative was to risk seriously injuring the female he he'd come to care about so much, he'd choose stupid every time. There'd never be any hesitation—Thargen would always choose to protect Yuri no matter the danger it might place him in. Besides, he'd put himself in far worse situations for far dumber reasons—usually just to let his Rage peak and burn out.

He clenched his fists at his sides and walked toward the shelter.

Left her in there all alone and cold. Good work, shit-for-brains.

Better than splitting her in half on my dick in a Rage-fueled fuck fest.

Thargen snorted, smiling for the first time since he'd left the shelter. "Would be nice if I could stop arguing with myself."

But conflict was nothing new; almost every memory he possessed involved some manner of it, usually the sort involving blasters and explosions.

Still, even if he was torn on what was best for Yuri, even if he was torn between his desires and the harsh reality he would face if he were to give in to them, he had no question of his feelings toward her.

Thargen adored his *zoani,* and that emotion was only growing as time passed.

The clouds strobed with more lightning, illuminating the dirt mound up ahead and making its opening seem impossibly dark compared to the dirt and roots around it. For a moment, the shelter reminded him of the burial mounds some of the vorgal tribes—including his own—had built in their ancient past. His imagination imbued this mound with that mystery, solemnity, and ominousness.

He sped his pace, nearly sprinting across the remaining distance. His Rage was already threatening to resurge, roused by the idea of this being a place of death—and Yuri having been left alone inside.

Thargen didn't slow down when he reached the entrance; he grasped a root, bent forward, and pulled himself through.

The overwhelming darkness inside made his heart quicken—he couldn't see her, couldn't see their packs, couldn't see anything. When his vision finally adjusted, his relief was so great that he nearly collapsed. Yuri was lying on the mossy floor in roughly the same place he'd left her, dressed in dry clothes with a second shirt wrapped around her shoulders.

He forced himself to take in a few steadying breaths. The emotions stirring in him at the sight of her were powerful and complex—far more complex than anything he was used to dealing with. Adoration was still the strongest, but it was mixed now with guilt, regret, desire, concern, and a hundred other things. He'd thought she provided him that simple sense of being alive he'd experienced in combat, but it was so much more than that—far more than he could put into words. Even before they were kidnapped, Thargen had felt a connection to Yuri as deep and powerful as the sort of bond typically born in battle, while waist-deep in mud and blood amidst a deluge of blaster fire, screams, and explosions.

Thargen had been in a lot of fights, had faced many challenges—most of which had put his life in very real danger—but nothing had been as hard as walking away from Yuri earlier. Nothing had been as hard as resisting this small, fragile looking terran.

I'm okay. I got some of it out. Enough of it out.

He filled his lungs with another deep breath and forced himself to hold it for several seconds as he willed away the tension in his muscles, opening and closing his hands, flexing and relaxing his jaw, and rolling his shoulders. He must've looked like a damned fool—naked in a hole, stooped over so he wouldn't hit his head, dripping water all over the ground as he tried to find some shred of inner peace.

The humor in that image wasn't lost on him; it eased him further, and he exhaled through his nose while chuckling silently.

He found the wet, discarded clothing on the floor nearby, and picked up the shirt to wipe away as much of the moisture from his skin as he could. It wasn't particularly effective, but it was something, and in situations like this, *something* was often the best you could do. When he was done, he hung the wet clothes—and the cloth strips he'd wrapped around Yuri's feet— from some of the exposed roots on the ceiling. Either they'd dry by morning or they wouldn't; he couldn't exactly leave them out in the sun right now.

Only then did he allow his attention to return to Yuri. She was still soundly asleep, though she'd curled up a little tighter than before. Was it because of the cold, or subconscious fear and loneliness?

Another pang of guilt struck him—not that *pang* adequately described something that hit like an industrial freight hauler. It was only made worse by the fact that just looking at her had his cock pulsing again despite everything that had happened. He glanced down at his erection, which was hit with just enough light to make his piercings gleam faintly.

"You're not helping," he whisper-growled.

Moving as quietly as he could, he stepped over to the backpacks, crouched, and reached into the open one. He kept his eyes on Yuri as he felt his way through the contents, wincing at every little sound he made. Though he couldn't explain it, his instinctual drive was to leave her slumber undisturbed; he owed her at least that much.

Finally, after what felt like a breathless eternity, his fingertips brushed against the thick, rough fabric he'd sought—the same material as the pants he'd been wearing earlier. He grabbed hold of it and withdrew it slowly, gritting his teeth as it caught on the other items and offered resistance.

Once again, his mind turned to how ridiculous he must look—crouched in the dark, face set in concentration and alertness, as he tried to silently withdraw pants from a bag.

Would make more sense if I was trying to steal her underwear or something, wouldn't it?

Heat flared in his chest—and his groin.

Fuck! Abort that line of thought, damn it!

He clenched his jaw harder. This wasn't a fucking night raid on an enemy encampment, he was just trying to put on some pants before lying down with Yuri. Why was he making it so dire, so complicated? The answer came to him just as the pants finally pulled free.

Thargen froze, and his heartbeat was suddenly loud enough to overpower the drumming rain. He'd watched far too many of those Volturian dramas Razi liked for his own good; they'd started to change his way of thinking.

Because the answer that popped into his head, the reason he was making this such a big deal, the reason he was fighting his desires so hard to keep her safe, was right out of one of those sappy shows—he was falling in love with Yuri.

Maybe I've already fallen.

For once, there was no dissenting voice in his head, no argument. He lifted his free hand and pressed his fingers to his right temple, running them over the scars on the side of his head. His mind was silent, and he felt oddly numb. He'd never thought about love before. Even seeing Arcanthus and Drakkal find it with their terran mates, Thargen hadn't once considered it for himself. It had seemed well outside the realm of possibility.

"Fuck," he whispered.

He fumblingly pulled on the pants, having to ultimately drop his ass on the ground to force his feet through the openings and get the pants started up his legs. These felt even more snug than the last pair, but he barely noticed. When they were finally on—and his throbbing dick was securely tucked away—he moved to Yuri.

A swelling warmth was radiating out from the center of his chest, chasing away that numbness. Though it was related to the fire of his lust, it was not the same—this was even deeper and more mysterious.

He eased down behind Yuri, who was lying on her side, and scooted close to her. Keeping his movements slow and gentle, he slipped one arm under her head and settled the other over her middle.

She stirred, turning to face him, and curled into his body.

"Thargen?" Her voice was broken and husky with sleep, and so fucking sexy. She placed a hand on his chest and released a slow, deep breath. A second later, that hand fell, and she was asleep again.

The way she was tucked against him, like there was nowhere safer in the universe than in his arms, only intensified the sensation in Thargen's chest.

This little terran really is going to be my undoing, and I'm not even angry about it.

He smirked. All those big, tough warriors he'd killed over the years probably would've been angry to know they'd been bested by a vorgal who himself had been handily defeated by Yuri—a tiny terran who'd probably never even held a real weapon before the crash. Of course, those warriors likely would've been more upset about being dead to begin with...

Thargen watched her as the light faded, keeping his eyes open even after darkness engulfed everything and shrouded her from his view. He'd have to add the dark to the list of things he needed to figure out how to effectively punch—just above hallucinatory rivers. It was so dark that his eyeballs itched, but the discomfort was more than a fair price to pay for the brief glimpses of her he was granted by the infrequent flashes of lightning.

Fuck, I want this terran. I want all of her.

He wanted to rut her until all either of them could do was lie there, moaning and panting, utterly spent, and then he would find the strength to take her again anyway. But that couldn't happen.

Would Thargen have joined the Vanguard if he'd known it would lead to his Rage leaving him like a ravenous beast that was constantly tugging on the corroded chain that was its tether? Would he have followed that path if he'd understood that it would one day mean he couldn't have the only thing he'd come to crave—no, *need*—more than anything else?

But that path led you to her in the first place, Thargen. And it's the only reason the two of you are alive right now. The only reason she is alive.

He drew in a deep breath, taking in her fragrance, which had remained strong despite the many competing scents—primarily dirt, roots, and rain. His cock was straining against his restrictive pants, but the onset of a sharp ache in his skull over-powered his yearning. Considering what could have been an endeavor usually reserved for a time long after the *gurosh* had kicked in, and it was rarely fruitful, presenting tangled webs of potential causes and effects that were particularly trou-blesome for him to navigate—especially layered atop his already complex feelings for Yuri.

Thargen tilted his head down to settle his lips on her hair. Experience told him that the headache wouldn't go away any time soon, especially now that it had crept behind his eyes, which already burned with exertion. But he didn't have to waste time contemplating the complexities of his growing rela-tionship with Yuri; it really was quite simple.

She was his. They'd figure out all the rest eventually. He just needed to tamp down his Rage enough so that he could please her without fear of losing control.

Right now, all that mattered was keeping his eyes open so he could enjoy those fleeting glimpses of Yuri in the purple-tinged glow of alien lightning. He'd lost so many memories from his life before the head wound. He sure as hell wasn't going to let himself lose a single moment of his time with her—even if it meant he had to punch his own memory right in the face to illustrate the importance of holding onto every second he'd spent with her.

That list of inanimate objects and abstract concepts to punch was getting really damned long, really fast.

The storm continued outside, marking time by the sounds of pouring rain and rolling thunder, but Thargen wasn't keeping track. He was content to continue existing beyond time and space with Yuri. There were no threats to confront, there was no Rage to resist, no future to worry over and no past to haunt him. He knew this serenity wouldn't last long. For Thargen, it never did.

When the darkness pulsed with a faint red tint for a fraction of a second, Thargen furrowed his brow and released a confused huff.

Something was wrong.

Red was for blood, or fire, or Rage.

His thumping heartbeat filled his ears.

The ground vibrated with a burst of thunder that dragged itself out over several seconds as though it were raking immense, booming claws across the mountainside one meter at a time. In his mind's eye, it shattered rocks and tore up great clumps of dirt in the process.

Lightning. The red tinge had been lightning, seen through his eyelids.

When had he closed his eyes? When had his exhaustion become so complete, when had his body grown so heavy, his mind so...so clouded?

He felt like he was sinking into the ground, sinking into himself, but he didn't fight it. Yuri was here, and the storm's sounds were soothing and familiar. So familiar...

The droning sound of rain pattering on trees, ground, and stone was safe, natural, serene. It was water—just water.

A soft moan rose unbidden from Thargen's throat. He felt heavy, so heavy, but there was something heavier still in his gut. Something cold. That relentless drumming wasn't falling water. It was the crackling of ravenous flames, the popping of distant gunfire, shrapnel raining into puddles and onto muddy, blood-steeped ground.

The darkness took on that crimson tint again, but it did not fade now. The boom that followed wasn't thunder—it was an explosion, the ground-shaking impact of an artillery shell. He knew it in his bones.

The gunfire sharpened and increased in volume. Distant shouts and howls echoed through the air. Thargen's skin tingled and itched, bathed in the heat of raging fires.

They were here. He knew they were here, and it was too late.

He opened his eyes to a world of fire, smoke, and blood—he was standing on a battle-scarred field made anonymous by widespread destruction. Dark figures charged from the haze and flames, featureless but for their jagged-toothed mouths. Their howls intensified, suddenly deafening and immediate.

The armored vanguards on either side of Thargen opened fire. None of them were wearing helmets. He knew the sweat-beaded faces of those vorgals; he'd served with most of them for years. But what were their names? Why couldn't he remember their names?

Yuri.

Eyes wide, he looked down. He was naked and unarmed in the rubble-strewn field, skin covered in muck and blood that glistened in the firelight. The pounding of his own heart drowned out the din of battle.

She wasn't there.

She'd been lying beside him, hadn't she? She'd been nestled against him, held securely in his arms, and her alluring fragrance had been filling his nose. Now he had only the smells of dirt, blood, and scorched flesh, the sting of smoke and singed metal.

Rage stirred in him, but it felt oddly distant—it felt impotent. His limbs were leaden, and his feet were sinking into the muck, and those howling fucking shadow-skeks were attacking. Thargen growled and pushed himself forward. Every muscle in his body strained to pull his foot up from the mud. It was like the whole planet sought to drag him down.

The blaster fire from the vorgal vanguards was tearing through the skeks, but two more of the grinning monsters emerged from the smoke for every one that fell.

A glimpse of pale flesh ahead momentarily stilled Thargen's heart. That was Yuri—it had to be her. But she was amongst the enemy. He had to get to her, had to get her out of here. He had to save her.

Growling, he tore his foot free of the muck and moved forward. The next step was no easier, but he simply clenched his jaw and willed himself onward, battling the hungry mud for each centimeter. The ground ahead was black with skeks, so many of them that he couldn't distinguish the living from the dead.

The vorgal soldiers around Thargen were dying. He saw them, even though he wasn't looking at them, saw their faces with stunning clarity. He saw skeks bullets punch through already battered vanguard armor. Saw skeks blades and axes split skulls. Saw comrades he'd known for years use their dying moments to kill more of their enemies and build their own burial mounds out of corpses.

And he felt a thousand knives plunge into his heart because he knew their faces, knew they'd died bravely, but he still did not know their names.

Yuri.

He would not forget her name. Wouldn't let her become another anonymous ghost in his memory.

Thargen roared and continued moving. She was just ahead; he'd get to her. He had to.

Skeks projectiles struck his body with dully, heavy thumps. The pain was distant, little more than points of warmth blossoming across his body, but each one slowed him a little more. The skeks swarmed, hacking at him with blades and gnashing teeth. Thargen lashed out at them wildly with fists, raked at them with his nails, bit into their filthy flesh with his tusks.

A small hand rose from amidst a pile of dead skeks ahead, its fingernails painted green.

Snarling, Thargen pressed harder. Rage refused to provide the strength he needed, roiling in an ineffectual little ball in his chest. He dug deeper, clawing at the core of his being for something, for anything, because he *had* to save her. He had to get his Yuri home.

He heaved howling skeks off him, shattered bone with his blows, and felt fresh, hot blood running over his skin. The mud sucked at his feet and pulled them ever deeper, hungry for more blood, for *his* blood.

Yuri dragged her torso out from beneath a corpse. Her eyes were wide with fear, her skin as covered in dirt and blood as Thargen's.

Powerful arms banded around Thargen's torso, legs, and

shoulder, and another curled around his neck. He thrust a hand forward, leaning toward Yuri and pushing with every bit of strength in his legs.

"We need to go," someone said in a calm, deep voice behind him. Urgand's voice.

"*No*," Thargen snarled. His joints strained, and his arm felt like it would dislocate in three separate places at once. He couldn't look away from Yuri's face, from her terror and desperation, from the pleading light in her eyes.

"You're seriously wounded," Urgand said firmly. "We need to evac."

Thargen couldn't leave without her. He wouldn't. She was all he had, she was everything he needed—and right now, she needed him.

Yuri reached for him. One of his fingertips brushed one of hers. Hope flared in Thargen's chest, pushing aside his useless Rage. He just needed a few more centimeters...

He caught her hand in his. For an instant, relief brightened her eyes.

The arms clamped around Thargen yanked him backward with sudden, immense force. He clutched Yuri's hand with all his might—but his might made no difference. The blood coating their skin ensured that her hand slipped from his.

No!

The terror in her gaze pierced his chest like a spear. He reached for her again, but he was lifted off the ground and swept away at an impossible speed, watching her grow smaller and smaller with distance. Though he couldn't hear it, he felt a roar tearing out of his throat.

What he could hear was Yuri.

"Thargen!"

The arms holding him were like bands of tristeel, unrelenting and unmoved by his desperate struggles. Yuri was a tiny, pale figure amidst blazing orange fires and black, shadowed corpses, left behind just like his comrades. His roar intensified, rattling his chest.

"Thargen!" she called again, her voice somehow louder even though she was so far away.

The shadowy assailants restraining Thargen forced him to turn around, ripping his eyes away from Yuri. He snarled and fought to break their grasps, vision flaring as his Rage finally produced a spark, finally built some heat. Baring his teeth, he drew back his fist.

When Yuri called his name again, her voice was startlingly close.

"Thargen!"

Thargen jolted awake, opening his eyes to total darkness. His body was tense, limbs trembling with an unsettling mix of fury and fear, and cold sweat coated his skin. He was on his knees with one fist poised to lash out at the foe pinned beneath him. He needed to get to Yuri. He couldn't leave her there, couldn't—

Gentle hands grasped his face, forcing him to look down. "Thargen, wake up."

He knew that voice, knew that touch. He drew in a sharp breath through his nose; the air smelled of rain, dirt, and Yuri. The fire, the blood, the skeks—all of it was gone.

Thargen opened his raised fist as ice blasted through his body, extinguishing the heat that had built within him. He wasn't on a nameless battlefield being overrun by skeks. Yuri hadn't been taken. She was here with him, she was *under* him, and he'd been about to...

"Fuck," he rasped. "Did I..."

Yuri stroked his cheeks with her thumbs. "No."

His lungs emptied with a heavy exhalation, and his body sagged. He dropped his hands to the ground to brace himself, but his limbs still trembled—not merely because of the chill inside him, but the thought of what he might have done to her had she not woken him.

Yuri slid her hands down the sides of his neck until they reached his shoulders. She coaxed him down atop her, guiding his head to rest on her chest, and cradled his torso with her thighs. She took his weight without any sign of discomfort. She shifted one palm to his back, smoothing the tension from his muscles with firm but tender motions, and settled the other on his cheek.

"It was just a dream," she said softly.

He knew she was right, but it hadn't felt like a dream—they never did. Even now, he could still see the faces of his fallen comrades in his mind's eye, could still see the bone-chillingly real terror that had been on Yuri's face. He released another breath, this time shaky and thin, and tried to focus on her warmth, her softness. Her closeness.

Thargen curled his hands up around her shoulders to hold her close.

"Stay with me," she whispered.

The combination of her hands, her voice, and her presence acted as a balm to Thargen, filling him with warmth and easing away the fury and fear that had seized his heart.

Stay with me.

She'd said those words before.

Thargen tightened his hold on her and turned his face into her breast, inhaling deeply her sweet, soothing scent. "Never leaving you, *zoani.*"

FOURTEEN

"Stay here," Thargen said as he hooked several knives on the waistband of his pants, using the little clips attached to the sheathes. The gray morning light, though still weak, lit his muscles in harsh contrast to the shadows inside the shelter.

Yuri flicked away the pine needles she'd just picked out of her hair and looked up at him, brows furrowed. "Where are you going?"

"I need to kill something," he said as he dipped to pick up one of the hardlight axes; the other was already in place along his thigh. His gaze shifted to the untouched meal bar sitting atop the pallet beside Yuri—the one he'd thrust at her when her stomach had growled a little earlier. "I'd prefer some*one*, but we're overdue for some real food."

She could totally go for some real food right now, but—

A pang of worry spiked through her chest.

"Wait," she said, pushing herself to her feet. "You're going out alone?"

Thargen stepped over to her. He still had to look down at

her despite having to stay hunched over to fit in the shelter. "You ever hunted?"

Yuri blushed, and smiled sheepishly up at him. "Well, no, not in real life..." *Way to be useful, Yuri! Those virtual games really paid off, didn't they?* "But what if something happens to you?"

He raised the axe and spun its haft on his palm, closing his fingers to stop it abruptly with the grip facing her. "Things don't happen to me, terran. *I* happen to them."

She frowned and took the weapon. Having it in her hand, feeling its weight and solidness, only increased her uncertainty; it was just a physical confirmation that he was about to leave. She knew he was strong and capable, knew he could fight, but however much he acted like he was invincible, he wasn't.

And I don't want to lose him.

Thargen hooked a finger beneath her chin and lifted her face toward his. "There's nothing on this planet that can take me away from you, *zoani*. I'll be back soon."

Yuri eased closer to him, slipped her free hand around the back of his neck, and pulled him down into a kiss. She closed her eyes and parted her lips, flicking her tongue along the seam of his mouth. He growled and cupped the back of her head in his hand, slanting his mouth to kiss her harder. His tongue invaded her mouth and stroked hers, beckoning it—no, *demanding* it—to do the same.

The kiss was heated and wet, charged with the sexual energy that had been crackling between them since the moment they'd met. Yuri swayed toward him, arching her back. Her body tingled with desire. Her breasts were heavy with the need to have his hands on them, and her nipples had tightened into achy little buds.

It wasn't until Yuri bit his bottom lip that Thargen grunted and pulled away from her. She moved to follow, to continue what they'd started, but he released the back of her head to catch her jaw, halting her movement. She opened her eyes to look up at him. His lips were dark, swollen, and glistening with a hint of moisture.

Thargen's tongue slipped out to lick his lips, and Yuri suddenly imagined that tongue licking a *different* set of lips. Heat flooded her core in a rush, and her sex clenched.

Can this man make me any hornier?

"So fucking sweet." His nostrils flared with a deep inhalation. "And I haven't even had a real taste yet."

Oh, eff me.

Yuri squeezed her thighs together. "You can. Like, right now."

He grunted, and the corners of his mouth curled into a wicked, sexy grin. "I'll save that as a treat for later. We need something a little more...savory right now."

She lifted her leg, brushing her thigh against the prominent bulge at his groin. "I could go for some meat right now."

Thargen shuddered and squeezed his eyes shut, releasing a long, low groan. "You're fucking killing me, terran."

Yuri chuckled and scraped her nails over the back of his neck. "I can cure you. I was trained as a nurse, remember?"

Well, kind of, but there's no need to get technical.

He lowered his mouth and pressed a soft kiss to her lips— tender rather than fiery, soothing rather than arousing. Before she could coax more from him, before she could escalate it, he pulled back.

Had that kiss been a gentle rejection?

You're a glutton for punishment, Yuri, that's what you are.

"Be back soon, terran," he said in that rumbly voice that only teased her more. "Stay here. I won't go far."

Yuri stuck her bottom lip out—she wasn't too proud to pout —as he withdrew, breaking all physical contact with her.

What was it going to take to get that giant club between his legs between hers?

Thargen caught his bottom lip with his teeth. "Fuck, *zoani*. I can't think straight when you look at me like that. Not enough blood for my brain."

Yuri laughed, and immediately after, her stomach decided to rumble. Her hand flew to her belly.

Damn you!

Now Thargen laughed.

"Doesn't mean anything," Yuri declared.

"It's my job to see to my female's needs." He moved to the opening and paused there, looking back at her over his shoulder. "Gonna take care of your hunger, first. Then we'll see if I can't do something about your *appetite*."

Yuri's toes curled into the moss, her sex clenched in anticipation, and she grinned. Thargen's eyes swept over her body, fire blazing in their golden depths, before he stepped out.

She stood there for a time, some small part of her hoping he'd change his mind, that his big body would reappear in the opening and block out the light, but she knew he was serious—and that he was right. They needed food.

The sky was still overcast, and the gloom outside was enhanced by the fact that this side of the mountain didn't get direct sun in the morning. The wind was still blowing, rustling foliage and making trees creak, but at least it wasn't raining.

Yuri blew out a long, slow breath, pushing the loose strands of her hair out of her face. She sat down in the pallet, laid the axe on the ground beside her, and glanced at the meal bar. Her stomach cramped again. If she was this hungry, she could only imagine how Thargen must be feeling. She doubted a single meal bar was enough to sustain a vorgal of his stature for a day—especially lately, with how hard he'd been pushing himself.

And he gave this one to me, not knowing whether or not he'll actually catch something out there.

Yuri picked the meal bar up and held it on her open palms. She had no idea what these bars were made of. Her best guess was hard-packed sawdust given their appearance, texture, and taste. Sawdust or insects ground to powder and glued together.

She shuddered.

What the hell, Yuri? Don't think about that!

Scrunching her nose, she broke the meal bar into two, tucked the larger chunk inside one of the open backpacks, and nibbled on the corner of the smaller piece. As she chewed, the meal bar broke down into something increasingly dirt-like and seemed to suck all the moisture out of her mouth.

And of course, they were out of water cubes.

Once she'd finished eating—and her arousal had finally cooled—another pressing issue made itself known.

She had to pee.

Yuri stretched her legs out her and crossed them, willing herself to hold it, to wait for Thargen to get back, but the need swiftly became unbearable.

She looked at the entrance. "Damn it. Guess I'm playing mountain woman again—by myself."

Wrapping her hand around the axe, she pushed herself up to her feet. Keeping her thighs squeezed together, she waddled to the opening and stuck her head out, peering left and right. She saw no movement save for the vegetation swaying in the wind.

She ducked out of the shelter. The wind swept over her, fluttering her hair and clothing and sending a slight chill up her spine. Raising the axe with both hands, she stepped forward, glancing around her.

It's fucking clear, her bladder yelled at her. *Go!*

Yuri ran to a nearby tree, shoved her pants down—nearly

falling over when they caught on her foot in her rush to get them off—and set them aside, dropping the axe on top of them. Relief came swiftly once she'd pulled up her shirt and squatted.

Once she was done, she used some of the soft leaves to clean herself. She snatched up her pants and bent down, meaning to tug them back on, when she noticed the sound of rushing water. Retrieving the axe, she straightened and walked forward, turning her head to scan her surroundings again. She paused when her gaze swung downslope; there, not a hundred meters away, a shimmer of moving water was just visible through the trees.

The river.

Her mouth ached with thirst and the memory of the water's taste.

Yuri glanced back at the shelter before returning her attention to the river. It wasn't too far. She could get a drink, maybe even take a quick bath—the hose on the ship and yesterday's rainstorm certainly didn't count—and get back to the shelter before Thargen returned.

Tucking her pants under her arm, Yuri made her way carefully downslope, picking the softest grass and smoothest stones to walk on. The hem of her shirt fluttered around her bare knees.

She paused when she reached a tree that was perched on the edge of a low drop-off, where she was granted her first full view of the river. Yuri was fairly certain this wasn't the same place they'd come to drink from yesterday, but she doubted she would've recognized it even if it was—the water was significantly higher today, having been swollen by the heavy rains.

Fortunately, that swelling had created a relatively shallow bulge in the river a bit farther upstream, where several large trees would provide at least partial cover. Those trees had likely been ten or twenty meters away from the water's edge before the rain had started.

Yuri walked on, keeping herself amongst the trees until she was closer to her destination. The slope leading down to the water was an easy one, and she was thankful for it; her aches from yesterday's long hike were making themselves known again now that she was up and about.

Focus, Yuri.

She forced herself to check her surroundings again as she approached the water's edge. The sound of the flowing river was soothing, but it was also a distraction, making all the other forest noises harder to hear in comparison. She needed to stay alert. Smugglers and skeks were her primary fears, but she couldn't ignore the fact that this planet had native wildlife. Just because she hadn't seen signs of anything big didn't mean there weren't large, aggressive, dangerous animals out here.

Yuri would just have to be quick about this so she could get back to the shelter. She dropped her pants and the axe on the ground and stepped forward to kneel at the water's edge. Bending over, she scooped handfuls of cold, clean, delicious water into her mouth, filling her belly. When she stood, she pulled her shirt off over her head and tossed it on top of her other belongings.

Her nipples hardened as the cold wind blew over her bare skin.

Water's going to be even worse, Yuri. Get it over with.

After taking a few deep, fortifying breaths, she stepped in.

The water was like ice around her feet. Goosebumps broke out over her skin, and she was wracked by a shudder as that bone deep chill invaded her body. She forced herself forward until the water was up to her thighs.

"Oh, f-fuck, fuck, fuck, fuck," she stuttered while hurriedly splashing water over her body, cleaning her hairless armpits, her backside, and between her legs. She chuckled despite her chattering teeth. "G-getting body hair removed w-was the best decision I m-made."

Though there wasn't any soap and she was freezing by the time she was done, she felt cleaner— and better—than she had in a long time. It was rejuvenating, really.

Yuri dashed out of the river, shivering anew as the wind only intensified the cold, and wrung her hair out. Water streamed down her body and limbs. She bent down and snatched up her shirt, dragging it over her head and tugging it down. It clung to her damp body, but at least it dulled the wind's bite.

She'd just pulled on her pants and was rolling the waistline down to make them fit more snugly when she heard a *snap* behind her.

Yuri's heart leapt, and she froze, clutching the pants in a white-knuckled grip. She swallowed and slowly turned, telling herself it was just a fallen branch, or a cute, cuddly animal, or a figment of her imagination.

But when she completed that turn, there was no adorable animal, there was no fallen branch, and she couldn't convince herself that the hulking being staring at her from a few meters away was the product of her imagination—though it would've been right at home in the worst of her nightmares.

The alien was powerfully built, his skin a burnt red-brown, dressed in an eclectic mix of furs, tattered cloth, and dingy combat armor. He had long, pointed ears that jutted out from either side of his head, a flat nose, and large, sunken eyes that gleamed with hunger. His oversized orange irises were made bolder by the contrasting smears of black paint across his brows and cheeks. Tangled, matted hair—adorned with bits of metal, beading, and bone—hung about his shoulders. But most horrifying was his mouth. He had no lips, just the pointed, yellowed teeth of a predator bared in an unwavering, menacing grin.

A skeks.

Cruel glee flashed in his eyes an instant before he charged at Yuri.

Her body moved before her brain could give it any commands, crouching to snatch up the axe. There was no time to struggle with activating it. Grasping the weapon in both hands, she swung as she surged upright, throwing all her strength behind it.

The flat metal head of the axe struck the skeks on the underside of his jaw, the impact resonating through the haft and nearly breaking her grip. The skeks' head snapped up and aside, and his charge faltered.

Yuri staggered backward, watching with growing horror as the skeks turned his face back toward her, his toothy grin unbroken. Blue blood seeped from a gash on his jaw. He took another step closer.

She turned and ran. "Thargen!"

Rock and pine needles bit at the soles of her feet, but she barely registered the pain. All that mattered was escaping —surviving.

I am not *becoming skeks food.*

A whimper escaped her. She clung to the axe as she ran, her breath sawing in and out of her constricted throat like it was made of broken glass. Heavy footfalls crashed over the ground behind her, drawing closer with every heartbeat.

"Thargen!"

She dashed between two trees and screamed when something big struck her from the side with enough force to throw her off her feet. The axe flew from her grasp, and she hit the ground hard, knocking the air out of her lungs. Pain shot through her body. Rock and pine needles dug into her side and belly. She squeezed her eyes shut and groaned, willing herself to get up, to keep moving.

A heavy weight fell atop her, caging her in on all sides. Yuri opened her eyes and looked up into the face of another skeks—this one with blazing red eyes and a jagged scar across his face.

The skeks spoke in a guttural language Yuri had never heard—but her translator provided the meaning of his words.

"Hello, little food."

THARGEN ADJUSTED his grip on the shaft of his spear as he crept through the brush—though spear might've been too generous a term. The makeshift weapon was simply a tristeel combat knife tied to the end of the strongest, straightest stick he'd been able to find in the area immediately surrounding their shelter within a minute or two. It wasn't pretty, and it seemed likely to either fall apart or break outright after a single blow, but a single thrust was all he needed.

Hopefully.

Even when alien creatures had outward appearances that were somewhat familiar in shape, proportion, and configuration, the internals were always a mystery. A killing blow on one species could be little more than a mild irritation for another.

The quadrupedal creature he was stalking—which stood a little shorter than Yuri and was covered in shaggy, reddish fur—was close enough to familiar that he'd decided to go with the usual strategy of aiming at its chest, just behind the front leg. That was the lungs on many such creatures. All it would take was for his not-quite-straight spear to strike true.

Well, that was all it would take once he was close enough to attack—he sure as hell didn't trust this spear to fly straight if he threw it. He'd lost much of his patience for all this sneaking and stalking long ago, and what remained of it was stretched particularly thin now thanks to the throbbing in his groin and the lingering heat of arousal pumping from his core.

By Vorga's flaming skull, his female didn't even have to try hard to get him going.

He eased forward a little more, parting the foliage with his weapon to clear his field of view.

His quarry was just ahead, neck bent and head down as it drank from the bloated river, which had swollen with runoff to reach all the way up to what had been a low, grassy hill the day prior. The spot was somewhat open, with no cover once Thargen left the thicker brush behind, but he was confident in his ability to cross that grass without making a sound; those were skills he'd picked up under far more dangerous circumstances. He just needed to move deliberately and with care. The wind was in his favor, and the river would help mask any of the tiny sounds he did make. The conditions couldn't get much better considering his lack of preparation and the unfamiliarity of this world.

But his body seemed willing to fight him on that. A steady stream of Rage and desire was running through him, the two so intertwined by now that he could barely tell the difference between them. As much as this was about obtaining fresh food, it was even more about venting that Rage, about finding a release that could not be obtained by throwing rocks and pummeling trees.

What he truly needed was a fight—a *real* fight—or to fuck.

He'd have to settle for just killing something for now.

Thargen emerged from the brush and stalked forward, keeping himself in a low crouch and feeling out every step. He forced himself to breathe slowly, taking in and expelling each breath through his nostrils, and willed his heartbeat to remain steady. Rage had risen enough to heighten his senses, but he could allow it no more purchase in his body and mind until the instant he was ready to make the kill.

The creature at the water lifted its head, tufted ears perking. Thargen froze mid-step and held his breath. The creature's ears flicked, and it turned its head left—the same direction as Yuri and Thargen's shelter.

Thargen's heartbeat increased in volume as the pressure in his lungs intensified. His prey continued staring downriver, and he continued to hold still. He'd been incredibly fortunate to come across this animal so close to the shelter, and he refused to lose this opportunity. He was going to kill this thing, cook it, and feed the meat to his little terran, letting her lick the juices off his fingers.

Then he'd lick *her* juices straight from her sex.

Fuck. Been away from her too long already.

Finally, the animal lowered its head.

Releasing a long exhalation that finally eased the pain and pressure in his lungs, Thargen proceeded forward. Centimeter by centimeter, he closed the distance to his prey, feet silent on the soft red grass. A new tightness built in his chest—anticipation. His Rage stirred anew, roused by the promise of action, of violence, of bloodshed.

He altered his path to circle around to the creature's left side, raising the spear slowly. His skin pulled taut as his muscles swelled, pumped up by Rage.

"Thargen!" Yuri's shout echoed off the trees and over the dark river water.

The creature darted away, crashing through the undergrowth in a panicked run upriver. Thargen barely noticed. The tone of Yuri's voice—the desperation, the fear—sent a chill through him that the wind and rain had not been able to match.

She was outside. She was downriver. She was in trouble.

He didn't resist his Rage this time; he let it carry him

toward her voice in a sprint. The hazards and terrain were lost on him. He didn't feel the needle-like tree growths under his feet any more than he felt the uncompromising surfaces of rocks or the tufts of soft grass. He barreled headlong through the undergrowth and low branches, slowing for nothing, oblivious to the scrapes and scratches he should've been receiving.

Yuri.

It was the only word in his mind, as strong and steady as his pulse, amidst a storm of instinct and emotion. He latched onto her name—and onto his fury. Nothing else would be any help now. The forest was a blur of red, brown, and yellow around him, the river a strip of wavering grays.

Somewhere ahead, branches snapped, and foliage shook. Thargen wasn't the only one racing through these woods. He sped his pace as he descended a low rise overlooking a part of the river where flooding had created a small, shallow pool butted by tall trees on one side. Two familiar scents struck him at the bottom.

One was sweet, exotic, and feminine, unmistakably Yuri's. The other was subtle, spicy, and smoky. Blackwhorl—a potent herb the skeks often smoked in their scavenging camps, meant to alter their awareness and make the more effective hunters.

"Thargen!"

Her voice had come from much closer this time—twenty or thirty meters ahead at most, around the same place as the other sounds he'd heard—and it was more desperate, more afraid, more strained.

When she screamed a moment later, there was sheer terror in the sound.

Rage sharpened Thargen's vision further, narrowing his focus down to the trail of broken branches and trampled vegetation leading toward Yuri's voice. He charged onto the trail without hesitation.

In the back of his mind, buried deep beneath the primal instincts that had seized control of him, he was vaguely aware of a multitude of thoughts that could've been swirling through his mind in a paralyzing, panicked maelstrom at that moment. All those possibilities, all those what-ifs. There were countless horrible things the skeks could do to her, things they might already have done. There were countless scenarios that might greet him when he found her, countless skeks that could be watching him from amongst the trees even now.

But none of those thoughts even began to take shape. If nothing else, Thargen had always been good at keeping things simple.

Skeks had found Yuri.

Skeks always ran in packs.

He was going to kill some skeks and save his *zoani*.

Yuri cried out again, her voice coming from a thicket just ahead. The sound was quickly cut off—and followed by guttural laughter and words spoken in the harsh tongue of the skeks.

Thargen growled and leveled his spear, angling himself toward a gap between two of the larger trees comprising the thicket. That familiar battle haze enveloped his mind; he *was* Rage. Fire blazed at his core, lightning crackled through his muscles, and molten fury flowed through his veins, pumped by a heart that beat with the thunderous cadence of war drums.

His legs pumped harder, faster, devouring the meters between him and his destination.

One of the skeks silenced the others and hissed, "Do you hear?"

A large figure clad in tattered furs and dingy armor stepped into the opening between those thick trunks. The skeks' sunken eyes met Thargen's and rounded an instant before Thargen burst through the gap.

The knife at the end of the spear hit the skeks in the abdomen, punching through the old armor to plunge into flesh. The skeks grunted.

Thargen kept running, pushing the skeks backward until the skewered enemy struck another tree. The sudden stop forced the blade deeper until it, too, hit the tree with a dull *thunk* that Thargen felt through the shaft just before the stick snapped centimeters away from his leading grip.

He was already turning as the skeks to his right shouted in alarm, dropping his left hand to snatch the hardlight axe from its place at his thigh. He swung the broken stick backhand, cracking it across the face of a second skeks who'd been approaching.

The skeks reeled aside, caught off guard by the sudden blow. Thargen lashed out with the axe in an angled arc, following the stick's path; he activated the blade mid-swing. The hardlight edge caught the skeks at his cheekbone, carving off a wedge of his head from cheek to mid-scalp.

Behind him, the impaled skeks released a choked snarl.

But Thargen's Rage had already shifted to the other two enemies beyond the faceless skeks. One was on his knees, twisted to look back at Thargen—with Yuri pinned beneath him. The other was closer, only four or five meters away, and had a large rifle in his hands, the stock against his shoulder.

The big-bore barrel swung toward Thargen.

Thargen lunged forward, ducking to catch the falling, faceless skeks on his shoulder. Blue blood poured from the gaping wound to shower Thargen's skin.

The rifle boomed, the sound deafening in the confines of the thicket. The skeks propped up on Thargen's shoulder shuddered, and a huge hole blasted open on its upper chest, centimeters from Thargen's head.

Fresh gore splattered Thargen's back, and the stench of burnt flesh hit his nose.

He heaved the dead skeks aside, and his left hand flicked out, releasing the haft of the axe. The weapon tumbled awkwardly through the air, but it didn't need to go far. The upper curve of the blade sliced through the rifle-wielder's thigh, opening a huge gash, before the weapon hit the ground.

The skeks' leg gave out immediately, and he staggered back onto his other leg just as his rifle went off with another burst of thunder. Dirt and debris leapt off the ground beside Thargen's foot.

Thargen growled and rushed forward.

A flicker of movement at the edge of his vision was his only warning before something heavy and hard slammed into the side of his head with a force that resonated through his bones, knocking him off course. Blackness descended over his vision, and the only sounds he could hear were his own pounding heart and heavy breathing.

That had either been a sledgehammer or a fucking space freighter. The skeks would have to hit him with a lot more than that if they meant to get out of this alive.

Grinning, Thargen braced his legs to regain his balance and lashed out blindly with the broken stick as his vision slowly cleared, swinging quick and hard enough to make the air itself bleed.

A figure took shape in front of him, stained crimson through the lens of his Rage—the scar-faced skeks who'd been restraining Yuri, standing up with a club in his hand.

A strong, thick arm looped up under Thargen's left armpit and over his shoulder, dragging him back as a second arm wrapped around his neck. Hot, strained breath sounded at his ear—and the splintered end of a stick jabbed at his lower back as the new assailant tightened his hold. But the cable-like tendons on either side of Thargen's trachea shielded his airflow from that crushing grasp.

The scar-faced skeks swung his weapon again, striking Thargen's cheek. Thargen's head snapped to the side, and there was an immediate metallic tang on his tongue. Now his vision was a field of red and black, shadows and blood.

Laughter ripped from his throat, raw and rough, delighted yet cruel. He laughed as he raised a leg and kicked the skeks before him in the chest, laughed as he straightened that leg to shove all his weight back onto the enemy restraining him. He laughed as the skeks fell backward and he crashed atop the wounded foe. That laughter strengthened in response to the skeks' pained grunt and continued as Thargen rolled with his momentum, swinging his feet over his head to flip over and land on his knees, looking down at the fallen skeks.

Thargen grabbed the broken bit of spear shaft protruding from the skeks' gut and pulled it like it was an emergency brake lever on a vehicle about to crash. The shaft—and the knife attached to it—jerked back with a wet, cracking sound, ripping open a huge hole in the skeks' abdomen until it finally caught on the underside of the skeks' ribcage. A flood of blue blood bubbled from the wound.

The skeks convulsed, grabbing at his gut and making choked, desperate sounds as his blood pooled on the ground beneath him.

Thargen released the bloody wood and flattened his hand on the dying skeks' chest, bracing himself long enough to get his feet beneath him. His laughter exploded into a savage roar as he sprang at the approaching club-wielder. The scarred skeks swung his club in a wide arc, but Thargen closed the distance in a flash, getting inside the swing. The skeks' arm hit Thargen's left shoulder in a strong but ineffectual blow.

Thargen's right hand—still holding the longer portion of his broken spear—darted up. The sharp end of the stick punctured the underside of the skeks' chin, pushing through soft flesh until it finally broke against the roof of the skeks' mouth.

The scarred skeks released a strained groan and staggered backward. Blue blood ran in rivulets through his exposed, pointed teeth. He dropped his club to grab at the stick with both hands, trying to pull it out or staunch the blood flow—it didn't matter which.

Thargen had already let go of the stick and drawn a pair of knives from their sheathes on his waistband. He lunged forward and plunged one of the knives into the skeks' right eye. He felt the squelch of the bursting eyeball through the weapon. The skeks stilled, his remaining eye blazing with fear and hatred as it held Thargen's gaze for a moment—until the life faded from that eye.

Thargen tugged the knife free as the skeks' knees buckled, turning to face the remaining enemy.

The skeks with the rifle had retreated farther, and now stood with his back against a tree trunk and his left leg—covered in glistening blood—stretched out before him. His eyes gleamed with malice and that intense light unique to the gazes of the dying. He raised his rifle to his shoulder.

Rage swelled in Thargen's chest, forcing another roar out of his throat.

Only empty air stood between him and the barrel of the rifle—nearly ten meters of it.

As the skeks steadied his weapon, Thargen charged.

A high, ragged cry sounded to the skeks's side, a bizarre combination of a defiant war cry and a frightened scream.

The skeks snapped his head toward the cry just as Yuri burst out of the foliage. She swung a hardlight axe from overhead in a downward, two-handed arc. The blade sliced clean through the skeks' left forearm before slipping out of her hands.

The weapon fell and hit the skeks in the left knee, chopping off his leg just below his prior wound.

Roaring with pain, the skeks swung his arm at her—and would have hit her, had she not just shortened his reach. Blue blood sprayed into her face from the stump.

Thargen leapt across the last couple meters between himself and his target, no longer seeing anything but the crimson of his Rage. His shoulder hit the skeks' torso, crushing the injured foe into the tree and forcing a gasping grunt from the skeks' lungs. Thargen's knives took over from there.

The skeks' cries of pain were soon drowned out by the wet thuds and squelching sounds of knife blades punching through flesh and being torn back out over and over, occasionally punctuated by the cracking of bone. Thargen roared, or laughed—or both—as he stabbed the skeks in the sides, chest, and abdomen repeatedly. Blood slickened his hands and arms, hot and sticky and sweet smelling.

A whole fucking lot more blue blood needed to spill before Thargen would be satisfied. He'd cover every centimeter of this whole fucking planet in blood until it seeped out of the ground with every step.

The skeks sagged to the side, and Thargen's next thrust missed. The blade of the knife hit the tree with a dull *thunk* just as the dead skeks crumpled to the ground. Thargen stood there for several seconds, his Rage uncertain—the threats were eliminated, but his bloodlust was not yet sated.

He tore the knife out of the wood and turned. Everything in him stilled when his eyes fell on Yuri.

She was the reason he'd fought these skeks, not some ancient feud. It had been to save her.

Yuri was staring at the skeks who'd fallen at Thargen's feet, her eyes huge and round and stark against the blue blood spattered over her face. Her dark hair was a tangled mess, filled with red and brown needles and even a small stick, and her shoulders rose and fell rapidly with her ragged breaths, all taken through flared nostrils.

Thargen's Rage stepped aside, and clarity swept into its place, cold and unrelenting. He'd won this fight, but the situation was little improved—and his *zoani* was in distress.

He took a step toward her. "Yuri—"

Her eyes flew up to meet his a split second before she bent at the waist and vomited. When she was done, she lifted a trembling arm and wiped it across her mouth, pausing when she lowered it to stare at the blood smeared on her skin. A high-pitched whine escaped her, escalating toward as scream.

She staggered back, wiping frantically at her arms, which only spread the blood more. "Get it off. Get it off. Get it off! *Getitoff!*"

Fuck.

Thargen bent forward, quickly wiping the blood from his blades on the dead skeks' tattered clothing, and returned the knives to their sheathes as he straightened. He closed the distance between himself and Yuri in two long strides, swept her into his arms, and raced back along the trail of broken foliage to the pool.

His eyes scanned his surroundings restlessly as he carried her into the water, stopping only when it was as deep as his mid-thighs. Her little hands clung to his shoulders. Tears spilled from her eyes, and her inhalations came in sharp, broken gasps.

"Hold your breath, *zoani*," Thargen said.

Yuri's watery eyes locked with his. They were filled with fear, vulnerability—and trust. Thargen's heart lurched.

"I got you, Yuri," he said roughly.

She nodded and drew in a deep, shaky breath, pressing her lips into a firm line, and closed her eyes.

He dropped onto his ass, submerging them both completely. The water was icy against his heated skin, creating a jolt that swept away Rage's lingering hold on his mind, but the current here was soothingly slow. Yuri's hold on him tightened, and her body trembled.

Thargen planted his feet on the ground and pushed up, standing only straight enough to lift their heads above the surface.

Yuri gasped and raised a hand to sweep her hair back from her face.

He lowered her to her feet and quickly but gently wiped away the remaining blood from her cheeks. "You hurt?"

"N-no. You...you c-came in time."

Shouldn't have left her alone to begin with.

Thargen cut off that line of thinking before it could continue; what was done was done. This was the reality, this was the situation, and how it had come to be was irrelevant. She needed comfort. That was the priority.

He eased back from her to run his hands over his own body, scrubbing it as clean as he could. His lips curled up in a small smirk. "Guess the color doesn't matter."

She peeked up at him while scouring her arms as though the blood hadn't been washed away. "Let's j-just...pretend th-that didn't happen."

"I'm not gonna forget the first time my female chopped off someone's arm."

A shudder wracked her, but one corner of her mouth quirked. "I w-was pretty badass, h-huh?"

"Fuck yeah, *zoani*." He stood up straight, splashing a handful of water over his face and shaking it off. "Need you to keep being a badass, all right? We gotta go back."

Yuri's face blanched, and her shivering intensified.

Frowning, Thargen picked her up, carried her to the riverbank, and set her back down. He framed her cheeks between his hands, placing his thumbs on her chin to keep her face toward his. "Nothing's gonna to happen to you. We need to take what we can from them, grab our shit, and get moving, and we need to do it all fast. I'll be with you the whole time."

She placed her hands over his. "Th-this is nothing like those VR g-games."

He shook his head and chuckled. "Nah, they tend to miss out on some important details."

"And they usually have options to turn off blood effects."

"Don't know if anyone told you, but I'm a walking blood effect. Guess you shoulda ignored my striking good looks at the club that night."

Yuri laughed, shaking her head as much as he allowed. "Worth it."

Thargen pressed a kiss to her forehead. "You might be crazier than me, *zoani*."

When he lowered his hands from her face, she grasped her shirt, twisting it to wring excess moisture from the fabric. Thargen skimmed his eyes over her to make sure she was unharmed, and he couldn't help the stirring of desire that warmed his blood. That wet shirt clung to her breasts, clearly outlining her hard nipples.

Gritting his teeth, he forced his gaze down until it caught on her feet—her bare feet. There were little scrapes and cuts on the tops of them, and he could only imagine the damage that must've been done to their soles.

"Fuck, terran," he muttered as he stooped to lift her into his arms again. "When we get back to Arthos, you're not allowed to walk for a whole damned week."

Shivering, Yuri grinned and wrapped her arms around his neck. "I-I kind of like y-you carrying me, anyway."

I do, too, zoani.

Thargen hurried back to the thicket. Only when he reached the two large trees through which he'd entered the small battlefield did he set her down, keeping her back to the carnage beyond the gap.

"Stay right here and keep watch, Yuri. I'll be quick."

She reached out and caught his wrist as he stepped away. "Thank y-you. For everything. And for, uh...making m-me feel useful when I know I'm not."

He sighed heavily and cupped the side of her face in his palm. Her skin was cool, even though there were splotches of pink on her cheeks, and her lips had a faint bluish tint. "You saved my life. I'd call that pretty useful."

She smiled wide. "I did, didn't I?"

"Damn right."

I fucking love this terran.

Yuri didn't have a warrior's strength, skill, or stomach, but she had a warrior's spirit right down to her core. Some training would go a long way with her—and this whole experience was likely to make every other challenge in her life seem a lot less daunting by comparison.

He lowered his hand. "You see anything out there, you come to me right away. Don't look down at all."

She straightened, squaring her shoulders, and snapped her hand up to her forehead as though shading her eyes, arm rigid. "Yes, sir!" When she dropped her hand, her posture sagged slightly, and the blush on her cheeks deepened. "That was so corny."

Even if he didn't recognize that particular gesture, Thargen recognized its intent—it was a salute. He couldn't understand what this whole mess was like from her perspective, and he could only imagine that the mental toll on her was immense, but here she was, finding humor in it along with him. She called it *corny...*

He called it sexy as hell.

I really fucking love this terran.

He almost reached for her again, but he forced himself to stop. They needed to get moving—too much time had been wasted already. This had just been a small skeks scouting party; there'd be more of them out on this mountainside, and those gunshots had likely been heard for kilometers around. Thargen and Yuri needed to get very far away from here very quickly.

He'd just have to show her his...*appreciation* once they found a safe place to stop.

FIFTEEN

Thargen grabbed a fistful of the dead beast's narrow mane and dragged the carcass toward the mouth of the cave.

"Thargen?" Yuri called from just outside. There was a hint of uncertainty in her voice.

He ducked slightly to fit through the opening, emerging into late evening gloom that was made thicker by the trees in front of the rocky cliff.

Yuri's shoulders sagged, and she breathlessly said, "You scared the crap out of me."

"Hope not, terran. I haven't dug a shitting hole yet."

Her nose scrunched. "Not literally, Thargen. You know what I mean." She tilted her head. "What happened in there? Those sounds..."

Grinning, Thargen hauled the beast out into the light, dumping it unceremoniously onto the ground before him. It was about as long as Yuri was tall, with a muscular hunched back, long front legs, and curved black claws on its toes. Its fur —relatively short and soft but for the bristly mane running along its spine—was mottled red and brown. Fortunately, that coloration made it harder to see the blood on the fur around its short, thick neck.

"Was just getting dinner," Thargen declared.

Yuri's brows shot up. "*That* was in there?" She narrowed her eyes and peered past him. "Are there...others?"

"Just the one. Woke it up, I think."

"Looks like you did a little more than that."

Pride swelled Thargen's chest, a welcome substitution for the Rage that had been driving him only moments before. This wasn't how he'd meant to provide for his female—he was supposed to have returned to her this morning with a fresh kill obtained through his patience, skill, and prowess. But he'd accept it; the only important thing was that they'd have fresh meat tonight.

"So...do you know how to make a fire?" Yuri asked.

Thargen arched a brow. "Doubting my abilities, terran?"

"Noooo, I'd never." Her lips twitched as though she were holding back laughter.

"Get your ass to work," he grumbled, waving her away. "Dry sticks and whatever else you think will burn. Stay close."

Her efforts to contain that laughter failed as she turned away, bending to pick up and gather sticks with her shoulders shaking gently. Thargen grunted and stepped over to his backpack, which he'd set on the ground before venturing into the cave. He grabbed the collapsible spade from the holding loop on the side of the bag—it was just one of several old-fashioned but practical items he'd found on the dead skeks.

He dug a small pit for a fire close to the base of a nearby tree, not resisting when his Rage sparked in response to the tough dirt making the task unnecessarily difficult. The light was failing, and he didn't intend to have a fire going any longer than necessary. Even with the flames hidden and the smoke largely dispersed amongst the trees, the smell would be clear to most creatures that came anywhere close.

When Yuri returned with an armful of tinder, most of which was drier than he could've hoped, he arranged a portion of it in the pit and scooped up a handful of dry fallen needles from closer to the cave. He used another of the items he'd taken from the skeks to light the needles—an old fire starter that sprayed sparks when the trigger was pulled.

He set the smoking needles at the base of the arranged wood, and after some coaxing—and several lungfuls of air slowly blown over the embers—the firewood caught.

"We have fire!" Yuri pumped her arms in the air above her head. "Achievement unlocked."

Thargen glanced up at Yuri. Her smile, the sparkling delight in her eyes, and the genuine cheer in her voice all hit him hard, like a solid kick to the chest that made his heart ache and his breath catch. He'd never imagined how *good* a feeling that could be before her.

Today had been another long, hard day in a growing chain of them, and Yuri remained unbroken.

Thargen grinned. "Not doubting anymore, are you, terran?"

She was shaking her sexy little ass when she glanced at him over her shoulder and grinned. "My male delivered."

His eyes fixated on that ass, and suddenly food was the lesser of his two cravings. "Got a few more skills to show you before the night's through, *zoani*."

Her eyes widened, and her cheeks flushed. Thargen wondered if the rest of her body was just as pink.

She lowered her arms and turned toward him, her smile taking on a wicked tilt. "Oh yeah?"

Fuck, he could eat her up right now.

But first, he needed to feed her. They'd gone too long

without any real food, and he planned to fill her belly before filling her *pussy* with his tongue.

Thargen licked his lips, anticipation thrumming through him. "It's a promise, terran."

He sat back on his haunches, watching smoke rise from the fire pit, travel up the trunk of the tree, and disperse as it got higher. He could only hope it wouldn't be thick enough to be spotted from higher elevations.

Thargen couldn't help but find some amusement in the radical change that had undergone his thinking lately; were he here alone, he'd *want* the skeks to spot his fire. He'd welcome the fight and throw himself into it with reckless abandon and no small amount of glee.

But he wouldn't do anything now to put his Yuri in danger. That death in combat that he'd long anticipated had become a bitter thought. She gave him a reason to want more, gave him a chance at a future and a path to obtain it.

His temples throbbed, and a sharp ache briefly pierced the center of his skull. It would've been easy to attribute it to over-thinking, but he knew it had more to do with the solid blows he'd taken from the skeks earlier.

And that reminder triggered another—his work wasn't done yet. If he wanted to sleep before sunrise, he needed to get moving.

There'd be plenty of time for contemplation when Thargen and Yuri made it back to Arthos.

"Fuck," he grumbled, forcing himself to stand up. "Find some good sticks to use as skewers, *zoani*. I'm gonna see to our food."

Yuri approached him, running her fingers up his arm and along the back of his shoulders. A thrill zipped down his spine, and his cock leapt in response.

"I love a man who can cook," Yuri said with a chuckle as she walked past.

He inhaled deeply as he watched her walk away, glad for once that her smell was mostly masked—this time by the sweet smoke of the fire. He forced his focus onto her belt instead of her ass. Sized for a skeks waist, it had been far too big for her, but Thargen's improvised adjustments seemed to be working well enough, and seeing the sheathed knife at her hip offered him a bit of comfort.

"Keep the cave in sight," he said as he strode to the dead beast and grabbed hold of it. "I'll be close."

"Yes, sir!" she called.

That was enough to make his cock twitch. He gritted his teeth and hauled the body away from the camp until he couldn't see Yuri anymore; he'd have to be content with just hearing her move around amidst the vegetation and fallen branches. This was messy work, and she didn't need to see any more blood today if it could be avoided—the goal was to keep food in her stomach long enough for her body to take some actual sustenance from it.

He worked in silence, bleeding, skinning, and butchering the alien creature as quickly and efficiently as he could—and feeling like a clumsy novice throughout. His talents had always leaned toward those bursts of brutal action. As good as he was with a knife in a fight, his hands felt unsteady and unsure once he had to slow down and think about what he was doing. It didn't help that the creature was unfamiliar to him.

Still, he returned to the campfire with several hunks of promising-looking meat that he was determined to enjoy no matter how tough, stringy, or gamey they were. Yuri was already sitting at the fire waiting for him, all her skewer sticks set out with their ends carved to points, and her belt laid on the ground next to her. She'd spread out some of the spare clothing to sit on, leaving plenty of room for him.

He grinned, eyed her with undisguised hunger for a few moments, and sat beside her to start slicing the meat into smaller pieces. To his surprise, Yuri took those pieces and skewered them neatly, her skin not even paling a bit.

Apparently, it really was just blood that triggered her spells.

When they were done, they had several meat-laden skewers ready to cook. Thargen laid a few over the fire pit before grabbing one of the canteens they'd obtained from the skeks—all surprisingly modern, with built in filtration and purification systems—and using it to rinse his hands. Yuri did the same afterward.

Thargen smiled as he recalled how they'd filled these canteens; it felt like that had been ages ago even though it had been only hours earlier.

They'd stopped at the riverside to drink around midday, when Thargen had finally deemed them far enough away from the dead skeks for a brief rest. Yuri had opened one of the scavenged canteens and plunged it into the water. When she lifted it out, she shook it vigorously, dumped it out, and repeated the process several times. Thargen hadn't needed to ask what she was doing—he just mimicked her with one of the other canteens.

Yuri and Thargen had rinsed—and eventually filled—all four of the containers that way, kneeling on the wet grass beside the chilly river water. There'd been no need to exchange words. The moment had been oddly soothing, and it had made him feel even closer to her than before.

It had also been further example of her immense resolve. He'd wrapped her feet again, but they'd been hiking at a brisk pace for hours by that point. He'd known she was in pain, but she'd never once complained.

Thargen had chosen to carry her later in the afternoon, after she'd begun to lag—not because she'd been unable to go on, but because he'd been unable to bear the sight of his *zoani* struggling. She was weak, hungry, and tired, and none of that was her fault. Still, he didn't doubt that Yuri would've kept walking until she collapsed had he not intervened.

With the added gear from the skeks—including the heavy rifle that had nearly put an extra hole or two in Thargen—he'd actually felt the burden when he'd picked her up. But he had strength to spare for her. He'd always find more for her.

Back in the present, Yuri shook excess water from her hands, closed the canteen, and returned it to Thargen. The meat was already sizzling over the crackling fire, and the aroma it emitted was mouthwatering.

The day had been long and hard, yes, and they'd brushed up against death this morning, but Yuri was safe, and they were about to have their first hot meal in...a week? A week and a half? He wasn't sure how much time had gone by, but he didn't really care. He had her with him. His terran, his female, his *zoani*. This was worth it. The hunger and thirst, the aches and pains in his body—both old and new—were worth it.

As he flipped the skewers, he said, "If I could be stranded on an alien planet with anyone, Yuri, I could do a hell of a lot worse than you. I'd do this all again so long as you were with me."

She lifted her gaze from the fire to look at him, one eyebrow quirked. "I'm not sure if I should take that as an insult or compliment."

"Meant it as a compliment, but I *am* much better at insults."

She chuckled, but her smile quickly faded, and her eyes

shifted back to the crackling fire. Some time passed before she asked, "Do you have family waiting for you back in Arthos?"

Thargen's smile fell, too, though his gaze lingered on Yuri. He missed his friends, but he hadn't thought about them much. It was always easier for him to focus on the immediate—and he didn't like the idea of them worrying over him. "Yeah. Not related by blood, but family all the same."

"Family is family." She drew her legs up and wrapped her arms around them, resting her chin on her knees. "Most of my family is still on Earth. Their lives are established there, and it would have been too much for them to migrate to Arthos. But Takashi and I... We had no direction. I mean, I knew what I had wanted to do, and when that didn't work..." She shrugged. "I didn't know what else to do with my life."

Yuri frowned, and sudden sorrow gleamed in her eyes. "He's going to be so worried. If something happens to me... I hope he doesn't get himself killed looking. Hope he didn't *already* get himself killed."

Thargen picked up one of the skewers to examine the meat; it was golden brown now and glistening with juices, its smell even more appetizing than before. "You were assaulted twice, kidnapped, kept naked in a cage for days, demeaned, survived through a crash, and have been attacked by skeks on top of having to hike through a rugged alien wilderness and survive with little food and no clear way home, and you're still worried about your brother?"

Yuri's brows furrowed as she looked at him. "Well...yeah. Why wouldn't I be?"

He bit down on one of the smaller pieces of meat and tore it off the stick, chewing thoughtfully. It was certainly tough—a tad overcooked, perhaps—but it was still savory, easily the best food he'd had in as long as he could remember. As he passed the skewer to her, he said, "Just figured you'd have more immediate stuff to concern you is all."

She took the offered stick. "Not much we can really do at the moment, right? No point in sitting here worrying myself to death about our situation. We're still alive. It...could be worse."

Somehow, Thargen's admiration of her—which was already immense and overflowing—only expanded.

"But I'm allowed to worry about my brother," she said as she turned the skewer on its side, holding one end in each hand, and bit into the meat. Her eyes rolled up, and she made an appreciative moan that went straight to Thargen's cock.

"So...effing...good," she said as she chewed. She took several more bites, barely swallowing one before taking next—and kept making those little moans.

Fuck. Gonna have to plug my ears if I want to get through dinner without throwing myself at her and tearing off her clothes...

Thargen removed the other skewers from the fire and replaced them with the raw cuts before allowing himself to eat. He struggled to keep his attention on the cooking food as he ate, but it was difficult with Yuri right there, making those pleased sounds, smelling so nice, looking so beautiful.

Soon. It'll be time soon... But only time for a taste.

Fortunately, it wasn't difficult for him to keep his attention on the food he was eating; he devoured the meat by the kilo, it seemed, and could barely cook it fast enough to keep up with the appetite it had woken in him. He'd been hungry for a long time, but he hadn't realized just how much so until that first bite of freshly roasted meat. Yuri put away a fair portion herself. They lapsed into that companionable silence, replacing conversation with the sounds of their chewing.

"No one's coming to save us, are they?" Yuri asked after a

while, reaching for another skewer. She kept her eyes on Thargen as she bit into the meat.

Thargen paused in his chewing and glanced at her. He knew she was looking for hope, but he couldn't bring himself to lie to her. She needed the truth. He swallowed his mouthful and took another bite, speaking around the food. "No one's coming for us."

"So we really *are* on our own here."

He licked the grease from his lips and offered her a grin. "Yeah, but we're alive. That's bad for the smugglers and skeks, but it's really good for us." He reached toward her and gently chucked her beneath the chin with a curled finger. "We'll find a way home, *zoani*."

She smiled, and her eyes softened as she lowered her food. "Thank you, Thargen. For everything. I wouldn't have made it this far without you. I really do owe you my life."

The look in her eyes sparked a deep warmth in Thargen's heart, the sort that he'd only felt since meeting her. He shook his head and dropped his gaze to the fire. "Fuck, terran, you don't owe me anything. I'm having the time of my life."

Yuri laughed. "You really get into this much trouble all the time?"

"Been in a lot worse trouble than this more times than I can count—and I can count at least to five."

"Guess your guardian *angel* needs to step it up a little."

Though Yuri's tone was playful, her words produced an unexpected pang of guilt in Thargen's chest. When she'd talked about guardian *angels* before, she'd likened Urgand to one—and she'd been right in a lot of ways. Urgand was undoubtedly worried by now, had probably been worried ever since Thargen hadn't shown up for his shift days and days ago. Everyone back home was probably worried.

And Thargen hadn't been kidding—he was enjoying his time here with Yuri, despite the downsides. However torturous his desire grew, however dangerous the obstacles facing them proved, he wouldn't have traded this for anything. Wasn't that pretty much like taking a big shit on his friends' concern?

"Urgand already does more than he should have to," Thargen said, voice low. "He's not responsible for me, or my safety. I don't want him to...babysit me. He's got this thing with Sekk'thi, this ilthurii we work with, and he's pretty much become the doctor for our crew. That's the stuff he should focus on. I'll be okay. I mean"—he lifted his gaze and locked it with hers as that inner heat spread and intensified with each beat of his heart—"I have you."

She smiled. It was wide and genuine, and so damned sexy. "Yeah, you have me."

Thargen grinned. "Fuck yeah, I do."

Placing her empty skewer on the ground, Yuri leaned closer to him and tipped her face up. Her eyes dipped to his mouth. "You know, Thargen, you could have *all* of me."

A single word blasted through his mind, resonating from every cell in his body—*Mine.*

She reached out and placed a finger on the center of his chest, slowly trailing it down his abdomen. "I recall someone promising to show me some...skills."

His cock twitched, and Rage brushed against his conscious mind, forcing a low growl up from his chest. He drew in a deep breath through his nose. Her scent was suddenly stronger, enhanced by the perfume of her desire. His muscles tensed, and he balled his hands into fists. Though the body beneath her clothing was no mystery, he was ravenous to see it again—and he knew those clothes would offer little resistance.

Tossing his stick aside, he curled his fingers around her slim wrist, stopping her hand before it could reach his groin. "I did, didn't I?"

He yanked her arm to the side. She fell across his lap, face down, and he released her wrist to pull up the hem of her shirt. Yuri flattened her hands on the ground and pushed up, but Thargen grunted and planted a hand on her back, holding her down. He hooked the fingers of his other hand beneath her waistband and tugged her pants down to her knees to reveal the curve of her ass and the backs of her thighs.

He hummed appreciatively as he settled his hand over her backside. Spanning his fingers wide, he smoothed his palm over her skin, slipping his middle finger between her thighs to tease at her slit. Her sex radiated heat, and his fingertip swept up a bit of the moisture gathering there.

Yuri whimpered and arched her back, reaching for his touch.

Thargen withdrew his hand and slapped her ass with a growl.

She gasped, her body jolting, and she turned her surprised eyes toward him.

"You move at *my* pace, *zoani*," he said, gently rubbing the spot he'd struck. "Understand?"

There was heat in her eyes as she nodded. That heat—that desperation, that need—only stoked the fires burning inside him.

"Good." Thargen continued to soothe her now pinkened flesh, somehow keeping his palm steady despite the building pressure within him. His nostrils flared as he inhaled more of her scent; her arousal was all he could smell now, and he took in as much of it as he could.

Her weight, though slight, was torturous to his cock, which throbbed beneath her, straining against the thin barriers of their clothing. So close. She was so fucking close...

He moved his hand down, squeezing her yielding flesh along the way, until his finger was back at her slit. The sound that emerged from him was the bastard offspring of a growl and hum. "Your little *pussy's* wet for me, *zoani*."

Yuri snorted, drawing his attention back to her face just as she dropped her head. A moment later, her body shook with near-silent laughter.

Thargen slipped his finger between her folds and brushed it over her clit. "Something funny?"

She gasped, her body stiffening. A moan followed as she eased back, pressing against his finger, but he kept it still— despite everything in him demanding more. Every moment he resisted her was the hardest of his life.

"Well?" he asked.

Yuri groaned, but she lifted her head and turned it to look at him, grinning. "You know the word *pussy,* but not *angel?*"

"The fuck, terran? I'm trying to set a mood here."

She laughed and lifted a hand off the ground, slipping it between their bodies to grasp his cock through his pants. "Oh, I'd say the mood is pretty well set."

Eyebrows falling low, Thargen clenched his jaw and closed his eyes, struggling to hold out against the overwhelming blast of pleasure caused by her simple touch. It wasn't just his Rage anymore—all his instincts roared at him to take her, to rip off his pants and bury himself in her heat.

And to tear her apart in the process?

"Fuck," he growled through his teeth. Without allowing himself another moment to hesitate, he withdrew his hand from her sex and hooked his arm under her belly. He simultaneously flipped her onto her back and pulled his legs out from beneath her to get onto his knees; she landed atop the clothing spread on the ground.

Yuri reached for him. He caught her wrists in one hand and forced them to the ground above her head, pinning them in place. He returned his other hand to her sex, cupping it as he stared down at her face. Her eyes were wide and gleaming, her lips were parted, and her cheeks were flushed.

He leaned down, moving his face closer to hers. "*My* pace."

"Okay," she rasped.

Thargen dipped his head farther to graze her neck with his teeth. He pressed his middle finger between her folds again, gathering her essence as he stroked up toward her clit. He slowly circled the little nub with his fingertip.

"You don't have a choice," he said against her throat, barely keeping his voice steady.

Her breath quickened, and Yuri moaned as she dropped her knees to either side, opening herself to him.

Thargen's hips rocked involuntarily, driven by another increase of pressure in his cock. Just her scent alone was almost enough to make him come. He lifted his head to watch her face as he slid his finger back down to her entrance and pushed it inside her.

Fuck.

Fuck!

His chest rumbled with a low growl. He was barely in past his first knuckle, and her sex had clamped down around his finger hungrily, squeezing to draw him deeper.

Yuri caught her bottom lip between her teeth as her eyes locked with his. "Is, uh, now the time to tell you I've never done this before?"

Thargen strained to keep from strengthening his hold on her wrists as he shoved aside thoughts of what her sex would feel like clamped around his shaft. Hot, wet, and tight; *so* fucking tight. "Not funny, terran."

"I'm not joking." Somehow, her flushed cheeks turned even redder. "I mean, I've had vibrators and whatever, but I've never...*done* anything with anyone."

FUCK!

Rage flooded his body, superheating his blood and swelling his muscles, blanketing his mind in a haze. He held himself still, breath caught in his lungs. His heartbeat was echoing like thunder in his ears.

Control. All comes down to control.

Yuri had never mated with anyone, had never even had anyone else touch her like this. How was that possible? How could a female as beautiful, sexy, kind, funny, and badass as her have never taken a male?

Thargen could be her first. He could lay that claim on her that no one else ever had, could be her *only*, could be her male more fully than he'd ever imagined possible.

All he had to do was give in to the primal urges that were blasting through his lust-fogged mind. All he had to do was push between her thighs and enter her heat. She was right here, willing—more than willing.

The feel of her sex clamped around his finger was a thrill, a tease, a promise of what could be, but it was also a reminder. A warning.

If he gave in, his Rage would take her. And her tight sex, her soft little body, would pay the price for his pleasure. He'd hurt his Yuri. He'd never forgive himself for that.

Yuri wiggled, scooting her ass toward his hand, pushing his finger a little deeper. "I want you, Thargen. I chose you."

And I chose you, too, but I can't have you. How'd we get it so right and so wrong all at once?

In the short time he'd known her—which had been a lifetime already by some measures—she'd come to mean everything to him. He couldn't risk her safety, couldn't bring her pain, not for his own pleasure or any other reason.

Thargen squeezed his eyes shut and finally released the air in his lungs, blowing it through his teeth. Yuri was all that mattered—her safety, yes, but her happiness too. Even if he couldn't give her everything she wanted, he could get close.

His Rage howled inside his mind, railing against his decision, but he wouldn't relent. It had been allowed its outlet today—he'd fed it four skeks. This was between Thargen and Yuri alone. This was *for* Yuri.

He opened his eyes and met her gaze. She looked at him with undisguised yearning, but also with adoration, with affection, with trust. It was that last one that solidified his resolve; he couldn't violate that trust.

Lifting his torso upright, he released her wrists and slipped that hand under her back. Her brow furrowed when he withdrew his finger from her sex to grab the hem of her shirt. Still, she didn't resist when he guided her to sit up, didn't question him when he drew the shirt off over her head, baring her completely to his hungry eyes.

He dropped the shirt onto the ground with the other clothing and lowered Yuri onto her back again before tugging her pants—now wadded up at her ankles—off her feet. The garment was forgotten as soon as he tossed it away.

Thargen stared down at her pale skin, admiring at her curves, which were accented by the deepening twilight shadows and the faint, soft glow of the fire. Her dark hair was spread out around her. Her breasts were full, tipped with bronze nipples, and Thargen's mouth watered for a taste of them.

"You're mine," he growled an instant before he dropped his head and sucked her hardened nipple into his mouth. He twirled his tongue around that bud and sucked harder, taking more of her breast into his mouth as he cupped her sex again, slipping his finger back into her welcoming heat.

Yuri gasped, and her hands flew to his head. She curled her fingers into his hair, nails scraping his scalp, as she arched her back. Her eyelids fluttered closed.

He thrust his finger deeper, pulling it back slightly only to thrust it in again and again until it went as deep as it could.

Thargen released her nipple and moved to the other, giving it the same attention he had the first. Soft, sultry sounds came from Yuri—little mews, whimpers, and moans. Each one drove him to give her more. He thrust his finger into her faster, its passage eased by the sweet-smelling nectar her body released.

When he lifted his head, he looked down at her breasts. Her nipples had darkened, beckoning him to take another taste —but it was her nectar he craved more, that nectar for which he'd hungered for what felt like an eternity. Its scent teased him, and the memory of its flavor on his tongue was potent enough to drive him mad.

Just a taste, he'd told himself before.

But why the fuck would he limit himself to just one?

He wanted to do this slowly, to tease her with pleasure, to make her beg. He wanted to take his time. But he *needed* to have her on his tongue now.

Thargen withdrew his finger from her sex, cupped the back of her knee, and swung her leg to the opposite side of his body, positioning himself between her thighs. He dropped onto his stomach, looped his arms around her legs, and dragged her toward him.

"Thargen, wha—"

He pressed his mouth to her sex and ran his tongue along her slit, lapping up all that sweet nectar.

So. Fucking. Good.

Yuri's breath hitched. Her thighs tensed, and she tried to

squeeze them closed, but Thargen forced them wider with a ragged growl. His lips brushed over her folds, and his tongue delved between them, its tip sliding up to flick across her clit. When she cried out and bucked her hips, he only tightened his hold on her.

The haze of his Rage was nothing compared to the headiness of her nectar. Only two thoughts were coherent through the fog in his mind.

Mine.

More.

YURI PRESSED her lips together and curled them into her mouth, biting down on them to keep from crying out as pleasure unlike anything she'd ever experienced blasted outward from her core. Thargen licked, kissed, and sucked every bit of her sex, and she was helpless, caught in in the trap of his arms. It was torture; it was bliss.

It was ecstasy.

She reached one hand out to him, digging her fingers into his hair. She didn't know whether to push him away or pull him closer. The sensations he was creating within her grew and grew, sending ripples of pleasure throughout her body. Her thighs trembled, her belly fluttered, and her chest heaved with rapid breaths.

Pushing herself up on an elbow, Yuri watched with hooded eyes as his tongue moved ruthlessly over her sex.

The sight of him there, between her thighs, was more erotic than she could have ever imagined. His green fingers with their black nails dug into her pale thighs, and his tusks were cool and hard against her heated flesh, so at odds with his hot, pliable tongue.

Thargen's eyes flicked up and caught hers. His golden gaze

burned with possessiveness, lust, and hunger. He growled and latched onto her clit, sucking hard.

Yuri's lips parted, and she squeezed her eyes shut. Her grip on his hair tightened as she ground her cleft against his mouth. It was as though her body had taken over, moving on instinct, demanding more.

He sucked harder still.

Yuri's arm gave out beneath her, and she writhed in his hold.

It was too much.

It wasn't enough!

Another burst of pleasure made her hips buck wildly, pulling away from his mouth. Thargen dragged her back. His hot breath caressed her sensitive flesh for an instant before his broad tongue licked from her entrance to her clit, which he teased with slow, firm flicks.

"*Mmmf*! Thargen!" she cried, grasping at the clothing wadded beneath her.

Something firm probed her entrance. An instant later, Thargen's finger thrust into her. Yuri moaned and bore down on that thick digit; it was enough to fill her all by itself. It felt so damn good, and she couldn't help but yearn for more. For *him*. To feel his pierced cock push inside her. The thought of it only made her wetter.

"You're so fucking beautiful." Thargen pulled his finger out and circled her entrance with its tip, spreading her essence. When he returned that finger to her opening, it was accompanied by a second; he pressed them into her together.

Yuri's toes curled against his back, and her body tensed as his fingers stretched her.

"That's it, *zoani*." Thargen's rumbling voice sent thrilling vibrations through her. "Take them. Take them into that sweet, tight pussy."

Yuri lifted her head and opened her eyes, looking down her body to meet his gaze again. He grinned and returned his lips to her clit, taking it into his mouth and sucking, teasing it with his tongue.

Every muscle within Yuri quivered. The pressure inside her sex built as he pushed his fingers forward, drawing them back only a little before thrusting them back inside her and spreading them to stretch her wider. The pain was minor compared to the glorious pleasure building inside her.

"Come for me, Yuri. Right into my fucking mouth," he said before sucking her clit back between his lips.

Her head fell back onto the ground. Heat blazed across her every cell. Soon, she was rocking against his hand and mouth, needing his fingers deeper, needing...needing...

Yuri's entire body exploded with sensations she could not describe. She squeezed her eyes shut and tilted her head back farther as a scream built within her throat.

Thargen released one of her legs and clamped his hand over her mouth. Her ragged cry was muffled by his palm as her sex contracted around his fingers. Liquid heat flooded her, and Thargen thrust his fingers faster, harder, deeper, sucking her clit relentlessly throughout. Yuri undulated her sex against his mouth and fingers and grasped his arm in both hands, digging her nails into his skin.

Thargen slipped his fingers out of her, and she whimpered at the emptiness left in their place as spasms continued to roll through her. Not a moment later, his tongue replaced those fingers, delving into her entrance, licking and curling with startling firmness and strength. That clever tongue coaxed another rush of liquid heat from her, and he drank it all down greedily.

Finally, she released her grip on him, letting her arms fall to the sides, and collapsed upon the rumpled clothing. Her thighs trembled in the aftermath, and she twitched with every leisurely flick of Thargen's tongue.

Thargen's hand slid from her mouth to settle around her throat. He rumbled against her and placed a kiss on her clit. "You taste so fucking good, *zoani*." He pressed his nose into her public hair and breathed deeply, causing her to giggle. "Smell good, too."

Yuri hummed. She'd never felt so relaxed. She could've sworn that her body was made of putty, all heavy and mushy. "I can't wait to taste you."

Thargen tensed. He lifted his head, braced an arm on the ground, and pushed himself up onto his knees. The sudden absence of his heat, weight, and nearness had her opening her eyes, confusion further clouding her lust-hazed mind.

His tongue flicked out to run across his lips. "Tough shit, terran. Time for bed."

She skimmed her eyes over his body. He looked bigger, broader, his muscles straining beneath his skin. But it was his thick, hard cock, clearly outlined in his pants, that her gaze fixed upon. She barely noticed the chill from the wind blowing against her naked skin; she wanted him. Now.

She caught her bottom lip between her teeth.

"Fuck, don't give me that look," he said as he stood up—his new position only enhancing the outline of his erection.

Yuri could actually see it throbbing, even in the poor light.

She sat up and held her arms out to him. "Come back to me, Thargen. You know you want to."

He clamped a hand over his shaft and squeezed hard enough to make his knuckles go pale, hissing through his teeth. His jaw ticked, and the reflection of the firelight in his eyes was suddenly brighter—suddenly wilder.

Yuri spread her thighs, calling Thargen's eyes to her sex. "I want you, Thargen. And I know you want me, too."

His chest swelled with a slow, deep breath. When he released it through his clenched teeth, he stepped closer to her and sank into a crouch. Yuri smiled and placed her hands on his shoulders, brushing her fingers over his solid muscle. Thargen's hands encircled her waist. Her heart fluttered with anticipation, and all she could do was stare into his eyes, basking in his heat.

Before she understood what was happening, he was lifting her off the ground and standing up. He threw her over his shoulder, wrapped an arm around her legs, and gave her ass a sharp *smack*.

Yuri shrieked and swiftly covered her mouth to silence the sound. It wasn't that the slap had hurt—well, maybe it had stung, but it was a *good* sting that only made her wetter—but more that it had surprised her.

"Thargen! What are you doing?" she demanded, bracing her hands on his back. Her already dark world was made even more so by the curtain of hair hanging around her face.

"I said time for bed, terran. Guess I should've specified I meant to sleep."

"But what about—" She bit off her words when he smacked her other ass cheek. This time, he soothed it with his palm afterward. Whatever his intentions, he was making her anything but sleepy. Every time he struck her backside, her sex clenched, and fresh heat flooded her.

Was she seriously getting turned on by being spanked?

She never, ever would have thought that'd be something she was into, but here she was, her ass sticking up in the air, still pulsing with the sting of the last slap, craving more.

Thargen crouched again, but he didn't let her down. She brushed the hair out of her face with one hand to see him quickly gathering the clothing she'd spread on the ground—and the clothing he'd taken off her.

"You're serious?" she asked.

"I'm always serious."

Yuri snorted. She couldn't help it. His response had been a bald-faced lie.

"Okay, so maybe that's a slight exaggeration," he grumbled as he rose and strode toward the cave, "but yeah, I'm serious. Gotta rest while we can."

"What about once we get settled in the cave?"

"Sleep."

Yuri groaned loud and dramatically. "What's a girl gotta do to get some orc dick? I'm dying here. A virgin death. How sad is that?"

Thargen snickered and turned his face to kiss her hip. "I'll spear you with my tongue again."

"I'd rather you spear me with your cock," she said as he entered the darkness of the cave.

This time, he groaned, strengthening his hold on her. "Survival situation, *zoani*. Take what you can get and be grateful."

Yuri reached down and slapped his ass.

"Fuck!" he snapped, his hips jolting forward.

"Be grateful."

"I think I just came."

Yuri buried her face against his back and laughed.

"Don't see why you're laughing," he said. "You just lost whatever chance you had. I'm spent."

"I never took you for being a liar." As if to prove it, she stretched her foot down until the tips of her toes grazed his erection.

He grunted, released a huff of air, and crouched again. Yuri heard fabric rustling in the dark but couldn't see anything.

"You're gonna be the death of me, terran. At least it'll be a fuck of a lot sweeter than the one I always imagined."

She ran her fingers over his back, tracing the contours of his muscles and the lines of his scars by touch. Just the thought of something happening to him—of him getting hurt or dying—sobered her up. They'd already gone through so much, and they weren't safe yet.

"Nothing is going to happen to you," she said softly.

Thargen gently set Yuri on her feet. His hands moved up to cup her cheeks, thumbs stroking her skin. "You already happened to me, *zoani*. Nothing else matters."

SIXTEEN

Yuri awoke to find weak gray light coming in through the mouth of the cave—it was enough to make the opening distinguishable from the dark stone around it, but only just. She blinked the sleep away from her eyes. She was lying on her side with Thargen's body curled around her from behind, his heavy arm wrapped around her, and his leg thrown over hers.

He'd carried her into the cave last night, forced a shirt over her head, and left her to gather the rest of their belongings and put out the fire. The shirt hadn't been enough to ward off the chill in the night air—that was until he'd returned to her, lying down and pulling her into the wonderous heat of his body.

She hadn't thought the insatiable lust coursing through her body and clouding her mind would allow her to sleep while she was tucked against him. All she'd been able to focus on was the oddly heavy emptiness between her legs, the rasp of fabric against her sensitive nipples, and his hard, twitching cock against her back.

Exhaustion must have caught up with her eventually.

But now...

She was wide awake, and her body reacted immediately to his nearness, his heady, honeyed amber scent, and the feel of his shaft—which was as hard as ever and pressed insistently into the curve of her ass.

Yuri grinned and, ever so carefully, turned in his arms until she was facing him. She could just barely make out Thargen's features in the gloom. His brow creased, and he tightened his hold on her, drawing her closer.

That was all right; she could work with that. The vorgal was being stubborn about his own arousal, and she didn't know why when it clearly caused him pain so much of the time. This morning, she'd just take matters into her own hands—literally.

She flattened her palm on his abdomen and smoothed it down his body, slipping it beneath the snug waistband of his pants. Her fingertips brushed the head of his cock. She sucked in a sharp breath, flicking her gaze up to his face. Thargen didn't stir.

Biting her bottom lip, she ran her fingers over the blunt, round head and along the slit at its tip. There was already moisture gathered there. Using her thumb, she smeared it around the rim.

Yuri eased her hand farther into his pants, sliding her palm down his shaft and over the little bumps of his piercings until she reached his root. She curled her fingers around him; her hand couldn't even fully encircle his girth. His pulse throbbed against her palm.

Watching his face, she stroked his cock from its base up to the first of his studded piercings, keeping her grip firm and her movements slow and steady. He felt *so* good. He was hot tristeel covered in soft velvet. Her sex clenched, and she squeezed her thighs together. What would it be like to have his length inside her, to feel his strength as he pumped in and out of her body?

Yuri imagined him between her thighs, thrusting his powerful hips, taking her, claiming her as his.

She wanted that. She wanted that so damned much.

Thargen's lips drew back to bare his teeth. A low growl rumbled from his chest, vibrating into Yuri and teasing her nipples, which were tender from his attentions last night. He shifted his arm, clutched her bare ass, and began pumping his hips in time with her hand.

The head of his cock bumped into her belly with every thrust, coating her with his seed. If his leg weren't draped over both of hers, trapping them, all she would've needed to do was hitch her thigh over his hips and open herself to him—then he'd be there, right there, where she needed him most.

Thargen's grip on her ass tightened. Ragged breaths huffed out of him as he quickened his pace, thrusting harder and harder into her hand, and another growl rumbled his chest. That bestial sound only made her wetter.

Thargen's eyes snapped open, gleaming with faint reflections of the weak light. Before Yuri could react, before she could so much as smile at him, he snarled and burst into motion, quick as lightning.

She was on her back in an instant, and Thargen was looming over her. He wedged his hips between her thighs, forcing her legs apart, and tore down his pants with one hand, finally freeing his cock. His other hand caught her by the throat, pinning her down.

But it was the feel of his thick cock shoving into her that made Yuri stiffen and gasp. He stretched her inner walls, evoking a sharp, stinging burn. Those piercings felt so much larger inside her than they looked as her too tight sex clenched around him.

His teeth were bared, his brows sharply angled down, and his nostrils flared, and his intense, wild eyes were fixated on

Yuri. The gloom only made his visage more savage. He looked down at her as though he wasn't there, as though he didn't know who she was. She had the sense that she might've been staring into the eyes of a beast.

Yuri placed one hand on the arm he was using to pin her and settled the other on his chest, over his pounding heart. "Thargen?"

Thargen stilled. He blinked, and his eyes ran over her with quick, erratic movements. They cleared slowly, the reflected light in them softening, but his expression didn't ease. When he glanced down at his cock, and Yuri followed his gaze with hers. He had his fist clamped around its base—firmly enough that it was trembling. Her sex clenched around him again, eager to draw him in deeper.

For a moment, the hand around her throat squeezed harder, and he shut his eyes, bucking his hips and pushing himself farther into her. Her breath hitched, and she dug her nails into his arm.

"*Fuck*," he growled, shoving away as quickly as he'd mounted her. Just like that, his hand was no longer on her throat, his hips no longer between her thighs, and his shaft had withdrawn from her sex. All physical contact broken in an instant.

She snapped her thighs together reflexively, but it did nothing to ease the empty feeling left in Thargen's wake.

Yuri rolled onto her side, propped herself up, and watched Thargen—reduced to a big, dark silhouette by the gray dawn light—storm out of the cave.

She stared at the opening long after his form had disappeared, speechless, motionless.

Numb.

No, that wasn't right. There was a terrible ache in her chest, one that spread with every passing second. Her eyes stung, and the light from outside became a blur as tears filled her vision.

"What's *wrong* with me?"

Yuri took in a shaky breath, sat up, and drew her knees to her chest, wrapping her arms around her legs. She didn't understand. She was confused. She was...

Hurt.

Every sign, every look, every word from Thargen was proof of his attraction to her—that he *wanted* her. So why hadn't he taken her? Why hadn't he, after all the times she'd made it known that she wanted him in return? Oh, he'd touch her, kiss her, lick her. But...fuck her?

She recalled all the ways he'd changed the subject or denied her, and the pain in her chest only intensified.

A short, humorless laugh bubbled up from her throat, and she wiped her eyes with her palms, shaking her head. "I finally decide on a guy I want to have sex with, and he doesn't want to have sex with me. Go figure. Just my luck."

But it was more than sex. She wanted him to be hers. Hadn't Thargen claimed her as his, as well? Hadn't he even said *mine* the night before?

What's wrong with me?

Yuri dropped her hands and frowned as she looked at the cave entrance again.

Maybe it wasn't about what was wrong with her, but what was wrong with Thargen. What if there was something troubling him, some hang up or past trauma that had left an invisible scar on him? Something he hadn't told her...

Whatever it was, Yuri wasn't going to give up. She was going to find out what was keeping him from fully taking her, what was making him run from her—though she had a sense that it was more about him running from himself, somehow.

And once she knew, she'd help him work through it so they could be together.

Yuri groaned and fell back onto the pallet of rumpled clothing, staring up at the dark cave ceiling.

She wasn't going to let this keep happening. She wasn't going to let their relationship turn into some stupid, overly dramatic romance story where the only thing keeping the leads apart was a lack of communication. She didn't care how big or bad he was—she'd get him to talk about his emotions, damn it.

"I'm yours, Thargen, and I'm going to make you understand that you're also mine." Muttering under her breath, she added, "And I refuse to die a virgin."

THARGEN STALKED AWAY from the cave, eyes open but unseeing. His skin was taut and hot, his muscles tense and thrumming with unspent energy, and—above all else—his cock and balls were throbbing with an ache so deep and pervasive that he could focus on little else.

Rage and pressure—they had become his existence. The former demanded he turn around and finish what had begun in the cave. He could almost feel her tight, wet sex clamped around his cock, creating pleasure so pure and powerful it hurt.

It *still* fucking hurt. Even the hand currently grasping his shaft provided no relief. His seed was hot as magma, and his cock was a volcano that had been building pressure for a million years—well fucking overdue for an eruption.

He was going to explode.

Thargen staggered to an abrupt halt, dropping his shoulder against the rough bark of a tree trunk. His limbs trembled, and his ragged breaths were just as shaky, coming out through his bared teeth in hissing snarls.

He could turn around and be back in the cave within a few seconds. He could be back in her heat...

Growling, he strengthened his grip on his shaft. His knees buckled against a surge of that tortuous, thrilling pressure, and only the tree held him upright.

Rage roared in his head, unleashing a sound of such fury and unbridled desire that it threatened to shatter his mind. It wanted the same things as him—Yuri and release—but those things were one in the same to his Rage.

He pressed his left hand over his abdomen, dug his nails in, and dragged them across his skin. The pain, dulled by Rage, offered no clarity.

Thargen growled again and pumped his fist along his shaft.

A shuddering breath escaped his lungs. The sensation was overwhelming, pleasure and pain coiled together so intricately they could not be distinguished from one another, and it wasn't at all what he craved. It wasn't at all what he needed. The phantom sensation of Yuri's sex around his shaft resurged, taunting him, further rousing his Rage and building that impossible pressure even higher.

She was so close...

But so was Thargen.

He stroked his cock quickly, mercilessly, fueling his arm with all his frustration and longing. His hips bucked to match the wild rhythm of his hand. The ache in his groin only grew further, becoming as massive and dense as a fucking star. Thargen squeezed his eyes shut and moved his fist faster still.

Yuri's face appeared in his mind's eye, her half-lidded eyes gleaming with lust, her cheeks flushed, her lips kiss swollen. She spread her supple thighs, offering her sex with its glistening pink petals and sweet nectar.

His body shook, rocked by spasms from head to toe, perched on the edge of that ultimate release. So fucking close, this whole time so fucking close... The pressure consumed Thargen, strengthening the tremors coursing through him, heightening his desperation, threatening to drop him to his knees.

He felt her sex around his shaft, tight, hot, smooth, and slick—unlike anything he'd ever imagined, better than anything he'd ever experienced.

Thargen's muscles seized, and a raw growl tore from his chest, clawed up his throat, and escaped through his clenched teeth. A heartbeat later, he finally exploded. Thick streams of seed sprayed from his cock, pushed by waves of unbearable pleasure. He couldn't stop the movements of his hands and hips. No matter how good it felt, no matter how much it hurt, he couldn't stop.

His legs gave out. He fell to one knee, scraping his shoulder on the bark, without missing a stroke.

When his spasms finally eased and his twitching cock was no longer spurting, Thargen stopped his hand. He leaned more heavily against the tree and bowed his head, panting. His throbbing pulse served as a reminder that all he'd done here was release a little pressure. He hadn't satisfied any cravings, hadn't appeased his Rage.

Even with the immediacy worked away, his cock ached for Yuri.

And he'd almost fucking had her a few minutes ago.

"Fuck," he rasped, lifting his head only to tip it against the trunk. Slowly, he opened his fist and moved it away from his shaft. His fingers were stiff, and the muscles along his forearm ached with strain. His hand was slick with seed. He let his arm fall to his side as he caught his breath and willed his heart to slow.

What had happened back in the cave should've been ecstasy. He couldn't think of a better way to wake than with

Yuri's hand—or her mouth—on his cock. But he'd fucked it up, just like he'd known he would, just like he did most things outside of winning fights. He'd fucked it up because he was broken, because he had no control. Because of Rage. It wouldn't settle for a handjob or a blowjob. It wouldn't be satisfied with merely tasting her, no matter how much pleasure he gave her in the process.

Maybe his biggest mistake had been in thinking *he* could be satisfied with those little tastes, too—in pretending Rage was a separate entity rather than something that had become an integral part of him.

He clenched his jaw as Yuri's cry of pain echoed in his mind. The sound had been small, easily forgotten or barely noticeable outside the context, but it had broken through to Thargen's buried consciousness, had pierced that veil of lust and Rage that had roused him from his slumber. His awareness had faded in over the course of several seconds, and his mind had pieced together the scene with building horror.

His Yuri, his sweet, soft little terran, had been under him, and he'd been inside her, and she'd been so, so tight. So much so that he'd hurt her just by entering. And he knew he would've kept going. He would've pushed deeper, deeper, as deep as he could go and then more, and he would've done it fast and hard because that was the way he did everything—especially when Rage was at the forefront.

Had my fucking hand around her throat...

Thargen's fingers twitched at the memory of being closed around her delicate neck. A little rough play was fine—it was, in fact, exciting—but he could've harmed her so easily, could've crushed her fucking windpipe if he'd squeezed just a little harder.

All those what-ifs he normally ignored assaulted him now, battering his already wounded mind as relentlessly as he'd battered his cock a few moments ago. They bore down upon him with immense, crushing weight, like boulders in a rockslide.

If Yuri's reaction hadn't shattered that haze, he would've ravaged her body. At the very least, she would've been bloodied and bruised by the end. And the worst case...

Even Thargen, with more bodies piled behind him than he could ever count, couldn't bring himself to reflect upon that worst-case scenario.

Maybe back on Arthos they could find some way, but out here... If he hurt her, he had neither the resources nor the knowledge to help her. He knew terrans could be tough as hell, that they could take a surprising amount of punishment, but he also knew they were just as prone to being fragile.

This had to stop.

Everything inside him roared in displeasure, creating a violent chorus led by Rage, as he forced himself to stand up on shaky legs. He flattened his hand against the tree to steady himself. His nostrils flared with a deep breath; he tried to ignore the fact that her scent, clinging to his skin, permeated the air and was overpowering every other smell that should've taken prominence.

Resisting Yuri was the most difficult challenge of his life, and it would have remained so even if she weren't throwing herself at him constantly. But failure was not an option. His priorities were the same as they'd been this whole time—keep her safe, get her home.

Thargen wasn't like his friends. He didn't have Arcanthus's cleverness and focus, didn't have Urgand's stability and calm, didn't have Drakkal's patience and ability to see the larger picture. All he had was a body built for war and his Rage. If he meant to protect Yuri and get her back to Arthos, he needed to throw everything he had at those goals.

He finally opened his eyes. Little spots danced across his vision; he shook his head sharply and blinked to clear them away. Twisting, he looked back at the cave. Only darkness greeted him from within...but he knew Yuri was in there, too.

His cock pulsed, as though eager to return to her.

Thargen curled his hand into a fist—only to be reminded of the now-sticky seed coating it. His balls already felt heavy with another load. At this rate, he'd blast through all the protein from last night's meal in a few hours of jerking himself off. That was definitely an elite-tier survival strategy if he'd ever heard one.

He couldn't trust himself to go back to her yet, especially not in this state. What the fuck would he say?

Sorry, Yuri, but I just thought the forest needed it more than you. Been looking dry out here.

Yeah, calling this a fuckup would be an understatement.

Focus, asshole. You have a lot of other shit to worry about at the moment.

And yet none of those other concerns—almost all life or death matters—felt as immediate, pressing, or dire as his need for Yuri. How did that make any damned sense? Why, if presented with the choice to eat or fuck, did he feel such a heavy pull toward the second option?

"This is your problem right here," he muttered. "All this fucking thinking."

He pushed away from the tree, meaning to walk to the river to clean himself up and cool off—he'd freeze his dick into flaccidity if that was what it took—but his feet refused to move, and his gaze lingered on the mouth of the cave. Everything inside him was all tight and hot and uncomfortable.

Thargen swore he'd figure out a way to kick himself in the balls if he didn't get moving.

Fortunately, his body received the message. He strode away

from the cave, forcing his eyes to ceaselessly scan his surroundings for signs of danger, while trying—and failing—to ignore the tingling itch on his back that intensified with his every step away from Yuri.

Going out unarmed and leaving her alone again. That skeks hit you harder on the head than you thought?

Shut the fuck up already. I've heard more than enough of your shit.

The ensuing silence in his head was restless and uneasy, soured by the maelstrom roiling just beneath the surface, but he accepted it, nonetheless. At least that silence made it easier to pay attention to the environment.

When he reached the river, he tore off his pants and waded in. The cold water was a welcome shock to his heated body, sending a shiver up his spine and finishing off his ailing erection. He submerged himself fully for a few seconds. The quiet but consuming sound of water flowing around him was almost soothing—*almost*. Deep down, he knew there'd be no extinguishing the fires that Yuri had lit in his heart. All he'd ever have were temporary releases of pressure, and those would always have to come at his own hand.

He scrubbed himself clean after surfacing and returned to the shore, pausing as he reached the bank. Something stood out amidst the mud, stones, and tufts of red grass—something pale. He crouched and dug up the object, expecting a stone unlike the rest in its color. But he knew as soon as he pulled it from the muck that it was no stone; it was an egg, as wide as his palm and almost perfectly round, with a solid, slightly yellow shell covered in little blue spots. A bit more careful digging turned up five more of the eggs buried just under the surface.

Thargen rinsed them off and set them aside to pull on his pants. This was good—an unexpected meal that had required no effort. He was still annoyed with himself about the meat from yesterday. He'd had to throw so much of it away because there'd been no time to dry it out or smoke it and he hadn't wanted to leave it near camp for fear of attracting other predators—including skeks.

Whatever, Thargen. You had time. You just wanted her more, and since you couldn't have her, you forced yourself to go to sleep.

Pretty sure I told you to shut up.

He returned to camp with the eggs cradled in the crook of his arm. Yuri wasn't outside when he arrived.

He'd need to get the fire going again, and it would be wise to put on a shirt to help them both avoid temptation, but he wanted to show her the surprise haul first. She deserved something to be happy about after he'd stormed out on her, and breakfast was the perfect thing.

"I'm back, terran," Thargen called as he neared the cave. He heard a whisper of movement from within.

A smirk tilted his lips; he could almost picture her standing just inside, holding up a big stick in both hands—ready to give him the beating he deserved. But that image wouldn't fully form. That wasn't his Yuri.

Fuck, do I really have any right to consider her mine after this?

The answer blasted through his mind in a Rage-backed shout.

Fuck yeah, you do!

Thargen stepped into the cave, eyes quickly adjusting to the gloom. He found her sitting cross-legged on their pallet with the backpacks open beside her and their supplies arranged on the floor, organized by purpose. His gaze flicked to her thighs; she'd put on a pair of pants while he was gone. Despite everything, he was hit by a pang of disappointment. He longed to see her bare flesh whether it was good for him or not.

She looked up, and her face instantly brightened with a smile. "You're back. Is...everything okay?"

For all that fucking thinking he'd done, he seemed to have forgotten the effects of her smile; that simple curling of her sweet lips was nearly enough to shatter his resolve. "About as okay as it can be while I'm stranded on an alien world. You all right?"

She pursed her lips and moved them to the side as she looked up and hummed. Her eyes sparked with a sudden heat as they returned to him, trailing up and down his body before they locked with his. "Hungry. Maybe a little...*thirsty*."

Ah, shit.

Play it dumb?

"Well, I found some eggs"—he lifted his arm to show her—"and two of those canteens should still be full."

Yuri's eyes rounded, and she pushed herself to her feet. As she approached him, she asked, "You found eggs?"

Thargen's stomach knotted, and he found himself battling the sudden urge to retreat.

What the fuck is wrong with me? I'm no damned coward, and I'm not scared of this little terran.

That only enhanced the sick feeling in his gut. He'd run from her twice already, hadn't he? He'd tucked his dick between his legs and fled. Maybe he wasn't afraid of her, but he was terrified of what she made him feel—and of what would happen if he gave in.

He stood his ground, feeling more like a fool and a coward than ever. "Don't, uh...know if they're any good."

"I was going to ask if you knew what they were, but..." She laid her hand on his forearm as she inspected the eggs. "They're pretty. Kind of like *Easter* eggs."

His skin tingled under her touch. How long did he expect

himself to hold out when the simplest, most innocent bits of contact had this effect on him?

"What's *Easter*?" he asked.

She grinned up at him. "Sorry. It's an Earth holiday that usually fell close to the start of spring. My dad would take us all up to this old cabin he had in the mountains. It wasn't much, and he usually didn't let us use any electronics while we were up there, but we always had so much fun there. We'd paint eggs and craft little baskets and stuff. Most people would do egg hunts for kids, too, where they'd hide eggs and treats for kids to run around and find."

Thargen chuckled and shook his head. "Every time I get used to you, you remind me just how weird you terrans are. A place in the mountains sounds nice, though. Guess we kinda have that right now, don't we?"

"Yeah, I guess we do." She glanced around the cave before returning her attention to the eggs. "Well, let's hope they taste good and that there aren't any creepy alien parasites in them." Her smile fell, her nose wrinkled, and she shuddered. "Ugh. You get first taste."

That word, *taste...* Fuck if it hadn't taken on a whole new meaning for him.

"Fair enough, *zoani*."

Yuri eased a little closer, enough so that her body brushed against his side. She lifted her hand from his arm, caught his chin, and forced him to look at her. "And you can tell me what's going on while you cook them."

Fuck.

She searched his eyes, lips falling into a frown. "I know there's something wrong, something that's keeping you from, well...from having sex with me. Don't think I didn't notice." Her frown flipped into a smirk. "I mean, how could I *not* notice? It's pretty hard to miss that club in your pants, and I've been pretty open about how much I want you. Like, it doesn't get much more blatant than me saying, *I want you, Thargen.*"

He released a heavy breath through his nostrils. This wasn't a conversation he wanted to have right now, and he knew how it would end—he'd still want her desperately, and she'd want him despite the potential danger. But didn't she deserve an explanation? Didn't she deserve some openness from him? Maybe he was only good at fighting, but he ran his mouth all the fucking time. Wasn't he at least capable of *talking?*

There was nothing to fear. He just had to talk, and he knew she would hear him out. Didn't mean she'd agree or understand, but it was something. And if nothing else, it had a tiny chance of improving their current situation.

"All right, terran," he finally said. "Get our shit packed up while I get the fire going."

She nodded. "Okay."

He let his gaze linger on her for a moment before he stepped away, stopping only to snatch his belt off the floor before he went outside and set to work.

Yuri joined him shortly after he had the eggs cooking beside the fire, which he'd kept small. She passed Thargen one of the two canteens she was holding and sat beside him. He could almost feel her body heat against his skin.

Shirt. I was supposed to put on a damned shirt.

"Now spill it," she said firmly.

Staring at her, he opened the canteen and slowly tilted it.

Yuri laughed. "What are you doing?"

"Following orders, terran."

"I didn't mean to literally spill"—she waved a hand at the canteen—"it. I meant, start talking."

Thargen grunted, shoulders sagging. "Yeah, I know. Just stalling."

She frowned again. "Why? I mean, I don't want to pry if you really don't want to tell me, but... I'm confused, Thargen, and a little hurt. I'd like to understand."

Even if she'd said he'd only hurt her a little, it struck him harder than that fucking onigox smuggler could have. He'd been trying to stop himself from hurting her only to cause her a different kind of pain in the process.

"Sorry, *zoani*." He turned his gaze to the fire pit, staring as though it could provide him with the right words, as though it could suddenly make him more articulate. "It's just...not something I've ever talked about. It's not anything my people really talk about. Vorgals have this...I don't even know what you'd call it. I mean, my tribe's old word for it is *Hruk*, but I don't..."

He shook his head and let out a huff of air. "I just don't really know how to explain it. I can swear in twenty languages without a translator, but this shit is over my head."

Yuri brushed her fingers over his arm before folding her hands in her lap. "Just do your best. Try to explain, and I'll try to understand."

Her gentle encouragement eased away the frustration that had started building in him, and he was more grateful for it than ever.

"All right, terran. Vorgals have had *Hruk* for as long as we can remember, but most people call it Rage these days. It's like...our *thing*, I guess. I don't remember the little bit they teach us when we're young, not that it would be all that helpful. It's kind of an emotion, and an instinct, and this...primal force that lives in us. It's really all hormones or brain chemicals or some shit, but they say everything is, right?

"What I do know is that it made us the alphas on our planet. It pushed us until all we had left to fight was each other, and it took a long time for us to overcome that. And Rage fucks with our biology, or biochemistry, or whatever, fucks with our minds. Dulls pain receptors, enhances strength, reflexes, and senses, kills our sense of self-preservation. Everything comes down to fighting and fucking when it's in control."

Thargen absently lifted a hand, running his fingers over the scars on the side of his head. "Our civilization likes to pretend we've evolved past it. And we have, in civilian life. Most people don't have to fight with Rage much, and there are drugs to suppress it for those who do. But in the military, they use the *shit* out of *Hruk*. They enhance it in us, make it stronger, pump us with chems to make it last longer and burn hotter.

"And we're all told going in what it may do to us. We all know, even if people on the streets don't really talk about it. It's the cost we accept when we choose to fight for our people, when we choose to follow those old warrior traditions. Those drugs, being high on Rage all the time—and when we're campaigning, we're running on that shit nonstop—it adds up. It becomes...an addiction, but it's one you can't kick without keeping yourself medicated into sedation. Your body gets to the point where its building *Hruk* all the time, and if you don't let it out, it's gonna find its own fucking way out."

Yuri's brows furrowed. "It sounds kind of like an adrenaline rush, though adrenaline in humans usually doesn't have as powerful an effect as what you go through. Your *Hruk* is...well, pretty fittingly, it's like a berserker rage in those VR games I played. There's...no reversing it? It's either sedation or you just deal with it?"

He nodded. "And I chose to just deal with it. Usually, I can. I have plenty of outlets, and if they fail me, I can always go to a bar and get into a fight."

Yuri caught her bottom lip with her teeth briefly and looked at the fire. "What about...sex?"

"Vorgal military is unisex." He leaned forward and checked the eggs through the holes in the tops of their shells, moving them away from the fire one by one as he continued. "And after battle, there's a lot of fucking, all of it on Rage. I tried a few times when I moved to Arthos. But even when I did something to vent beforehand"—his lips peeled back in a cringe—"fucking Rage always fired up, and things always got rough. Some species can take that. But the last one...she was small. Small enough to make me hesitate, but she wanted it. And...fuck, it was too much for her. Too rough. She was a volturian."

"Was?"

Thargen drew back, his brows slamming down as he turned his face toward Yuri. "*Is* a volturian. I didn't fucking kill her or anything. But...that's not saying much. Everything started out fine, we were into it, until she bit me, and Rage took over. I think she started screaming and struggling, but it was all fuzzy, like it was happening somewhere else. I just thought she was enjoying it, you know? All I could focus on was..."

He cleared his throat. "By the time I came, she'd stopped fighting. She was crying when I shook off the haze. I had her pinned face down, and a lot of her bruises were in the shape of my hands. Her knees were scraped up from the floor, too."

"And you think that'll happen to me?" Yuri asked.

"I *know* it will. She was a delicate little thing, and you're even smaller than her, Yuri. And she took that *after* I'd already let off a lot of Rage."

She was silent for a time, her eyes searching his. Then she rose on her knees, reached out, and cupped his face in her hands. "I'm stronger than I look, Thargen. You won't break me." She stroked his cheeks with her thumbs. "You'd never hurt me."

Her gentle touch, paired with the soft sincerity of her words, wrapped around his heart and squeezed. She trusted him so completely, so unquestioningly. But he didn't have a fraction of that trust in himself. He couldn't share in those beliefs; such hope would only lead to mistakes—and damage—that couldn't be undone.

He settled one of his hands over one of hers. "I've hurt everyone I know at least once, Yuri. And if I hurt you out here, there's no one to help. I can kill just about anything, but I don't know how to heal."

"Thargen—"

"Not taking the chance, *zoani*," he growled. "Not with you." He guided her hand down from his face, turned it to press a kiss onto her palm, and then placed one of the eggs atop it. "Now eat. We got work to do today."

SEVENTEEN

Five days passed in the blink of an eye, though they'd felt like
the longest days of Yuri's life when taken one at a time. She
loved every moment she spent around Thargen—which was
more or less *every* moment. Sure, they'd been hard at work,
doing all sorts of survivalist type stuff that Yuri was slowly
starting to pick up on, but all that hadn't distracted her from the
questions growing increasingly louder in her mind.

Would they be all right? Would they find a way off this
planet? Was Takashi okay, and had he told their parents that
she was missing? Were *they* freaking out? What would happen
if they were here long enough to experience winter on this
planet? How many skeks were out there?

Was it possible for a person to die from sexual frustration?

Because Yuri felt like she was going to die. Despite
Thargen endeavoring to keep some distance between them
whenever possible during their days, he held her every night—
not that *held* seemed like the right word. It was more like he
locked her against him, her back to his chest with his arm
banded around her torso and his legs thrown over hers, barely

giving her any leeway to move. And damn if she didn't like it as much as she was frustrated by it.

Even though their bodies were pressed together, he wouldn't let her *touch* him, and he hadn't been intimate with her since that first night in the cave. No matter how she tried to persuade him—subtly, blatantly, quietly or loudly, he didn't budge. She could see the battle in his eyes, but he held firm— just like the cock he wouldn't let her have!

Yuri understood his fear. She really, really did. His experience with that volturian had shaken him. But she honestly believed he wouldn't hurt her. Every time she'd made a sound of discomfort or pain, every time she touched him, or spoken his name, he always snapped out of what he'd called *Hruk*—his Rage.

Even when he'd mounted her and put his hand around her throat, he hadn't really hurt her. Yeah, his cock was big, and there'd been discomfort while her body stretched to accommodate him—which is absolutely normal considering she was a virgin—but everything had been fine. In truth, his reaction had turned her the hell on. Even his hand clutching her neck. Yuri *liked* him overpowering her. Freaking *loved* it.

Which wasn't to say she didn't take his story about the volturian seriously. As much as Yuri didn't want to think about her vorgal with another woman, she could imagine that the experience must've been frightening and traumatic for the volturian, especially if it had been unexpected. Yuri had seen Thargen's Rage build over days and days, but she'd also seen it ignite in an instant; it was a volatile force.

Clearly, it had been bad for the volturian, and Thargen had taken that to heart, had accepted it as proof that he was damaged. As confident as he was, he didn't trust himself. Yuri felt for that faceless volturian—but Yuri wasn't that woman.

She still wanted Thargen regardless of the risk he thought he posed to her.

Right now, as Yuri followed Thargen through the trees, her gaze was practically glued to his ass. He had such a fine ass. It was round and toned, and his snug pants hugged it like a second skin. All Yuri wanted to do was reach out and cup it in her hands. Maybe even smack it.

The memory of him slapping her ass sent a spear of arousal straight to her core. She wanted to feel that sting again, wanted the rush of heat that would follow, wanted the soothing palm of his hand rubbing her tender flesh to ease away the lingering pain.

Yuri rolled her eyes and barely held in her groan. Even her damned nipples were aching.

I am seriously going to die.

Fuck me.

Just ahead, Thargen knelt to check something on the ground—a set of tracks, probably. The position only pulled the fabric around his ass tighter.

Fuck me, please?

After a moment, he huffed and stood up. "We'll check a few more traps and head back. It'll be getting dark soon."

It felt like traps had taken over their days—large ones and small ones, all of them crude and simplistic, some made to catch game, but most meant for bigger prey. For people. She and Thargen had set more traps than she could count in the area around their cave.

No, that was wrong; she *could* count them, right in her head. Thargen had made her help with every trap, had made her memorize their locations and triggers. He'd said he wanted her to be able to walk through the woods in the dark without setting off a single trap.

Thargen had become obsessed with keeping the cave

protected—with keeping *her* protected. That mission seemed to have become the outlet for all his frustration and discomfort. Despite how tired he should have been, he never showed signs of slowing, not even while he was digging in tough, root-tangled dirt or slicing chunks of wood with one of the hardlight axes.

When he glanced at Yuri over his shoulder, she offered him a playful smile. "We could stop by the river and get naked first."

Yuri refused to give up. She wanted him, and damn it, she was determined to make him hers.

His shoulders stiffened, his nostrils flared, and his lips pressed together firmly. "We could. And I could run my hands over your body slowly, washing away all the dirt and sweat, making sure every last bit of you was clean." He turned away and kept walking—not at all in the direction of the river. "But we're not. Get your ass moving, terran."

"Hey!" Yuri picked up her pace, having to take two or three steps for every one of his. "Are you saying I stink? And I am not covered in sweat and dirt."

"Then we really don't need to go to the river."

Damn it.

"Wait! I lied," Yuri hurried to say. "I'm filthy. I'm in dire need of a bath. You'll need to run those hands all over me. My breasts, my ass, between my—"

Halting abruptly, Thargen spun to face Yuri, wrapped her in his arms, and swept her into a kiss that had her dipping backward, supported only by him. Her eyes flared before fluttering shut, and she kissed him back. Surrounded by his heat and strength, powerless against his hungry mouth, she lost all sense of where she was and what was happening. Feeling was enough.

And damn, he felt good—smelled and tasted good, too.

Prickles of awareness skittered along her skin, and pleasure coursed down her spine straight to her core. That needful ache only intensified, leaving her slick between her thighs. She moaned against his mouth, nipping at his bottom lip as her hands clutched the waistband of his pants.

Just as quickly as he'd initiated it, Thargen broke the kiss, pulling his mouth away. When she moved to follow, one of his hands caught her hair, holding her head in place.

She opened her eyes to look up at him just as his tongue swept across his lower lip. Fire danced in his eyes.

"That's all you get, terran."

Son of a—

Yuri glared at Thargen. "Oh, you're playing so dirty, vorgal."

His smirk was equal parts wicked and tortured. "That makes two of us."

"I can show you dirty." Grinning, she slipped her hand into his pants.

Thargen growled and pulled her hard against him, trapping her hand between their pelvises before it could get any farther.

She chuckled. "Or you could put your hand in my pants and feel how hot and wet I am for you instead."

He sighed heavily, and a faint tremor ran through his arms. He dropped his face into the crook of her neck and shoulder and breathed deep. "Fuck, Yuri, you—"

Somewhere not far off, branches snapped and vegetation shook in a burst of sound. Thargen's head jerked up, his body going rigid, and Yuri's racing heart skipped a beat. Before silence could settle in to reassure her that there was nothing out there, that all was well, that it had only been an old, dead branch falling, someone screamed in pain.

Her eyes widened, locking with Thargen's. Those sounds had come from downriver—the direction from which they'd fled the crashed ship, the direction in which they'd laid the majority of their larger traps.

"Was that one of the pits?" she whispered; even that felt too loud now.

Thargen straightened, tipping Yuri upright, and turned his head toward the disturbance. "Yeah."

She'd felt useless while he'd dug those deep pits. The ground had been too tough for her to make much progress, even with the shovel they'd taken from the skeks days ago. But she'd done her part by gathering long branches and clumps of foliage to conceal the holes—and by sharpening some thick sticks for him to stick in the ground at the bottoms of those pits.

Sticks that would easily puncture flesh when someone fell in.

A horrifying thought chilled Yuri's blood, making her shiver. "Thargen, what if that was one of the slaves? What if we—"

He pressed a big finger over her lips. "Shh."

Another cry rose between the trees, not as loud but just as pained. Even less distinct was the voice that answered it a moment later, too faint for Yuri to make out the words. Thargen's pointed ears twitched.

Yuri could just make out the babbling of the river, which was steady beneath the sound of the breeze sighing through the trees, and, from somewhere out of sight, the murmur of strained voices.

"We need to go check it," Thargen said, lowering his finger.

"We?"

"Yeah. Just like I've been showing you, terran." He tugged one of the deactivated hardlight axes from the loop on his belt and held the haft out to her. "Stay low, quiet, and on my ass."

She closed her fingers around the weapon's grip, swallowed, and nodded. Her stomach was knotted and fluttering for entirely different reasons than it had been a few moments before. Because yeah, it *could* be other escapees out there, but she knew in her heart that wasn't likely—not after what Thargen had told her about those slave collars.

What would be worse to find at that pit—slaves, smugglers, or skeks? Somehow, the unknown was less unsettling than her inability to decide which of those things she'd prefer. Whatever they were, they were too close.

Thargen swung the skeks rifle off his shoulder, taking it in both hands, and moved toward the voices without even a hint of hesitation. Yuri followed immediately behind him, grateful that his pace was slow and deliberate.

Thargen's path led them across terrain that had become quite familiar to Yuri over the last five days. She could almost liken it to a video game starting area, where new characters could get their bearings and pick up a few skills, the sort of place veterans knew in and out after countless playthroughs. This chunk of alien forest had become the real-life version of that for her.

And now, her novice stealth skill was about to be put to the test.

Maybe I should've grinded out a few more levels instead of lusting after my tank...

The voices grew more distinct as Yuri and Thargen advanced, though she couldn't quite make out their words. She forced her breaths to remain even, now more aware than ever of how she placed her feet with every step. Her eyes darted up and down constantly, torn between watching Thargen, the ground in front of her, and the surrounding woods. She repeatedly adjusted her two-handed grip on the haft of her axe. The weapon felt overly heavy, her palms clammy, fingers weak.

Though it wasn't visible through the vegetation, she knew the pit was directly ahead—another fifty meters, maybe. Those voices were still going, one in hushed whispers and the other in something between hissing and shouting, the latter broken occasionally by sharp intakes of breath and agonized groans. They were speaking Universal Speech.

Thargen veered upslope well before the pit came into sight, and Yuri didn't question him. The new course brought them onto a small ridge overlooking the spot where they'd dug the pitfall. They crouched and moved up to a boulder at the edge of the ridge, where they pressed themselves against the stone and peered down through the trees.

Well, we can cross off two of the three S's.

Even though the clothing of the two aliens down at the pit was dirty and tattered, the orange accents on it were unmistakable. Not skeks or slaves—smugglers from the Zulka gang.

"Didn't expect them to be out this far," Thargen said, his voice little more than a low rumble.

Neither had Yuri. She hadn't forgotten about the smugglers, not at all, but after the storm, the skeks, and days of hard hiking and harder work just to keep themselves marginally safe and fed, the smugglers had become something of a distant concern.

The smuggler kneeling beside the pit looked like a borian, though he clearly wasn't Taeraal—this one had red-orange hair right out of a New England autumn. He was holding one of those large auto-blasters that had been strewn about the ship's cargo hold, and Yuri didn't doubt that it would fire very real, very deadly plasma bolts when he pulled the trigger. The borian was currently looking down at his companion, who was in the pit. From this vantage, she could only see what she thought was an arm and a leg of the second smuggler. But that one's strained voice, a whisper right on the cusp of becoming a shout, was quite clear now.

"Just get me out of this fucking hole, Auris!"

"Shut up, Garegon," the borian replied, his voice lower, calmer, and much harder to make out. He lifted his head to scan his surroundings; Yuri reflexively ducked behind the rock, heart thundering.

That name, Garegon, sounded familiar. Was that...was that the kaital who'd been with the onigox and volturian at Starlight Trance?

"You try shutting up when *you* have a small tree run through your guts," Garegon snapped.

Thargen eased over to Yuri's side of the boulder, flattening his hand against it just over her head and leaning over her to peer around its side. He was only centimeters away, big and powerful and radiating heat, a living shield from all the fear and uncertainty threatening to close in on her. While Thargen was near, she'd be okay. Everything would turn out all right. Bloody, probably, but ultimately all right.

He was silent for what felt like a long while. Yuri stared at his chest, which swelled and relaxed with his deep, slow breaths. Though he'd taken to wearing shirts since the morning he'd talked about his Rage, the fabric did little to mask the muscle beneath. If she just put her hand out, she could touch his chest, and she'd feel the powerful thumping of his heart beneath her palm. And if she looked a little lower, or dropped her hand a little lower...

"Only see two," Thargen said as he sank back into a squat.

Yuri's eyes darted up to his face.

Yuri, this is so not the time to let that sexual frustration run rampant.

"Me too," she forced herself to say, "Not that I got a great look. Forest is pretty thick around here."

"That's a good thing."

She frowned, settling the haft of the axe across her thighs. "So...what do we do?"

"You stay here, quiet and out of sight. I'm gonna go take care of them."

Her gaze dipped briefly to his rifle, but she didn't say anything. This was a stealth mission, after all. The goal was to avoid drawing attention to this slice of mountainside they currently called home. Firing the loudest gun in the history of the universe would take out those smugglers quick and easy from all the way up here—but it would also give every smuggler and skeks on this side of the galaxy a pretty good idea of where Yuri and Thargen were.

"Be careful," she said.

Paired with the wild light that had sparked in his eyes, Thargen's grin was outright wicked. "No promises, terran."

Before she realized what she was doing, Yuri grabbed the neck of Thargen's shirt in her fist, pulled herself toward him, and smashed her mouth against his. Thargen stiffened for a moment, but that was all it took for him to give in; her hulking, savage male practically melted against her.

The instant she felt him lean closer, felt his lips demanding more, she forced herself to pull back. Her tongue slipped out to run across her tingling lips as she met his gaze. That light in his eyes was only more intense.

"Wrong answer," she rasped.

Baring his teeth, Thargen leaned forward, tipping his forehead against hers. "Be right back, *zoani*. And that's a fucking promise."

That wasn't exactly what she'd been after—but considering the fire his words lit in her lower belly, she accepted them. The thrill of getting him to give in, even in this small way...well, that was something she'd have to explore further when they didn't have enemies within throwing distance.

She smirked and gave him a shove—not that he budged—releasing his shirt. "I'm holding you to that."

He lingered there for another second or two, nostrils flaring with a deep inhalation; she had no doubt that he was smelling her, no doubt that his low groan afterward was one of apprecia-tion. When he finally pulled away and left, she let herself fall back against the boulder, fully aware that she would've likely fallen on her ass and tumbled right off this little ridge were the stone not there to bolster her.

Yuri willed her heart to slow, her breathing to ease, and her mind to focus, reminding herself that Thargen was currently crouch-walking his way into a dangerous situation. The reminder only helped the latter of her struggles—now she was fully focused on Thargen being at risk.

For once, it was easy to ignore the ache at her core; the tightness in her chest was more than enough of a distraction.

You'd better be careful, damn it.

Taking up the axe in one hand, she turned toward the rock and peeked around it.

Thargen slipped in and out of sight as he crept down the slope, vanishing behind trees, rocks, and dense foliage. He seemed to be giving the smugglers a wide berth; his current trajectory would put him at least thirty meters to the left of the pit, by Yuri's reckoning. But that made sense—that route would make it harder for them to hear him thanks to the added distance while allowing him to circle around to the thicket near the pit, which would provide him some cover on his final approach.

Yuri pressed a hand against the boulder and leaned aside just a little farther to bring the pit into view. Both Auris and Garegon were in the same places as before—not that the kaital was likely to go anywhere without help—but the borian seemed even more alert now, head turning from side to side as though he were carefully scanning his surroundings. As his gaze shifted up toward the ridge, Yuri eased back behind the boulder.

Was Auris just worried his companion's cries had alerted

nearby skeks, or was it possible that he'd heard Yuri and Thargen speaking even though they'd kept their voices so low?

Borians looked a lot like elves from many fantasy settings back on Earth—if elves were around two meters tall and had the physiques of world-champion swimmers. Did they have the same heightened senses, too? She was pretty sure they did, but she'd never made it far enough into nursing school to take any of the courses on alien species, and knowing all the racial bonuses from RPGs sure as hell wasn't going to help her now.

Drawing in a deep, steadying breath, she glanced back toward Thargen's projected route. Panic sparked in her chest as she raked her eyes across the landscape, seeking some sign of him, *any* sign of him, and a hundred possible scenarios flitted wildly just beneath her conscious thoughts. How could he just be *gone?*

Talk about overreacting.

That was her voice in her head, her thought, but its cold, practical tone dampened her panic before it could fully take root.

Yeah, this situation was scary—but so was almost every situation she'd been in since leaving Starlight Trance with Thargen that night. It felt like a lifetime had passed since then. And when scary became normal, it lost some of its power. Regardless, her mother had always said Yuri had a very solid spirit at her center that would keep her strong through bad, stressful times. This was nothing new—not really. She and Thargen had been through worse together already.

After a second calming breath, she slowed her eyes and really *looked.* The forest colors had become so familiar that they seemed to bleed together, but she wasn't looking for the forest's colors. She was looking for Thargen's colors.

A flash of gray amidst the vegetation farther downslope

caught her attention—Thargen's shirt. For being so brawny, he sure could move quickly and quietly when he wanted to.

She peeked out at the smugglers again, only leaning far enough for one eye to look past the boulder.

Despite his alertness, Auris hadn't moved, not even to ready his auto-blaster. That had to be a good sign, right? But her heartbeat gradually quickened as she watched Thargen continue his silent journey, her eyes constantly shifting from him to the smugglers and back again. It became a little harder to breathe every time he was blocked from view by some obstacle—which seemed to happen with increasing frequency as he moved closer to his destination.

"Not going to survive this if you leave me here much longer," Garegon said, calling Yuri's attention back to the pit.

"You'll die quicker if I pull you out and can't patch your wounds," replied Auris. The first signs of irritation had entered his tone, echoed in his movements as he lifted his right arm to access something on his wrist.

Though the projection that flickered into view over the borian's arm was much too small and far away for Yuri to make out any details, she knew it was the screen of a holocom. She flexed her left hand absently. After two years of wearing a holocom on her wrist, she felt almost naked without one now. Seeing the borian's was just a reminder of how oddly light and off-balance her arm felt due to that absence.

"They're just uphill from us," Auris said. "Not much longer."

Yuri's blood turned to ice; she barely managed to duck behind the rock again before her whole body froze.

They're just uphill from us.

So he *had* heard Yuri and Thargen? Did he know Thargen was sneaking toward him even now? Was this Auris sadistic enough to use his wounded companion as bait?

Swallowing thickly, she leaned over to search for Thargen again. He was closer to the smugglers than her, and he must've heard Auris's words, must've known he was walking into a potential trap—one laid in response to his. But where was he now? She couldn't see him again, couldn't spot any movement down there that wasn't caused by the wind.

And even if she had been able to see him, what would she have done to get his attention?

"What if the skeks come back before then?" asked Gargeron.

"Keep your mouth shut, and they won't," Auris said.

Yuri's mouth was suddenly dry, and her throat constricted. Tension bristled in the air, charging it with an ominous, unsettling energy even stronger than it had held preceding the thunderstorm. The forest seemed preternaturally quiet—a silence that would gladly betray Thargen's slightest sound, that would turn the high-pitched thumps of Auris's auto-blaster into deafening booms.

A flash of movement caught her attention, jolting her heart. It was Thargen, everything below his shoulders hidden by the uneven ground beyond which he was walking. He vanished into the thicket a moment later.

"Where the fuck is Mortannis?" demanded Garegon.

Mortannis? Wasn't that the oni—

A branch crunched just behind Yuri, slowly—as though a great weight were gradually being settled over it.

Yuri's back stiffened, and that ice inside her was suddenly so cold it burned. She slid her thumb to the depression on the axe's grip. She sprang to her feet, squeezing hard to activate the blade as she spun to swing it at her uninvited guest.

She saw a huge body and red skin in her peripheral vision before she'd fully turned. A huge hand caught her forearm in a viselike grip, stopping her swing in an instant. Yuri clenched her teeth and turned to look up at the face of a towering onigox—the same one from Starlight Trance. The bastard with the hose.

A bronze-scaled ilthurii stood just beyond him, reptilian eyes narrowed.

Mortannis's lips stretched into a wide grin. "I've missed you, terran."

Later, Yuri wouldn't be sure whether any conscious thoughts crossed her mind in that instant. There was that fear, of course, as cold as ever, but there was something else there, too—something deeper. Maybe it was just that old fight or flight instinct buried in every human, roused to action by a surge of adrenaline. No matter the science behind it, she'd only have one way to think of it later—it was her *what would Thargen do* moment.

Her free hand dropped to her belt and tugged her knife from its sheath. The weapon came free just as Mortannis yanked her toward him, and she used that momentum to thrust the knife into the onigox's abdomen.

Mortannis released a startled grunt and staggered back a step. Yuri threw all her weight away from him; paired with his brief shock, it was just enough to break his hold on her arm. The knife slipped out of her hand, but it was okay. It had served his purpose.

With her *what would Thargen do* moment thus complete, Yuri ran as fast as she could. She wasn't dumb—she didn't stand a chance against a four-armed, two-hundred-plus-kilo wall of muscle.

Her legs carried her over the uneven terrain in a hectic flight that could easily have resulted in her breaking an ankle or falling and accidentally hacking off a limb with the axe, but somehow, she made it off the ridge and reached a point where she could turn downhill with minimal risk of unintentional dismemberment.

Her heart was racing, and panic blazed in her chest. A scream gathered in her throat—it would've taken the shape of Thargen's name had she not clenched her jaw, refusing to let it out.

She guessed that those smugglers still wanted her alive. Terrans were good money, and she was small and weak—easily manageable. But she doubted they'd have any qualms about killing Thargen on sight by this point. If they thought she was alone, it might be enough to give him a better window of opportunity to take them by surprise.

And besides, even her looming panic couldn't make her forget that golden rule—always pull adds to the tank.

Oh God, I better be right about this.

Yuri turned toward the pit—which was temporarily blocked from view by the trees—and cried, "Keep your hands off me!"

"The fuck?" Auris shouted. "Mortannis? Ir'esh?"

Yuri's feet slammed down with bone-rattling impact as she ran, driven on adrenaline alone.

"Found the terran," Mortannis called from behind her. From much too close behind. "Don't shoot her!"

It's not much, but I'll take it.

She raced around a large, gnarled tree, and the pit came into sight—but it was Auris and the auto-blaster he was aiming at Yuri that commanded her attention. The borian was standing up, eyes cold and weapon steady. With that look on his face, Yuri was convinced that he was about to shoot her no matter what Mortannis had just said.

She came to an abrupt halt a few meters away from Auris and locked her gaze with his, hoping her eyes were blazing with all the anger, frustration, and defiance roiling inside her.

Heavy footsteps behind her were the only warning that the onigox had caught up. She tightened her hold on the axe's haft, and for a wild second, could almost imagine herself turning and launching herself at the big red asshole like a fucking Valkyrie out of myth.

Then Mortannis's huge, strong hands caught her. He clamped a hand around each of her arms, just above her elbows, grabbed a fistful of her hair, and pried the axe from her grasp all at once.

"You've been making me work way too hard for this ever since we met, *ji'tas,*" Mortannis said. He raised the axe and tugged on her hair, forcing her to tilt her chin up and expose her throat. The translucent hardlight blade came closer, and Yuri shrank back, but he didn't allow her to retreat. The blade stopped a hair's breadth from her nose.

"Boss has been looking for these. Been looking for you, too, and that crazy vorgal of yours." Mortannis chuckled. "But you and the axes are the only things he wants returned."

Yuri pressed her lips together, trying to focus her attention on anything but that deathly-sharp blade. She refused to show them any fear.

The ilthurii walked past her and strode to the edge of the pit. "Fuck, Garegan."

"Just get me out, Ir'esh," the wounded smuggler pleaded.

"I'm not going down there," Ir'esh replied.

Auris reluctantly lowered his weapon, keeping those cold eyes on Yuri. "Apparently, she's got claws. You all right, Mortannis?"

Come on, Thargen. You've never waited to jump into a fight before...

Mortannis laughed, finally lowering the axe. Before Yuri could even let out a sigh of relief, the onigox bent forward, craning his neck to look down at her. "Oh, I know. But they're just little ones. Barely even stings."

At the lower edge of her vision, something moved in the

thicket behind Auris. Yuri's lips curled into a smirk as she caught a glimpse of gray through the foliage.

"I don't need big claws," she said through her teeth. "I've got my own berserker."

Mortannis's brow creased. "A what?"

Thargen emerged from the thicket immediately behind Auris, knife in hand and rifle strapped to his back. Moving so fast the motions seemed simultaneous, he wrapped an arm around the top of the borian's head, pulling it back, and dragged the blade across Auris's throat. The borian's eyes widened, and he opened his mouth as though to speak. The only sound he managed was a choked gurgle.

Yuri quickly shifted her gaze away from the borian; just the brief glimpse of crimson pouring from his slit throat like it was one of those wall-mounted waterfall fountains was more than enough to make her stomach churn and her head spin.

Mortannis lifted his head, strengthening his grip on Yuri. Thargen was already moving; he darted toward Ir'esh, who was turning to face him, auto-blaster swinging up. Thargen lashed out with a powerful kick. His heel struck the ilthurii's shoulder.

Ir'esh hissed as the force of Thargen's blow knocked the ilthurii off his feet and directly into the pit. The sound of him landing was one Yuri would be glad never to hear again. It was followed by a scream—not from Ir'esh, but Garegan.

"What the fuck?" Garegan yelled.

Apparently, Ir'esh *was* going down there.

Growling a curse, Mortannis released Yuri's arms and pulled hard on her hair, yanking her back and to the side. She cried out at the agony on her scalp and stumbled backward, grabbing his forearm with both hands in a desperate attempt to alleviate some of the pain and keep her feet beneath her.

"Shooting you this time," Mortannis said.

Thargen's answering roar shook the forest—it wasn't just a

roar, but a bestial battle cry that rumbled straight to Yuri's core. She'd never heard anything so full of possessiveness, rage, and lust. She'd never heard anything so frightening—or so sexy. That roar was Thargen, was the wildness in his heart, but it was his dedication, too.

From the edge of her vision, Yuri saw the onigox's lower arm drop to take hold of the auto-blaster slung at his side. He swung the barrel up toward Thargen, who was rushing toward them with an axe in hand.

Yuri gritted her teeth, dug her nails into Mortannis's forearm, and pushed up off the ground, curling her abs to lift her feet high. Tears welled in her eyes, blurring her vision, and a ragged growl tore out of her throat, fueled by both the surge of pain on her scalp and her fury.

This onigox—this big, stupid, brutish bastard—was the reason she and Thargen were here. Because he couldn't keep his damned hands to himself.

With all the strength she could muster, she slammed her feet down on the auto-blaster. Mortannis grunted as the weapon knocked out of his grasp.

Mortannis jerked Yuri farther back before she could get her feet on the ground, producing another flare of pain that forced fresh tears to her eyes.

An orange blur streaked past her head.

The onigox's arm went slack, and Yuri fell, landing hard on her ass. Though his hand remained in her hair, it suddenly seemed like her grip was holding him up instead of the other way around.

Someone was snarling. Yuri looked up to see Mortannis still on his feet, a hulking blotch of red and black, backpedaling frantically as the living whirlwind that was Thargen advanced on him mercilessly. The onigox was already several meters away.

If the onigox was there...then...

Yuri angled Mortannis's heavy forearm to the side; it swung like dead weight. She recoiled and closed her eyes when she saw the bloody stump—ending just before the elbow—from the corner of her eye.

Oh God.

Drawing in a shaky breath, she untangled the thick fingers from her hair.

Gross, gross, gross!

As soon as it was free, she released the limb and threw herself forward onto hands and knees, opening her eyes after she'd crawled away. She stopped there, panting, and stared at the ground as her stomach twisted and bitter bile threatened to rise in her throat.

Somewhere ahead of her, Garegon was blubbering, his cries weak, disjointed, and desperate. And somewhere behind her—no more than ten meters away—something heavy crashed into the undergrowth, shaking leaves and crunching branches. The heavy, growly breathing from the same place, reminiscent of an agitated lion or bear, was familiar to her; that was Thargen.

Yuri pushed her torso upright, sitting back on her calves and bracing her hands on her thighs. She expected a wave of terror to wash over her, to set her to shaking uncontrollably, but it didn't come. Neither did the blissful numbness of shock. She felt...

What did she feel?

Heavy footfalls approached her; even the rhythm of Thargen's walk had become familiar during her time here.

"The fuck is going on up there?" Garegon moaned. "Auris? Mortannis?"

Thargen strode past Yuri. The instant during which he was beside her was enough for her to feel the immense heat radiating from his body, but she didn't let herself look at him directly—he was likely covered in blood. She watched from the corner of her eye as he moved to the edge of the pit and aimed what looked like an auto-blaster toward the hole.

"Oh shi—"

Garegon's curse was cut short by a burst of blaster fire.

Yuri suddenly knew what it was she felt—*alive*. She found no pleasure in the death around her, took no satisfaction from it. She hadn't asked for any of this—well, not any of it except for Thargen—but having her life constantly in danger sure had a way of putting everything in perspective. These smugglers had wanted to hurt her and someone she'd come to care about very deeply. They'd probably hurt a lot of other people before Yuri and Thargen. Now they were dead, but she and Thargen were alive.

That felt good. Surviving. Beating the odds, getting a few more moments. Everything was sharper, clearer. And she knew it wasn't just being alive—it was also Thargen himself.

Snarling, Thargen stalked to the fallen borian, fired the blaster into him, and crouched to grab a few items off the corpse. Yuri didn't care what he took. So long as he took her, too, none of it mattered.

Placing a hand on the ground, she carefully climbed to her feet. Surprisingly, her legs held her up just fine, no wobbling or trembling. Heat pumped through her body as Thargen approached. She forced her eyes down; as desperately as she wanted to see him, she didn't want to faint or puke right now.

"Close your eyes," he growled.

EIGHTEEN

Yuri snapped her eyes shut without hesitation. Thargen's guttural voice sent a shiver through her; despite everything that had just happened, her body was responding to him as though their last kiss had only been a moment ago.

She felt his burning gaze upon her, felt him draw closer, felt his breath through her hair as he leaned over her, felt tension and heat roiling off him as he inhaled deeply. She even felt the vibrations of his low, deep groan. Her heart sped, fluttering with a mix of desire and anticipation. She didn't have to see his expression to know that same desire was on his face, made primal by the wildness in his eyes.

His hands closed around her upper arms.

Yuri took in a sharp breath; the air was thick with the tang of blood.

"Thargen, the blood," she said quickly. "Please."

His hands flexed, tightening infinitesimally—but it was more than enough to express his inner turmoil. She knew he was holding his Rage back, knew he was on the edge of losing control.

He withdrew his hands abruptly. Not a moment later, he swept her feet out from beneath her, catching her in his arms, and clutched her against his chest. She scarcely had time to put her arms around his neck before he was running—and her hands bumped into not one, but three guns slung over his shoulders on their way into position. There were wet, sticky spots on his skin and shirt. She tried hard to imagine those spots were anything other than what they were.

Yuri turned her face away from Thargen, away from the scent of blood wafting off him, and opened her eyes as she filled her lungs with fresh air.

Thargen crashed through the forest, crushing foliage and snapping branches, darting across patches of bare rock, leaping over exposed roots, using his body to shield her from the thick vegetation through which he charged.

They arrived at the river so quickly—and by following such a hectic path—that it annihilated Yuri's sense of direction; she no longer knew where she was, and she didn't care.

Thargen stopped at the bank and set her down. She looked at him, swallowing hard seeing the blood spattered on his arms and shirt, the flecks of it on his face. She glanced away as a wave of dizziness struck her.

Stop it, Yuri. You are stronger than this.

In her peripheral vision, Thargen pulled the guns off his shoulders, tossing them onto the ground, and tugged his belt off —axes, knives, and all—to throw down beside them. He tore his shirt off over his head, wadded it up, and used it to wipe away some of the blood on his face, neck, arms, and hands before fixing his intense gaze upon her.

Yuri turned toward him and met those burning, golden eyes, forgetting the blood, the violence, the death, forgetting everything but him.

When he clutched the waistband of his pants and shoved

them down, her gaze dipped. His cock sprung free, fully erect with its piercings gleaming in the late afternoon light. Yuri's mouth went dry. His shaft was darker than the rest of him, and the bulges along its sides throbbed with his pulse. Her lips parted, and her nipples stiffened into hard, achy points.

She swore his muscles swelled infinitesimally with each of those throbs, their definition being enhanced as his skin stretched a little tighter.

Thargen hooked his fingers on her belt and pulled her closer. He unclasped it quickly, letting it fall. Before the belt had even hit the ground, he'd grasped the hem of her shirt. He whipped it off over her head and didn't waste a moment in moving on to her pants.

He crouched, and Yuri caught his shoulders as he tugged her pants down; just as they reached her knees, his head dipped toward her pelvis, and he stilled. She heard him take in a deep, ragged breath, felt it come out in a hot huff against her skin—against her sex—that sent a thrill straight to her core. Heat flooded her.

There he remained, as still as a statue except for his heavy breathing. Veins stood out on his arms, his jaw muscles bulged, and the cords of his neck were taut. His shoulders and chest swelled with another inhalation, and his hands trembled.

His eyes snapped up and met hers. They were fierce, fiery, *ravenous*, and they stoked the flames in her core to new heights. His nostrils flared.

"You smell so fucking good," he grated through his teeth. "Need you."

Yuri touched her fingers to his cheek. "So take me."

He dropped onto his knees and swept her pants down to her ankles, his hands moving so fast that she felt cool air flow over her bared skin in their wake. She lifted one foot and shook it free of the garment. Before she could even set it down,

Thargen caught her leg behind the knee, threw it over his shoulder, and swept her to his waiting mouth with his hands palming her ass.

She stumbled, startled by the suddenness of his actions, and caught herself with one hand on his shoulder and the other on his head. He sat back on his heels, easily accepting her weight—and then his strong, thick tongue made her forget about everything else.

Yuri moaned, curling her fingers in his hair. His tongue swirled over her, dipping into her entrance to gather her slick, drinking her desire and lavishing her sex before it flicked over her clit. Her belly fluttered and her hips twitched closer to his mouth.

He growled against her, clutching her ass hard enough to bruise, but Yuri didn't care. She didn't even care about the blood speckled on his face, or that some of it was smearing on her thighs. All that mattered was him, was this feeling growing inside her, this desire that burned hot and bright.

She lifted her hand from his shoulder and cupped her breast, squeezing her yielding flesh as she stared down into his eyes and eagerly rocked her pelvis against his mouth. When she pinched her nipple, adding to the pleasure building in her core, she couldn't hold in a whimper.

One of his tusks grazed her thigh as he withdrew his tongue just long enough to say, "Ride my fucking face, terran."

Thargen's words, so forceful, so crude, only aroused her more. She loved it.

She loved *him*.

She'd known it the moment she had seen him standing at the bar, had known it since the first time he smiled at her.

This vorgal was *hers*.

Gripping his hair, Yuri gyrated her hips. His tongue pushed deep, sweeping along her inner walls, twisting and thrusting mercilessly. Yuri's hand returned to his shoulder for support, and her head fell back. Her breasts bounced and her thighs quivered as she teetered on the verge of release, her entire body straining for it, desperate for it, trembling with the need for that explosion of pleasure.

Dragging his tongue out of her sex, Thargen moved his mouth up and took her clit between his lips, sucking hard.

Yuri's consciousness shattered into a million flickering stars.

She curled forward, pulling his hair and releasing a ragged cry as heat burst over every centimeter of her body. She tried to move, to draw herself closer to him and to escape, but he allowed her no leeway; Thargen held her firmly to his mouth, drinking from her greedily.

Yuri's breathy moans filled the air, and she made no effort to silence them, letting the river sweep them away into eternity.

The fluttering in her stomach intensified suddenly; she didn't realize she was falling until her back was on the soft grass. Thargen's arms banded around her thighs, spreading them wider, and his mouth took on a new ferocity. He devoured her, the sounds of his licking and sucking only broken by his snarls, his huffing, ragged breaths, and his growls, which pushed her to an even higher peak.

Pleasure wracked Yuri's body. She grabbed his head, scraping her nails over his scalp. That only drove him on harder. His insistent tongue lapped at her sex and plunged into her channel, his nose pressed down on her clit, and his tusks framed her slick, tender flesh.

Her mouth opened to cry out, but no sound emerged—overwhelming ecstasy, overwhelming *pressure*, stole her breath and constricted her throat.

Thargen tore his mouth away abruptly, releasing one of her legs to push up on his arm. Panting, Yuri lifted her head to look at him. He sucked in a hissing breath and squeezed his eyes shut, lips peeling back further to display his teeth and those wicked tusks. His muscles bulged, and she could feel him trembling.

"Need more," he growled. When his eyes flashed open to meet hers, they were wild as ever. "Fucking need more of you."

In a burst of speed, he moved onto his knees, dragged Yuri to him, and wedged himself between her thighs. Then the broad head of his cock was *there.*

"Forgive me, *zoani,*" he said, his voice raw and strained. "*Forgive me.*"

Before Yuri could ask what she was meant to forgive, he thrust into her.

The breath left her in a *whoosh.* She stiffened, lips parted, brows low. His thick shaft stretched her painfully, demanding her body accommodate it, blazing like a heated iron rod. Even the wetness slickening her inner walls wasn't enough. Her body was just too untried, too small, too...*virginal.*

Yuri had never hated being a virgin more than she did at that moment.

Thargen dropped down with his hands to either side of her, caging her in between his arms, and pulled his hips back. His slight withdrawal eased her pain, but that relief was short-lived. He slammed his hips forward again with a grunt, sinking even deeper than before.

Yuri cried out and slapped her hands against his chest. She instinctively tried to close her legs, to alleviate the pressure, the discomfort. Thargen snarled and bucked again, pushing deeper still, forcing her body to take more of him.

Tears stung her eyes, and she dug her nails into his chest. "Thargen."

He tensed, and his fingers curled into the ground, tearing at the grass.

Yuri reached up and took his face between her hands. "Look at me, Thargen."

With a huffing exhalation, he angled his head down to meet her gaze. His teeth were still bared, his unfocused eyes blazing, but there was something more in his strained expression. Thargen was still in there.

"You take me. Not your Rage. *You.*" She stroked his cheeks with her thumbs, trying to ignore the painful pressure between her thighs, trying to keep her voice steady despite it. "You have to be here with me."

Thargen's body froze, his pulsing cock still buried within her. Sudden awareness rounded his eyes. "Yuri," he rasped, and started to pull away.

Yuri wrapped her legs around him, keeping him where he was. Her inner walls clenched his cock, causing him to groan and shudder. The vibration of that shudder traveled into her and chased away a little of her pain with a thrill.

"Kiss me, Thargen. Touch me. I won't break," she said, knowing what that glimpse of fear in his eyes meant. "Make me feel good, ease me into this, and show me you're with me. You're stronger than your Rage. It isn't you, it's just one piece of you."

For several moments, he remained unmoving but for his heavy breaths, keeping his eyes locked with hers. Then he lifted a hand and brushed it over her cheek, wiping away the tear that had fallen. Something in his expression changed—somehow, it softened while heating further.

He bent at his middle, lowering his mouth to hers as his hand trailed down her throat. His kiss was hard, demanding, claiming—but it was *him.* Yuri slipped her arms around his neck and returned his kiss, opening to him as his tongue moved ruthlessly against hers.

His hand continued down, his rough palm rasping over her

breast and her beaded nipple, across her stomach and belly ring, and brushing past the patch of hair on her pelvis until it finally reached the place where their bodies were joined. Her breath hitched as his fingers grazed her sex, sliding over the flesh wrapped around his cock before moving back up to her clit and circling it.

The pleasure wrought by his touch sent a shiver through Yuri that made her arch her back, forcing her hips up—thus taking in a little more of his shaft. Her sex was taut around him, and she could not deny the burn as he stretched her further, but the discomfort was fading in the face of the building sensations as he stroked her clit.

"Yes," she breathed against his mouth, letting her thighs fall open. "Just like that."

"You know just what you want, terran," Thargen said as he pulled his shaft back, allowing her to feel every one of the little metal studs lining it. His body strained as he pushed his cock in again, slower than before but more firmly, his passage eased by her gathering slickness. He released a shuddering breath. "So fucking hot. So fucking *tight*."

Yuri squirmed beneath him, panting as heat coiled within her core. She bit his bottom lip and tugged before releasing it. "I want you, Thargen. I've always wanted you."

He growled and gnashed his teeth, punctuating the sound with a hard, fierce thrust of his hips.

Yuri gasped. There was a flash of pain as his cock slammed home, stuffing her full, but that pain was swiftly replaced by a burst of pleasure as Thargen increased the speed and pressure of his finger on her clit.

"Thargen," she moaned, lashes fluttering as she tipped her head back—but she could not look away from his eyes. She grasped his shoulders and tried to undulate her hips, but she was pinned beneath him, trapped, forced to endure anything and everything he gave her, and he...

He wasn't moving. She ground her cleft against him, needing...wanting...

Thargen withdrew his hand from her sex, lifting it to his mouth. He groaned as he slid his glistening finger over his tongue. When he lowered that hand, he didn't return it to her sex; he slipped it beneath her head, grasping a fistful of her hair.

"You want me, *zoani*, you get *all* of me." His voice was a harsh rumbling, rolling into her through their connected bodies, and his eyes were molten gold. "Give me all of you."

"You have me," she rasped.

His hips drew back. "You are fucking *mine*."

On that last word, Thargen slammed into her again. He angled her head back, exposing her neck, and grazed the sensitive flesh of her throat with lips, tusks, and tongue as his hips pumped with a rapidly quickening rhythm.

Any pain she'd felt before was gone, its memory fading a little more with each stroke of his cock, crushed beneath her growing pleasure. She came to love the faint burn and the incredible fullness each time he shoved into her. His piercings only added to his width and enhanced her stimulation, their smooth studs hitting all the right places.

"Give me everything," Thargen snarled against her neck, tightening his hold on her hair. "I want it all."

Yuri hissed at the sting in her scalp, but the sensation became a thrilling tingle that quickly spread through her whole body. Her nipples ached, craving his touch. She dragged her nails down his back, clawing him as hard as she could.

He shuddered, his chest vibrating with a growl. Releasing her hair, he shoved his torso upright, grabbed her hips, and lifted her ass off the ground and onto his thighs. He was like an engine suddenly switched into overdrive. He pistoned his pelvis at a brutal speed, using his hold on her hips to slam her against him and meet his every thrust, driving himself impossibly deeper.

She panted, barely able to catch her breath with his wild rhythm—barely able to think through the pleasure that was consuming her. She tried to keep her head up, to keep her eyes locked with his, but it was all too much.

Thargen's grip was too tight, but it wasn't tight enough. She needed to be closer to him. She was too full, but she needed more inside her, needed more of him filling her, she needed *everything*.

"Come for me, *zoani*," Thargen commanded, words raw and guttural. They were all she needed.

Yuri fractured. Her back arched, forcing her head onto the ground, and she clawed at the grass as rapture rocketed her past all the previous peaks Thargen had lifted her to. She released a choked cry, and her mind was torn asunder, leaving only the waves of ecstasy sweeping outward from her core, each stronger than the last.

A bestial roar tore out of Thargen's throat. His grip on her hips was relentless, and somehow, his frantic speed increased, taking on a new desperation that forced another cry from Yuri. She felt his shaft swell impossibly larger just as his rhythm faltered.

"Fuck!" He bucked hard, driving his cock right up to her damned womb. The flood of liquid heat at Yuri's core became an outright deluge as his seed blasted into her. Thargen clasped her to him, grinding against her as his shaft twitched with his prolonged release.

Yuri felt every single spurt. She moaned as her sex contracted around his cock, milking him for more.

Finally, his hips stilled, and he leaned forward, propping himself over her on one arm. Yuri glanced up at his heaving chest, watching a bead of sweat run down to catch on the stud of his pierced nipple before closing her eyes.

I am so going to bite that nipple next time.

She practically hummed with the endorphins running through her veins. Her body felt bruised, but it also felt delightfully languid, sated, and *pleasured*. She didn't think she could even lift her pinky finger at this point—and had never known until now just how good a feeling that could be.

"Achievement unlocked," Yuri said, grinning wide.

His low, rumbling laughter sent another pulse through his cock—and right into her. Yuri nearly purred. She opened her eyes and looked at him.

"Anyone ever tell you that you have a sexy laugh?" she asked.

"I've got a sexy everything, terran," he replied with a smirk.

"Yeah, you do."

He returned his hand to her hip and slid both of them up over her belly. He paused briefly to stroke his thumbs around her belly ring, sending fresh tingles over her skin, before his hands moved higher to cup her breasts. "None of it's as sexy as my female."

This time, Yuri did purr as she pressed her chest into his calloused palms and settled her hands over his. Her sex clenched around his cock. "Say it again."

Thargen grunted, slipped his hands under her back, and lifted her as he sat on his heels, resulting in her straddling his lap—and his still-hard cock pushing a little farther into her. Could he seriously get any deeper? She slipped her arms around his neck as her hair fell around her shoulders.

"You're fucking sexy, *zoani*."

"Not that," she said. "The other part."

He moved a hand up her spine, sliding his fingers through

her hair to cradle the back of her head. "You're fucking *mine*, female."

Yuri smiled and leaned close until their lips were a hair's breadth apart. "That's right. Yours. And you are mine." She lifted her hips slowly, relishing the feel of every little stud on his shaft, and lowered herself back down. A shiver stole through her, but she kept her eyes locked with his. "You'd better give your Rage the message. Yuri's in charge now."

A deep chuckle rumbled his chest, and he tipped his forehead against hers. "Have I mentioned that you're really, *really* fucking sexy?"

"You might've." She twirled her fingers in his hair. Several of his braids had worked themselves loose, allowing his black locks to flow freely. Yuri's heart fluttered with her next words. "Have I mentioned that I love you?"

Thargen pulled his head back and looked into her eyes, his expression uncharacteristically solemn. "No. But you've shown it." He moved his thumb in small, slow circles, rubbing the back of her head. "I love you, too, *zoani*. Love you like it was always meant to be, and I don't even care if that sounds like those sappy fucking Volturian dramas."

Yuri was sure she was wearing the biggest, goofiest smile that had ever existed. "You do?"

"Fuck yeah, I do."

She closed her eyes and pressed her lips to his, tightening her arms around him. He twined his fingers in her hair and kissed her back.

It wasn't the most heated kiss they'd shared, wasn't the most desperate, wasn't the most breathtaking, but it was her favorite one so far—because it so perfectly echoed the words they had just exchanged.

When she bore her hips down on him, Thargen hissed

through his teeth and pulled back suddenly, dropping a hand to Yuri's waist to still her.

"Can't. Not now," he said.

Yuri drew back and frowned. "Thargen, you're not going to hurt—"

"We gotta get moving. Not safe around here anymore."

She blushed and lowered her eyes; it wasn't like she'd tried to be quiet or anything. But...damn it, she *really* liked where she was currently.

Thargen released her hair, curled his finger under her chin, and tilted her head back, guiding her gaze back to his. "Don't worry, *zoani*. You'll be getting as much of this as you can handle from here out."

Yuri's skin heated further, and she laughed. "I can still handle a little more."

He hooked both his hands under her thighs and stood up, groaning slightly as his cock shifted inside her. Her breath hitched, and she squeezed him harder.

"If the water's not too cold for you, you can have some more," he said, walking toward the river. Each of his steps, though not particularly heavy, made her bounce on his shaft, creating a little of that sweet, maddening friction.

Yuri wrapped her legs around his waist and smiled as she leaned forward and brushed her lips across his. "I have something to keep me warm."

NINETEEN

Thargen floated up from a deep, dreamless slumber—a sort of sleep he'd not had in recent memory. His slow awakening, during which his senses eased into awareness one at a time like a ship's systems booting up for a prelaunch check, was just as unusual. Most of the time, he snapped to wakefulness with a jolt, instantly alert even if he didn't always know exactly where he was or what was happening. The state of high-alert confusion was particularly common following those haunting dreams, many of which felt more immediate and vivid than reality.

The world behind his eyelids was completely dark, and the quiet cocooning him was broken only by the soothing sound of Yuri's slow, even breathing.

She and Thargen lay on their sides together, his front to her back, in the position she called *spooning*. At some point, he'd have to ask her what it had to do with spoons—but he loved this no matter what it was called. Her little body was soft, warm, and relaxed, and had somehow become even more perfect a fit with his than it had already been.

This is what peace feels like.

That should have been a simple thought, a passing reflection on his current state, but it held a startlingly profound weight that made his chest ache and something warm spread through it. His mind hadn't been so calm, so still, in...well, in as long as he could recall. He knew his Rage wasn't gone; it was a piece of him, just like Yuri had said, and it would be with him forever. But it was silent for now, slumbering in its cave in the depths of his subconscious. The beast had been lulled to sleep by his female.

There'd been times when friends had helped Thargen back down from his Rage, had helped him curtail the worst impulses it triggered until he could find a healthy outlet, but no one had ever been able to penetrate it like she could. Yuri was like a Rage-piercing rifle, able to shoot straight through to his heart every damned time. She hadn't just met his Rage head on, she'd made it flinch.

She'd made it her bitch.

And he fucking loved her for that—for that and a million other things. There were people he cared about enough to die for them, but only Yuri made him care enough to really *live*, to do more than just...exist.

Even if he never felt this degree of serenity and contentment again after today—even if he never felt either again at all —he wouldn't have changed a single step along the path that had brought him here. His time with Yuri was worth any price. However short it had been up to now, it was the greatest part of his life.

A small part of him wished he hadn't held back, hadn't waited, hadn't wasted so many of those precious moments, but he couldn't regret even that. The chances of harming her had been too great, the potential consequences too dire, and choosing her safety—which had been the most fucking difficult fucking decision he'd ever made—hadn't been a mistake.

Thargen inhaled deeply, drinking in air perfumed by her alluring fragrance and the lingering scent of sex. A low rumble sounded in his chest. He tightened his arm around her just a little, drawing her more firmly against him—which only served to remind him that his shaft, already throbbing and swelling to erectness, was caught between their bodies, tucked in the cleft of her ass and along her spine.

It was a delicious taste of torture.

He grinned to himself. His cock had probably seen more use last night than it had over the entirety of the last few years. He and Yuri had fucked beside the river, then *in* the river, had rutted in the cave—and then in the cave a couple more times, depending on how he interpreted the blurred lines between mind-shattering orgasms. And here he was, still craving more.

Once again, that seemed like it should have been such a small thing—he'd craved her this whole time. But it was *Thargen* wanting her. It wasn't just instinct, wasn't just Rage. All of Thargen wanted all of Yuri; heart, body, mind, spirit, and whatever the hell else there was to have.

Just yesterday, he hadn't believed it possible for her—so small and delicate looking—to make it through sex with him unharmed, much less to have enjoyed any of the experience. But she'd taken everything he could give—she'd taken all of him. She'd proven his fears to be unfounded. She hadn't broken or run away; she'd dug those little claws of hers in deeper and demanded more.

His *zoani* was just as tough as she was smart, kind, funny, spirited, and beautiful—and she was almost as insatiable as Thargen.

His arm curled tighter still, increasing the pressure on his shaft. He refreshed her scent in his nose with another deep inhalation. Her heady aroma settled over his mind in a sweet, hazy cloud.

Fuck, she smells amazing. Looks, sounds, feels, and tastes amazing, too.

Barely suppressing a hungry growl and an aroused shudder, Thargen finally opened his eyes, leaving his eyelids slitted. Only the merest hint of gray light came in through the cave opening—the sort of gloomy light that was only a suggestion of sunrise, that made it seem like the sun wasn't sure if it wanted to get out of bed or sleep off its hangover.

Thargen and Yuri needed to get an early start today. They'd risked a stop at the pitfall after leaving the river yesterday, with Yuri keeping watch while Thargen checked the smugglers more thoroughly for supplies than he had in the throes of Rage.

The search had taken longer than he'd intended thanks to the holocoms on the smugglers' wrists. Those devices had made the little spark of hope in his chest flare—at least until the trick Arcanthus had shown him to bypass simple security codes confirmed that there was no network, or long-range communication available. The only thing the holocom he'd picked up could interface with were the other holocoms close by.

It had been near dark by the time they'd finished and returned to the cave. He likely would've insisted on leaving immediately—considering this area was compromised—but he had no desire to wander the nighttime woods while skeks and smugglers were on the prowl, especially with no guarantee of finding a new shelter.

All his desire had been directed toward Yuri...and it sure as fuck still was.

She shifted slightly, brushing that soft skin over his hard shaft. Thargen hissed softly through his teeth, unable to ignore the burst of pleasure caused by that tiny movement. He slid his hand down from her stomach toward her pelvis.

Yeah, they needed an early start. But not *too* early.

"Mmm." Yuri stretched against Thargen when his fingers brushed across that neat little patch of hair on her pelvis, arching into his touch. "Is it morning already?"

"Barely," he murmured, dipping his hand lower.

She parted her thighs without hesitation. He slipped his fingers into her slit to find her soaking wet. Somehow, his cock stiffened further, his balls aching for release despite how many times he'd emptied his seed the night before. His terran was a needy little thing, and he fucking loved it.

"Guess I could let you get back to sleep..." He grazed her clit with light strokes, back and forth, teasing the sensitive flesh.

A sound escaped her—half purr, half moan—and she tilted her pelvis, pressing into his touch. Thargen chuckled and eased his fingers away from her clit to circle it, applying just a little more pressure. Yuri's breath hitched.

He nuzzled the place between her neck and shoulders, inhaling her sweet scent. Her soft hair tickled his nose and cheeks. She reached up and curled her fingers around the back of his head, her thumb brushing over his scars. Every one of her panting breaths and little mews of pleasure made his cock twitch, coaxing seed from its tip as they escalated in volume.

"Thargen," she whispered, rocking her pelvis—and rubbing her ass against his shaft—in time with his fingers.

His balls tightened, and pleasure coiled low in his belly, forcing him to part his lips and release a shuddering breath. That little bit of friction would be enough to finish him if it continued for long—and not even for all that long.

He moved his fingers down, gathering her essence, and slipped his middle finger inside her. Her *pussy* contracted around the digit, drawing it in like it would devour any part of him it could get a hold of. Thargen groaned and pressed his palm down on her pelvis, putting pressure on her clit and squeezing his cock between their bodies. His muscles tensed as his Rage finally stirred, narrowing his focus down to *her*.

The fragrance of her arousal had overtaken all other scents; between that smell, her feel, and those sounds she was making, he was in danger of spilling his seed right then and there.

"Are you sore, Yuri?"

"A little," she breathed, curling her fingers into his hair. "But I don't care. I need you inside me. Now."

"I fucking love you." He nipped her neck, and she moaned, bucking her hips and grinding her ass against him.

Thargen refused to spill his seed now, not while her sex was dripping and ready for him. He withdrew his finger and moved his hand to the back of her thigh. Forcing her leg up, he opened her wide. He didn't waste a second in angling his hips to slide his cock free—gritting his teeth against the pleasure of that friction—and thrust it into her slick channel.

Yuri tilted her head back with a gasp. Her sex gripped his cock more firmly than his fist ever could, and for an instant all he could do was hold himself there, muscles rigid, and growl as he willed away the threatening explosion. The fires of his Rage intensified; it demanded movement, demanded release, demanded he lose control—demanded *her*.

When he allowed himself to move again, he withdrew just enough to give his next thrust extra momentum, plunging back into her to the hilt. He felt every millimeter of her hot, wet sheath, and its ruthless grasp created pressure on his piercings that catapulted his pleasure onto a whole new level.

Thargen kissed her neck and jaw, and she turned her face toward him so he could capture her lips. He angled his mouth to kiss her deeper, harder, pumping his hips with increased strength to match the force of that kiss. Liquid heat flooded her, coating his cock in her essence. He breathed deep their mingling scents and growled appreciatively.

She panted against his mouth, and he swallowed her moans, claiming them along with every other bit of her. It was all fucking *his*.

He tore his mouth away and gritted his teeth, staring at her face. Her eyes were closed, her dark brows furrowed, and her lips, swollen from their kiss, were parted. Yuri was beautiful all the time, but seeing this passion on her face, seeing this plea-sure, made his heart constrict with more emotion than he'd ever thought possible. She wasn't just beautiful; she was so fucking beautiful that there weren't the right words in any language to describe her.

Not that words mattered—only Thargen and Yuri mattered now, only this connection between them, only the love he felt for her, which grew every moment of every day.

"You feel so fucking good, *zoani*."

Yuri opened her eyes, and those green, green orbs met his. "So do you." She moaned when he slammed into her harder, shutting her eyes again. "I'm so close."

Her *pussy* contracted, her breaths came short and fast, and her thighs quivered. That pressure in him was near to bursting, having become an equal blend of pleasure and pain; a few more strokes, and he could finish them both off.

But he wasn't done yet. Thargen wanted more, wanted as much as he could have—wanted to give as much as he possibly could. He cut those mental bindings and released his Rage.

The lustful haze that her scent had settled over his mind thickened into an impenetrable fog, blocking out all the universe but for her. Yuri was his everything—his sight and sound, his taste, his touch, his hunger, his whole reason.

Without pulling out of her, he shoved himself up onto his knees, flipping Yuri onto her front in the process. He caught her hips between his hands and slammed his cock into her, burying himself fully with a ragged snarl.

Yuri cried out, sliding her palms over the rumpled pallet beneath her. She caught her bottom lip with her teeth and turned her face into the fabric, muffling her moans.

A thrill shook Thargen's entire body, making him sag toward her; this new angle altered the way her sex slid around his shaft, producing powerful new sensations for which he'd not been prepared—and he had to have more.

Forcing her legs wider with his, he pulled back and slammed into her again with a harsh grunt, but he allowed himself no pause this time. He set a ferocious pace, driven on by raw sensation, by wicked, consuming pleasure, his grunts and growls mixing with her breathy moans and tortured whimpers, underscored by the slapping of their flesh in an unrelenting rhythm.

And even through his Rage, he felt her moving—her position was submissive, but her participation was not. Each time he tugged her back with his hands, he felt her push toward him with lustful desperation.

Suddenly, Yuri's body seized. Her sex clamped around his cock, and her essence, hot and wet, surged around his shaft. She came with a choked cry and squeezed fistfuls of clothing in her hands, hips bucking erratically.

Thargen threw his head back and lost himself in that pleasure, in her climax, pushing his pace even wilder, thrusting even harder. The pressure in him soared; it was too much, too painful, dangling him over the edge of oblivion.

Somehow, he only rutted her with greater frenzy.

Squirming, Yuri cried out again with a fresh flood of liquid heat just as a savage roar erupted from Thargen's throat and his body convulsed. His spasming cock pumped seed into her while overwhelming pulses of ecstasy swept through him, obliterating any conscious thoughts that might've remained in his mind.

He sagged forward, bracing one hand on the ground and wrapping the other arm around Yuri's middle to keep her pinned against him as he gyrated his hips, seeking every last modicum of pleasure, desperate to fill her with every last drop of his seed.

Yuri's moans faded into ragged breaths as his movements slowed and the haze slowly lifted from his mind. He peered down at her. Her face was turned to the side with lips parted, eyes closed, and cheeks flushed, and her black hair was a tangled mess. She trembled in his grip, her sex still quivering and contracting around his shaft.

Thargen moved his hand up and cupped her breast. He kneaded the soft mound and pinched her nipple, wringing a gasp from her. "When we get back to Arthos, terran, I'm dragging you into bed and keeping you there until we're too exhausted to move."

She chuckled, and her sex was still so tight around him that he could feel the tiny vibrations of the sound, could feel every tiny movement it caused in her, through his cock.

Raising a hand into the air, she stuck her thumb up. "Sounds good to me. No complaints here."

"At least not until I tell you we're gonna have to get moving soon, right?"

Yuri groaned, letting her hand drop. "But the morning started *so* good." She wiggled her bottom, grinding it against him and pushing him in deeper. "I like you where you are."

"*Fuuuuuck.*" Thargen squeezed his eyes shut and tightened his hold on her breast, fighting off another pleasure-laced shiver. "Trust me, if we could actually cover some ground like this, I'd fucking do it."

She laughed. "You paint an interesting mental picture."

Opening his eyes, he dipped his head to kiss the back of her neck before pushing himself upright. He placed his hands on her sides and ran his gaze down the line of her spine. He couldn't deny that he was tempted to start moving his hips again, to rut with her until well after the sun had come up.

But that temptation died when his gaze reached her waist.

Brow furrowed, he carefully slid his trembling hands over her pale skin—over the dark bruises around her hips and waist. Suddenly, his heartbeat was thunderous, rattling his bones, and his throat was constricted. He turned one of his hands; a set of the bruises matched his fingers almost perfectly.

He tried to speak, but no words came out when he opened his mouth. He had hurt her. He had hurt her, and she hadn't said anything about it, hadn't mentioned it, had just pretended everything was okay.

I fucking marked her.

And more disturbing than that was the knowledge that some part of him took pride in that. Fucking *pride.*

"Thargen?" Yuri said.

His body tensed, muscles coiled and ready to spring away from her, to withdraw before he could do any more damage. But what had that done for him so far? It had only cost him time with her, had only delayed the intimacy they'd been sharing since yesterday.

He covered a patch of bruising with each of his hands as gently as he could and released a huff of air through his nostrils. "I hurt you, Yuri."

"What?" She pushed up on her hands and turned to look back at him. Her brows shot up when her eyes landed on the bruises. "Oh, wow."

Thargen's jaw ticked. This wasn't okay, was it? It wasn't okay, whether he'd meant to do it or not, and it wasn't okay that he found it kind of sexy. "Why didn't you tell me?"

"I had no idea. They must've formed overnight." Her eyes met his and she grinned. "It's kind of hot."

If there was already a crease between his eyebrows, it must've deepened to a fucking canyon just then. "What?"

She stared at him for a moment, her smile fading. Finally, she pulled forward, forcing his cock to slip free from her. She winced; that made his heart break a little even as primal pride swelled in his chest at the sight of his seed seeping from her sex.

Yuri rose on her knees, turned, and moved closer to him, placing her hands on his shoulders. She searched his face and frowned. "Don't you dare."

That firmness in her tone made his cock twitch.

"It's just... *Fuck*, terran." Thargen shook his head and laughed, uncertain of whether there was any humor in the sound. "You really think it's hot?"

She slid her hands down his arms, took hold of his hands, and guided them to her hips, right over the bruises that matched them. "I do." She reached up and cupped his jaw. "You didn't hurt me, Thargen. Well, I mean, I *am* sore, and we might need to slow it down a little, but...I feel pretty damn delicious right now. Like, wow, what a way to wake up in the morning. I hope we do *that* again. But those bruises? They're nothing but proof of how much you want me. Of how good you made me feel."

"Guess I don't need to feel shitty about thinking they were sexy, too," he said, flexing his fingers. "Proof that you're mine."

Yuri grinned. "You don't need proof. I just am. And you..." She ran her hands down the sides of his neck to his chest. Suddenly, she flattened her palms against him and shoved.

He didn't budge.

One corner of Thargen's mouth tilted up. "And me, little terran?"

"Well, that didn't work out how I'd hoped." She laughed. "Lie down."

"That a command?"

"You bet your ass it is."

When she pushed against his chest again, Thargen didn't resist; he let himself fall backward onto the clothing spread beneath him. Yuri climbed atop of him, straddling his waist and giving him a clear view of her sex and its glistening petals.

Even if he were to come within a few meters of a blazing star, he could never see anything hotter than the image before him—his female over him, her curvy little body baring his marks, her tousled hair hanging about her shoulders and curling around her bronze-tipped breasts.

Yuri lifted herself and wrapped her hand around his cock.

He groaned, scraping his nails across the cave floor. His every muscle was tense with anticipation, but he dared not touch her yet—he was too interested in seeing what she would do, in letting her be in control.

If only for a few moments.

Her lips curled up into a saucy smile. "And you, my sexy green beast"—she positioned the head of his cock at her entrance before lowering herself, taking him into her body centimeter by slow centimeter—"are mine."

"Fucking take me, *zoani*."

TWENTY

"Gotta take a piss," Thargen declared.

Yuri dropped her bag on the ground and turned her head to see him walking toward a nearby tree. She couldn't stop her eyes from dipping to his ass—still visible despite the gear and weapons with which he was laden. He definitely wasn't human, but announcing that he was about to pee on a tree was probably the most universally *male* move in existence, apparently transcending species.

She chuckled, shaking her head, and knelt on the riverbank. Opening her bag, she withdrew the two empty canteens, setting one on the ground beside her. Popping open the other, she dunked it into the river, lifting it to her mouth and drinking deeply once it was full. The cool water felt wonderful going down her parched throat. She only stopped when she had to take a breath, and immediately plunged the canteen into the water again.

Who knew having sex for most of the night and a chunk of the next morning was such thirsty work?

She still couldn't wipe the goofy grin off her face. Not even the disappointment of discovering the smugglers' holocoms were utterly useless had been able to dampen her mood.

Thargen was hers.

Every muscle in her body, even ones she didn't know she had, was sore in the most satisfying way—like she'd had the greatest workout of her life. And there was still a delicious ache between her thighs. Were it not so urgent that they distance themselves from the scene of the fight and find new shelter, Yuri would have eagerly continued what they started this morning. There were still so many things she wanted to do with Thargen—*to* Thargen.

There were still so many things she wanted him to do to her.

Most of all, she wanted to taste him. She wanted to have his cock in her mouth, wanted to feel his hard, throbbing shaft on her tongue, wanted to look up and see him shatter as he came.

Yuri groaned as that ache between her legs grew; squeezing her thighs together only enhanced the sensation.

Why am I torturing myself? Just need to focus on something other than my hyperactive libido.

She lifted the canteen out of the river, closed it, shook off the droplets of chilly water from its exterior, and returned it to her bag. After she'd filled the other, she clipped it on her belt next to the small blaster at her front. Gathering her feet beneath her, Yuri stood and turned.

And found herself suddenly face-to-face with an alien, her eyes locking with his—one of which was vibrant magenta, the other rich cerulean.

She froze, unable to speak, unable to breathe, unable to do anything but stare. Her skin prickled, and the hairs on the back of her neck rose.

The teal-skinned male daevah in front of her stared right back. His purple hair was tousled, with a loose braid hanging down one side of his face. Short eyebrows of matching color rested over his mismatched eyes. Markings, almost like raised scars, stretched out from the corners of his mouth up to his pierced, pointed ears, with another cutting through his lips and down his chin. A final set ran from his hairline to his cheekbones, lined up perfectly with the centers of his eyes. His lean, athletic body was clad in black, form-fitting armor, which was comprised of hundreds of interlocking plates that covered him from his feet all the way up to just under his jaw.

The daevah's gaze shifted to look past her for an instant. It was only then, during that brief break in eye contact, that she noticed the blaster in his hand.

A soft whine started in the back of Yuri's throat.

The alien shook his head and brought a finger to his lips.

Eff. That.

Yuri spun and ran. "Thargen!"

The alien spat out a curse behind her.

"Busy," Thargen growled.

His voice led her eyes to him; he stood in front of a tree a few meters away with his back toward her, hands positioned as though they were on his dick—but his head was turned to the side to stare at *another* daevah, this one holding a long, sleek rifle with the barrel aimed directly at Thargen.

Though his hair was styled differently—it was gathered in a neat ponytail, and the sides of his head were shaved—the second daevah looked exactly like the first.

Yuri halted, eyes flaring wide. Her fear shot up several notches.

"We've come to help you, terran," said the daevah behind her.

"You're not fucking touching her," Thargen snarled, turning toward Yuri.

"I will shoot," the second daevah said. "Hands up, vorgal."

"No!" Yuri dropped her hand toward her blaster.

Before she could close her fingers around the grip, a strong hand clamped around her wrist and yanked her arm away, spinning her to face the first daevah. He dragged her closer, and something moved behind him—a long, thin tail, flicking either in restlessness or agitation. It swept up between their bodies and plucked Yuri's blaster from its holster.

"Thank you for the warning, brother," he said, though he did not look away from Yuri. His tail lifted the blaster high, dangling it by the trigger guard. "Why would a slaver allow his slave to carry a weapon?"

Yuri yanked on her arm, but she couldn't break his hold. "I'm not a slave."

"Release my *zoani*," Thargen said with a snarl. "Now."

She turned her head to glance back at him. He hadn't moved from his place, and though he'd raised his empty hands into the air in surrender, his lips were peeled back, and his golden eyes held that primal fire. He was on the verge of Rage. She could almost feel the heat baking off him despite the distance separating them.

"*Zoani?*" the first daevah asked. "A vorgal calling his slave *zoani?*"

"I'm not a slave, and he's *not* a slaver," Yuri gritted through her teeth.

"Not slavers, Kier," the second daevah said in a flat voice. "These are more smugglers."

Kier tightened his hold on Yuri's arm, making her cringe. "Kidnapping, transporting, or selling, it's all one in the same, Kayl."

"You take your fucking hand off her," Thargen roared, lowering his hands and taking a step closer to her.

Kayl's weapon jerked slightly and fired, producing a

piercing but barely audible sound. A cloud of dirt sprayed from the ground within a few centimeters of Thargen's foot.

Yuri's heart leapt into her throat.

Thargen snapped his head toward Kayl, teeth bared, and snarled, jutting his hands back into the air.

"Don't shoot him!" Yuri turned her face to the daevah holding her. "I don't know who you are, but we're not smugglers. We were kidnapped on Arthos and escaped when the ship crashed here. Just *please* don't hurt him."

Kier stepped back slightly without relinquishing his grip and ran his eyes over Yuri from head to toe and back again. "Rather well equipped for escapees, aren't we?"

"Her clothes are twice her size and we don't even have any fucking shoes," Thargen said. "You wanna talk well equipped, how about you tell us where you got those weapons and armor? That shit isn't cheap."

A corner of Kier's mouth drew back, altering the angle of the scar-like line leading away from it. "All the others we have seen had orange markings on their clothing..." After a moment's pause, he glanced at his companion. "Yes, I *do* know it is possible to change clothing. I've done so on a few occasions, myself."

Kier narrowed his eyes, shifting them between Yuri and Kayl. "I'm sure terrans are capable of it, but this one? It does not seem likely." Another second or two went by before he huffed through his nostrils, released her arm, and took a step back. "I am not taking her side!"

Yuri frowned, brow furrowing. Confusion blanketed her mind, making her fear suddenly less immediate and the situation seem more surreal. "Um...what would I be capable of?"

"Being a slaver," Kier replied before rolling his eyes and shooting another glare at Kayl. "*Smuggler.* Is it really the time to correct my terminology?"

"What the fuck is wrong with you?" asked Thargen.

"My brother, currently. He seems to enjoy making me look foolish when I need to be intimidating."

"Must you speak out loud?" asked Kayl, still betraying no emotion in his voice.

Kier threw up the hand holding his blaster and shook his head. "Yes! That is what people do, Kayl. They speak."

Yuri glanced at Kayl, whose eyes matched the colors of his brother's perfectly except for the fact that those colors were flipped—they were like mirror images of one another. His weapon was still trained on Thargen; she would've sworn the daevah hadn't moved a centimeter since she'd last looked at him.

Thargen growled. "Berrok's bare ass, am *I* gonna have to be the voice of reason here?"

"Are you two speaking to each other? Like, in your minds?" Yuri asked.

"Yes. But Kier prefers the sound of his own voice," replied Kayl.

"Sounds like a friend of mine," Thargen muttered.

Yuri looked between the two brothers, a flare of excitement brushing aside both her confusion and her lingering fear. "That...is so cool!"

"Nothing cold about it, unless you are referring to his personality," Kier said in a low voice.

"Are you two capturing us or what?" Thargen asked. "If you need some time to punch each other until you have this figured out, we can just go. Won't even kill you."

"We are not letting smugglers escape," said Kayl. "You will give us information on your camp."

"We're not smugglers," Yuri and Thargen said in unison.

"Then where are your collars?" Kayl asked.

Yuri reached up—slowly—to touch her neck. "We never had collars. We weren't part of their original...cargo."

"Convenient story," Kayl said flatly. "Likely a lie."

"Call her a liar again and see what fucking happens," Thargen said with a growl.

"You will force me to shoot you, and I will continue my work."

"It's not a lie," Yuri said hurriedly, glancing at Thargen. His muscles were bulging, his skin was tight, and barely perceptible tremors were running through his raised arms. She had the sense that it was taking him more effort to remain still than it would have for him to launch a vicious attack.

She returned her gaze to Kier. "You mentioned the orange markings. Those were on the males that came into Starlight Trance, the nightclub I work in back on Arthos. One of them got aggressive with me, but Thargen"—Yuri pointed at her vorgal—"beat the crap out of them before they could hurt me. They got kicked out, but they were apparently waiting for us when we left because the next thing I knew, I was waking up in a cell on their ship. Their leader, Tae-something—"

"Taeraal," Thargen interjected.

"Yes, thank you. Taeraal said they were taking us to Caldorius. But then we crashed here."

"And you simply tossed off your collars and strolled into the wilds?" Kier asked, one of his small eyebrows quirking.

"I told you, we never had collars. We weren't part of the original cargo. We were just...a bonus. They were pissed off that Thargen kicked their asses. All the other captives had collars on."

"And all this equipment?" Kayl asked.

"Shit they were smuggling in the cargo hold," said Thargen.

"I was not asking about fecal matter."

"I think it's an expression," Kier offered.

"And you could have informed me of that when you sensed my confusion, brother."

Kier snickered. "Would you also like me to hold your hand and carry your gear?"

Yuri couldn't keep a smirk off her lips. As alien as they looked and spoke, the interactions between these daevah reminded her so much of the way her and her siblings interacted with one another.

"Anyway," Thargen said, "we took some of this sh—*stuff* from the hold on our way out. Some of it was from a skeks scouting party we killed about a week ago. The rest came from those fuckers we killed yesterday."

"That was you?" Kier smiled, and light sparked in his eyes. "Would that I'd been around to see it happen. How did two of them end up in that pit?"

Thargen chuckled; there was humor in it, but it was also laced with Rage, making it almost threatening. "First one wasn't paying attention while he was walking. Second wasn't fast enough to stop me when I kicked him."

"So...I think we've established that we aren't slavers or smugglers, right?" Yuri said, offering Kier a tentative smile.

Thargen grunted. "I'd say so. Now who the fuck are you two?"

"Hunters," replied Kayl.

"Well, that's descriptive."

"Annnd what are you hunting?" Yuri asked.

"Slavers," said Kier. "We've an official Consortium endorsement to bring them to justice by any means necessary."

"Great, we're on the same side," Thargen said. "Can I put my fucking arms down now?"

Kier ran his eyes over Yuri again and frowned slightly.

After a few moments, his tail drifted forward and offered her blaster to her. "Yes, I am serious, Kayl."

Yuri lifted her hand and hesitated before carefully taking the end of the blaster's grip between her forefinger and thumb, letting the weapon dangle as she lowered it into its holster. "Thanks."

After giving Yuri a nod, Kier shifted his gaze to Thargen. "You may lower your hands, vorgal."

Yuri turned to face Thargen. His hands were still raised, and his muscles still looked pumped up, full of Rage, even though his eyes were a touch clearer than before.

Thargen tipped his head toward Kayl. "He gonna lower his railgun?"

"Perhaps," Kayl said, "after you place all your weapons on the ground."

Thargen's answering laughter bubbled up from his gut, making his shoulders shake. "How about you kiss my ass?"

Yuri stepped away from Kier and went to Thargen, wrapping her arms around him. He didn't hesitate to return her embrace. His heat baked into her, as reassuring as it was concerning; he always ran hot, but this was definitely at a level he only reached through Rage.

"Kayl..." Kier warned.

"Don't touch my *zoani* again, and we won't have any problems," Thargen said.

Kayl's eyes—so similar to his brother's and yet somehow so much darker and deeper—ran over Yuri and Thargen slowly. She felt more like she was being scanned by a computer than a person. Several seconds of silence passed, during which Kayl offered no sign of his thoughts or intentions, displaying not even a flicker of emotion—and during which Thargen's hold on Yuri strengthened and he infinitesimally shifted his body as though to shield her with it.

Finally, Kayl lowered his railgun.

Thargen's tension eased, though not by much. "Perfect. Now we're all friends. You have a ship?"

Kayl's tail swished from one side to the other and went still again. "We do."

"Then let's get off this planet already."

"Our business here is not complete."

"You said you hunt slavers," Yuri said. "How did you know they were here?"

Kier moved to stand next to his brother, dropping his blaster into a holster at his hip. "We've been monitoring Taeraal and his branch of the Zulka gang for several months. When they left Arthos with their cargo, we followed."

"You knew they had a hold full of slaves and let them leave?" Thargen asked.

"It is about more than just the slaves, vorgal," said Kayl.

Just like that, the heat and tension in Thargen's body was rising again. "Enlighten me then, daevah. We were in that cage for close to a week, at least. Who knows how the fuck long everyone else was behind bars with those fucking collars on. So what else was there to wait on if you already knew about all those other people?"

Yuri slid her hand under Thargen's backpack and smoothed it over his heated skin.

"There were whispers that Taeraal would meet with another slaver during his journey to Caldorius," Kier said, brows falling low. "Someone far more powerful and far more influential."

"Someone we have been hunting for many years," his brother added. "A tretin pirate called Vrykhan."

"Vrykhan?" Yuri asked. "That sounds familiar. Didn't... didn't Taeraal mention that name?"

"I think he did," Thargen said with a grunt. "Something about having him lined up as a buyer on Caldorius."

The twins' faces lit up.

"Tell us everything," Kier said.

"Not much else to say. He was bringing the shipment to a buyer on Caldorius, said that name. That Vrykhan doesn't like to wait and they didn't want him pissed off or something like that."

"That is all?" demanded Kayl. "There was nothing else?"

"That's it," Yuri said. "He only spoke to us that one time, and that's all he said about Vrykhan."

"We followed the smuggler ship for six days," Kier said, "waiting for the Zulka to meet with Vrykhan's ship."

"But the information we received was incorrect," said Kayl.

"They were meeting *on* Caldorius. That is rare for Vrykhan, based on what we've learned about him over the years. But after those six days, we were drawing too near to Caldorius, and we are not welcome there. We could not let the smugglers land. So we fired on the ship."

"That's why we crashed," Yuri said.

Thargen thrust an arm forward, jabbing a finger at the daevah even as he clutched Yuri a little tighter. "You fuckers almost killed everyone!"

Kier scowled. "We sought only to disable the engines."

"And I did not miss my mark," said Kayl. "I never miss."

Thargen's voice dipped toward a growl as he said, "And yet here the fuck we are."

At that, the corners of Kayl's mouth dipped. The movement was infinitesimal, but it was undeniable, and it was the strongest display of emotion Yuri had seen from him thus far.

Kier sighed, tipped his head back, and shook it. "If you are angry, Kayl, feel free to *say* something. Why must I be the one to hear it? And don't you dare say—"

"Because I hear it every time you are angry, Kier. Is it not enough that I must feel it regardless?" Kayl said. "Do you prefer it this way? Do you prefer for our new *friends* to hear it?"

"Yuri, when we get home, I'm gonna need you to tell everyone I know about this. About how I was the fucking reasonable one," Thargen said. "Can I get you two to stay on subject for a minute?"

Yuri pulled her lips into her mouth and bit them to prevent herself from smiling.

"They engaged their jump drive despite the damage to their engines," Kayl said firmly, glaring at his brother. "That is why the ship crashed."

Kier returned his attention to Yuri and Thargen. "It took days to track the jump path. We came as soon as we knew where the ship came down."

Kayl also swung his eyes back to Yuri. "The outcome is regrettable."

"We've never wished harm on innocents."

"But so long as there are survivors remaining, our task is incomplete. We need to extract what information we can from Taeraal and eliminate his crew."

"And save the captives," Kier said from the side of his mouth.

"Is that not obvious? Must I state every detail?"

Thargen cleared his throat. "If you want to just let us know where your ship is, we'll go wait for you there while you work out your family issues." He leaned his head closer to Yuri's, and in a loud whisper said, "I say we just take the ship. They're so busy arguing they won't even realize."

Yuri drew back her arm and poked him in the side.

He flinched and released a soft grunt.

"I cannot say that you are giving us much reason to trust you, vorgal," said Kier.

Thargen straightened. "Goes both ways. Anyone who can't take a joke is worthy of suspicion."

"It is my understanding that jokes are meant to be humorous," said Kayl.

"Not necessarily," Thargen countered. "So, we going to this ship or not? I'm getting my *zoani* home one way or another, and I'm not gonna stand here until another pack of skeks show up because they were lured over by your arguing. How the fuck did you two manage to sneak up on us without giving yourselves away?"

The daevah were silent for several seconds, turning their eyes toward one another. Little changes in expression flicked across their faces; were they having a whole conversation in their heads? Oddities aside, this was a stroke of luck, a chance for Yuri and Thargen to get home—and it was real. She couldn't stop the hope flaring inside her, outshining all else.

"However else it may appear to you, we are very good at what we do," Kier finally said. "We will provide you passage back to Arthos, but we must ask for your aid in return."

"What do you need help with?" asked Thargen.

"We do not *need* help," said Kayl.

Kier closed his eyes, raised a hand, and caught his braid, squeezing. "I am rescinding my earlier argument. Please, Kayl, just close your mouth and let me talk."

"Help with what?" Thargen said with a bit more gravel in his voice.

Yuri set her hand back into motion, rubbing her palm up and down his back. She understood his frustration, but frustration wasn't going to help them here.

Kier lowered his arm, shot his brother a glance, and looked back at Thargen. "The Zulka have established a camp at a large cave six kilometers from here. They've built barricades, presumably to fight off the skeks, and are armed with the same type of auto-blasters you are carrying. There are ten smugglers there, not including the ones you killed yesterday."

"Fuck, how many people did they need to run a cargo ship?" Thargen muttered.

"It is common for such crews," said Kayl. "They bring so many along to ensure they have presence enough on Caldorius to defend their cargo until it is offloaded to the purveyors."

"Is it just the smugglers at the camp, or are there other survivors?" Yuri asked.

Kayl nodded. "We have accounted for six surviving captives. The smugglers seem to be utilizing them for menial labor, despite their weakened states."

"And you want us to help take out this camp and rescue the captives before you'll get us off this planet?" asked Thargen.

"Yes."

"You really can't take ten of them between the two of you?"

Kayl's frown returned, just as subtle as before but entirely unmistakable. "We do not *need* your help, vorgal, as I have stated."

"But it would be greatly appreciated," said Kier. "An extra warrior on our side will undoubtedly prove beneficial to our goals and help us save innocent lives."

"All right," Thargen replied. "What are we waiting for? Let's kill some smugglers."

Kier's brows rose. "Now? Would it not be wise to await the cover of darkness to make our attack?"

"Do I look like someone who worries much about wisdom?"

Kier glanced at his brother. "I know the tattoo means he was a vanguard, Kayl. Why do you think I requested his help?"

"Fuck, I thought it was because you liked me," Thargen said.

"The chances of that are low," Kayl replied.

Yuri chuckled. "I find him quite charming."

Kayl's frown deepened slightly. "Terrans are strange beings."

Thargen snickered and shook his head. "Not often I meet people with less self-awareness than me."

"All that aside," said Kier, "I believe this undertaking would be best approached with stealth and caution. It would be best if we could eliminate any sentries and enter the cave before our targets are alerted. We'll only grant our enemies a chance to bolster their defenses and potentially harm the captives if we expose ourselves."

"Done that a time or two unintentionally," Thargen said. "Amazing how many people don't enjoy seeing a bare-assed vorgal."

Yuri turned her head to look up at him; there'd been humor in his voice, but she didn't think he was lying or even exaggerating. The seriousness of what the daevahs were discussing wasn't lost on her. She hadn't shaken the trauma of being caged like that, and the images from the time following the crash were still fresh in her memory, but she couldn't stop herself from saying, "Well from now on, nobody gets to see *my* vorgal bare-assed but me."

Thargen's lips stretched into a grin as he met her gaze, and that hungry fire ignited in his eyes. "Yes, sir."

"So, she really is your *zoani*," Kier said.

Yuri turned her face toward the daevah. They were both staring at Yuri and Thargen intently. Almost...longingly?

Her brows furrowed. "He hasn't told—"

"She is." Thargen settled his hands on her shoulders and gently squeezed, rotating his thumb along her collarbone. "And she's my main priority. If she's not safe, no one on this planet is. That too metaphorical or whatever for you, or do you understand it?"

The daevah nodded in unison. Seeing them move in such

perfect sync while standing beside each other was almost eerie, the exact sort of thing that would've been right at home in a horror movie from a hundred years ago.

Thargen grunted. "Good. Now for fucking real, we going to this ship or not? Starting to think you don't even have one."

TWENTY-ONE

The daevahs had a nice ship.

Really fucking nice.

Probably *too* fucking nice. Definitely a lot nicer than its simple name—the *Fang*—had implied.

Thargen couldn't stop his eyes from roving over the complex arrays of controls and displays before him. He could drive a hovercar with competence, and had been trained to operate a few classes of armored ground vehicles back in his Vanguard days, but this ship was clearly beyond him. It looked like all the controls for a battle cruiser with a crew of hundreds had been crammed into this four-seat cockpit, and he couldn't begin to guess what ninety-five percent of it was for.

He suspected that lack of familiarity was behind his odd but insistent urge to touch *everything*.

He glanced at Yuri to find her looking around too, awe and excitement gleaming in her wide eyes. She didn't need to say it out loud for him to know what she was thinking just then—*This is so cool!*

I should be suspicious. On guard.

His attention shifted to the daevahs, who were standing in front of one of the control consoles, their fingers flying through commands on a pair of projected holo screens. Their armor and weapons were high-quality—even better than the undoubtedly stolen military equipment from the smuggler ship—and this spacecraft was on a whole different level somewhere far above that.

Its cloaking system was advanced enough that Thargen hadn't sensed the *Fang* at all when the daevahs had first led him and Yuri into the clearing where they'd landed. He'd thought it an empty field—the perfect place to be ambushed—and his Rage had flared in response.

This big, black, sleek ship materializing at the center of the field in front of him had been like a bucket of icy water poured on his Rage, and, despite his better judgment, that had been enough for him to set aside his suspicions.

This wasn't one of those *no other choice* situations—Yuri and Thargen had countless choices laid out before them, and trusting these daevahs was only one. Maybe not even the best one, or the smartest one.

But regardless of the warning signs—like this ship, which would've been more at home with an elite special forces unit or in the Inner Reach Syndicate's criminal fleet—he believed Kier and Kayl. They were strange, but who in Thargen's life wasn't without their quirks? The twins struck him as genuine. At the very least, they hadn't harmed Thargen or Yuri despite having had ample opportunity to do so, and that had to say something, didn't it?

His eyes drifted back to Yuri again. When it came down to it, she was all that mattered. So long as she was safe, he cared about nothing else.

She met his gaze and smiled, making the light in her eyes even brighter. It wasn't just awe and excitement—it was hope.

That glimmer of hope she must've been nurturing to keep herself going all this time was shining brighter than ever now, and seeing it made Thargen's heart swell. He hadn't lied when he'd told her he would gladly go through all this again for her. He'd do it without hesitation, over and over again.

All for her.

"Almost done, *zoani*," he said softly. "We'll be on our way home soon."

She slipped her arms around Thargen and squeezed him. "I know. Hopefully we'll be able to help some of the others get home, too."

Thargen wrapped an arm around her shoulders, leaned down, and inhaled deeply, taking in her sweet scent. He hummed appreciatively. His terran possessed a noble heart, and he was not above taking pride in it—in her. At some point in his life, he must've done something good to have earned a female like Yuri.

She turned her face toward the daevahs, pressing her cheek against Thargen's chest. "So, what's the plan?"

"Go in, kill the smugglers, and get the slaves out," Thargen said.

"That sounds reasonable to me," said Kier without even a hint of irony.

Yuri looked up at Thargen with her brow furrowed. "You can't be serious."

Thargen frowned. "Why wouldn't I be?"

"Because this is dangerous," Yuri said flatly, "and we should make a plan to minimize that danger."

"And the situation is not a simple one," Kayl added. "There are too many variables to simply storm in and expect an acceptable outcome."

"Complex problems do not necessarily require complex solutions." Kier turned around to lean his backside on the console, bracing a hand atop it to either side of his hips. "Sometimes simple plans are the most elegant and effective."

"Less to go wrong with a simple plan," Thargen said. "Start getting too complicated and all you're doing is guaranteeing something's gonna go wrong."

Kayl's nostrils flared, but his expression remained otherwise unchanged. He tapped something on the holoscreen in front of him, and a free-floating, three-dimensional holographic map appeared in the center of the cockpit. Though Thargen didn't know that particular chunk of land, it was clearly a little piece of this planet—and it looked like that piece fit somewhere near their current location.

Kayl strode to the map and manipulated it with his fingers, altering the view angle and zooming in on what could only be the smuggler's camp. The cave opening on the cliffside was tall but narrow, and the rocky landscape outside boasted ample cover for any would-be defenders, bolstered by crudely constructed wooden barricades.

Thargen stepped closer to the map, drawing Yuri along with him. He lifted his right hand and ran it absently across the side of his head, making his palm rasp over his scars. "Not a bad position. Good cover, good lines of sight."

"We assumed it was a defensive position they claimed because of the skeks," said Kier, joining the others near the map. "We found evidence of an attack around the crash site. Was that when you escaped?"

Yuri tensed and shook her head. "No. We were already out in the wilderness when that happened. Just...not far enough away to avoid hearing it in the middle of the night."

Thargen gave her a gentle squeeze, and she leaned against him as though it were the most natural thing in the universe. He was coming to understand the fear she must've been feeling throughout this ordeal, if only to a small extent—because the thought of her coming to harm was terrifying to him in a way nothing else ever had been or could be.

"It was difficult to piece together what happened. The skeks stripped the wreckage quite thoroughly, and the few tracks we were able to locate were days old at best," said Kier.

That wasn't surprising. The skeks were notorious scroungers, scavengers, and hunters—and the crashed smuggler ship had offered them a chance to employ all those skills. Really, the only unexpected part of all this was that the smugglers had managed to get such a large group so far away from the crash site and survive for so many days despite the skeks presence in the area.

Thargen met Kayl's gaze. The daevah had steady eyes, unflinching eyes, and his stare was deep and determined.

"Still wanna hit them at night?" Thargen asked.

Kayl dipped his chin in a slow, deliberate nod. "Darkness may be our best cover in approaching the camp."

Yuri tipped her head back to look up at Thargen. "Don't the smugglers have those scopes or optics or whatever that have night vision?"

"Yeah, they do," Thargen replied, offering her a small smile.

"That may eliminate any element of surprise we might've hoped to gain under darkness," Kier said.

Kayl turned his face toward his brother. "But it remains our best course. The species we observed in that camp were largely diurnal, meaning they will be at a disadvantage whenever they are not using those optics. It also means a greater likelihood of more of them being asleep."

Thargen frowned and tilted his head, studying the holographic map. His instinct remained unchanged—attack head-on—but he knew that wasn't exactly correct here. A simple plan was absolutely the right answer, just not *that* simple of a plan.

Yuri reached forward, turning the map slightly before trailing her finger along one of the cliff faces. "What about here? It's not perfect, but the angle should keep you hidden from anyone at the camp until you're pretty close."

Kayl's short brows fell slightly. He flicked his hand through the hologram to angle the place Yuri had indicated toward him. For several silent seconds, he continually turned and zoomed the map, following the rock face toward the cave entrance. Kier watched, eyes just as intent and intense as his brother's. Finally, Kayl grunted thoughtfully.

"You can tell her, Kayl. It will not hurt you to say it out loud," Kier said.

"Nor would it harm you to relay the sentiment," Kayl replied.

"My brother believes it will work. I am in agreement. What of you, vorgal?"

Thargen ran his eyes along the holographic cliff one more time. They'd have to keep right up against the cliff, but it wasn't a bad angle of approach—and he'd get to kill some smugglers before everything was said and done. "Looks good to me. Name's Thargen, by the way."

"We really haven't done actual introductions this whole time, have we?" Yuri asked.

"Been a bit preoccupied."

"Forgive us for forgoing the usual formalities," said Kier, dipping his head in a shallow bow. "Such are not often employed in our profession. I am called Sol'Kier Sevris, and my brother is—"

"Sol'Kayl Kortanis," Kayl said.

Kier simultaneously glared at his twin and offered Yuri a smile. "Kier and Kayl will suffice."

Yuri smiled in return. "Yuri Eriksen. Pleased to officially meet you."

Thargen frowned. "I didn't know we were doing full names. Kinda steals the impact my full reveal would've had."

Yuri tipped her head back to look up at him again, quirking a brow. "You have a last name?"

"More like a title. Earned in battle by ancient vorgal tradition."

"Well?"

"Thargen Skullbreaker, Bane of Skeks."

"That sounds as though you just made it up," said Kayl flatly.

Yuri's shoulders shook with silent laughter.

"I didn't make it up," Thargen grumbled. "And I didn't make fun of your flowery daevah names, did I?"

Yuri placed a hand on his chest, rubbing it over his heart. Even through his shirt, that was more than enough to call his full attention back to her. She was looking up at him with a sudden lustful light in her eyes. "I think it's kinda hot. Very *orcish*."

Heat spiraled low in Thargen's belly and spread outward through his body. He covered her hand with his and grinned, making an appreciative growl in his chest. "Feel free to say it all you want, *zoani*."

"Can we focus on the matter at hand?" asked Kayl.

Kier snickered. "It is fine, brother. Perhaps they want an audience."

Those words caused a moment of paralyzing turmoil in Thargen. He wanted Yuri badly enough that part of him didn't care where or when he had her—or even who was nearby. But a much larger and stronger part of him, a part with a superheated core of pure Rage, refused to let anyone else see her because she was fucking his and his alone.

Yuri's cheeks flared pink, and she cleared her throat.

"Nope. Absolutely not. I'm, uh, more of a one-on-one, in private kind of girl."

And oh, the things I'll do with her once we're alone...

"We got a plan now," Thargen said, reluctantly tearing his gaze from Yuri to look at the twins. "What else do we need to worry about?"

"The details," replied Kayl.

"We're gonna sneak in there after dark, kill the smugglers, and free the slaves. Think that about covers it, doesn't it?"

"The leader, Taeraal," Kayl said. "We want him alive."

Thargen's nostrils flared with a heavy exhalation as that old beast that was his Rage slithered a little closer to the surface. "If you two know what a vanguard is, you know I don't really take prisoners in situations like this. Especially not when that spawn of a skeks is the one who made this whole thing personal."

Kier stepped toward Thargen with fire in his mismatched eyes. "That doesn't matter."

Yuri tightened her arm around Thargen and pressed her hand more firmly to his chest. It was just enough to keep him from lunging forward to meet the daevah's challenge. It said a lot that Yuri could hold him back with a simple touch; he'd always wanted to fight a pair of daevah, and even if these two were scrawny by vorgal standards, he had a feeling they'd put up a good fight.

"He may have information about Vrykhan," said Kayl. A flicker of his brother's fire gleamed in his gaze.

"Whom we have been hunting for a *very* long time." Kier's voice was strained, spoken through clenched fangs.

Thargen recognized that look in the daevahs' eyes, that tone in Kier's voice. He'd seen that hatred before in Arcanthus and Drakkal both when they'd talked about their past, when they'd talked about the person who'd betrayed them and destroyed everything they'd built—the person who'd killed everyone they'd cared about.

This was personal for the daevah—not necessarily with Taeraal, but with this other slaver they were after. Whatever emotions were behind it, whatever reason they had, it was clearly a vendetta that ran deep. That didn't negate the grudge Thargen had with Taeraal, but it put it into perspective. All Thargen had to do was get through this last bit, and he and Yuri could be free. They could move on from what Taeraal had done.

He doubted that the twins would be able to move on from whatever had happened to them even if they found their target; the hatred they'd displayed just now suggested that their pain was too great, that the trauma inflicted by the wrong they'd been done was too scarring.

Thargen tucked his Rage away; he'd have chance enough to let it out later. "I'll try, but that's the best I can promise you. Tend to lose the meaning of *mercy* while I'm in the thick of it."

The daevah stared at him, their solemn expressions perfect mirrors of each other. Tension crackled in the air. Normally, Thargen would've thrived on that sort of tension, would've pushed it further. What would that gain him in this situation?

"That good with you, or we gonna stand here staring at each other like a bunch of creeps?" he asked.

"It's nice to have people to stare at other than *him*." Kier tipped his head toward Kayl, a corner of his mouth tilting up.

"I assure you, the feeling is mutual," Kayl said.

Fuck. Strange as they are, I kinda like these two.

Kayl manipulated the map again, indicating a copse of trees downslope from the smuggler camp with a clear line of sight to the cave. "I will position myself here, in one of these trees. That will allow me proper vantage to ensure no one escapes."

"Where's the *Fang* gonna be?" Thargen asked.

"Here, until we need it for extraction," said Kier. "This is as close as we could safely land to the camp without coming down directly atop it."

"You can have it remotely fly to us?"

Both twins nodded.

"Good." Thargen squeezed Yuri a little tighter. "She's staying here."

Yuri looked up at him again, brow furrowed, and caught his gaze. "Thargen, I—"

"Will stay on this ship." He leaned his head down to kiss her forehead and whispered, "We both know you're not ready for this, Yuri. You have a warrior's heart, but not the training. At least if you're here, I know you're safe."

Her lips were downturned when he lifted his head away, but she offered him a nod. "I know. I'm not stupid. I know I'd only get in the way and, well, we both know how I react around blood. I'd only be a liability. I just don't like having to sit here being useless while you go put yourself in danger."

Fucking hell, she was beautiful even when she was sad. Leaving her, even for a little while—even for a fight he'd been looking forward to since Taeraal had jumped him in Arthos— was going to be hard. A lot of things were hard when it came to Yuri, and the easiest one to deal with these days was his cock. But none of that was her fault, and he wouldn't have wanted it any other way. All the things he felt for her, all the emotions she showed for him, it was all worth it. She was worth it a million times over.

Thargen cupped a hand under her jaw, keeping her face angled toward his. "You're definitely not stupid, and you sure as fuck aren't useless, terran. Don't ever think you are."

That reversed her frown, though he could still see the turmoil in her eyes. He understood that frustration—he under- stood wanting to make a difference, wanting to be helpful, and knowing that you couldn't be in a particular situation. Fuck, he felt like that pretty damned often outside of combat.

"It is many hours until dark," Kier said. "We need not pass them standing around this map. Would the two of you care for some food?"

"Fuck yeah," Thargen replied.

At the same instant, Yuri' said, "Heck yeah."

Her lips stretched into a grin almost as wide as Thargen's just before they burst into laughter.

And that laughter felt *good*—better than it had any right to feel. He guessed it was because they were finally so close to the end of this, because the escape he'd promised her was finally in sight...and because he'd found the missing piece of himself, which had always been her.

The twins led them to a small galley, where they all sat and ate together. Even though the food was just those typical pre-packaged, instant-rehydration meals served on a lot of small ships, it ranked amongst the most delicious meals Thargen had ever eaten. As much as he loved meat, especially when it had been roasted over an open fire, having some fruits and vegeta-bles—even if he didn't know what those fruits and vegetables were—was a welcome change.

Kier was talkative throughout the meal, a bit awkward but friendly enough, and even Kayl seemed to relax a little. Thargen had the sense that, despite having one another, these daevahs were lonely at heart. He wondered if it had to do with their psychic bond—were they just so connected to one another that being together for them was just like being alone for everyone else? But he didn't spend much time contemplating that—or talking. He was far too occupied with shoveling food into his mouth.

Yuri ate an entire second meal on her own, and Thargen cut himself off after his third, giving in to the obnoxious little voice in the back of his mind yammering about manners and being a gracious guest or some shit like that—a voice that sounded oddly like Drakkal.

After the food, Kier took them into the cargo hold—which had been converted into a bunk space with fold-up cots along the walls. He opened a row of storage lockers, revealing dozens, perhaps hundreds, of pieces of clothing in a variety of cuts, sizes, and colors.

"For many of the slaves we rescue, choosing their own clothing from here is the first thing they do that shows them they are free," Kier explained when Thargen gave him a questioning look. "A small thing, perhaps, but it helps them feel more like people again rather than possessions."

He told them to help themselves to some fresh clothing if they could find anything that suited them. Thargen claimed a pair of boots that were a bit snug but mostly comfortable but decided to wait on anything else—he was likely to stain whatever he was wearing with blood tonight.

Yuri selected a shirt, pants, and shoes that were actually sized for her little terran body, holding them up to show him. The pants were black, like her hair, and the shirt almost perfectly matched the color of her eyes. Though he longed to peel off her current clothing himself, though he yearned to have his hands on her bare skin, there was still the matter of having an audience— and the looming battle, which was a distant second concern.

Kier eliminated one of those problems by leading Thargen and Yuri to private quarters—apparently one of three such chambers on the *Fang*.

The room was small and sparsely furnished, containing only a bed, a little table built into the wall, a shower stall, and a door that opened on a toilet room. Compared to the accommodations Thargen and Yuri had been sharing for the last couple weeks, this was outright fucking extravagant.

"Feel free to clean yourselves up and get some rest," Kier said. "We will check with you in a few hours." With that, the daevah slipped out.

Thargen's blood was already flowing hot before the door had even closed; cleaning up and resting were not the activities at the top of his priority list. He set their gear and weapons down on the floor near the door and turned to Yuri, who'd already moved deeper into the room.

When she tossed the folded pile of new clothing onto the table and flopped down on the bed with a content groan, Thargen *knew* there'd be no rest now—and that there'd be no point in cleaning up just yet. Seeing her lying on that bed, the fabric of her oversized gray shirt sculpted to her full breasts and nipples, sent his Rage into a frenzy.

His clothes were off before he'd even reached the bed; his cock sprang free, already hard, throbbing, and hungry. Yuri stared up at him with those beautiful green eyes, her lower lip caught between her teeth. The fire in her gaze said all that needed to be said—*You know what I want, vorgal.*

Damn right, he did.

He whipped off her pants, tore her shirt open, and unleashed himself, worshipping her with his hands, mouth, and tongue, leaving no part of her delectable little body untouched. He was aware only of Yuri through the haze created by her heady scent and intoxicating taste, and when he joined his body with hers he was overcome anew with the need to brand her, claim her, possess her as thoroughly as she did him.

Their fingers roved, squeezing flesh, pulling hair, clenching fistfuls of the bedding as they thrust and writhed, panted and moaned, and completely lost track of where one body ended and the other began.

Thargen kissed her repeatedly, kissed her everywhere. He kept his body in constant motion, pressing ever closer to his own climax as Yuri's breathy cries of pleasure filled his ears. His Rage roiled beneath the surface, relishing every sensation, pushing him to give more and more to her—more pleasure, more of himself.

They came undone simultaneously, bodies shuddering, lips locked together with Yuri's blunt nails digging into the skin of the back of his head, and pushed through the overwhelming ecstasy that wracked their bodies.

By the time they'd begun to descend from those heights, Thargen had already changed positions, flipping onto his back so Yuri could ride him. The squeezing of her thighs on his hips and the scrape of her nails over his chest drove him mad.

He lost himself on those building waves of pleasure, falling so deeply into her that he could not recall carrying her out of bed—though he must've, as they wound up in that narrow shower stall, Yuri's ass against his lower belly. Her hands were on the stall door, and his were clamped around her waist, holding her up as he drove into her with ragged breaths. Hot water sprayed on his back and sluiced down their naked bodies.

He was well beyond words by then, able only to grunt and growl as he pumped his hips. When he reached his climax, his seed shooting deep inside her, his mind blanked out for a moment; there was room for nothing else but pleasure and heat.

Eventually, they must've caught their breath and calmed, and Thargen withdrew from Yuri, lowering her to the shower floor. She stood, limbs languid, with a pleased smile on her lips as he gently cleaned her. She made little humming sounds throughout—and those sounds were almost enough to get him going again. But he held back now, tamping down his Rage to save for later.

His *zoani* needed rest, and it wasn't a bad idea for him to get some, too. However quickly and quietly he and the daevahs hoped to raid this camp, no one could predict what would happen, and Thargen would need to be rested and alert.

The shower's automated dryer kicked on a few seconds after he'd turned the water off, bathing Thargen and Yuri in a warm light that made the moisture vanish from their skin over the course of a few thumping heartbeats. He stepped out of the stall and carried her to bed.

She turned to face him as he lay down beside her, and he drew her into his arms.

They remained like that for a long while, with Thargen content to simply listen to her breathing and enjoy the feel of her against him.

"Guess we need to expand your title," she said once the blush had finally begun fading from her cheeks.

"How's that?" he murmured.

"Thargen Skullbreaker, Bane of Skeks and Slayer of Yuri." She offered a satisfied smile that heated his blood all over again.

Thargen hummed appreciatively and leaned his face toward hers, capturing her lips in a kiss that he had no qualms about stretching out. He wasn't sure how much time had passed since they'd come into the room, and he didn't care. He would squeeze as much as he could out of these moments.

"I accept this honor, *zoani*," he said when he pulled back, "and offer you the titles *Conqueror of Thargen* and *Master of Rage*."

She beamed at him, and it pierced straight to his heart—which only made it hurt all the more when her smile faded, and her expression became somber a few moments later. "Just so you know, Thargen, you haven't been released from your promise."

"To get you home?"

"To come back to me." She cupped his cheek, brushing her

thumb over his cheekbone. "You're required to come back. I'm not done with you yet...not even close."

"Ah, Yuri"—he turned his face toward her hand to kiss her palm—"I only just got started with you. There's nothing in this whole fucking universe that could keep me away."

Now it was Yuri who kissed him—one of those sweet, tender kisses he'd come to enjoy so much, the sort of kiss that made it clear that she was here for him, even with everything else put aside. He understood now that a kiss like this was love in its purest form, love without conditions or modifiers, love simply for its own sake. And it stole his breath just as thoroughly as their most heated, passionate kisses.

When she finally withdrew her lips, Thargen pulled her closer and rasped, "I fucking love you, terran."

TWENTY-TWO

Kier—who was little more than a shadow amidst darkness, even to Thargen's eyes—flattened his back against the cliff and lifted a hand to his wrist. With a barely audible click and a gentle hum that was more a feeling than a sound, a small, spherical object detached from his wrist armor and floated into the air.

Thargen adjusted his hold on his auto-blaster and suppressed an impatient growl. They were close enough now for him to smell not only the smugglers' fire but the sweat of the camp's inhabitants. His Rage demanded action; it had no patience for all this slinking around in the dark. It wanted *blood.* And Thargen agreed with it—just not enough to give in. Not yet.

"*Three sentries at the barricade, one of whom is monitoring your angle of approach,*" said Kayl through the commlink in Thargen's ear. "*All armed with auto-blasters.*"

The orb silently drifted around the corner.

"*I see him,*" said Kier. His words also came through the commlink even though he was only a meter away from Thargen; his fully enclosed helmet was not currently transmitting his voice in the open air. *"Drone is inside the cave. I see five captives, all in collars."*

"Is that really all that's left?" Yuri asked over the comms. *"You said there were six before, didn't you?"*

How much guilt was she feeling because she was alive and well while so many of the others had suffered and died? How much weight was she carrying on her shoulders because she hadn't been able to help them before, because she was safe aboard the daevahs' ship now while the other survivors were trapped in a cave with the remaining smugglers?

Part of Thargen wanted her with him even though logic said she was in the best place she could possibly be right now. He never could've imagined just how adversarial his instincts to keep her safe and keep her at his side could be with one another.

"It would seem so. One of them did appear to be in exceptionally poor condition when we first scouted the cave, and it is possible she has already passed. Considering the circumstances, this is more than we could've hoped for." Kier tapped his wrist controls again. *"Seven of the smugglers are inside. Only one appears to be sleeping."*

"And there's Taeraal." Yuri's voice was darker than Thargen had ever heard before. He could almost picture the expression that must've been on her face as she sat in the *Fang's* cockpit, watching the holo feeds from the twins' drones.

"Taking him alive remains a priority," said Kayl.

Kier lowered his arms. *"We will eliminate the closest sentries. Be prepared to end the third, Kayl."*

If they could kill the lookouts quickly and quietly, they'd catch the rest of the smugglers off-guard, which would be more than enough to swing the fight to Thargen and Kier's advantage—and was likely the only way they'd catch Taeraal alive.

Rage pushed against Thargen's mind, seeking entry, demanding control.

Not yet, damn it.

Kier turned his head toward Thargen and nodded as he drew a blaster from his hip.

Thargen returned the nod stiffly, dropping a hand from the foregrip of his auto-blaster to draw a knife. He sank into a crouch as Kier did the same.

Not yet. Soon, he told his Rage. *Soon.*

Kier leaned forward ever so slightly to peer around the cliff. Despite the daevah being clad in armor from head to toe, Thargen sensed Kier's muscles tensing as though preparing to pounce.

"*On my mark, vorgal...*" Kier's tail flicked—whether with restlessness or eagerness could not be determined. "*Now!*"

Thargen stood up and pushed himself away from the cliffside.

"*Hold!*" Kayl's command, though little louder than his usual volume, cut through Thargen's rising Rage, halting him in his tracks.

For an instant, Thargen was beyond the cover of the cliff, staring toward the smuggler camp—toward a bokkan with craggy skin who was positioned beside a two-meter-tall boulder at the edge of the wooden barricade, torso twisted while he looked back toward the other guards. The alien shook his head and began turning toward Thargen.

Both Thargen and Kier leapt back against the rock wall. Thargen's back hit hard, but he barely registered the pain over the thundering of his heart. He held his breath and listened for the shouts of alarm that would call the other smugglers to arms.

Coward, his Rage growled, raking its claws across his mind.

"What is it?" Thargen whispered through his teeth after a few seconds of taut silence.

"*Skeks*," both daevah replied simultaneously, their voices almost indistinguishable from one another.

Fuck. Leave it to the skeks to show up to a party uninvited.

"*They are approaching the camp from the far side, relative to your position,*" Kayl said. "*I do not have a clear line of sight, but I estimate more than twenty-five of them.*"

A sound rose into the night sky—no, not a singular sound, but a chorus of undulating howls. Skeks war cries. They were like fresh chunks of wood being tossed into the fires of Thargen's Rage, instantly heightening his bloodlust.

And it sounded like a fuck of a lot more than twenty-five to him.

The howls were answered by shouts from the camp. Within a moment, the high whining of auto-blaster fire was echoing off the cliffside. Blue-white light cast the nearby forest in a faint, ghostly glow. The booming of skeks guns retorted, swelling to overpower all other sound and make the blaster fire seem pathetic in comparison.

"That's a fucking warband," Thargen said with a snort.

"*Smugglers are rousing inside the cave,*" Kier said. "*They're taking up weapons and going to reinforce the barricade.*"

At least the comms were clear despite the din of battle.

"*I see nine outside now,*" Kayl said.

Kier touched the wrist controls. "*One remained behind with the captives.*"

"*My earlier estimate was low,*" Kayl said. "*This looks closer to one hundred. They are using the trees and rocks to cover their advance.*"

The thundering of those skeks rifles was followed by the sharp cracks of projectiles striking stone, which only became more piercing as they increased in frequency.

With each inhalation, Thargen's Rage burned a little hotter, and fresh strength pumped into his muscles. Those battle sounds called to him, beckoned him to come, to join. He'd have all the bloodshed he could desire if he just charged around the corner.

"*The smugglers are focused entirely on the attacking skeks,*" Kayl continued. "*Their position is defensible. They may yet hold.*"

"They *will* be overrun," Thargen said. "Smugglers must've pissed them off. When skeks organize into a warband like this, they won't stop until they destroy their enemies. They aren't here to hunt, just to kill."

"*And they won't stop with the smugglers,*" said Yuri, her sense of helplessness evident in her every word.

"*We must reassess this situation, and you are too close to the chaos,*" Kayl said with a new layer of hardness in his voice. "*The two of you must withdraw.*"

Thargen clenched his jaw and tensed his muscles, fighting the draw of the ensuing combat, trying to ignore that his heartbeat had become a thunderous, insistent drumming that urged him onward to war. There were only two possibilities for those captives if Thargen and Kier retreated now—remain slaves should the smugglers win—which was highly unlikely—or become food.

Too many of Thargen's comrades had fallen prey to these forces—the ravenous infestation that was the skeks and the slow, cancerous death promised by slavery. Even his Yuri, more precious to him than anyone or anything, had not managed to get through her life unscathed.

"Fuck that," Thargen growled—or perhaps it was his Rage speaking with his mouth.

Kier snapped his head toward Thargen, who could almost imagine those mismatched eyes being wide behind that black helmet. "*Thargen, there are—*"

"Run your fucking drone thing." Thargen pushed away from the cliff face again, bracing the end of his auto-blaster on his forearm to retain his hold on the knife. "Find us another way out of that cave."

"And if there isn't another way?"

"We'll make one."

If Kier responded, Thargen didn't hear.

Thargen darted around the corner and charged the undefended section of barricade ahead—the bokkan had moved to join his companions on the other side of the defenses. The forest was flashing with plasma pulses and the orange muzzle flashes, creating a strobe-like light that made the movements of the figures amongst the trees stuttering and erratic.

Without slowing, Thargen leapt over the barricade. Firelight from just outside the cave mouth cast a soft orange glow on the backs of the smugglers along the defensive line, an almost surreal contrast to the more intense bursts of illumination from the gunfire.

Rage whispered for him to join that chaos, to embrace his place as its agent, its embodiment. He could kill all those smugglers before they even turned around. Kill them like the fucking animals they were.

You're with me *this time*, he told his Rage.

Those smugglers were the only buffer between the skeks and the captives at the moment. Killing them now would only complicate things.

Thargen forced himself onward into the cave. A sharp turn after the narrow entrance opened into a large chamber lit by intense white light; he had the impression of electric lanterns set up around the chamber, but it was an unimportant detail. His attention fixed on the group of captives deeper within the chamber and the smuggler standing guard over them. Thargen's arm moved without thought, lashing out and releasing the knife as he broke into a run.

The lone smuggler spun away from the huddled captives just in time to catch the knife in the side of his neck. He grunted and staggered aside a step. Then Thargen was there, slamming his palm against the knife's pommel to hammer the blade in to the hilt. Blood bubbled from the smuggler's mouth, and with a choked gasp, he sank to the cave floor.

A whisper of movement had Thargen spinning, auto-blaster raised.

"*It's Kier,*" Yuri said, her voice punching through Thargen's Rage. "*He's there with you.*"

Thargen forced his finger away from the trigger and lowered the blaster. He spat a curse. "Fucking tell me you're following next time."

Kier's helmet peeled back in segments, revealing his face. His brows were low. "I did."

"Then say it louder next time. Fucking skeks are making a ruckus out there."

"Noted," Kier replied with a smirk. He dropped his blasters into their holsters and hurried to the captives, several of whom recoiled from the approaching daevah.

The female sedhi and ilthurii were still together, just as they had been since Thargen had awoken in that cage. The female kaital who'd been locked up beside Thargen and Yuri was here also, along with the male azhera who'd escaped the crashed ship, and a young male borian who'd been caged toward the front of the cell room.

All five were dirty, naked, and noticeably thinner than they'd been the last time Thargen had seen them. Their hair was tangled, the azhera's fur was matted, and many sported healing cuts and bruises on their bodies.

Kier crouched, placing himself closer to the captives' eye

levels, and said, "My name is Kier, and he is called Thargen. Do you remember him from the ship?"

A few of the captives glanced at Thargen and nodded.

"He was caged with the terran," said the sedhi, her third eye's pupil dilating and contracting. "How are you alive, vorgal?"

"Do I look that fucking easy to kill?" Thargen turned his weapon toward the cave's entrance. The battle sounds from outside seemed to be intensifying with each moment.

"What of the terran?"

"She's fine, too. Damn fine."

"We are going to escort all of you out of here." Kier accessed the controls on his wrist armor again. "My drone has scouted through a tunnel at the rear of this cave that will lead outside. We must move swiftly."

"What about these collars?" asked the azhera. "They used them to shock us, to track us."

Kier pulled up a small holo screen at his wrist. "Just a moment."

"There is another large group of skeks advancing from the other direction," Kayl said, a hint of static in his voice. *"The smugglers are being spread thin now, forced to defend along the entire barricade."*

Thargen growled, flexing his hands on the auto-blaster's grips.

Should be out there fighting. Out there killing.

But that was his Rage talking, irritated that it had been pushed back again, that it was being held on a leash. His muscles were rigid in his struggle to hold it back. He was here to defend these people, to get them out of here, to do what he hadn't done before. And it was Yuri's voice in the back of his mind that helped him win that struggle—her voice, so sad and dismayed, asking, *Is that really all that's left?*

He fucking loved her, and he was going to make sure she knew it when they were reunited.

"There," Kier declared, tapping his wrist.

A rapid series of soft clicks ran through the group of captives—their collars disengaging. The captives tugged the metal collars off and tossed them onto the cave floor, the azhera and sedhi spitting curses in their native tongues.

"Everyone on your feet," Thargen called over his shoulder. "We need to move."

"The skeks are gaining ground," Kayl announced. *"They are advancing cautiously, providing covering fire for each other."*

Fuck.

If this warband had been worked up into a frenzy, it might have bought Thargen and the daevahs a little more time—the skeks made easy targets when they were rushing headlong into blaster fire, even for assholes like these smugglers. But if they were making an organized attack...

The smuggler ship must've crashed in a skeks tribe's home territory.

Kier helped the sedhi onto her feet, who in turn helped the ilthurii beside her. Within a few seconds, all five were standing—and as difficult as that had proved for them, Thargen didn't expect much speed during their escape.

"Come. I will show you to the tunnel. It is narrow, but we can all fit through." Kier led the captives toward the rear of the cave.

Thargen followed, keeping his blaster directed at the entrance. The battle sounds spilling into the cave were made ghostly and distant as they echoed off the stone walls and ceiling. Thargen's Rage wanted the skeks to break through, wanted a chance to build a mound out of their corpses high enough to block the mouth of the cave.

"*Riniya*," someone said behind him in a thin, wavering voice.

Thargen glanced back to see the kaital looking at him. It was hard to believe she was the same female that had been their neighbor only a week ago. She looked diminished, dehydrated, broken.

"*Riniya*," she repeated, voice cracking. She pointed toward the far side of the cave with a trembling hand.

Thargen's Rage intensified to an inferno, fueled by the sight of this kaital in such a state; none of the smugglers he'd seen were nearly as dirty, malnourished, or battered as these captives. This could've been his Yuri, had things gone differently.

But his Rage was also fueled by a pang of guilt; could he have prevented this? Could he have spared this kaital and the others the hardships they'd endured? Could he have kept more of them alive?

No. I wasn't in any state to help them and keep Yuri safe.

Regardless, there sure as hell wasn't any time to contemplate that now, but he let it pour into his Rage all the same.

"Don't understand what you're saying, but we gotta go," he said.

"*Riniya*," she said more firmly, jabbing her finger in the same direction again—toward a clutter of pallets on the cave floor. "She's alive."

One of those pallets, piled higher with ratty cloth than the others, moved slightly.

"Go with the daevah." Thargen didn't linger to see if the kaital obeyed. He jogged to the pallets and knelt beside the one that had moved, tugging off the tattered clothing and blankets piled atop it. "Ah, fuck."

"*Thargen, what is it?*" asked Yuri.

The female volturian—Riniya—who'd been beneath the

cloth turned her head to look up at him with one eye gleaming feverishly. The other was swollen shut. Beads of sweat stood out on her skin, which had an ashen pallor. She met his gaze and held it.

Fuck.

"Kill me," she rasped. "Don't let them…" Her eye fluttered shut.

"*Thargen?*" Somehow, Yuri managed to squeeze a hell of a lot of worry into his name.

"The volturian who hurt her leg. She's alive," he said.

Should've helped her at the crash. Should've helped her get away.

Fuck, haven't I been through this? They all had collars on, the smugglers had guns, and me and Yuri were both battered and half-starved ourselves. What the fuck should I have done?

"Thargen!" Kier called. "We need to help everyone up into the tunnel."

Thargen's heart quickened further, and he gritted his teeth as a fresh wave of Rage blasted through him. He swung his blaster onto its shoulder strap and, gently as he could, scooped Riniya into his arms. She groaned, curling in on herself, features contorted in pain. She was even lighter than Yuri, even more delicate.

His mind flashed back to the volturian he'd slept with back in Arthos years ago, back to her cries, her—

Fuck! I didn't do this, it was those fucking smugglers!

The rest of the group was gathered at the rear of the cave, standing below a nearly two-meter-high ledge.

"Up there," Kier said as Thargen approached, frowning when his gaze fell on Riniya, "and a little farther back."

"Didn't see any openings when we came in," Thargen said through his teeth, struggling to keep his breaths measured, to hold back a wave of raw fury.

The commlink in Thargen's ear crackled.

"*Uh, Kier,*" Yuri said, "*the feed from your drone just went out. Like...its black now.*"

Kier lifted his arm and fiddled with the controls on his wrist again. "Likely just interference from the surrounding stone. Signals seem unreliable on this planet."

Thargen set Riniya down and hurried to the ledge, trying to ignore the itch crawling up his spine—he knew it was just an instinctual reaction to having his back turned to a battle. He hauled himself up smoothly and followed the ledge back, moving around a bulge in the rock to find an open passage just as Kier had said—a narrow, pitch-black gap in the stone. A faint, cool breeze flowed out from the opening.

He almost hated that part of himself was disappointed to have found an escape route after only a single kill. The smugglers and skeks deserved a lot worse before Thargen was through with them. All he needed was a few minutes to release his pent-up Rage and he could be satisfied.

Of course, he should've kept in mind what he'd expressed earlier—things rarely went according to plan.

"*Three smugglers down at the barricade,*" Kayl said. "*I am thinning the skeks as best I can, but a precision railgun is not exactly the most efficient weapon against a ravening horde.*"

There was a chance the smugglers could hold out all night —more improbable shit happened all the time—but it was just as likely they'd be overrun in the next few seconds. Either way, Thargen and Kier needed to have these captives moving *now*.

Thargen rushed back to the others, knelt at the edge of the ledge, and offered a hand. "Let's get going."

The female sedhi urged the kaital forward. The kaital's trembling hand caught Thargen's, and he pulled her up; she was nearly as light as Riniya. Once she was balanced on the ledge beside him, he reached for the next captive—the ilthurii.

Just as his fingers closed around her scaled wrist, a sound pierced the battle din—a small, insignificant sound he shouldn't have been able to hear, given the situation, but one that made him freeze for an instant.

It was the sound of a pebble clattering in the passage behind him.

Releasing the ilthurii's arm, Thargen pushed onto his feet and ran to the opening, swinging his auto-blaster into his hands. He raised the weapon to look through the optic. The stone walls, floor, and ceiling were lit up through the optic as though bathed in pure daylight.

So was the grinning skeks working his way through the narrow passage.

Fuck. When will I learn my damned lesson and stop asking for shit to go wrong?

The skeks opened his jaws to release a howl as he struggled to raise his rifle in the cramped space. Thargen cut that howl short with a burst of plasma; the last he saw of the skeks was its half-melted face just before it hit the floor.

At least half a dozen more skeks picked up their fallen comrade's war cry, their howls so amplified by the walls of the tunnel that there might as well have been a hundred of the fuckers crammed in there—and there very well could've been for all Thargen knew.

"Tunnel might be a bit tighter than you thought, Kier," Thargen shouted, firing another stream of plasma bolts into the passage.

Skeks snarled, growled, and howled, their large, sunken eyes gleaming with reflections of the blaster fire. One of their weapons went off, producing a fiery muzzle flash and a deafening crash of thunder. Projectiles cracked off the stone around Thargen, and heat flared on his bicep.

Rage pulsed through his veins, curling his lips into a grin.

He kept the trigger depressed, filling the tunnel with the blue white of plasma bolts and the orange glow of melting stone where those bolts struck the walls, floor, and ceiling. "Gonna have to do a lot fucking better than that if you want to eat tonight!"

When that stream of plasma sputtered out only seconds later, Thargen snarled and threw himself aside, pressing his back against the rock wall as another volley of return fire erupted from the darkness. He opened the auto-blaster's power cell chamber. A puff of smoke coiled out of the compartment, revealing a melted, sizzling power cell.

High-end weaponry and those stupid smugglers loaded them with cheap-ass ammunition?

He ejected the deformed power cell and dropped his hand, intending to reach for another, but the sound of heavy, shuffling footsteps in the passage had him tossing the blaster aside to pull his axes free of their loops on his belt. He already had the weapons activated and swinging by the time the first skeks emerged from the tunnel. One of the hardlight blades cleaved off the top half of the skeks' head.

"Kier, get over here!" Thargen's second axe lashed out to hack off the next skeks' arm at the elbow.

There were even more of those bastards howling in the tunnel now.

Thargen kicked the disarmed skeks into the wall once it had stumbled out of the passage and set into the next foe, his axes moving in blurred orange arcs that were complimented by sprays of blue blood.

"How many are there?" Kier asked as he appeared in Thargen's peripheral vision. He fired two quick bolts from his blaster, finishing off the one-armed skeks.

"Too many."

Or maybe not enough...

Thargen growled and hit another skeks with both axes, barely registering the immense damage wrought by the blades. The entrance of the tunnel was already slick with blood—and was fast running out of room for bodies.

"Will we be able to fight through them?" Kier asked.

"Tunnel's too narrow. Too dangerous."

Thargen's Rage purred at that. *Since when is anything too dangerous for you?*

There are people depending on me. Yuri's *depending on me.*

Another skeks charged out, and Thargen tackled him, crashing atop one of the fallen enemies. The skeks thrashed and struggled, striking Thargen with claws and fists, gnashing his teeth. Thargen hammered a forearm across the skeks' throat, reared back, and buried an axe in the bastard's face. He twisted to see Kier behind him, firing his blasters into the tunnel.

"Kayl, we may need to exit the same way we entered," Kier said.

"*I have difficulty imagining the situation is worse in there than out here,*" Kayl replied, his voice distorted by static. "*I have downed twenty, at least, and yet there seem to be only more.*"

Thargen climbed to his feet. "How big a fucking tribe they have living out here?"

Yuri's words were even more garbled by static than Kayl's when she said, "*Guys? Um, there are...on Kayl's drone feeds, and...like they have, uh...*"

"Zor atkoshai," Kayl spat. "*Rocket launchers.*"

Gunfire boomed in the tunnel, and Kier grunted, staggering back. Flattened skeks shells dropped to the floor at his feet, and as he swung aside to take cover against the wall, Thargen saw the chipped outer coating on his armor where the rounds had hit.

"Call in the *Fang*, Kayl," Kier said.

Thargen's eyes dipped to Kier's belt, locking on an armored

container clipped to it. Even if the specs were different between various military forces, those things seemed fairly universal—he knew almost instinctively that it was an explosives case.

The commlink crackled and broke Kayl's response. *"The automated weapons...at great risk... whole cave down."*

Kier turned his face away from the passage as a ricocheting bullet sprayed chipped bits of stone at him. His helmet emerged from the back of his neck, sealing around his head again, and his voice sounded both out loud and in the commlink when he said, "So could the skeks, Kayl, if they start firing rockets!"

The exchange had just enough context for Thargen to glean meaning from. "Yuri will shoot."

"What?"

Thargen was fairly certain that all three of his companions had asked that simultaneously. Dropping one axe, he reached across the mouth of the passage, opened Kier's explosives case, and grabbed everything inside before leaning back into cover.

A howling skeks lunged out of the darkness. Thargen lashed out reflexively, hitting the skeks on the thigh with his remaining axe. The skeks fell forward—and was hit by at least four shots from Kier before crashing to the ground.

"Those are powerful," Kier said.

Thargen looked down at the small, disc-shaped explosives on his palm. "Good."

He pressed the activation buttons on the discs quickly. Kier fired several more shots into the passage before darting aside. Thargen followed the daevah's path, tossing the handful of explosions into the tunnel as he passed it.

The cave shook with an explosion, and rocks, debris, and dust sprayed from the passage to clatter everywhere. Thargen slapped a hand against the wall to steady himself, grinning despite the ringing in his ears.

"Thar...ou okay?"

"Fuck yeah," he growled. "Be even better when you swoop in to save my sexy green ass."

Another explosion shook the cave, this one from outside; fresh dust and debris rained from the ceiling.

"Guess they want their food well done," Thargen muttered. He pressed himself against the wall and moved back to the passage, waving away the dust. There was just enough light for him to make out the stones blocking the tunnel—and a mangled skeks arm jutting out of the rubble, its fingers unmoving.

One less problem, at least.

More static crackled across the commlink; if there were any words in there, Thargen couldn't decipher them.

Clenching and relaxing his jaw, Thargen scooped up his fallen axe and blaster, stowing the weapons as he returned to the others. He dropped to the lower level of the cave beside Kier, turning to lift the trembling kaital down from the ledge as soon as his feet were on the floor.

Kier was tapping the controls on his wrist armor again, shaking his head.

"How's that air support coming along?" Thargen asked as he ejected the melted power cell from his auto-blaster.

"I cannot establish a connection with the *Fang*," Kier replied.

"Ske...ference...blocking si..." Kayl's voice cut out completely after a few seconds of broken speech.

"They're blocking local signals," Thargen growled. He tugged a fresh power cell from his belt—if any of the pieces of shit cells he'd taken from the smugglers could be considered *fresh*—and loaded it into the open chamber.

"Are vorgals psychic, too?" Kier asked, brows drawing close together.

"No. We just fight skeks a lot."

"Kayl cannot connect to the ship either, and he has also lost contact with Yuri. He must relocate to try again."

"They've got a portable signal jammer somewhere close by. Do it to cut off their quarry's communication, prevent them from sending out warnings or calling for help." Thargen ran his gaze over the survivors. The kaital had fallen to her knees beside the injured volturian, and the ilthurii had moved to put her arms around the shaking female. The adolescent borian was squatted down, head bowed, chest relaxing and expanding with erratic breaths. Only the azhera and the sedhi were on their feet, the first holding the dead smuggler's auto-blaster. The sedhi was unarmed, but she stood tall, naked, and unbroken with fire in her violet eyes.

"How long, Kier?" Thargen asked.

"He is moving as swiftly as he can, but there are a great many skeks," the daevah replied. He turned toward the prisoners on the floor. "I swear to you, we will see you all out of this. Your ordeal is nearly over."

The shooting, howling, and shouting from outside only seemed louder and more frantic than before; the battle lines had drawn closer. It was a matter of minutes now, at best.

I'm getting back to you, Yuri. There aren't enough skeks in this whole fucking galaxy to stop that.

Thargen strode to the sedhi and offered her the auto-blaster. "Ready for a fight?"

She accepted the weapon without hesitation, settling the stock against her shoulder. Her long, thick tail was as steady as her unwavering gaze. "I am a crimson raider, vorgal. I'm always ready for a fight."

Thargen grinned, baring his tusks, and tugged his axes free. "Friend of mine back in Arthos used to be a Crimson Raider."

"There is no used to be. Once a raider, always a raider. It is the same with you vanguards, isn't it?"

"Fucking right it is. Remind me to buy you a drink when we get to Arthos. We can swap war stories—not that I actually remember many."

"No point in making plans. All that awaits us here is death," the azhera snarled. "We can only hope to make it honorable."

"Are all you furballs so pessimistic?" Thargen activated the hardlight blades. "We aren't dying, and there's no honor to be had. Just a fuckton of skeks to kill."

Thargen strode forward. The cave was narrowest where the entryway curved into the main chamber; that was the best point from which to defend.

Kier moved up alongside him, flanked by the azhera and sedhi. "What is a *fuckton?*"

Thargen laughed, probably harder than he should have—but it was as much the result of Rage as it was of amusement. "Terran saying. Means a fuck of a lot."

Another explosion went off outside, vibrating the ground beneath his feet.

"The rockets are missing the smugglers," Kier said. "The smugglers are retreating."

"Missing on purpose. Just want to drive them into this cave, knowing they'll be cornered."

The skeks war cries swelled, overpowering the other battle sounds outside for the space of a few heartbeats. Thargen drew in a deep breath; he caught a hint of Yuri's scent, undoubtedly lingering on him. The core of his Rage solidified into something hard, deadly sharp, and white hot.

Shouts from the approaching smugglers echoed into the cave.

"*Kraasz ka'val,*" the azhera rumbled.

Crimson flooded Thargen's vision; he didn't fight the spread of his Rage now, didn't hold it back.

"With me," he shouted.

"With you," replied Kier, the azhera, the sedhi—and Thargen's Rage.

The first of the smugglers rounded that bend, his gaze snapping to Thargen immediately, but the hardlight axes had already hacked him down before he could swing his blaster toward Thargen, too.

A tall, silver-haired borian was the next to come around the bend. Taeraal. Thargen kept his weapons in constant motion, turning them toward his new target.

Taeraal frantically staggered back from the swinging axes. His auto-blaster fired wildly, spraying plasma bolts into the floor and walls as he struggled to aim at Thargen. Bits of molten stone sprayed Thargen's skin, but the pain was too distant to slow him down. In the corner of his vision, he saw two more smugglers falling back, firing at a mass of writhing skeks beyond them.

A plasma bolt darted past Thargen's side and hit Taeraal's weapon. The auto-blaster hissed, and Taeraal, eyes rounded, flung it toward the mouth of the cave.

The auto-blaster exploded in a blinding white flash, vaporizing the other two smugglers and turning a three-meter-diameter section of the entrance into a glowing orange pocket of melting stone and ash. Rocks loosened by the explosion tumbled down from overhead, but none of them were nearly big enough to block the entrance.

The skeks beyond the blast opened fire. Thargen backed around the bend, out of their line of sight, but Taeraal was not so fast this time. Several projectiles pierced his chest, the wounds oozing blood.

"Thargen fucking Skullreaver," Thargen roared.

Taeraal spat a curse, dropping a trembling hand to his waist to draw a blaster pistol.

Thargen lopped off his head with a quick swing of his axe.

So much for taking this fucker alive.

The howling tide of skeks crashed into the cave an instant later. Thargen laughed and threw himself into the writhing mass of flesh—hacking through it would be his only way back to his *zoani.*

TWENTY-THREE

Sol'Kayl pressed his back against the tree and sank into a crouch. Skeks darted by to either side of him. The sounds of branches snapping and undergrowth being crushed beneath their feet were almost entirely swallowed by the cacophonous shouting, shooting, and howling. The forest was chaos—and the roiling thoughts just beneath the surface of Kayl's mind were straining to mirror that chaos. But he would not allow himself to succumb to that inner turmoil.

He stomped down his concerns as harshly as the skeks trod the surrounding dirt, thrusting the infinite possibilities of what might've been and what could yet be into the tristeel vault at the back of his mind, and clamped his fangs down on his emotions. This was a simple situation despite all the chaos.

Kier was trapped in the cave. Only the *Fang* possessed the firepower necessary to effectively combat this flood of blood-thirsty enemies. But Kayl could not connect to the ship because somewhere amidst this mass of grinning skeks was a device jamming communications.

He needed to either get out of the signal blocker's range—

which could've meant making the two-kilometer trip through these skeks-infested woods to return physically to the ship, for all he knew—or destroy the responsible device, which could itself entail repositioning several times to scour the tumultuous battlefield.

Thus far, Kayl had only managed to cross thirty-two-point-seven meters since descending from his original position. Either of his options would take hours at that rate. Kier had minutes, at best.

Kayl could feel Kier's heart pounding, driving his own to quicken in turn, could feel the anger and passion burning in his brother's chest, could feel the desperation of that life and death struggle just as readily as he could feel the crushing weight of his own looming failure.

He swung his gaze from side to side, scanning the information relayed through his helmet's HUD—distances and measurements, primarily—seeking a higher vantage point from which to survey the battlefield. One tree in a nearby thicket stood out amongst the jumble of information; it was farther downslope, but still towered eight meters higher than the first perch he had chosen. He would have reduced visibility of the cave from the new position, but that was a necessary price.

He hoped the extra elevation would make a difference—but he couldn't know until he was up there.

That just left the simple matter of crossing another forty meters of ground where the vegetation was too thinly spread to conceal his movements.

Kier would not have hesitated; Kayl did not allow himself to, either. Springing upright, he darted toward his destination, running parallel to the cliff.

The skeks collective gunfire came together like a perpetual peal of thunder, an ominous backdrop for their battle cries. They had been whipped into a frenzy when the smuggler's defensive line collapsed. And what cause had they for caution now? Their prey was trapped.

Even with his armor, he felt the skeks' projectiles whizzing through the air around him. He pointed his railgun downslope, keeping his face forward, and targeted the attacking skeks through the scope's feed within his helmet's display.

He snapped the railgun in a tight arc, squeezing the trigger three times. He felt the weapon's faint thrum and silent click thrice as it fired its magnetically propelled projectiles, and the trio of skeks he had targeted fell almost instantly.

Kayl's forward momentum carried him behind a thick tree trunk. The tree shook, and its wood splintered as skeks gunfire hit it from the opposite side.

Hold on, Kier, he pulsed.

We are holding, came Kier's reply, as clear as one of Kayl's own thoughts.

A pang of guilt hit Kayl—*we.* Kier was not alone; Thargen and the surviving captives were in there, too. But there was no time for guilt—and he would not let himself feel it, regardless, for prioritizing Kier over the others. They had already lost Taeraal, their only current lead on Vrykhan's whereabouts. He would not also lose Kier, who was so much more to Kayl than what other species considered a brother—Kier was Kayl's *na'dival,* linked forever in heart and mind. One corner of incomplete triad to which they belonged.

The instant he was close enough to the thicket, he dove in, somersaulting through the undergrowth and stopping on one knee. He twisted his torso to angle his railgun toward the skeks who were shooting at him, picking out their glowing, high-lighted forms through the dark vegetation and tree trunks in the scope's digital feed. He fired answering shots of his own—one for each skeks he could see.

The skeks' rounds zipped around him, cracking against

wood and rustling the foliage. The thicket shielded him from most of the gunfire, and his armor stopped the few bullets that hit their marks, leaving him only to feel the thumps of their impact. The projectiles from Kayl's railgun were not quite so forgiving to his enemies; they punched through wood and armor unhindered to destroy the flesh beneath.

He could not count the number of skeks charging him. All he could do was keep his weapon moving, keep his finger on the trigger, keep his breathing firmly under control despite his racing heart. The ammunition counter in the scope feed was quickly running down, but he did not need to see it to know he was about to go empty—he had accounted for every shot.

Tell me you've found a connection, Kier pulsed.

I am somewhat preoccupied at present, Kier.

The final projectile left his railgun just as a pair of roaring skeks charged into the thicket. Kayl flicked on the energy blade attached to the underside of the railgun's barrel and leapt backward to avoid the wide arc of a swinging club.

Some haste would be appreciated, said Kier's thought-voice.

Kayl thrust the railgun forward, plunging the energy blade into the ribs of the skeks who had just missed with the club. The skeks hissed in pain.

Please, forgive the delay. Kayl twisted the blade and wrenched it aside, tearing a huge wedge of flesh out of the skeks' side. *It was certainly selfish of me to have stopped to defend myself from these ravenous savages.*

Gritting his teeth, Kayl turned to face the other enemy, who lunged at him with a wicked looking axe, sunken eyes gleaming and sharp teeth glistening in that unwavering grin. Kayl danced backward to avoid the weapon until his back struck a tree trunk. Halted abruptly, he batted aside the skeks' next attack. The impact of haft against barrel jolted up his arms. A few more such blows, and his railgun would be ruined.

I am sorry, he thought.

Were you apologizing to me or your weapon, Kayl? Kier's pulse came with a psychic smirk.

Kayl ducked under the skeks' follow-up swing. The axe lodged into the trunk over his head, striking hard enough for Kayl to feel the tree vibrate through his armor. He stabbed his energy blade into the center of the skeks' chest and pulled his weapon up as hard as he could, tearing the skeks open up to its clavicle.

To my weapon. Do you not have more pressing matters with which to concern yourself, Kier?

Releasing its axe, the skeks staggered backward. Its companion was struggling to its feet nearby, sucking in short, wheezing breaths.

Kayl drew his blaster from his hip and fired three plasma bolts into each skeks in quick succession. Shouts from outside the thicket—and a fresh volley of rifle fire around him—suggested that this skirmish had not gone unnoticed.

Kayl's hands moved of their own accord, returning the blaster pistol to its holster, grabbing a fresh magazine, and reloading the railgun. He hurried to the tree he'd targeted, slinging the railgun over his shoulder as he ran, and activated the climbing pads on the hands and feet of his combat suit. He scrambled up the tree just as the undergrowth at the edge of the thicket shook violently and a skeks shouted from nearby.

I have loaded my last magazine, he pulsed to Kier.

I suppose I'll be on my way to save you shortly, then, came Kier's reply. The humor on the surface of that pulse could not mask Kier's underlying fury; the flame in his breast had become an inferno.

Kayl harbored fury of his own, but it was not a barely contained firestorm, was not a star on the verge of exploding. His was cold, a black hole devouring light and heat, hungry but focused on a single point—he and Kier could not die here. Not with the purpose that had driven them for so many years left unfulfilled.

Not until Vrykhan's body was a smoldering heap of ashes.

Kayl wove around the trunk as he climbed, avoiding the largest branches. The confused calls of the skeks below soon became just another part of the din. Only when he was teetering on the uppermost few meters of the tree did he halt. Between the wind—which was noticeably stronger up here— and his weight, the tree was swaying heavily, its wood creaking.

He looped his tail around the narrow trunk and hooked it back around his waist, leaning back on it to anchor himself in place and free his hands. As he sent another summon signal to the ship, he said, "Yuri? Yuri, can you hear me?"

The commlink remained silent, and his HUD flashed the same message he had been seeing for the last several minutes —*NO CONNECTION.*

Clenching his jaw, Kayl swung his railgun into his hands and turned his attention downward. The branches below him blocked some of the battlefield from view, and a smoky haze was forming on the ground, but the trees were relatively sparse leading upslope.

The skeks were rushing toward the cave like swarming insects, and the crowd of them at the cave's entrance—where their movement was restricted by the narrow passage—was growing larger and thicker by the moment. How could Kier and the others stand against that?

But not all the skeks were moving; there were several groups of them hanging back, watching the attack. He swung his railgun toward each such group, expanding the scope feed in his helmet's display to allow himself a closer look. The optics cut through the haze easily.

Most of those unmoving groups were centered around

skeks holding those shoulder-mounted rocket launchers, all of which looked as likely to fire a rocket as explode in their operators' hands. Each skeks carrying a launcher was accompanied by several of its kind bearing small racks loaded with spare rockets on their backs. From his vantage point, he could see five such groups.

He had the sense that this was not some mindless raid—this had been planned, and it was being coordinated somehow.

Where were the directors of the assault?

Kayl kept his scope in motion, raking it over the battlefield, searching through the jumbled chaos. But it was something at the upper edge of his vision, outside the scope's feed, that ultimately caught his attention—something not on the forest floor but atop the cliff. He had been at too low an angle in his first position to spot the trio of skeks gathered directly over the cave.

Two were kneeling beside a crude, two-meter-tall device with uneven antennas jutting from its top. The third was a few meters ahead of them, lying on its belly at the edge of the cliff to watch the events below.

Kayl steadied his railgun and exhaled. When the tree's gentle swaying shifted the weapon's crosshair onto the base of the device; Kayl pulled the trigger.

Sparks and fire flared from the device's casing, and the skeks flanking it recoiled.

"*—hear me? Is anyone there?*" Yuri asked over the commlink, voice high with desperation.

Her words were only just discernable over the battle sounds undoubtedly coming through Kier and Thargen's commlinks.

"I am here, Yuri," Kayl replied, releasing the grip of the railgun to press the remote pickup button again. The message on his HUD was quite different this time—*INBOUND...19.25s.*

The counter was ticking down.

"*Is everyone okay? What hap—*" She yelped. "*The ship's moving, Kayl!*"

"Hold tight, Yuri."

The skeks beside the broken signal jammer seemed to be arguing with another. The one at the edge silenced them; its eyes were locked on Kayl. It lifted its arm and pointed.

Kayl fired a shot that struck the front skeks between the eyes. Its skull burst apart. As Kayl swung the crosshairs to the next target, Yuri made another startled sound—likely in reaction to the ship suddenly accelerating. He squeezed off another round, hitting the second skeks in the chest. The third was already bellowing a warning as it rushed to the edge of the cliff —a warning that had no business carrying over the battle din.

But skeks were nothing if not loud, apparently.

"The trees! In the trees! They are—" The skek's echoing call was cut short by a projectile through the throat that tore its head off.

INBOUND...12.55s.

Growling laughter crackled over the comms, overpowering a series of pained snarls and guttural cries and drowning out the skeks war howls in the background.

"*Thargen,*" Yuri breathed.

"*Fuck yeah,* zoani," the vorgal roared.

We will only hold so long as Thargen is standing, pulsed Kier. *He is the only thing holding them back.*

For most of his life, Kayl had never depended on anyone but Kier. Together, they had overcome every challenge they had faced. Now, all he could do was hope that Kier had been correct—that the reputation of vorgal vanguards was not exaggerated.

Shouts called Kayl's attention down again. Several skeks

were looking up at him from the ground, calling out to one another.

"Yuri, listen to me carefully," he said, angling the railgun toward the new targets and dropping a skeks with a snapshot as bullets whizzed and cracked through the air around him. "There is a screen on the console before you. The fourth option down"—he grunted when a bullet struck his shoulder, hitting with enough force to disrupt his aim and make his next shot miss its mark—"accesses the weapon systems."

An indicator appeared on the leftmost edge of his vision. He fired two more shots, taking down two more skeks, as he turned his head toward the indicator. The HUD highlighted the cloaked ship in orange and tagged its distance from him—two hundred meters and closing fast.

"I'm in. Now what?" Yuri asked.

"Activate the underside cannon turret and place it under manual control."

The ship came to a sudden halt in the air a few meters away from Kayl, and the plasma cannon turret lowered from its belly. Though the craft was silent, Kayl could feel the hum of its antigrav engines in the air.

Below, two of the skeks rocket teams turned their attention toward him.

Kayl, you need to move, Kier pulsed, likely sensing Kayl's alarm.

Both rocket launchers angled up toward Kayl.

"A big wraparound holo screen came up," Yuri said. *"I can see the ground below, and—"*

"Control stick on the armrest, Yuri." Kayl's heartbeat quickened further, but he kept his hands steady as he fired.

His projectile hit the rocket loaded into one of the launchers, triggering an explosion that lit up a section of the forest and completely engulfed the group of skeks that had been around the launcher's operator.

Kayl was already pivoting to his next target. "Shoot anything moving on the ground."

Splinters of wood blasted off the trunk, and two more bullets hit his armor. The tree shook more intensely. His next shot missed the rocket launcher he had been aiming for, hitting its bearer in the thigh instead. The skeks dropped, but caught itself on one knee.

"Shoot, Yuri!" Kayl said.

"*You got this, terran,*" Thargen growled.

The turret dipped suddenly, and big plasma bolts blasted from its dual barrels, casting a new blue-white glow on Kayl and the battlefield below. The group of skeks Kayl was currently aiming at were hit by one of those bolts and were swallowed by an even larger explosion than before.

"Keep firing," Kayl said as he swung his railgun over his shoulders. He brought up the remote piloting commands in his HUD, opening the rear entry ramp and angling it toward him.

The cannons continued firing, their heavy thumps echoing off the cliffside as the plasma cut huge swaths through the skeks scrambling below. Now there was gunfire striking the underside of the ship, doing no damage but causing the faintest flickers in the cloaking field around the points of impact.

Kayl did not believe a rocket would be quite so ineffectual, should one strike the ship's hull.

"*This is just like a game I used to play with my brother,*" Yuri said. "*He always made me play gunner because he* had to *be the pilot.*"

"Excellent," said Kayl as the ramp drew within a few meters of him. "Utilize that experience."

Placing his hands on the tree, he unraveled his tail and tipped his weight toward the ship. The tree swayed before rebounding, and Kayl shifted his body with it, seeking that pendulum like momentum that would get him close enough to reach the ramp.

"*I was never very good at it. We'd always fail missions because I caused too much collateral damage.*"

The tree creaked, protesting Kayl's treatment of it, but he pushed on. "Focus, Yuri."

"Right, sorry!"

Just a little farther...

Kayl thrust his weight toward the ramp one last time—just as an explosion went off at the base of the tree, sending violent vibrations all the way up the trunk. Wood snapped and cracked below him, louder than everything else for an instant.

His heart skipped a beat; the tree was no longer swaying, it was falling—falling away from the ship.

What's wrong, brother? Kier's mind-pulse was bristling with alarm.

Kayl shoved away from the broken tree, throwing his arms out. He hit the edge of the ramp with his chest, legs dangling with forty meters of open air between his feet and the ground. He slipped a few centimeters before slapping his hands down. The climbing pads on his palms latched onto the surface, halting his fall.

He released a huff. *Nothing, Kier.*

Irritation joined the concern thrumming through his empathetic link with his brother.

Do not lie to me, Kayl. I know when you're lying.

Busy now, Kayl pulsed.

He drew in a deep breath and glanced down. The battlefield was fire and smoke, fraught with shadowy figures and muzzle flashes that were like stars flickering in and out of existence. Projectiles pinged off the ramp and the hull.

Lifting a hand, he quickly tapped the control to put the

ship into a holding pattern—at least they'd make a harder target for those rockets if they were moving, and that was the best he could manage at the moment.

The ships cannons were still firing, blasting down trees, obliterating ground and stone, vaporizing skeks. And its line of fire was following the same path the attacking skeks had taken —up the slope and to the cave.

A pair of plasma blasts struck the ground not five meters from the mouth of the cave, annihilating the skeks there and spraying superheated debris against the cliffside.

"Yuri, do not fire too near the cave!" Kayl hauled himself up onto the ramp. "It may cause a cave in."

"*What? Why didn't you say that before?*" Yuri asked hurriedly. "*Didn't you hear what I said about causing collateral damage?*"

As soon as he was on his feet, Kayl slammed the button to close the ramp and raced to the cockpit. Yuri was in the gunner's seat, her hands white-knuckled around the control stick.

Her eyes flicked toward him for an instant. "So you're taking over, right?"

Kayl leapt into the pilot's chair adjacent to her and took the controls, disengaging the autopilot. "I need to pilot the ship. I fear we will be able to touch down for mere seconds, at best, before we are overwhelmed. I need you to keep the landing zone clear."

"You mean, like...right in front of the cave?"

"Yes."

The holographic view screens wrapping the cockpit— including the floor and ceiling—switched on to display the view outside the ship, creating the illusion that the controls and chairs were floating in open air.

"The cave you told me not to hit a minute ago?" Yuri asked.

"You got this, zoani. *Kill all these fuckers,"* Thargen growled over the comms. *"Just don't kill* us."

"Thanks, sweetie. No pressure or anything, right?"

AHEAD OF KIER, Thargen beheaded a skeks with a quick strike, adding to the mound of corpses on the cave floor. Kier fired his blasters simultaneously, hitting a skeks that was lunging over the bodies of its comrades to attack the vorgal. Four plasma bolts to the chest dropped that one; a few of them had taken more punishment than that before staying down.

Kier and the other defenders had already been forced several meters back from the chokepoint where the entry tunnel curved into the main chamber—partly because of the onslaught of skeks, and partly because of the gore and bodies. Even Thargen, who had become an unrelenting whirlwind of death, could not maintain his footing amidst that mess. His axes were blurred orange arcs, and the air around him almost seemed misted with blue skeks blood. He laughed, and growled, and roared, daring his enemies to come, and cut down any of them that attacked.

And despite his ferocity, skeks were getting through. He'd been pushed to a portion of the cave too wide for him to fully hold by himself.

For now, it was only one out of every five or six that managed to break past Thargen alive, and all of those had been shot down by Kier, the sedhi, and the azhera, but that number would only grow as the battle lines shifted ever toward the rear of the cave. Kier kept his blasters firing, picking off skeks around Thargen, covering him, but the monsters kept coming.

The sedhi was already showing signs of fatigue, no matter

how determined her expression remained, and the azhera looked unsteady on his feet.

The situation was not ideal. Kier and Kayl had been at this hunt for slavers—for Vrykhan—for a long while, and he couldn't recall another time when things had gone so quickly and immensely *wrong*. They'd fought a lot of slavers and pirates, but they had never fought an army. Now, all these captives were in grave danger, and the main reason Kier and Kayl had traveled all this way and undergone all this trouble was at the bottom of that damned corpse pile.

Kier accepted that frustration, that hopelessness, and channeled it into his movements; his blasters were but conduits for his wrath, and the skeks who had denied him precious information on his prey would suffer it.

Stones rattled at the back of the cave, but the noise of the screaming enemies, firing blasters, and thumping plasma cannons outside made it difficult to focus on so small a sound. Kier kept shooting, firing at everything around the blue and orange blur that was the blood-soaked vorgal and his dancing weapons.

That clatter of stones came again, more insistent and prolonged than before. After a brief lull, it resurged, becoming a clamor loud enough that it might have been a landslide.

"Kier?" one of the captives behind him called fearfully.

Kier looked over his shoulder, past the huddled survivors and up to the ledge beyond them just as a dust-covered skeks emerged from the passage.

Throat constricting, Kier spun toward the back of the cave. The skeks charged toward him—with a second one rushing out into the open behind it.

The creatures filled the cave with their unnerving howls.

Kier opened fire on them, already running to meet the new flood. The lead skeks reached the edge of the ledge before a pair of Kier's plasma bolts took out its eyes. It toppled forward and crashed in a heap amongst the captives, all of whom scrambled away save for the unmoving volturian. Kier was certain that someone—the kaital, perhaps—was wailing, but he brushed the sound aside as he put a burst of plasma into the next skeks' chest.

More of the beasts were storming out of the passage.

Bit of a problem, Kier pulsed to his brother. *They've reopened the rear tunnel.*

Kayl's concern flowed through their empathetic bond, but his mind-pulse was calm when he replied, *We should have clearance to descend soon. Hold out a little longer, brother.*

Behind Kier, Thargen was still roaring and laughing, taunting the skeks, and the sedhi and azhera's auto-blasters were firing in short, erratic bursts. Thargen would hold; though Kier had not known the vorgal for even a full day, he was confident in that. And Kier would not die here. He refused to accept death while the pirate Vrykhan still drew breath.

Kier and Kayl had lost a link in the chain leading to Vrykhan today, but they would lose nothing else.

He planted a foot on the fallen skeks' back and vaulted up onto the ledge, firing half a dozen shots before his feet had even touched down.

Kier followed the ledge back toward the passage, blasters spitting plasma into every skeks in his path. Each bolt was driven by his willpower, a messenger of his rage. Skeks fell before him, smoke curling from their plasma wounds, and he moved over the corpses like a rising tide swallowing a beach. Within moments, he'd closed to melee range with the invaders. The snarling skeks attacked him with clubs, axes, and rifle stocks.

Gritting his teeth, Kier dodged and swayed, avoiding the

blows without slowing his rate of fire, and lashed out with knees, elbows, and feet whenever there was an opening. His body was the weapon; his blasters were merely an extension of it. Centimeter by centimeter, he pushed toward the passage.

All the while, he sensed his brother, just as always—Kayl was a steady, solid presence no matter the situation, no matter his own underlying emotions. Kier could feel his brother's concentration, fear, and anger, but it was all wrapped in cold, hard tristeel.

"We will only have seconds for you to board," Kayl said over the comms. *"Be prepared to move."*

The plasma cannon thumped just outside the cave. The ship was close.

Not quite so simple as that, brother, Kier pulsed.

It must be, Kier. The skeks are scattering but not withdrawing. The ship will be an easy target for them when we land.

Kier risked a glance toward the front of the cave. Thargen's swinging axes were holding back a group of four skeks, but two others had slipped past him. One of those was facing off against the sedhi, who was beating him with her auto-blaster as though it were a club. The other had the azhera pinned on the floor, their bodies a tangle of bloody claws and snapping jaws.

Growling, Kier fired a quick succession of bolts into the torso of the skeks in front of him, rammed his shoulder against the creature's broad chest, and ducked to use it as a shield as he swung an arm back to shoot at the skeks attacking the azhera, which he could barely see at the edge of his field of view.

He couldn't tell if he'd hit his target. There were powerful blows raining down on the body he was using as a shield, and the dead skeks was much too heavy for him to support for long. He shifted his arm to fire blindly around the dead skeks' torso before shoving the corpse aside. The next enemy in line was already wounded and reeling, scorched plasma wounds smoking on its gut. Kier finished it quickly—and then he was finally at the opening to the passage.

The optics of his helmet saw easily through what must've been complete darkness in that tunnel—more skeks were approaching, their large bodies blocking the narrow passage too thoroughly for him to get an accurate estimate on their numbers. He could only assume their line stretched back for the tunnel's entire length.

Kier fired indiscriminately into the tunnel. Both blasters flashed warnings—overheating was imminent.

"We're nearly clear up there," the sedhi called. She entered Kier's peripheral vision a moment later, leaning against the wall as she moved toward him; her right thigh had a long gash across it, bleeding freely. "Something has stemmed the tide."

"*Our extraction window is open,*" Kayl said over the comms.

"*I still see them all over the woods,*" said Yuri.

Thargen's voice, hoarse but gleeful, carried back to Kier as he shouted, "Keep shooting those toothy fuckers, terran."

Skeks howled in the tunnel, and their guns boomed. Projectiles bounced off Kier's armor. He ignored the pain of the impacts. He had to keep shooting; he and his companions would be overrun before anyone reached the ship if this tunnel were left unguarded.

"*Are you ready?*" Kayl asked.

"We require a few moments." Kier shoved himself aside, taking cover against the wall while keeping one blaster firing into the tunnel. He holstered the other blaster and reached for the explosives case on his belt.

The *empty* explosives case.

A hard lump of dread sank in his gut.

I do not like sensing that from you now, pulsed Kayl. *You are supposed to be on the verge of escape.*

A minor complication, brother. Feel free to kick your feet up while I resolve it.

"How many more?" the sedhi asked from beside Kier.

"Too many, I fear," Kier replied. "And I will need to change power cells soon."

Realization struck him suddenly. He dropped his gaze to the sedhi's auto-blaster—the same one Thargen had been using minutes ago. "Give me the power cell."

"It's almost fried," the sedhi said. "It's cheap, unstable and probably unshielded." Her eyes rounded for an instant before she opened her blaster's chamber and ejected the power cell onto Kier's waiting palm.

The power cell was smoking, but not yet melted. That meant it wasn't depleted.

One chance at this.

All other sounds faded as Kier planted his foot on a dead skeks, leaned in front of the tunnel opening, and threw the power cell inside. He squeezed off three shots with his blaster.

The third hit its mark.

His helmet's optics flared with a white flash as the power cell exploded, briefly silhouetting the approaching skeks before obliterating them. Kier tossed himself back against the cover of the wall as debris, glowing orange with heat, sprayed from the tunnel's mouth. The howls of the skeks in the passage were drowned out by the sound of falling stone.

Kier knew without looking that the damage would only grant them a temporary reprieve. "We need to go."

The sedhi preceded him along the ledge and dropped down quickly despite her injury. At the front of the cave, Thargen brought an axe down on the skull of the last standing skeks, splitting its head and neck in two. The vorgal was covered in blood—most of it blue, but there were spats of red mixed in.

The azhera was on his feet again, chest and shoulders heaving with ragged, panting breaths and dirty fur matted with glistening blood. He had the butt of his auto-blaster on the ground and was leaning on the weapon like a crutch.

Shouts echoed out of the passage as Kier dropped onto the cave floor; those voices hadn't come from close to the opening, but they were not nearly far enough away.

Riniya was still curled up on the floor, and the kaital was beside her again, head down and body shivering. The sedhi was already helping the ilthurii to her feet, and the young borian was standing nearby, albeit unsteadily.

"*We will be down in thirty seconds,*" said Kayl over the commlink.

Flicking blood off his weapons, hands, and arms, Thargen jogged over to Kier and the others, deactivating the axes and attaching them to his belt as he moved. "Time to get the fuck out of here."

Kier couldn't help but sweep his gaze over the vorgal. Thargen was covered in cuts, and one of his eyes was squeezed shut; a gash over his eyebrow had poured blood over that half of his face. But he was grinning, and the wild light in his eye was undiminished. Beyond him lay dozens of corpses, a field of death and gore. How many had the vorgal killed?

"Thought we were past the creepy staring." Thargen laughed as he crouched and lifted Riniya, settling her over his shoulder. The kaital recoiled when the vorgal reached for her.

"Can you walk?" Thargen asked.

She shook her head.

"Come on, then," Thargen said with surprising gentleness in his rough voice. "Promise no one's gonna hurt you anymore."

Kayl's voice pulsed in Kier's mind. *Make haste, brother.*

"This ordeal is nearly through," Kier said, retracting his helmet. The stench of blood, scorched flesh, and unwashed bodies stung his nose immediately. "We need but walk a few meters farther."

For a few precious seconds, the kaital simply remained trembling on her knees. Another howl from the rear tunnel set her into sudden motion. She flung herself at Thargen, wrapping her arms around his neck, and he scooped her up and stood as though completely unburdened by the two females he was carrying.

The azhera wobbled, one of his legs buckling.

Kier hurried over to him, ducking to get his shoulders under one of the azhera's big, furry arms to support the weakened being's weight. The azhera leaned against Kier heavily; even in his current state, he likely outweighed Kier by at least fifteen kilos.

"*We are touching down now,*" Kayl said.

"We must move quickly." Kier walked forward, grunting as the azhera struggled alongside him, and crossed the corpse-littered cave as fast as he could. The sedhi and ilthurii were at the corner of his vision, helping one another along. Outside, the plasma cannon was still firing with its rapid, one-two cadence. It was the predominant sound, but it was not enough to silence the pops of skeks gunfire and their ragged war cries.

Almost, brother, Kayl pulsed. *You are almost here.*

As Kier reached the bend that would lead to the opening—where the bodies were piled three-deep—a chorus of howls sounded from the rear of the cave. Kier twisted to look back, and every curse he knew flitted through his mind simultaneously.

The skeks were already out of the tunnel.

One of them fired its rifle as it charged toward the drop-off.

The bullet struck the floor beside the borian, who was at the rear of the group. The borian reflexively stumbled aside. His legs gave out beneath him, and he fell with a cry.

Thargen's lips peeled back—not in a grin but in a furious sneer. His open eye met Kier's for an instant before he turned to face the oncoming skeks.

No. Oh, no.

Kier spun around, raising his blaster pistol. The azhera staggered, clamping a hand on Kier's shoulder to keep himself upright.

The skeks—a group of at least half a dozen—leapt down from the ledge. Thargen took a long step forward and roared. Kier had never heard such a sound from any creature in all his life—it was thunderous, raw, brimming with a fury so primal it may well have predated the universe itself.

And it made the skeks hesitate.

Kier leveled his blaster and opened fire.

There were voices in his ear, voices in his head, but he ignored all of them, focused entirely on his weapon, his targets, and the people between the two who he did not want to hit.

Unfazed, Thargen heaved the kaital up, swinging her so she lay across his shoulders and partly atop the volturian, and closed the remaining distance between himself and the borian with another long stride. He crouched, muscles bulging, and caught the borian by the bicep.

More skeks emerged from the tunnel. The azhera tightened his hold on Kier's shoulder and raised his auto-blaster, spraying bolts of plasma toward the passageway.

Thargen surged upright, turned toward Kier, and ran, dragging the panicked young borian behind him. Sweat trickled down his face, cutting paths through the blood spattered on his skin.

"They are bringing up—" Kayl's voice was cut off by an

explosion from outside that rocked the cave. Bits of stone and dust fell from the ceiling, clouding the air.

Kier's heart froze, and the entire universe went still.

"*Rockets,*" Kayl finished flatly. "*That one missed, but they are likely to bring the whole cliff down atop us even if they do not land a direct hit on the* Fang."

Thargen hurried past Kier, stomping over dead skeks. "Do I need to take your fucking tails in my mouth and drag you, too? Move!"

Skeks stirred toward the back of the cave, their figures obscured by the dust. Kier squeezed off a few more shots as he turned. Then he and the azhera scrambled around the bend.

The *Fang's* entry ramp and cargo hold were all that was visible outside the cave; the cloaking field was holding, at least. The sedhi and ilthurii were already up the ramp, and Thargen stormed up just after them, the borian struggling to get onto his feet as he was towed along.

Skeks shouted from just around the corner behind Kier. He gritted his teeth and pushed harder, driving the heavier azhera as fast as he could. His feet finally came down on the ramp, and the azhera threw himself forward onto hands and knees, chest heaving even harder than before.

Kier sent a mind-pulse to his brother. *Go!*

The *Fang's* engines thrummed, and the craft lifted off the ground.

A hand closed around the end of Kier's tail. He glanced over his shoulder to see a bloodied skeks grinning up at him from the ground. It yanked hard on his tail, tugging him backward—opposite the motion of the ascending ship.

Kier's stomach lurched as he rocked on his heels and his torso tipped past the edge of the ramp. He felt the ship slipping out from beneath him.

Kier! Kayl's thought-voice yelled.

Something snagged on the front of his belt, halting his backward motion and increasing the strain on his tail tenfold as the skeks, still holding on, was lifted off the ground. Kier gritted his teeth. The ship gained altitude quickly, making the fires, trees, and enemies seem to shrink below.

The dangling skeks growled a single word. "Food."

Kier swung his arm back and fired two plasma bolts into the skeks' face. Its grip went slack, and the skeks plummeted to the ground at least fifty meters below.

Drawing in a ragged breath through his nostrils, Kier turned his attention ahead to find Thargen in front of him. The vorgal's feet were planted wide apart, and one of his hands was braced against the doorframe. His other hand—or rather two of its fingers, as a quick downward glance confirmed—was hooked under Kier's belt.

Thargen tugged Kier away from the edge and slapped the button to raise the ramp. Kier forced himself to breath slowly, seeking some semblance of calm.

You have greatly exceeded the limit on brushes with death I have afforded you, brother. Kayl's mind-pulse was dry as ever, but that dryness could not mask the relief beneath.

If I recall correctly, Kayl, so have you.

"Thank you, Thargen," Kier said.

Thargen was covered in blood and dirt, his clothing tattered and torn, and several of his cuts seemed to be actively bleeding, but he grinned all the same. "Woulda been funny if I had to actually catch your tail in my teeth, huh?"

Kier chuckled and shook his head. Whatever failure they'd suffered tonight, this had not been a loss. The surviving captives had been rescued, and Kier and Kayl had survived to carry on their hunt. That was thanks in no small part to the vorgal in front of him. "It might have taken me some time to find the humor in that."

"Thargen?" someone called from deeper within the ship.

Thargen turned around. Kier sidestepped to look around the broad-shouldered vorgal.

Yuri was running down the corridor, her little boots clanking over the floor. Her eyes were wide, and her skin was pale.

"Sorry, *zoani*," Thargen said, taking a step toward her and putting his arms out to the sides, "I'm covered in blo—"

Yuri leapt at Thargen, slamming into him hard enough to knock him back a step, and wrapped her arms around his neck. Thargen embraced her in turn and drew in a deep breath, tipping his face against her hair.

The two did not speak, did not acknowledge the exhausted, battered captives huddled around them nor the daevah within arm's reach, did not even move save to squeeze one another tighter.

Even without sharing a psychic link with either of them, Kier could feel the love reverberating from Thargen and Yuri, could feel it flowing from their hearts like rays of light from a star.

And that light, for those few seconds, only deepened the shadows in the gaping chasm in his heart, drawing attention to the void in his triad, his incomplete *daevalis*. Until he and Kayl found their mate, their *na'diya*—which seemed unlikely, given their singular purpose in life—they would not know anything like what this vorgal and his terran shared.

Such is not for the likes of us, Kayl pulsed, a hint of melancholy coming through with his words.

For I am wrath, Kier replied.

And I am vengeance, Kayl continued.

Their minds finished the mantra together. *And our only fate is to slay the tretin called Vrykhan.*

But for the first time in many, many years, those words—

which Kier and Kayl had exchanged so often—did not feel quite right. They did not feel quite so...inevitable. And though there was much to say and much to do, Kier couldn't pull his attention away from Yuri, Thargen, and their uninhibited, unfiltered display of love.

TWENTY-FOUR

They were home.

It was almost unreal to Yuri after everything they'd gone through, but she and Thargen were finally back home in Arthos. Yuri stared out the hovercar window, looking down at the bright neon lights, towering buildings and walkways, and crowded streets of the Undercity.

A shiver ran up her spine, and she clutched the small, gift-wrapped box in her lap. Looking down on the crowds like this, she couldn't help but flash back to the horde of skeks charging toward the cave where Thargen and the others had made their stand. That was one of several memories from the last few weeks that would haunt her. Fortunately, she had many, many more good memories to outweigh the bad.

She glanced down at the big, warm, green hand possessively covering her thigh. As if sensing her thoughts, Thargen squeezed her leg. Yuri trailed her eyes up along his thick arm to meet his gaze briefly before he returned his attention to driving.

Nearly every moment with Thargen on Sotera—the planet they'd been marooned on, according to Kier and Kayl—had been wonderful. If it hadn't been for the skeks and smugglers, it would have been a little taste of paradise. She'd miss those autumn colors, the clear water, the fresh air, the soft red grass, and most of all, the beautiful open sky.

Of course, the air had burned her lungs when she'd first breathed it, the days were chilly and the nights had been downright freezing, the thunderstorms were a level of terrifying she'd never imagined possible, there'd been little food to be found, and the rocks and fallen needles had torn the soles of her feet to pieces—but she stood by her prior thought. Under different circumstances, with the right equipment, their time on Sotera would've been the sort of vacation she'd needed for a long while.

But now they were home, and Thargen was taking her to *his* home to meet his family and friends...and to reunite her with her brother. She was both anxious and excited.

The hovercar sped up suddenly, making Yuri's stomach flutter. Thargen banked to the side, tilting the hovercar at a harsh angle to dart past a slower vehicle.

"Why does it feel like everyone here drives even slower than before?" Thargen grumbled.

"I am sure that our destination will not go anywhere," said Kayl from the back seat. "Would not some patience be prudent?"

Yuri turned her head and looked back at the twins. They were dressed in the same sort of form-fitting black jumpsuits they'd worn throughout the return trip on the *Fang*. The high-collared suits made the twins look leaner than they appeared while wearing their armor, but the daevahs were in no way weak or lacking muscle definition. Their tails were resting on the seat between them, hooked around each other with their ends flicking leisurely.

They both met Yuri's gaze, and Kier smiled.

"I've been away from home for weeks, daevah," Thargen said. "If I didn't let an army of skeks stop me, I sure as hell won't let the Infinite City's infinite fucking traffic do it."

As though to illustrate his point, he increased the vehicle's speed further, cutting across the wide airway and passing directly in front of several other vehicles in the process.

"You are even more reckless a pilot than my brother," Kayl grated, brow creasing.

"I believe *skilled* is the correct word," Kier said. "I suppose now I've something more to aspire to. Thargen has set a new standard."

Yuri settled her hand over Thargen's. "I think I'm with Kayl on this one. I'd rather not puke before we get there."

Thargen blew out an exasperated huff. "Nobody's bleeding, Yuri. You're not gonna puke. Sit back and enjoy the ride." His eyes flicked toward her again, suddenly heated. "This is just the first of many now that we're back."

"Were you not sated enough by your couplings aboard our ship?" Kayl asked.

"And I would not call this the first since arriving," added Kier with a chuckle. "When we landed, it certainly sounded like you were—"

"Are we there yet?" Yuri asked, cheeks flaring with warmth. Had they been *that* loud?

"Yeah, almost." Thargen guided the hovercar out of the main traffic lane to follow one of the streets below. "Now I know that daevahs like to stare at people like creeps *and* listen in on private moments. You two aren't winning any points for your species."

"It was no fault of ours. At times, there seemed to be nowhere on the *Fang* we could *not* hear you," Kayl said.

"The only thing louder was your snoring during our first

day of travel," added Kier. "I feared the *Fang* would be rattled apart by it."

Yuri's relief when she'd seen Thargen, bloodied but alive, standing in that cargo hold had been immense—even stronger than her aversion to blood. She'd hugged him as hard as she could for a long, long time, reluctantly releasing him only when he'd put his hands on her hips and guided her back. He'd told her to help with the others, that he was going to get cleaned up.

He'd managed three steps before collapsing. Yuri's heart had leapt into her throat, and she'd rushed to his side. His skin had been more heated than she'd ever felt, but his heartbeat had been strong and steady. That hadn't eliminated her worry, but she'd seen it before—the day of the crash, when he'd sat down in the middle of an alien forest and just gone to sleep despite everything.

When he'd started snoring there on the floor, she'd been unable to hold back a smile.

She and Kier had seen to the rescued captives, tending their wounds, showing them where to clean up, opening the lockers full of clothing, and fetching several of those instantly rehydrated meals from the galley. They were all in poor condition—the smugglers had driven them hard and provided barely any food or water—but most of their wounds were minor.

Unfortunately, Riniya's had been in significantly worse condition than the other survivors. Her broken leg had not been set, and the bone had already begun healing while misaligned. She'd been feverish, likely the result of an infection, and her body had been covered in bruises and scrapes. According to the others, the smugglers had taken their frustrations out on her—and if the camp had been moved again, it was unlikely that they would have brought her along.

Yuri had tended Riniya during the return trip as best she could, and had seen improvement during that time—but her conversations with the volturian, always brief, had suggested the damage went far, far deeper than physical.

Thankfully, the only stop the twins had made before coming to Arthos had been at a waystation they called Avarius Reach, which they described as a safe haven dedicated to the rehabilitation of liberated slaves. The staff of the waystation had said they could grant Riniya the help she needed. Tsirisa, Corgen, and Harukan—the kaital, borian, and azhera, respectively—had all chosen to stay there as well.

Apparently, Kier and Kayl had brought hundreds of freed slaves to Avarius Reach, and most had eventually recovered from their ordeal.

Vireesi and Fyr'ta, the sedhi and ilthurii—who'd been inseparable during their time on the *Fang*—had decided to continue on to Arthos with Yuri, Thargen, and the twins. They'd departed shortly after landing, hands intertwined and tails touching. The two had not known one another before being kidnapped, but their time in that cell together had apparently forged a very deep bond between them.

THE HOVERCAR CRUISED over side streets and alleys, its speed reduced despite Thargen's earlier arguing. Judging by the lights and buildings within view, they were near a busy part of the Undercity, but Yuri lost sight of them when the vehicle dropped into a dark, deserted alley. After several turns along similar alleys, Yuri would've been entirely lost— had she not already been clueless as to where they were. Everything around here looked abandoned or, at best, neglected.

That only increased her surprise when the hovercar pulled up to a large bay door that opened to reveal a large garage in which everything was polished to a shine.

Thargen pulled the hovercar inside, and the door closed as soon as the vehicle was clear.

Yuri's eyes darted left to right, taking in the hover vehicles lined up in neat rows along the walls. This place looked like one of those garages super wealthy people had in their ultra-modern, thirty-thousand-square-foot mansions.

The hovercar drew to a stop in the center of the garage. It was only then that Yuri pried her eyes off the other vehicles and noticed the people standing near the interior door ahead. There were six of them, and five of those looked as tall as Thargen, if not taller—a sedhi, an azhera, a cren, and another vorgal, all males, and a female ilthurii. But it was the smallest figure amongst them that stood out to Yuri the most. A human woman with her blond hair pulled back and a blaster on her hip.

That must be Thargen's friend, Shay.

She's pretty.

And she looks like she could kick my ass.

But the one person she wanted to see wasn't there.

"Where's Takashi?" Yuri asked.

"Inside, probably." Thargen squeezed Yuri's thigh again. "Don't worry. He's safe."

Yuri nodded, tamping down the anxiety rising in her chest.

"Now everyone be on your best behavior or whatever," Thargen said as he disengaged the hovercar's engine. "Drakkal looks kinda pissed. Not that that's unusual for him."

Yuri had but a moment to glance back at the group. Drakkal was the burly azhera, Shay's mate. Yuri couldn't deny that he *did* look angry. He was staring at the hovercar hard enough that she wouldn't have been surprised if it burst into flames.

Thargen shoved open his door and climbed out of the car.

All right, Yuri. This is the easy part, right? No reason to be nervous.

She took in a quick, steadying breath, and exited the car.

The twins did so just after her. She followed her vorgal as he approached his friends, clutching the gift to her chest and peering around him. It was strange to know so much about these people despite having never met them. Thargen had told her a lot about all of them.

Drakkal folded his arms across his chest.

"You saved some of that cake for me, right?" Thargen asked when he was in front of them.

"*Kraasz ka'val*, the first thing you ask about is fucking cake?" Drakkal snarled, fur bristling.

"No, there isn't any fucking cake," Shay said. "What the fuck, Thargen?"

Yuri curled her lips in to keep herself from laughing.

Thargen lifted his hands, palms up. "It was really good cake, and I promised some to my *zoani*. It so fucking wrong for me to ask about it?"

"Your *zoani*?" the other vorgal asked. He was brown-skinned and just a bit shorter than Thargen, and his cheek tattoo had slightly different symbols around the central axe. He was Urgand.

The aliens' expressions had shifted toward confusion—or maybe disbelief.

Thargen lowered his hands. "Yeah. Why the fuck are you all looking at me like that?"

Urgand turned his face toward Yuri and ran his eyes—a startlingly clear blue—over her. "Is this terran... And you..."

"Magama's flailing teats, stop acting so shocked."

"I expected a heartfelt homecoming, perhaps even a few tears, but this is far more entertaining," said the sedhi, Arcanthus, who was leaning casually against the wall, his silky black robe open to reveal his sculpted chest. His lips were curled in a smirk.

"No, it's not fucking entertaining, Arcanthus," Drakkal's

nostrils flared, and he pinned his gaze on Thargen. "Last trace we found of you was some gang, the Zulka, taking you down in an alley with this terran and dragging you off, and we had to hack into Consortium security feeds just to find that."

"Doesn't Arcanthus do stuff like that all the time, though?" Shay asked.

"That's not the point, *kiraia*," Drakkal said. "We went three weeks tracking that fucking gang, chasing any lead we could find, thinking you were *dead*, only for you to call us out of nowhere from a shielded comm ID—and you don't tell us what happened or where you were, just that you want us to fucking kidnap a terran. And here you are, in our secure compound, with three more strangers you did not clear with us."

"Your...*zoani*?" Urgand asked again, his expression still confounded.

Yuri's brows creased. Now she *really* needed to know what that word meant.

Thargen threw his hands up again, this time in frustration. "Anything else? Gonna get on me for forgetting to take out the trash or something?"

"I knew that was you," the ilthurii, Sekk'thi, said.

"Yeah, it was. Now before I address anything else...did you really think I was dead?"

"When someone like you disappears, Thargen, it doesn't tend to be temporary," Arcanthus said. "You do have a habit of looking for fights."

"All right, I guess that's fair." Thargen jabbed a finger toward Drakkal. "But I didn't tell you to kidnap him. I just said pick him up and bring him in."

"Whether he wanted to come or not," Drakkal said.

"Wait, are you talking about Takashi?" Yuri asked, stepping out from behind Thargen. "Is he okay? You didn't hurt him, did you?"

"No, but he nearly knocked Razi on his ass," Drakkal replied. "That terran packs a surprising punch."

Yuri smiled. "He's been into martial arts since he was a little kid."

"We were aware of your brother before Thargen called," said Arcanthus, pushing away from the wall. His tail languorously swayed behind him. "We IDed you from the holos we pulled looking for Thargen, and finding your brother was easy afterward. He was quite zealous in his search for you."

Relief flooded Yuri knowing that he was all right.

"He's in back, waiting for you," Shay said, offering Yuri a smile.

"But nobody is going back until I know who the fuck *they* are." Drakkal dipped his head toward the daevah twins, who'd been standing behind Thargen, largely ignored, the whole time.

Thargen ran his palm over the scars on the side of his head. "I kinda...offered them Arc's help."

Drakkal's eyes narrowed to a furious glare. "You did *what?*"

"Didn't think you'd have trouble hearing with ears that big, azhera," Thargen replied.

"You offered them Arc's help and brought them here without talking to any of us about it first? *Vrek'osh!* You must be stupid."

"He's not stupid," Yuri said, giving Drakkal a glare of her own. "They saved our lives."

Thargen gave Yuri a quick look—a *you're so fucking hot* kind of look—before returning his attention to Drakkal. "And you and Arc have brought people here without asking anyone, too. Don't act like you haven't."

"We run this fucking place!" Drakkal roared.

"I know that!" Thargen roared back. His voice was normal when he added, "We can talk about the three weeks' backpay you owe me later."

Drakkal's hackles rose, and he stepped toward Thargen. "*Kraasz ka'val*, you fu—"

Shay reached out and grabbed Drakkal's belt, tugging him to a halt. "Calm down, kitty. He's right. You offered me a place here before even knowing me."

Drakkal's lips twitched, revealing his fangs, as he stared at Thargen. Tension crackled in the air between them.

"Regardless of any precedent that may have been set, this is still an issue," said Arcanthus, his lower eyes shifting toward the daevahs while that third eye at the center of his forehead remained on Thargen. "We have all had to learn some difficult lessons over the last two years, haven't we?"

"Yeah, we have." Thargen held Drakkal's gaze for a few more moments before looking at Arcanthus. "But you barely knew me when you offered me a job. You took a shot on me and when I recommended you hire Urgand, too, what did you ask me?"

Arc's eyebrows fell. "I asked if you trusted him."

"Right, because you trusted me and my judgment for whatever reason."

"Because you're open and honest, vorgal."

"And I am fucking loyal. I would die for anyone in this building, and you know I've come fucking close plenty of times. I told you I trusted Urgand that same way because he saved my life more than once." Thargen twisted his torso slightly, pointing back at the twins. "Same with them. They saved me and my *zoani*, fought alongside me, and rescued people who didn't deserve what was done to them. I didn't offer them a fucking room next to yours or anything, Arc. But they're doing good work out there, and if you want us to be making a real difference in this universe, we should at least consider working with them."

Arcanthus pressed his lips together and lifted a hand, brushing his metal fingers along his jawline.

"Shit, Thargen," the cren said, "you write that speech beforehand or what?"

"Fuck you, Koroq," Thargen replied, one corner of his mouth lifting.

With a thoughtful hum, Arcanthus stepped past Thargen and Yuri, stopping immediately in front of the daevah twins. Seconds passed as the daevahs and sedhi studied each other, all three silent and seemingly wary.

"I suppose there's no point in aliases by now," Arc finally said. "I'm Arcanthus. Forger, hacker, pit fighting champion, sex god—"

Shay snorted, rolling her eyes.

Arc glanced at her over his shoulder. "I'm deducting that from your pay, terran."

"Again, Arc, *I* handle payroll around here," Drakkal said, finally seeming to ease.

"*Anyway*"—the sedhi turned back to the twins—"you're here, so the very least we can do is have a chat and determine whether or not we can be of any use to each other."

"We must know if you or any of your people have ties to slavery," said Kayl, face betraying no emotion.

"What a blunt and oddly specific demand." Arc's tail lazily swished as he raised his arms—both of which were cybernetic. "My only ties to slavery were fighting my way out of it in the pits and arenas of Caldorius, as were Drakkal's." The sedhi turned so he was perpendicular to the twins and everyone else. "Shay was captured by slavers and sold to a wealthy businessman who kept her in his private zoo to be bred until Drakkal broke her out. Sekk'thi was born into a livestock pen full of people meant to be traded to skeks as food. And Razi, who is inside, spent ten years enslaved in a mine, extracting raw materials in the dark, usually with an electrolash tearing up his back."

Arcanthus returned his gaze to the twins. "Does that satisfy your curiosity?"

The daevahs looked at each other, and Yuri could almost sense the unspoken words flitting across their psychic link. When they returned their gazes to Arcanthus, it was Kayl who spoke first.

"We were taken as small children, after our parents were slaughtered by pirates."

Kier said, "We were sold to a mistress on a planet we'd never heard of and were trained to be her personal servants—"

"And to pleasure her at her whim," Kayl finished.

Kier offered a slight bow. "I am called Sol'Kier Sevris, and my brother is Sol'Kayl Kortanis."

Kayl mimicked that bow as he was introduced. "We hunt slavers."

"Really? Well, it seems we will have much to discuss." Arcanthus walked toward the interior door, waving the daevahs along. "Drak, let's speak with our new friends in the workshop. And shall we call for a party in the break room in... two hours?"

"Better be cake," Thargen said.

"No promises, vorgal." Drakkal paused to nuzzle Shay's hair before joining Arcanthus.

"So the kid gets cake, but I don't?"

"It was her birthday," Shay said.

Kier and Kayl offered Yuri and Thargen nods as they passed, following Arc and Drakkal through the interior door.

"Yeah, but what does that even mean?" Thargen said. "That she didn't die for a year? Well I didn't die for three weeks, and my circumstances were just a little more dangerous. Isn't that worth at least one slice?"

Koroq laughed and slapped Thargen's shoulder. "Glad you're back, vorgal."

"As am I," Sekk'thi said.

"You owe us a story," Koroq said as he walked to the door. Just before he slipped through, he added, "And the drinks are on you!"

"That bastard," Thargen muttered.

Sekk'thi brushed her fingers lightly across Urgand's shoulder. "I will see you soon." Then she, too, left them.

Shay arched a brow at Thargen. "Let's not pull that kind of disappearing act again." She turned to Yuri and grinned. "Hi. I'm Shay, Thargen's best friend. Don't let Urgand tell you otherwise."

Yuri smiled, glancing at the other vorgal who was still staring at her, seemingly in shock. She cleared her throat and returned her attention to Shay. "I'm Yuri. Thargen's told me a lot about you...about everyone really. Oh!" She held the gift out to Shay. "And, uh, this is for you. Well, not for you, but for Leah. It's from Thargen."

The other woman took the gift carefully. "Should I be worried that it's going to explode?"

"Damn it, I didn't know explosives were an option," Thargen said.

"I can't tell if you're serious or not, vorgal. You keep things interesting, I'll give you that much."

Thargen laughed. "This one is not nearly as great as a knife or a bomb, but it's appropriate for a little terran." He slipped his arm around Yuri and drew her against his side. "I had some help picking it out."

Shay's eyes dipped as though absorbing the way Thargen was holding Yuri, and her brows rose high. "Oh. Oooooh. Damn it! Are you serious? Now I owe Sam."

"Ah, shit, me too," Thargen grumbled.

"Owe Sam for what?" Yuri asked, glancing up at him.

"The pool we had running. Everyone was putting credits on who they thought would end up with a terran next. I'm telling you, Sam's either a fucking genius or totally insane to have put money on me."

Shay smiled wide. "I need to learn to stop betting against her. Can't say that I'm mad, though." She turned the gift in her hands. "So, what is it?"

"A vorgal toy," Thargen replied, grinning.

"A vorgal toy?" Shay asked flatly. "So what, like a battle-axe or something?"

"No, not a *vorgal* toy, a vorgal toy."

"It's a mini Thargen," Yuri said. "Much, much safer than the real thing."

One of Shay's brows arched.

"It's one of those stuffed things," Thargen said. "Like that stupid cat Razi ga—"

Shay jabbed a finger against Thargen's chest. "Leah *loves* that fucking cat, vorgal. Don't you talk shit about it."

"Woah, all right, terran. This was way fucking better, anyway. She's about to have a new favorite."

Shay laughed, shaking her head. "We'll see. It'll be hard to pass up her kitty. Hell, even Drakkal is her favorite over me right now. Know how much that hurts? I'm sure she'll love it though."

"I almost forgot." Thargen unhooked a pair of sheathed knives from his belt and held them out to Shay.

"What are these for?" Shay asked, the wariness returning to her expression as she took the weapons in one hand.

"One for you, and one for Leah's second birthday."

Shay rolled her eyes and shook her head. "You asshole. First thing I'm going to teach her with these is how to stab you." When she turned her gaze back to Yuri, there was amusement in her gaze. "Anyway, welcome to the family, Yuri."

Warmth flooded Yuri's chest. She glanced up at Thargen, and he grinned down at her. *Family.* As odd as that should have been coming from someone she'd only just met, it felt good. But it would feel even better when she finally saw her brother again.

"Can you bring me to Takashi?" she asked.

"Yeah. I think he was in the break room with Sam, Leah, and Razi. We can pass this gift on to Leah and reunite you with your brother all at once. Come on."

"Thargen," Urgand said, calling everyone's attention to him. He reached out and placed a hand on Thargen's shoulder. "Is she really your *zoani*?"

Thargen's hold on Yuri tightened. "Yeah. Without a single fucking doubt."

"And you've..." Urgand's eyes flicked toward Yuri.

"Yeah. A lot."

"But she's..."

"Yeah. Fuck, Urgand, you've never had a problem just saying what's on your mind any time before this."

"I'm also right here. Am I missing something?" Yuri asked, blushing and looking between the two.

"I'm wondering the same thing," Shay said.

Thargen raised his free arm, cupping the back of Urgand's neck. "She breaks through it. Right to my fucking heart. With her...I'm good. It's not like she magically fixed me or anything, but I'm good."

"Good," Urgand said, lips spreading in a slow smile. "I'm glad to hear that. Really fucking glad. This place wasn't the same without you."

Thargen released Urgand, only to punch him on the shoulder. "Someone's gotta be the interesting one, right?"

Urgand grunted and replied with a punch of his own, making Thargen rock slightly. "Crazy and interesting aren't necessarily the same thing."

"So, um...you're the one who saved Thargen's life, right, Urgand?" Yuri asked. "Thank you for that. Not that you did it for me or anything. It's just that...I'm *really* happy I got to meet him, even considering what we had to go through to get here."

Urgand laughed and shook his head, turning his blue eyes toward Yuri. "I patched him up as best I could. Just enough to keep him on his feet. But Thargen is the one who got *me* out of there. Don't even think he could remember his name at the time, but he dragged me and another grunt out of that place and got us onto the evac ship when he should've been on the ground dying."

"You don't gotta make up stories about it to make me feel better, Urgand," Thargen said. "Everyone already knows I'm a badass without the embellishments thrown in."

"Damn straight," Shay said with a chuckle.

But having seen Thargen in action—and having heard Kayl and the rescued captives recount their escape from the cave—Yuri knew Urgand was telling the truth.

The interior door whirred open, and Takashi ran through, his dark eyes immediately falling on Yuri.

A wave of excitement flooded Yuri. She'd missed her brother, had worried about him, but she hadn't realized just how much until right now. "Takashi!"

She pulled away from Thargen to charge at her brother. Takashi caught her in a crushing embrace, lifting her off her feet, and she clung to him.

She'd done a pretty good job of not thinking too much about the chances of never seeing him again while she was stranded, and all the emotions she'd set aside crashed upon her now. Tears stung her eyes, and a small whimper escaped her throat. She clutched him tighter.

"You scared me half to death," Takashi said. "More so than that big ass cren showing up at our apartment. Who turned out to be pretty cool, actually, even though I punched him in the jaw."

Yuri laughed.

"I spent so much time looking for you, Yuri. I just...I didn't know what to do," Takashi said, his voice thickening with emotion.

"It's okay. *I'm* okay. I had my own big ass alien to protect me."

"And you gotta tell me everything."

They held each other for a while—until the tears were done, and Yuri could breathe steadily.

"So, you're the stripper?" Thargen asked from just behind Yuri.

"What?" Takashi asked, drawing back. His brows furrowed when he looked at Thargen.

Yuri shook her head, laughing again as she wiped the moisture from her eyes. "Thargen, this is my brother, Takashi." She lowered her hand and smiled, returning to Thargen's side and slipping her arms around one of his, hugging it to her chest. "And this is Thargen, my big ass protector."

Takashi's eyes moved over Thargen. "Wait. You and *him*?" He raised a hand and ran his fingers through his long, black and pink streaked hair and chuckled. "I don't even want to picture how that's possible."

"Tak!"

"You're not the only one," Urgand muttered.

"Wow. I'm surprised that you males have such tiny imaginations. Hopefully that's not proportional to something else,"

Shay said, walking toward the door. "Are we going to stand in the garage all night, or are you coming inside?"

Urgand chuckled and followed Shay.

Takashi crossed his arms over his chest and narrowed his eyes on Thargen. "You break my sister's heart, and I'll break you. Got it?"

Thargen reached out and gave Takashi a slap on the shoulder, making him stagger slightly. "While I'm around, *no one* is going to hurt her. Disregarding the stuff that already happened, of course."

"I mean it, vorgal." Takashi looked at Yuri and lowered his voice, grinning. "It's about damn time you got some dick!"

Thargen scoffed. "What do you mean, *some*? She gets *all* of it."

Yuri's cheeks flamed. "Ooookay, we're going back to not talking about this stuff."

Takashi snickered. "Let's go in and party," he said as he turned toward the door. "You have *got* to see their VR system!"

Yuri grinned as she and Thargen walked behind her brother. She enjoyed the VR games she and Tak had always played together, and she knew she'd continue enjoying them—hell, they'd probably helped her a bit while she was stranded—but they'd lost a little of their luster. The last few weeks had been filled with experiences she'd never imagined going through in real life, and they'd been so much sharper, so much more frightening, so much more thrilling, so much more immediate and unforgettable.

She smiled up at Thargen, and those butterfly wings fluttered in her belly when his golden eyes met hers.

And how much appeal could those games really hold for her now that she finally had her own orc, right here in the flesh?

EPILOGUE

Thargen strode down the hall with Yuri over his shoulder, his eyes locked on the entrance to his room. He couldn't get there fast enough. Yuri was giggling, but she didn't understand the seriousness of the situation—he was palming her ass, and it was taking all his willpower to keep from tearing off their clothes right then and there in the middle of the damned hallway, where someone was guaranteed to show up just as he was balls deep in his terran.

He fucking needed her, but he refused to subject her to that sort of embarrassment—that, and he was a selfish, possessive fucker. No one got to see her naked except him.

Yuri smoothed her hands down his back and cupped his ass. "Old habits, huh? Just can't resist throwing me over your shoulder *caveman* style?"

Thargen's cock twitched. "Don't even care what that means right now. Just tired of having to share you."

He loved the people here—they were his friends, his brothers and sisters—but he'd have been lying if he said he hadn't grown used to having Yuri all to himself. Their time on

Sotera had spoiled him for that. And of course, Yuri had charmed all of them. She was talkative and friendly, and had no trouble flowing from conversation to conversation during the party in the breakroom. It was just like that first night he'd seen her—these were the qualities that had made her such a popular bartender at Starlight Trance.

There'd been some solemnity, some good-natured insults, a lot of laughter—especially when Sam collected the pool that no one had ever believed would be paid out—and that overall feeling of being home, of being where he belonged. Yuri fit right in with that, as did her brother. Hell, even the daevah twins had joined in, adding pieces to the story Yuri and Thargen told about their ordeal.

But Thargen was well overdue for some alone time with his *zoani.*

He lifted his wrist to the scanner beside his door, muscles tense, ready to spring though the moment it opened.

It did not open.

He glanced at his arm—and the barely perceptible scar where his ID chip had been removed. The same ID chip that had been coded to unlock this door.

"*Fuck,*" he growled. A hundred different options flashed through his mind—foremost was trying to knock the door down, which would only have harmed him considering it was a reinforced tristeel blast door. After that was a mental run through of every other room in the compound, like he was on an imaginary tour of the place to seek doors that weren't locked.

Not taking her in a fucking supply closet.

"What?" she asked, flattening her hands on his back. He could just imagine her pushing herself up to see around him.

Thargen could override the lock himself, but that would mean a trip back to the security room, and that was way too far to go while his cock was about to burst out of his pants.

Fuck. Guess it's last resort time.

He pressed the call button at the base of the scanner panel.

"*Yes?*" Arcanthus said through the speaker, his voice somehow more smug than usual.

"Open my door," Thargen answered tightly.

"*Ah, yes. Your chip was removed, wasn't it? You could come down to the—*"

"Just open the fucking door, Arc, or there's gonna be a mess out here you don't wanna clean."

"*Didn't you say something about Yuri having a soothing effect on you?*"

"Well, sex does release *endorphins* that can induce a state of serenity," Yuri said.

"Yeah, all that shit. Open the door so I can release some fucking *endorphins*," Thargen said, "or they're gonna be released all over this carpet."

Yuri buried her face against his back and laughed.

"*You're right. I don't want to clean that up,*" Arcanthus replied.

The room door slid upward; Thargen was darting through before it was even fully open. He slapped the control to close it again, turned to the wall, and set Yuri on her feet. He tore his shirt off and braced his arms against the wall, caging her in with his body. There were no conflicting scents here to battle with hers—only his own, which he'd make sure was all over her by the time they were done.

Who the fuck am I kidding? We're never gonna be done.

Thargen met her eyes and grinned. "Now that I have you all to myself—"

Yuri reached up and cupped his face. "We can finally talk."

"Terrans definitely pick funny words to have double meanings." He leaned down, drawing in more of her scent, and pushed his pelvis against her. "Let's *talk, zoani*. With our bodies. All fucking night."

Yuri moaned and pressed her pelvis right back against his, grinding against his cock. "Mmm. I like the sound of that. Actually, I *love* the sound of that." She abruptly withdrew her hips and angled his face down, so he was looking at her fully. "But first, we really do need to talk."

He sagged and released a frustrated huff. "But we've been talking for fucking hours, Yuri."

She chuckled, stroking his cheeks with her thumbs. "Just a little longer. Promise. Then you can bang me to your heart's content."

Thargen snickered. "So you think you can take that much, huh?"

Yuri tilted her chin down and raised her brows. "Vorgal, I can take everything you have to give me. Haven't I proven that already?"

"Yeah, you have." He eased his pelvis back, removing some of that pressure from his throbbing cock; he couldn't ignore the fact that it had been *her* body pressed against it, and that was too much to resist for long. "What do we need to talk about?"

"You told me the truth about being a security guard, right? You didn't lie to me."

"I didn't lie, terran. That is what I do. But I'm obviously not guarding the sector bank or some shit."

"Obviously. I managed to put together that much when we get here. Dank alleys, discreet entrances, and talk about surveillance hacking don't really scream *legal business*. And I've overheard a lot of conversations at Starlight Trance, Thargen. People talk when they drink, and the way Arcanthus introduced himself... Is he *that* forger I've heard about? Alkor, or something like that? He said something about not using aliases with the twins."

He grunted appreciatively. "Alkorin. Was one of his more popular aliases before some shit went down that encouraged him to let that name fade away."

"Well...it hasn't. Are you all criminals, then? Hacking, forgeries, what else?"

"Personally? Mostly assault, trespassing, and murder. But we've already done at least two of those together." He slid a hand down to cup her cheek, brushing his thumb over her skin when she frowned. "We've all done bad shit, *zoani*, but we're not the bad guys. We're just...I dunno, morally flexible or something. Arcanthus is the best forger in the city, but he's always been very careful about who he accepts jobs from. More careful in the last couple years than ever. Mostly that means helping people who really need an ID chip but can't do it legally. Escaped slaves and people who had bounties put on their heads by corrupt corporations and that kinda shit.

"The people we've killed, there usually wasn't much choice. He's gone out of his way not to make enemies, and it's pretty rare that we have to do anything drastic. Only thing bound to set him off is betrayal—or threats to his people. To us. Fuck, that's the only reason I go out to bars sometimes, because we keep things so damned quiet around here. I can't go *that* long without a fight."

Yuri smiled and slipped her hands around the back of his neck. "Okay."

Thargen's brows dropped. "Okay? All that and you just say *okay*?"

"I trust you, Thargen. I *love* you. You've never given me reason to doubt you."

Warmth bloomed in his chest, so different from his Rage and yet just as powerful. He stroked his thumb across her bottom lip. "Yuri, you could stay here. With me. Make this your home if you want to."

Yuri grinned, her eyes lighting up. "Are you kidding? You're stuck with me, Thargen. I found myself an orc, and I'm *never* letting him go."

The fire in her eyes stoked the flames in his heart.

"Good, cause I'm pretty fucking needy, and I really need to fuck you." He dipped his head down to kiss her, but was stopped by her finger pressing against his lips. "Killing me, terran."

"I have one more question."

Thargen could only groan.

"You're not the only one suffering, believe me, but you gave me your word," Yuri said.

"My word on what, *zoani*?"

"That. You said you'd tell me what *zoani* meant once we were back in Arthos, and well, we're back. And some of your friends were acting pretty strange when they heard it, especially Urgand."

Thargen chuckled despite everything. "I did promise that, didn't I? It means..." He sighed, searching for the right words to explain; it was one of those terms that didn't seem to translate quite right into any other languages. "It gets used like *mate* or *wife* sometimes, but it's more than that. *Zoani* is the missing part of a vorgal. The person who completes them. The one a vorgal chooses to be with forever, through life and death. Like a...soul mate, I think Sam called it once. There's actually a saying that goes with it. A vow."

"What is it?"

He looked into her eyes, and that sense of calm only she could instill in Thargen washed through him, if only briefly. "I will live for you. I will fight for you. I will die for you. I will *be* for you. And when we are reunited in the next life, I will live, fight, and die for you again."

Yuri caught her bottom lip with her teeth. Thargen's eyes

dipped, and he nearly groaned, wanting to nip that lip himself, to taste her on his tongue.

"And you call me *zoani?*" she asked. "That's what I am to you?"

"You are my *zoani* and more, terran. You're my whole fucking universe."

"What would I call you?"

"Just call me yours. That's all I want. Well, that and your tight little *pussy.*"

Laughter burst from her. "You've been mine, and you know that's all yours, too."

Thargen's muscles tensed, and his cock pulsed in anticipation. "Any more questions, *zoani?*"

"No. No more questions," Yuri said with a smile, placing her hands on his shoulders. She tipped her face up and kissed him. Her lips were warm, teasing him with her flavor, and gone too soon. "You are mine, Thargen. I will live for you." She kissed the base of his throat and trailed more kisses down his chest and abdomen, speaking between each one, her hands smoothing down his body in the wake of her lips. "I will fight for you. I will die for you. I will be for you."

Thargen's breath caught in his throat as Yuri as knelt and pressed her lips against his belly, right above his belt. Heat flared in his groin and tingled across his skin, making his abs contract in anticipation, and he slapped his hand against the wall for support. A low growl rumbled in his chest.

She reached for his belt and turned her eyes up to meet his as she undid it. "And when we are reunited in the next life, I will live"—the belt fell to the floor with a *thud,* and her fingers were on the clasp of his pants—"I will fight"—she yanked the flaps open, allowing his painfully hard cock to spring free—"and die for you again."

"You are *mine*, Thargen," she said, wrapping her fingers around his shaft and closing her lips over the head of his cock.

"*Fuck*," Thargen hissed. Just that little bit of contact was so much, too much. He was so aroused in that moment—so needful of her, so in awe of her—that it was both the greatest agony and greatest ecstasy of his life.

Yuri took more of him into her mouth and moaned, sending little vibrations through his shaft. Thargen gritted his teeth. It took everything inside him to keep from thrusting his hips and burying himself in the warm depths of her mouth.

Tightening her grip on the base of his shaft, she pulled her head back and brushed her lips along his length, her tongue flicking out to lick the studs of his piercings. A shudder wracked Thargen's body, and seed seeped from the tip of his cock. His fingers curled against the wall. He watched her from above, watched her head dip, watched her little pink tongue each time it emerged from between her lips; he watched, and *felt*, and barely held himself together.

"Take me back into your mouth, *zoani*," he growled.

Her green eyes flicked up to meet his, and she held his gaze as she ran her tongue back along the underside of his cock and dipped it into the slit at its tip, lapping at his seed. He almost spilled completely right then.

She hummed in appreciation before she closed her mouth around the head of his cock again and sucked, stroking him with her tongue.

Thargen banged his fist on the wall and bucked his hips. "Fuck, yes. Like that."

She took him as deep as she could, her lips stretching around his shaft, and the same hunger and need that burned in his belly was ablaze in her eyes. His Rage refused to be held back any longer. It needed her.

I fucking need her.

He shoved himself back, pulling out of her mouth. His cock throbbed desperately in the open air, lingering on the verge of explosion, but he would not spill his seed in her mouth. He needed to look into her eyes while he was inside her, needed to kiss her, to taste her, to feel her body against his.

His hungry little terran lunged forward for more, but he caught her with his hands and drew her onto her feet.

Yuri's brows slammed down. "Thargen, what—"

Thargen ripped her clothes off, barely registering the sound of tearing fabric. She gasped, a faint flush blossoming across her naked skin, and the hungry gleam in her eyes only intensified. He didn't stop until she stood naked before him, her bronze nipples hardening into little points.

When he hooked his hands behind her legs and lifted her, she threw her arms around his neck and wrapped her legs around his waist, slamming her mouth against his. The tip of his cock pressed against her wet sex.

Breaking the kiss, Thargen tipped his forehead against Yuri's and opened his eyes to meet her fiery, loving gaze. "I am for you, *zoani*." He thrust into her, burying himself fully in her heat, and she gasped, tightening her grip around him as her sex clenched his shaft.

"And you, Yuri... Fuck, you are for *me*. Forever."

AUTHOR'S NOTE

We hope you all enjoyed Thargen and Yuri's story! Rob and I had so much fun writing *Savage Desire*, even during the more difficult times when we'd sit at our desks, stare at the screen, and wonder 'wut r werdz?' It's a crazy process when we write a book. We go through a myriad of emotions—eagerness, excitement, uncertainty, paralyzing doubt, depression, hope, and finally relief. It's always worth it in the end, especially when we hear from our readers, all of you, how much you loved the story and the characters. You guys have no idea how much your kind words mean to us. Thank you.

What's next in the Infinite City? Well, if you haven't already guessed, our daevah twins, Kier and Kayl, in *Tethered Souls*! Their story will be a ménage (mfm). If you don't usually read ménage, we hope you'll still give it a chance. We're really, really loved writing their story. The Infinite City has been a blast as it combines the two things we love—fantasy and science fiction. We hope you all continue to enjoy them.

If you're on Facebook, come join our private reader group! And please, if you have a moment, we've love it if you could leave a review. <3

Thank you all again for reading!

The Weaver

The Delver

The Hunter

<u>THE CURSED ONES</u>

His Darkest Craving

His Darkest Desire

<u>ALIENS AMONG US</u>

Taken by the Alien Next Door

Stalked by the Alien Assassin

Claimed by the Alien Bodyguard

Saved by the Alien Crime Boss

<u>STANDALONE TITLES</u>

Claimed by an Alien Warrior

Dustwalker

Escaping Wonderland

Yearning For Her

The Warlock's Kiss

Ice Bound: Short Story

<u>ISLE OF THE FORGOTTEN</u>

Make Me Burn

Make Me Hunger

Make Me Whole

Make Me Yours

<u>VALOS OF SONHADRA COLLABORATION</u>

<u>Tiffany Roberts - Undying</u>

<u>Tiffany Roberts - Unleashed</u>

<u>VENYS NEEDS MEN COLLABORATION</u>

<u>Tiffany Roberts - To Tame a Dragon</u>

<u>Tiffany Roberts – To Love a Dragon</u>

ABOUT THE AUTHOR

Tiffany Roberts is the pseudonym for Tiffany and Robert Freund, a husband and wife writing duo. The two have always shared a passion for reading and writing, and it was their dream to combine their mighty powers to create the sorts of books they want to read. They write character driven sci-fi and fantasy romance, creating happily-ever-afters for the alien and unknown.

Sign up for our Newsletter!
Check out our social media sites and more!
http://www.authortiffanyroberts.com